WITH SILENT SCREAMS

By Steve McHugh

<u>Hellequin Chronicles</u>

Crimes Against Magic

Born of Hatred

With Silent Screams

WITH SILENT SCREAMS

STEVE MCHUGH

47NORTH

Text copyright © 2014 by Steve McHugh

Published by 47North
P.O. Box 400818
Las Vegas, NV 89140

ISBN-13: 9781612184586
ISBN-10: 1612184588
Library of Congress Control Number: 2013947610

Cover design by Eamon O'Donoghue

For Faith.

You have the sweetest, kindest soul. All wrapped up in a bundle of naughty 3-year-old.

WITH SILENT SCREAMS

PROLOGUE

New York City, New York. 1977.

I do not like flying. I've been told it's perfectly safe, that it's the future of travel and about a hundred other things which I'm sure the sane part of my brain agrees with. The other part of my brain doesn't like the idea of being tens of thousands of feet in the air, in a small metal tube, with large quantities of jet fuel. I don't like the fact that my life is in the hands of people I've never met— from the pilots to the repair crew.

More than all of that, though, I really don't like the fact that flying makes me *feel* mortal. And as a nearly sixteen-hundred-year-old sorcerer, that isn't a very nice feeling at all. But when friends call saying they need my help, I'll brave this ludicrous form of travel and get there as quickly as possible. Even so, as the DC-9 came to a standstill outside the gate, allowing all of the passengers to exit into the terminal, I felt a moment of relief.

JFK Airport is massive on a scale that's hard to convey, and that's not just including square footage. The sheer number of people inside the airport was almost overwhelming, and I was grateful to finally get outside.

"Nathan," a man shouted as he walked away from a red Ford Mustang and took my hand in his, shaking it vigorously.

"Roberto," I replied with a smile as I dragged my hand free of his grip. "You said you needed my help with something."

The smile on his face vanished and he placed a hand on my shoulder, moving me toward the car. "We'll talk once we're on the road. We've got a bit of a drive ahead of us."

"And where would that be to?" I asked across the car's roof as I put my bag in the boot.

"Portland, Maine."

I paused. "You still work for Avalon, yes?"

Roberto nodded and got into the car. I sighed and followed suit.

"How long is this drive?" I asked after he turned the engine on and pulled away from the airport.

"Seven hours, give or take a few minutes."

"So, you've got plenty of time to tell me what the hell is going on."

Roberto was quiet for a while as the traffic around us began to get heavier. I didn't want to disturb him too much when he was driving; he was new to the concept of driving and I wasn't sure he could drive and hold a conversation at the same time.

"Why didn't you have me land there, then?" I asked as we entered the highway and Roberto appeared to relax with the monotony of going in a straight line.

"Because New York is neutral ground. It's the closest neutral state to Maine, and the safest place for us to meet without anyone being alerted to either of our presence. Technically I have not, and never will, set food inside Maine without official permission."

"I assume you don't have that permission."

Roberto's silence told me all I needed to know.

"So, do you feel like telling me why you're risking some serious trouble heading your way?" I asked, getting more confused by the minute.

"Glove box."

Inside the glove box was a manila envelope, which contained a photograph of a young woman with long, dark hair. There was a sheet of paper attached to the photo, which gave information about the woman.

"Sally-Ann," I said, reading the information. "Nineteen. She was born in Green Bay, Wisconsin, and she's a college student studying fine art at Yale, which makes her smarter than the average college student, I guess."

"She was incredibly smart, and sweet, and a good person."

"Was?"

"Her body was found outside of Stratford, Maine, four days ago."

I was silent for a moment. "I'm sorry, Roberto. How did you know her?"

"Her father worked for me. He was a doorman—he died four years ago in a car crash just a few miles from safety."

"Safety?"

"I mean home. It's been a long few days."

"That's fair enough. So, what happened to Sally-Ann?"

"She lived with her grandparents in Augusta after that. I made sure she was well taken care of."

Humans in positions of power or influence often also work for Avalon or some of the more powerful individuals who make up the council. Humans are a good way to find out who's who in a city, and I knew from previous experience that Roberto was very protective of anyone who worked for him.

"So, why was she in Stratford?"

"She went there a lot; she'd met some artistic types a few years ago and she liked to go there to meet them and draw. She was supposed to be on her way there when she was murdered. Whoever killed her dumped the body in a shallow ditch and let the heavy snow-fall cover her. We only found her because a local fell into the ditch. Sally-Ann's grandparents contacted me to let me know. They're heartbroken. She was going to be something very special."

"That's why you're risking your job?"

"Avalon won't fire me, Nathan."

He had a fair point. But they would make his life very difficult for a few years. Roberto was a head of a division of the SOA, or Sword of Avalon. The SOA are the internal security agency for Avalon. They're a mixture of an Internal Affairs department and the Secret Service.

"Here's the thing I don't understand," I said, sliding the picture of Sally-Ann back into the envelope. "Why me? You're more than capable of investigating this yourself."

"You'll see," he said. "I promise all of your questions will be answered in Portland."

"Then put your foot down, because this whole thing is making me nervous."

The rest of the journey was done in silence, allowing me to get a few hours sleep. Roberto woke me once he'd pulled up outside a bar called the Mill and switched off the engine. I yawned and opened the car door, stretching as the cold air of winter in Maine made sure I was fully awake.

The snow had let up for the day, but it covered everything in an inch-thick layer of whiteness, which crunched under foot as

I made my way around the car to join Roberto, who was waiting for me.

"In here," Roberto said as he pushed open the bar door.

I glanced up at the sign that hung above the window and stepped inside.

The warmth flowed over me like a welcome embrace. I glanced around the spacious bar and saw half a dozen people sat at various tables, either talking amongst themselves or eating. I spotted Roberto talking to the bartender, and he waved me over.

"Nice place," I said. "I remember it being a bit more of a hovel."

Roberto opened his mouth to speak when a woman walked up to us, her heels clicking on the bare wooden floor. She wore a beautifully tailored dark suit and heels that put her just a few inches below my own height of five-nine. Her eyes were deepest blue and contrasted nicely with her long, almost black hair.

"Mister Garrett, Mister Cortez, my name is Rebecca Dean, please follow me," she said and turned to walk away. Her accent placed her from New York, but I thought I caught something else in there, a little Irish maybe.

I watched her walk and received an elbow in the ribs from Roberto for the trouble. "Watch yourself," he said with a slight grin.

"I'm more interested in watching her," I said.

Roberto pointed to the woman's heels, which were four inches long, and glinted as light hit them. "Those heels have blades on them," he whispered. "Like I said, watch out."

The woman led us up a flight of stairs and down a corridor, where she opened door and beckoned us inside.

"Please take a seat," she offered, pointing to the two black leather armchairs that sat opposite a couch made of the same material. A glass coffee table lay between the chairs and couch, and as I sat in one of the chairs, I took the opportunity to survey the room.

It was a fairly large office at about thirty by thirty foot, but it contained nothing out of the ordinary. A large desk sat at one end, next to a window that bathed the room in light. The walls were adorned with paintings of various landscapes from around the world—they were very impressive, and whoever had done the work had certainly had a good eye.

"So, are we here to see you?" I asked Rebecca who had sat down on the couch in front of me, regaining my attention as I stared at an exquisite watercolor painting of Camelot.

"I'm just the bar's manager," she said. "I'm only here as a witness."

"A witness to what?" I asked.

"To why I asked you here today," a man said as he stepped into the office.

I was on my feet immediately, making my way over to the stocky man and embracing him tightly in a hug.

"Nathan, my old friend," he said with genuine warmth as we parted. "I'm glad to see you again."

"You too, you look good," I said. He looked almost exactly the same as he had when we'd last met over a century previous. He'd let his dark hair grow to shoulder length and had a small scar on his cheek, but it was his eyes that gave away the pain as if he had the weight of the world on his shoulders.

He stepped past me and shook Roberto's hand as the bar's manager bowed deeply.

"My liege," she said and he motioned for her to stand.

"Liege?" I asked. "When did you get people to call you that?"

My old friend turned back to me and smiled, but this time it didn't reach his eyes. "Have you not heard? I am the king of Shadow Falls."

My mouth dropped open in shock. I'd heard nothing about it. Even away from Avalon, I would have thought I'd have picked up little traces here and there. "How long?"

"Three years now," he said. "Although it feels much longer."

"King Galahad," I said. "Damn, if it doesn't suit you. Now can someone please tell me what the hell is going on?"

CHAPTER 1

Toronto, Canada. Now.

Sirens wailed as I parked the Mitsubishi Warrior next to a row of police cars and climbed out into the cool night air.

"You can't park there," one of the cops said as he made his way over to me. "You're going to have to move."

"He's with me," Sky said as she followed me out of the truck and showed the cop her ID.

"Sorry, ma'am," he said and stepped aside, allowing us through.

I pushed down the part of me that screamed to run toward the house—it wouldn't do anyone any good. Body bags were already being carried into the house. The building itself was a fairly old brick structure, with two floors and probably four bedrooms. It certainly looked big enough. The nearest neighbor was a few hundred feet away, and with all the open ground and trees around it, I doubted anyone had heard a thing while its inhabitants died.

"Damn it," I said as we reached the front door and I saw the splatter of blood inside.

"Hey, who the hell are you?" a male detective shouted as he strode toward us. Sky flashed her ID again.

"Oh great, a spook, that makes things much better."

Sky's ID just had a badge and a picture of Hades' logo on it—a raven sat atop a shield. Like all of the more powerful members of the world, Hades had his own business empire and security force. Very few humans knew that the Hades from mythology was real, although the two barely matched up in reality. The majority of law enforcement in Canada had heard of Hades as an organization, and most thought it was a secretive, CIA-esque authority. They were only partially correct.

"I'm not here to argue, just look around," Sky told him, replacing her ID in her pocket. "What can you tell us?"

"Well as you can see," the detective said waving his arms behind him, "it's a home invasion gone wrong. Some punks probably broke in and started searching, the old lady found them and they fought. She died with a stab wound to the throat."

"And the man?" I asked.

"Yeah, I figure the little bastards enjoyed killing her and took their time with him. Probably figured he was holding out on riches or some shit. We'll find them, though."

"No, detective, you won't," I said and walked passed him and into the nearest room.

Blood saturated the carpet and a man in white overalls was examining the body of an elderly lady, looking for clues, while his colleague searched the room.

"Did she die in here?" I asked them.

The one kneeling beside the body turned to face me. "Yes, on the floor just here. It looks like she was stabbed in the throat. The spray of blood on the wall there suggests she was standing when it was done."

I stared at the wall, and as the man said, the blood spray suggested she was standing when stabbed.

"Have you found a knife?" I asked.

He shook his head. "We're still looking."

"Can I see the body?"

The man glanced over at his colleague, neither of them wanting to say yes.

"He's with me," Sky said again. I got the impression she enjoyed showing off her ID.

Hades would probably get a call about an employee of his walking onto a murder scene, but I doubted he'd be too concerned. Hades allowed his employees the freedom to work as they needed to, and Sky, as his daughter, was given more than her share of allowances.

The coroner moved aside, and after placing some gloves on my hands, I crouched beside her and took a look at the body of Mrs. Vivian Moon. She'd bled out from the massive gash on her throat.

"You okay, Nate?" Sky asked as she joined me.

"No," I said softly, hoping to keep my temper in check.

"Where's the male?" Sky asked the coroner.

"He's been taken out already, but you can go to the bedroom where he died," he said. "First on the right."

I removed my gloves and threw them into the hazardous waste bag as we left the room, then followed the man's directions upstairs, the smell of death growing ever stronger. I grabbed a second set of gloves from a box outside the room, with Sky following suit, and we opened the door to whatever horrors the coroner had warned us about.

There were two detectives inside, one male and one female and both of them did their best to not glance at the blood-soaked bed. At some point the man who'd been on it had been a detective by the name of William Moon. He'd been a good man, an ex-Marine who had served his country during the Vietnam War and who had come back determined to do something good in the world. That good had eventually gotten him killed.

"Bill," I said softly and made my way to the bed. "What the hell did they do to you?"

"You knew the victim?" one of the detectives asked.

"Yeah, he was a cop," I said. "Retired a while back, but we worked together on something a long time ago."

"Can't have been that long," the man said. "You're what, thirty?"

"I'm older than I look," I said. *About sixteen hundred years older.* "What did they do to him?"

"They cut him up and beat him pretty badly," the woman said. "The coroner says they broke a lot of bones, and then they decided to partially skin him. They eviscerated him in the end. He died hard. The coroner had the body removed about twenty minutes ago."

"Can you both give us a minute?" Sky said, showing them her ID. They nodded and left the room.

"Nate, what did he call you for?"

"He said people were dying and he needed my help. He told me to be here at six and he'd explain everything. That was four hours ago, which is pretty much exactly how long it took to get you and drive here. The call was cut off when he was about to tell me something else, though."

"Any idea what?"

"Don't know. The phone just went dead. There are storms in the area, so I assumed it was a problem with the phone itself. When I couldn't call it back, I rang you."

"I'm going to talk to my father. I'll see if I can get him to take the case over. I know this is human on human, and not even Avalon touches those, but I figure we can make an exception. We'll find out who did this."

"I know," I said. "And then I'm going to kill them."

Sky placed a hand on my shoulder and I placed my hand on top and squeezed slightly. There was a time when we had almost been more than friends, but time and personalities had ensured that it never happened.

Sky removed her phone from her pocket as I noticed a business card that had fallen onto the carpet beside where Bill would have lain on the bed.

I picked up the black card and found that it belonged to a hotel in Manhattan, the Scepter Hotel. A bloody mark stained both sides of one corner. At one point, I would have used my Blood magic to try and get some insight into who the blood belonged to. But those days were gone. Since my necromancy had reared its head nearly a year ago, my Blood magic had vanished. Hades had told me that necromancy and Blood magic can't coexist, but it was a huge thing to lose, and something I still had trouble getting used to.

"You ever heard of this?" I asked Sky, passing the card to her as she told someone on the other end of the phone to wait a moment.

"It's a fancy five-star place. You think this blood is Bill's?"

"Maybe. It's worth looking into."

"I'll bag it up," she said and took it from me as she started talking on her phone again.

I walked over to a nearby door and pushed it open, revealing a clean en suite bathroom. Directly in front of the door was a mirror above a white sink. Someone had written "welcome back" on the glass in blood. I noticed the small camera, positioned on top of the mirror. And then my world exploded.

No amount of magic at my disposal could have stopped the destructive power of the explosion as it rushed toward me. A hastily assembled shield of dense air robbed it of its potency and left me alive, but the shockwave still picked me off the ground as if I were made of paper, flinging me back through the nearest window with a crash.

I slammed into the solid earth with a crunch, tumbling backward until a large tree stopped any further movement with a definitive thud.

I lay there, covered in blood, dirt, and brick dust as my brain tried to catch up with what had happened.

The first port of call was pain. It washed over me, hunkering down in every conceivable place on my body. My ribs felt as if on fire, turning even the simple act of breathing into a battle. My left arm was numb, and my back felt wet, but I couldn't move enough to find out what had happened. I coughed and the pain roared through my body until I spat bright blood onto the grass beside me. Probably a punctured lung.

All in all, I was lucky. I might not have felt it, but if I'd been human I would have most certainly died.

My magic had started to heal me—my ringing ears faded back to normal within a few seconds, so I just sat still as the thoughts of Sky and the officers in the house filled my head. Were they okay? Did I take the brunt of the blast? The more I thought about it, the angrier I got. Unfortunately, I couldn't move.

A short while later, a young woman walked out of the woods beside me toward the ruins of the house. She glanced around briefly as flames leapt from the giant hole where the bedroom and bathroom used to be, then turned toward me. Her high heels and knee-length dress were an odd sight, but the smile on her face suggested she was not here to help.

She ran her hand through her shoulder-length brown hair and stood a few feet in front of me, the smile never wavering from her beautiful face. I'd never seen her before—there wasn't even a glimmer of recognition on my part—but from the callous grin on her face, I got the impression that she certainly knew me.

She took a few steps toward me and breathed deeply before placing one of her heels against my shoulder and pushing down. The strength of the woman was incredible as the heel tore into my shoulder, causing me to yell in pain as she turned her foot left and right.

"I'd love to make you my new pet," she said and removed her foot, her heel dripping blood onto my arm. "My last one didn't make it."

"You triggered the explosion," I said. A cold rage began to fill me, but I couldn't have fought her on rage alone—I'd have been killed. Instead, I was forced to sit still, watch, and listen, which did little to improve my mood.

The woman made a contented sound, like a purr. "Of course. I wasn't meant to come say hello, but I just couldn't stay away. I wanted to see how you'd handle this...warning." She raised her head and listened as the sounds of voices came closer.

She sighed and bent down in front of me. "Such a shame we have to cut our relationship short. I'd kill you, but I don't want you to leave the fun just yet. See you soon, Mister Garrett." She pressed one finger into the hole she'd made with her heel a moment ago. I yelled out once more until she withdrew the finger and licked it clean. "You taste good. Maybe when we meet again, I'll be able to get my fill of you." She kicked me in the head so hard, it would have moved a car. I blacked out.

CHAPTER 2

"**H**ow long was I out?" I asked as I found myself in the back of an ambulance with Sky next to me. Her brown eyes held a look of concern, along with anger at what had happened. She drummed her fingers of one hand against the metal railing beside her, a nervous habit, while running the other through her long dark hair.

"An hour, give or take. Your wounds finished healing a few minutes ago."

I pushed myself upright; I felt sore and achy, but I'd live. More than that, I was *really* angry. "They didn't use silver in the bomb."

"You were lucky."

"No, they wanted me to live. They wrote 'welcome back' on the bathroom mirror. I was standing there for a good two or three seconds. They let me read that message and notice the camera before detonating the bomb."

"Any idea who *they* are?"

I shook my head. It hurt. "I'm gonna find out though." I swung my legs off the bed and the blanket covering me moved. I was naked except for my boxers. "Did you take my clothes off?"

"Nope, the human paramedics got to you first and started cutting your clothes off. They were a little surprised when your wounds started to heal in front of them."

"Yeah, that takes some explaining at the best of times."

"Fortunately, my people arrived. One of them had an ambulance, so we thought it best to get you out of there before the cops started asking questions."

"I need to go back and look around."

"You need to rest for a bit. Your magic still has some work to do."

As a sorcerer, my ability to heal injuries is far in excess of anything a human can hope to achieve. Magic will mend broken bones in a matter of hours, and near-death injuries in days. It all depends on how powerful the sorcerer, but our ability to survive is still quite impressive. A few years previously, my magical ability had increased, and that meant injuries which used to take hours to mend now took minutes. Along with the vast increase in power available to me, it was something I was still getting used to.

"I'm fine," I said.

"How about those marks? Any more of them gone?"

For my entire life, I've had six black marks on my torso. Each one about the size of a fist, and each of them constantly changes, making the discovery of their purpose impossible. It didn't help that they only show up when I use magic, and that only people who also have a Blood magic curse can see them. For over a millennium they sat there, doing nothing, and then someone sacrificed themselves to save my life and they started to vanish. The first one that went increased my magical power, and the second gave me the ability to use necromancy alongside my wind and fire magic. The final four remained in place, but I'd started to see the beginnings of the third mark starting to fade.

"Nothing yet. How are you doing? You were in the room when the bomb went off."

"I was just outside it, but the blast was directed away from where I was. Apart from some ringing ears, I'm fine. A few cops were in the room behind you when it went off. They were rushed to hospital with some slight injuries and a few cases of shock. But there was nothing too serious."

That was a relief. Although I doubted the bomb makers cared one way or the other who was going to get hurt, it was good to know the casualties were minimal. I turned to look out of the window behind me. "Where are we going?"

"My father's hospital. I arranged for the bodies of your friend and his wife to be sent there. My father wants to talk to you too."

I lay back on the gurney. "Yeah, I sort of expected he'd want to discuss how his daughter was in the vicinity of a bomb blast."

"He was worried, not mad."

"That'll change once he sees that I'm okay."

"He's not going to blame you, Nate."

Somehow, that didn't make me feel better about it, but I didn't have time to voice my concerns as the ambulance stopped and Sky opened the double doors.

"You coming?" she asked.

"I'm naked."

A sly smile crossed Sky's lips. "Oh, is it the cold? No one will say anything, it happens to every man."

"You are a witty woman to mock the naked man who was just blown up. Do you go kick orphans at Christmas too?"

Sky laughed. "Hey, Tiny Tim was asking for it. Wait there, I'll go get you some clothes."

"It's not like I can go anywhere else," I shouted after her, which earned me a glance at her middle finger as she walked into the hospital.

While I sat in the back of the ambulance, earning glances from people who entered and exited the hospital, my thoughts drifted back to just before the explosion. The words *welcome back* were meant to mean something to me, I was sure of that; otherwise, why wait until I'd read it and seen the camera before detonating?

Sorcerers are blessed, or cursed, depending on your view, with fantastic memory recall. I can tell someone exactly what I was doing on the 17th November 1078—sleeping with the sister of a chieftain's wife. But I can't remember details like faces or names very easily—she'd had long red hair, green eyes, and her name began with an R ... maybe. Unfortunately, messages written in blood weren't exactly new to me; so who might have written it, and why, would have to remain mysteries until something else jogged a memory loose. But for some reason the message on the mirror bothered me a lot more than being blown up.

I tried to get my brain to figure out a connection until Hades arrived at the front of the ambulance and threw me some clothes.

I quickly pulled on the blue t-shirt and dark jeans, but was happier to put on some clean shoes and socks. When finally dressed, Hades passed me a cup of hot tea.

"You're a good man," I told him as I inhaled the green tea and savored a quick sip.

"Could you tell that to the people who wrote those fairy tales about me, I could use some good PR."

The myth of Hades kidnapping Persephone and forcing her to marry him was just that, a myth. One perpetrated by Persephone's mother, Demeter, as she was embarrassed that her only daughter married a necromancer. In fact, Hades and Persephone probably have the strongest relationship I've ever known two people to have. And they're two of the people I'm proudest to call my friends.

"So, you got blown up," Hades said as I stepped out of the ambulance and pulled on the black hoodie he'd given me.

"Yeah, not my finest hour."

"Sky's okay." Hades' comment was said very matter-of-factly, but there was a barely concealed anger in his tone. No one with half a brain would want a pissed-off Hades running after them. And hurting one of his children, adopted or otherwise, was a very quick way of ensuring your life expectancy was about to reach zero.

"I'll find who did this."

"I know." Hades passed me a card, which turned out to be the one I'd found in Bill's bedroom. "Sky seemed to think this was a clue to their whereabouts."

"It was in a blood-soaked bedroom, right next to where they tortured Bill. I'd say it was planted there. Someone wants me to follow them."

"I assume you want to go back to the house first and look around."

"I'm hoping they left something for me to work with. Did any of your men find any trace of the woman I met?"

"She was long gone by the time they got to you. Werewolves have been sent to see if they can pick anything up. By the time you get back there, we should know more."

We walked into the hospital, and the people we passed said hello to Hades, who returned the greeting without pause.

I was certain that if asked, he would have known the names of every single person he met. It was that kind of attention to those who worked for him that gained him devotion amongst his work force.

The hospital itself was large enough to house a few hundred patients and staff, but not so large that you'd get lost wandering its identical corridors. Like all hospitals, signs pointed the right way. But unlike most hospitals, protection runes were etched onto every single door and window we walked past. If I knew Hades, they'd be marked on the very brick and concrete that made the building. I didn't know what they did, but I was very sure I didn't want to find out firsthand.

We entered the lift and Hades selected the second underground floor. I knew from experience that it contained the morgue and I felt a twinge of anger inside me at the thought of Bill and his wife lying cold and motionless while their killers roamed free.

Once out of the lift, we rounded a corner at the end of a long corridor and found Sky in a reception area, sitting on a chair next to a Coke machine.

"There's a reaper in with the bodies," she said as I sat opposite her and Hades continued to walk past us and through a nearby door.

I placed the heel of my palms against my forehead and shut my eyes. If I could get tension headaches, I'd have had a huge one. "Reapers?"

"Standard protocol in situations like this, you know that. We may learn something."

As much as I try to keep an open mind about all the species that inhabit the world, reapers are one of the few that I absolutely hate spending time around. It's not that they're inherently evil or anything quite so dramatic; it's just that they're so damn creepy. Talking to them feels like something is inside your brain trying to get out. After they've gone, you're still left with an itch in your psyche that can take hours to leave. It's sort of like when you wake up from a horrific nightmare and for a brief moment you're unsure if it's real or not.

The door that Hades had gone through opened and a tall man walked through. He wore a well-tailored dark-blue suit and a black fedora. Reapers aren't overly skinny, even though they can't eat or drink in the normal sense of the word. They sustain their energy by siphoning off the emotions from the spirits they talk to. Which is probably a big reason why I find them creepy. Contrary to myth, reapers do not help spirits cross the underworld or even kill people themselves. They're a type of necromancer. One that can communicate with the recently deceased. When a person dies, their spirit, or soul, or whatever you wish to call it, is still connected to their body for seven days. The Spirit itself can't move far from the body it was recently inhabiting, no matter where that body might be taken. So wherever the body is, reapers can find their spirit and talk to them.

"So, how'd it go?" I asked the man.

"Not well," he said, his voice was barely a whisper, but for some reason his words hung around in your head after he'd said them. "I managed to connect with the woman easily enough. She told me that she let in four people, three men and a woman. Once in the house, they attacked her and her husband, dragging him off upstairs. Two men took her into the room she was found in and started searching it for information. Her memory is jumbled about the details, as she has no idea what they were talking about. When she pulled a gun on them, they killed her. Like all spirits, she doesn't remember her death, and won't until she's no longer linked to her body, but I put two-and-two together."

"And the man?" I asked.

"His death was prolonged and unnecessarily cruel. He was tortured very horribly. Any thoughts I have from him are fractured. Mostly just thoughts of his wife, of being unable to save her. Of knowing that he was going to die. Whatever was done to him broke his mind before he died." There was no emotion in the reaper's voice. Everything was said in an even tone. I wasn't even sure they had emotions. Like I said, creepy.

"Thanks for trying," Sky said.

"I never said there was nothing," the reaper said, with what was almost irritation. "There were a few things he thought over and over again." He pointed at me. "Your name was repeated a lot. As was a hotel in New York. "

"The Scepter?" I asked.

"Yes, that's the one. And lastly there's laughter."

"Are you sure?" Sky said. "What he went through wasn't funny."

"He wasn't laughing. He's remembering the laughter. The person who tortured him was laughing while she did it. And yes, it was a she. There was a flash of an image of her. A youngish woman, most would consider her attractive. I don't really have a frame of reference for how attractive, however. She had shoulder-length brown hair. There's one sentence that his memory didn't fracture. *We'd have never found you if you hadn't started checking again.* She said it several times during his ordeal."

"Can you tell us more about her?" I asked.

The reaper shook his head. "Other than she enjoyed herself, no. If this woman is the one you seek, she is very dangerous. I would advise caution."

"Thanks," I said. "I think we've already met."

"Then you should be very happy that you're still alive," the reaper said. And with that he nodded to Sky and walked back toward the lift as Hades made his way over toward us.

"Well, now I have extra motivation to find her," I said.

"You will have to be very careful," Hades told me. "These people appear to be playing a game. One that we do not yet know the rules of. Nor do we know the point they're trying to make."

I took the hotel card from my pocket and turned it over in my hand. One side just showed the hotel name with the picture of a golden scepter behind it. The scepter shimmered slightly as the light caught it. The rear listed the address, which was on Lexington Avenue, along with the hotel's website.

I typed in the address on my phone's web browser and was greeted with some stunning photos of the hotel during the night and day. I flicked through the pictures, which were of both the outside and interior, and quickly came to the conclusion that Sky had been right, it was a very upmarket place. If the people who did this were staying there, then they had some serious money.

I passed Sky my phone and gave her a moment to flick through the photos. "It could be a trap," she said.

"Quite possibly. But it would be rude not to go see what they want."

"I'll join you," Sky said. "Quite frankly, you could use backup considering they seem to want you involved."

I nodded a thank you in Sky's direction.

"And what will you do if you find them?" Hades asked. "Like I said, you don't yet know the game they're playing."

"That's okay, Hades," I said. "I plan on cheating anyway."

Sky and I left the hospital after promising Hades that I would do nothing stupid and that anything we found out, we'd let him know first. He then gave me the keys to his Range Rover Evoque, a deep-blue beast of an SUV. Unfortunately, Sky hadn't shut up complaining about it from the second the keys had fallen into my hand.

"Why do you get to drive?" she asked for the fifth time since we'd set off on the road.

I'd stayed silent the previous times, because doing anything other than agreeing with her when she was annoyed was a recipe for an argument, but my willpower had officially run out. "Because you are not a good driver," I said honestly.

"The hell I'm not!"

"Number of cars written off by me, less than ten. Number written off by you . . . Can you even remember?"

"Look, they're not my fault."

"All of them? Really? Because I once saw you pull the hand break in a car doing nearly a hundred miles an hour. How many times did that one flip over?"

"I don't remember," Sky said coolly. "Someone was trying to kill me at the time."

"Because I was in the car behind you and it looked like something out of a Hollywood movie. It just kept flipping."

Even though I wasn't looking at Sky, I could tell that she was staring a hole through me. "You blew up a Nissan GT-R."

"Technically, yes, but—"

"No buts, you blew up a Nissan GT-R to get rid of a gargoyle."

"It wasn't moving at the time, and it wasn't like I had a lot of options. Also, remind me to thank Tommy for telling you that."

Sky was silent for a moment, then she started to laugh. "I'm driving on the way back."

"Okay, if you promise not to crash the car."

"I promise nothing of the sort. It depends on how much you piss me off."

I chuckled and was immediately grateful for Sky's company. She had the ability to take people's mind off whatever horrific thing they were dealing with. Even if she did it by starting an argument.

"Any idea why these people clearly wanted you at that house?" Sky asked after a few minutes silence.

"No," I said. "But they were there when Bill called me."

"How can you be sure?"

"The number of people who have my mobile number barely reaches double digits. So he either got the number from one of them, or—"

"Or they gave him the number."

"Exactly. Which does bring up one big question."

"How did they get your number? You think someone in our organization gave it to them?"

"There are people in the UK with it, but I very much doubt Bill's murderers contacted any of them. I'd have been called about five seconds after they'd finished on the phone. And there's no way you, Hades, Persephone, or any of your family handed it over. Which means, you have a leak."

"Fucking hell. Dad's going to crucify someone if that's true."

I was pretty certain that wasn't a figure of speech.

Sky's phone rang and she answered the text message. "They couldn't get a track," Sky said after replacing her phone in her pocket.

"What?"

"The werewolves that Dad sent to the house, they couldn't get a track on the woman. By the time they arrived, the winds were too strong and the scent had been muddled with about fifty other people. Apparently the only scent they could pick up was one of a cave troll. Was she a cave troll?"

"No," I said. "She spoke in clear sentences and she wasn't the size of a truck. Not a cave troll."

"Could she have used a troll to mask her scent?"

That made me pause. "Maybe, although would you want to ask a cave troll if you could use their scent?"

"It's a mystery then. But no other scents were in that wood except for what belonged to the troll."

"Why would a cave troll be this far from any caves?"

"A good point. You okay here?"

"They killed my friends and tried to blow me up. No, I'm *not* okay."

Sky placed a hand on my shoulder. "We'll find them." Her words were spoken with such conviction that it was hard not to believe them.

Sky went to sleep soon after, only waking to wave her ID at the border, which allowed us to go through without delay. Once in New York State, she went straight back to sleep.

We stopped in Syracuse for something to eat, and then I let Sky drive the rest of the way, even managing to relax enough to get a few hours sleep myself. It took in total over eight hours of driving, and probably would have been quicker to fly, but by the time we'd arranged for a jet, we would have only saved a few minutes at most.

We pulled up in front of the hotel and Sky threw the keys to the valet before we walked inside. The foyer was huge and very impressive, with some interesting artwork on the walls and massive windows that let in an extraordinary amount of light. Sky left me to look around while she walked over to the reception desk. Her ID would do little good in New York; neutral territory was just that. There was a time when the most powerful creatures on earth fought over the state, including Hades, but Avalon had eventually managed to calm everyone with a proposal that suited no one. New York was off limits to the influence of any of the major powers. It was one of only five states in America that could say they were neutral territory; Illinois, California, Louisiana, and Texas made up the rest. A number of cities also fall under the "neutral" banner, although apart from Washington, D.C., most of them are only neutral in the broadest sense of the word.

Sky had been talking to a young man behind the counter for a few minutes when she made her way back to me as I flicked through one of the hotel brochures.

"Any luck?" I asked.

"That black card, it's only available on the top three floors." She reached over and picked up a white card from the table beside me. "Everyone else gets these."

"Why would they bother?"

"Apparently it's been proven to make those who pay the extra dollars feel more exclusive. All of the cards and menus up there are different colors from those of the floors below. It's a marketing idea."

"Okay, so where do we go from here?"

"I slipped him a few hundred bucks and he said the third floor from the top hasn't been used for a few weeks. Remodeling."

"That's out then."

"The second floor is occupied at the moment by some Wall Street types. They've taken the two suites there to use for some sort of bonding retreat."

"And the penthouse?"

"In use for the last three weeks. All paid in cash, two men and two women. Apparently they scare the shit out of the staff."

"You got a lot for only a few hundred bucks."

"I'm very persuasive, and I also gave him my phone number."

I chuckled. "Penthouse it is then."

The lifts, which were just as opulent as every other thing I'd seen in the hotel, were quiet and no one else got on as we rode it to the penthouse on the twenty-second floor.

The polished lift doors opened to show a corridor filled with natural light from the huge windows that ran down one side. Arrays of colorful flowers had been placed on small tables and, apart from a door marked stairwell and the lift doors, there was only one other door on the floor.

"You going to use magic to open it?" Sky asked me.

Over the years I'd learned how to use my air magic to open locked doors, but it's time-consuming and difficult to do. It's also impossible to do with a lock that requires a card. "You fancy kicking it down?"

Sky smiled—it was sly and full of mischief. I stepped aside so she could use the keycard that appeared in her hand.

"Your phone number got you the door key card?"

"I'm not sure if you're aware of this, Nate, but I'm incredibly hot." Sky swiped the card through the door lock and then pushed the door open.

Whatever playful banter we had before the door opened ceased the second the living room was revealed. The expensive decor, and stunning views, did little to sway me as we searched the suite together. We started with the left side of the room, which contained the bedroom and an en suite bathroom, both of which were clean and tidy, with no clothes or toiletries around to suggest that anyone was staying here. We moved back into the living room and made our way through it to the second bedroom, which was also empty.

I pushed opened the frosted glass door to the second bathroom and paused to take in the scene before me. A man was lying in the bathtub; he was completely naked and covered, almost head to toe, in blood. The deep gouge across his throat, along with the huge number of cuts and gashes on his body, told me that it was his own. The back of his head rested on the rear of the bathtub, his eyes open, staring at the wall behind him. His body had clearly been staged.

"Holy shit," Sky said as she stood beside me. "I know this guy."

That was a bit of a surprise. "Who is he?"

"His name is—sorry *was*—Jerry Brown. He was a cop in Toronto. He also worked for my father."

It was a regular thing that people in positions of power within a community also worked for the more powerful members of the nonhuman world. Mostly they just fed back relevant information, but on occasion they would be required to spy on someone, or push forward legislation that would benefit their employer.

"Any ideas why he was here?"

She shook his head. "Dad didn't mention anything about any of his people vanishing in the last few days."

I glanced up at the wall, which contained another message. Like before, it was written in blood. *House of Silent Screams.*

I immediately knew who had written the message and why I was involved. And a shiver went down my spine.

CHAPTER 3

Portland, Maine. 1977.

"If you're not going to be honest with me, then you can take your offer and shove it up your ass," I said as we both stood on the roof of the Mill. The bar had seen a pretty heated discussion between Galahad and myself when he'd told me what he wanted, and I'd needed some air before I did or said something stupid.

Galahad sighed.

"Don't fucking sigh," I snapped. "You tell me you need me to find someone. You won't tell me why or what's going on. So my answer is no." I turned to look at my friend. I wasn't used to him being less than completely open. Maybe being king had changed him in more ways than I cared to think.

"How many times have you kept things from me?" Galahad asked, his voice containing more than a little anger. My secretive activities for Merlin had long been a thorn in the side of our friendship.

"This is different, and you know it. You want me to search the state for one guy who has wronged you. I get that he killed the daughter of Roberto's friend, but I don't get what you want out of it."

"Is it not enough that you'll be stopping a killer?"

"Don't do that. Don't you dare use someone's murder to get me interested. Merlin did that, and you left Avalon to get away from him, not become him." I hadn't really meant what I said. I doubted that Galahad would ever cross the lines that Merlin was willing to cross. But I was angry, and I knew how much Merlin boiled Galahad's blood, so I lashed out.

Galahad punched me in the mouth.

I fell to the ground and touched my blooded lip, but before I could get back to my feet, the bar's manager, Rebecca, was standing in a defensive position between Galahad and me, a dagger in one hand.

"You will not harm my king," she said.

I spat blood onto the floor and stared at the woman. "In case you didn't notice, he punched me first."

"You will not—"

"Yeah, yeah, I heard you the first time." I got to my feet and rubbed my mouth again. "You feel better?"

Galahad had turned away and was staring out across the streets below us. "Rebecca, leave us for a moment."

"But—"

"I will be fine."

Rebecca gave me one last glare, but did as she was asked and left the roof via the stairwell door.

"I'm sorry," Galahad said. "I should not have struck you."

"I pissed you off, you hit me, let's call it even," I told him. "You feel like telling me what's going on?"

"I can't."

It was my turn to sigh. "Can you at least tell me who this Simon guy is? Apart from killing students, why do you need him found?"

"I can tell you this. Simon Olson is a very dangerous man. He's aligned himself with several equally dangerous people, and they're committing murders. I can't tell you anything about Simon other than the fact that he's an alchemist."

"So, let me get this right: the king of Shadow Falls, a place full of alchemists, is asking me to track down and apprehend another alchemist? Do you think I'm an idiot?"

"No, but if you'd just read the file about him instead of telling me to fuck off, you would have known that he has no affiliation with Shadow Falls."

"So, why can't you go after him yourself? And if you feed me a bullshit answer, I'm going to walk."

Galahad looked up at the sky and sighed again. "This doesn't leave this roof. Simon used to work for the old king of Shadow Falls, Charles Whitehorn."

"Well that puts an interesting spin on things. You're worried that he still is working for him? That whatever Simon is doing, Whitehorn is involved."

Galahad nodded. "If I send my people up there, Simon will figure out that I'm sniffing around and disappear. We won't get justice for the people he's killed until he resurfaces, and I have no idea when that might be. If Simon goes, any link to Whitehorn will go."

There was something else, something I was certain he was holding back. I filed the information away for future reference. "So what does that really have to do with Sally-Ann?"

"Simon is killing people for a reason, but no one is able to figure it out. Until Roberto came to me with information about her murder, we didn't even know she'd existed."

"So, what would you have done if she hadn't been found? Would you still have involved me? Do you see my problem?

There's something that happened that made you want my involvement. Political bullshit aside, which I understand, *why me?*"

"Because I asked them to involve you," Roberto said as he arrived on the roof. "I came to King Galahad with information about Sally-Ann's murder. He said he would look into it. I didn't trust him enough not to brush it under the rug when he was done. So I asked for a neutral party we were both happy with. You have no standing with Avalon, you hold no rank with them or anyone in a position of power. You are, for all intents and purposes, a Ronin. Your reputation for what you used to do for Merlin and others affords you a lot of privilege in our world. People know of your name and reputation, either through fear or respect. But you hold no allegiance. You're perfect to look into cases like this."

"Why would he sweep it under the rug?" I asked.

"Because, apart from being a very talented artist, Sally-Ann was an alchemist," Roberto said. "Her mother was an alchemist. But she died when she was very young. Sally-Ann had only just started coming into her abilities."

"Her grandparents, were they alchemists as well?" I asked.

"Human, on her father's side. Sally-Ann and her father were in Maine visiting her grandparents when he died. After her father's death, Sally-Ann stayed in Maine until she went to college."

"So, I'm here because you think that Galahad and his people will deal with this in-house and you'll never really find out what happened?"

Roberto nodded. "Avalon does it enough, as you know. And I don't know Galahad well enough to say that Shadow Falls doesn't operate the same way. Sally-Ann's family deserves closure. You're my safest bet that they'll receive it."

It was a perfectly reasonable answer, I had no information that might suggest that something else was going on, but something told me I was stepping into trouble. "Okay, anything else I should know?"

"I can't go any further with you," Roberto said and offered me his hand, which I took. "I have to go back to New York. Drop you off and leave, that's the deal."

"I'll contact you when it's over and let you know it's finished."

"Thank you, Nathan. And you, too, King Galahad. You've been more than generous with your time." And with that, he left the roof.

"This whole Avalon and Shadow Falls never working together is stupid. He could have helped."

"I still have to answer to my people. And none of them would have been happy with a member of Avalon conducting an investigation in Maine. We are totally separate states, and changing that in any way is to invite danger to my people; I won't do anything that may put the lives of people that I'm duty bound to take care of, in danger."

"Yeah, I get that," I said. "You never answered my question though. If Roberto hadn't contacted you, would you have involved me?"

"Yes, I had plans to contact you. I trust you and know you'll do a good job and won't betray me or my people."

The links clicked together. "You don't know who you can trust in your own organization. That's why you came to me, because you know I'm not working for Whitehorn."

Galahad nodded once. "I don't know who's with me and who isn't. That's why only a select few people know about it—and why I can't just send my security force to go find him."

"So, I find this guy and turn him into a very dead bad person. I can manage that."

"About that. While I agree that Simon should be buried in a deep hole, I need him alive."

I really should have read the file. "Why?"

"Sorry, Nathan. There are some state secrets I can't tell you."

He genuinely appeared sorry, too. Galahad had always actively hated cloak-and-dagger shit, and having to operate in that way was probably alien to him.

"Okay, I'll go find your little problem and bring him back here. Who are these people he's with?"

"No idea. It sounds like he's allied himself with a cult of some kind in Stratford, but we don't have more information."

"Do they need to be brought back here, too?"

"They're responsible for, at the very least, helping Simon murder that young girl. Do with them what you will. I will contact the detective in the area who's leading the case and tell him you're on your way."

"What's his name?"

"William Moon—good cop from what I hear. I am loath to interfere in their investigation, but with the knowledge that Simon is involved, I no longer have that luxury."

"This guy pisses you off, doesn't he?"

"Nate, don't fuck around with him. He's a killer, and he's not a man to treat lightly. Be careful."

"Is there anyone else I need to see while I'm there?"

"If you can find them, there's a colony of wood trolls in the woods around Mount Bigalow." He passed me a small map with a red circle drawn on it. "Some of them may have an idea about what's happening."

I sighed. "Needle in a haystack–style search?"

"That depends if any of them wants to be found."

"One last question: why the hell did you become king of Shadow Falls?"

Galahad laughed. It was deep and throaty, a laugh you could hear from some distance away. "Do you not think I have regal bearing, my friend?"

"You're a soldier, Galahad. A very good one, at that. Politics and governing were never things you had any interest in. You were always more concerned with honor and finding a good woman to lay with."

"Unlike my father, I learned a long time ago that everyone has to grow up sometimes."

Galahad's father was Lancelot. The same Lancelot who had betrayed the knights and his friends for a woman. Before that event, Galahad had always wanted to emulate his father, but afterward, he did everything he could to separate them. Maybe by becoming king, Galahad had finally achieved some measure of satisfaction that the apple had fallen far from the tree. Whatever his reasoning, I really hoped he knew what he was doing.

CHAPTER 4

Roberto had gone by the time I left the bar, and taken his Mustang with him. Fortunately, as I was leaving, Rebecca had thrown me the keys to a 1976 Plymouth Trailduster, which turned out to be bright red and was probably big enough to be its own moving house. Still, it was better than walking the 150-odd miles to Stratford. I threw the bag onto the backseat and climbed inside.

The journey took a few hours. The snow and ice on the roads made driving at speed dangerous, and when it started to snow heavily, my movement dropped to a crawl. By the time I reached the small town of Stratford, it was dark.

The roads were relatively abandoned, the weather and time of night combining to keep people inside, but I passed several open fields and some farmland that gave the town a picturesque look. Once in the town itself, it looked like the kind of place that gets put on postcards for tourists. Unfortunately, as I made my way through the town, the thoughts of a group of murderers operating out of there dampened my enthusiasm for the place.

The police station was a large building, considering the "Welcome to Stratford" sign had said it had a population of only 9212 people. There were six patrol cars out front, and the rapidly falling snow had covered them in a thick layer of whiteness.

I parked the Trailduster on the street and immediately wished I could use my fire magic to keep me warm as I dashed to the front door of the building. Once inside, I reveled in the warmth that washed over me.

I glanced around, noting the elevator to the far left and stairs just next to it, alongside two closed doors, although I was in the wrong place to read what was on the nameplates attached to them.

"Can I help you?" a surly-looking cop asked from behind the desk in front of the door. I noticed from the three inverted chevrons on his shoulder that he held the rank of sergeant. He drummed the tip of his pen against the wooden counter and did not appear happy to see me.

"I'm here to see William Moon," I said.

"The detective know you're coming?"

I nodded. "Apparently."

"And you are?"

"Nathan Garrett."

He scribbled something down on a piece of paper. "Sign here." He placed a book in front of me, with a pen tied to the spine. I flicked to the front cover and found it was a visitors' log.

"You going to read the whole thing, or just do as I asked?"

I filled in my name and who I was there to see, but left my address blank.

"You need to put something in there."

"I've just gotten to town; I don't live anywhere at the moment."

The desk sergeant shook his head and mumbled something about out-of-towners that I chose to ignore. He wrote "no fixed abode" on the page and slammed the book shut.

"Second door down the hallway." He pointed in the direction, presumably just in case I got lost on the thirty-foot walk. "Second door."

"Thanks," I said with as cheerful a tone as I could manage and set off in the direction.

"Second door," the sergeant called after me.

"Sorry, I didn't quite catch that?" I called back. Sometimes I can't help myself.

I didn't wait for a response and opened the second door, letting it shut behind me as I entered the short gray corridor beyond. There was one door on my left, with the word stationery written on it, and another door in front of me, which led to a sizeable open-planned office space.

Two men and a woman all sat in silence, each of them at their own desk, either reading something or typing on a typewriter. A glass office with the word *Captain* stenciled onto the door sat at the far end, but it was dark inside, its occupant clearly gone home for the day.

The woman, a youngish brunette with a small button-like nose, on top of which sat her equally small glasses, asked, "Can we help you?"

"I'm looking for Detective Moon," I said.

She pointed to a desk at the far end of the office where a man turned around to look at me. "Detective Moon?" I surmised.

"And you are?" he asked, standing up. He was easily a foot taller than me, and also much wider, with the build of someone who regularly worked out. As I got closer, I noticed the nasty scar just above his cheek. It stretched to his ear and was jagged enough for me to think it was probably the result of broken glass, maybe a bottle, rather than a knife. The words "Semper Fi" were tattooed on his right forearm, just below the rolled-up sleeves of his light-blue shirt.

"Nathan Garrett," I said, offering my hand.

William took the hand in a comfortable shake. You can tell a lot about a man from his handshake. Is it too firm, too loose, does he try to overcompensate for something by trying to crush your hand in return? William didn't go for the crush, not that he would have succeeded. He was more likely to have lost the hand for good, but it was nice to know I was dealing with a grown-up.

"I got a call telling me to expect you." He started patting his pockets and removed some cigarettes. "Let's go outside, I need a smoke."

As we both left the building, I smiled at the desk sergeant and stood outside in the cold while Bill fumbled with a cigarette.

"You want one?" he asked, offering me the packet.

"No, thanks."

He gave me a "please yourself" expression and finally got one lit, taking a long drag before breathing it out. "So, you're here on the behalf of Galahad."

"I'm here to find Simon Olson and stop him and his friends from murdering people. I was told that you were dealing with the case."

Detective Moon took another drag, making me wait for his response. "That's right. Galahad has given me instructions to hand Simon over to him once the case is solved. But someone is going to pay for those murders, and if that means his friends get to see the inside of a jail cell instead of him, then I'm okay with that."

"Simon will see the inside of a place worse than any jail you can imagine," I said.

"I spent eighteen months in Vietnam, I can imagine a shit-load of bad things."

"You were a Marine," I said.

"Yeah, left the corps in seventy-three. Moved here and became a cop. I had a nice quiet life until about four months ago, when the first body showed up."

"How many have there been?"

"Officially? Four. Unofficially? At least a dozen."

"Why the discrepancy?"

"Most of the people are still missing; we've only found four bodies, so that's the official count. It's lucky the captain works for Galahad, too, otherwise the FBI would have been called in. Serial killer cases in a rural town like this, we don't usually have the manpower to solve them."

"Do you know where Simon or any of his friends are?"

William shook his head. "Up near Mount Bigalow is our best guess, although I can't say more than that. The four bodies were found all around the same area. I figure we wait till daylight and then go hunting."

"Anyone else know why I'm here?"

"Captain told everyone you were a external consultant to help bring the killer to justice. People around here are wary of newcomers, but you'll find them friendly enough when they decide you're not here to piss them off. The captain and me are the only two who know who you are."

"Good, that should make things easier."

"Oh, I almost forgot." William took a key from his pocket and passed it to me. "There's a motel about a half-mile down the road. Your room is already booked. Do you have anything with you?"

"A bag with a few bits of clothing and a toothbrush, but nothing that's going to last long."

"There's a clothes shop nearby. We'll get you sorted out in the morning. Can't have you traipsing around the woods and not looking the part."

"Thanks," I said and flicked the red leather key ring over, showing the number 4 in gold.

William walked me back to my truck. "Get some sleep, tomorrow is going to be a long day."

We shook hands once more and I climbed into the Trailduster and started the massive engine. The possibility that there were twelve victims made my skin crawl, and made me wonder what the hell was going on in this small Maine town with its picturesque scenery.

I drove to the motel, which was easy to find due to the number of lights it had on the front, and after making myself known to the overweight, balding man at the reception desk, I found my room and dumped my bag on the freshly made bed.

The room was small, but well kept. A small bedroom, with a door that led to a small bathroom with a shower and toilet. The bedroom had a nice desk, a bedside table, chest of drawers, and small TV. I put my clothes away, then glanced out the window, which overlooked the woods behind the motel. For the briefest of moments I thought I saw movement just inside the end of the tree line.

As soon as I'd convinced myself it was a trick of the ever-increasing wind, it happened again. There was no mistaking that there was definitely someone there.

I threw my coat and shoes back on and stepped outside, making my way around the side of the motel complex to where I'd seen the movement. But by the time I arrived, whoever, or whatever, had been there was nowhere to be found. So, after searching for a few more minutes, and finding nothing of interest, I made my way back to the motel room.

Before I'd even stepped inside, I knew something was wrong; the door was unlocked. I stood to one side of the entrance and pushed open the door with one hand, readying a ball of fire in the other. The room was empty, but someone had been there. And they'd left me a gift. They'd used a dagger to pin a piece of paper to the wall. I stepped inside the room and made the fireball vanish, pulling the dagger out a second later and catching the paper as it fell.

The dagger was called a misericorde—a long, thin, edgeless blade used in medieval times to kill a knight in full armor. The blade was thin enough to slip between the plates or get in between the eye slots on a helmet. It was widely used for mercy killings, to end the suffering of those who were too injured to be helped. I knew of several assassins throughout the years who had used one to kill someone in one-on-one combat. I hadn't seen one quite like it in several centuries, but it appeared to be new. I dropped the dagger on the bed and picked up the note. *You'll find no mercy here. Leave.*

Apparently I was making new friends already.

CHAPTER 5

New York City, New York. Now.

"So, do you feel like sharing how you know who's behind this?" Sky asked as we both left the bathroom and re-entered the main room of the penthouse suite.

I was about to speak when I heard someone trying the door handle. I motioned for Sky to follow me into the main bedroom, keeping the door open just enough to see as someone in a dark hoodie entered the suite and made their way to where the body of Jerry lay.

"It's a woman," I said when the door to the second bedroom closed.

"Pervert."

"Yes, clearly that's why I know it was a woman. The skintight trousers sort of gave it away, as did the fact that she has breasts under that black hoodie. We should go say hello; how do you want to take this?"

Sky opened the bedroom door and sauntered into the middle of the penthouse suite, taking a seat on one of the expensive couches, opposite the door to the second bedroom.

I knew the routine and crouched behind a glass cabinet next to the door, so that whoever the mystery guest was, she wouldn't see me when the door was opened. The idea was simple. They come out, see Sky and their attention is taken for just long enough for me to grab or subdue them. Sky and I had used it before to great effect. It was simple and relatively low risk for all involved.

The woman walked out of the bedroom and saw Sky sitting cross-legged on the sofa with a smile on her face. I was about to move when the woman crouched down and suddenly the wooden floor beneath me was no longer solid. It jumped up, grabbing my ankles and wrists and pinning me in place, solidifying into something much stronger than it had been before. Sky was already moving when the ground beneath her did the same, but instead of keeping her in place, it flung her into the far wall, which enveloped her legs and arms so that only her torso and head was free.

"Fucking bitch," Sky snapped, trying to free herself. "What the fuck is this shit?"

"Alchemy," I said and the woman's head snapped toward me.

A second later, she was up from her couched position, sprinting through the door.

"Come back here," Sky shouted, full of rage at her situation.

I threw a blade of air magic from one hand, into the wood that held the opposite wrist. It was a tricky maneuver—too close and I'd have sliced through my wrist—and it took me three attempts, but I managed to cut through the bonds of wood and dropped to the ruined floor.

"Go get her," Sky shouted. "I'll be fine."

I took after the alchemist at a sprint, making it through the door maybe a minute after her. The illuminated numbers above the lift said that it was still near the lower floors, so I ruled that out as an escape route. That left only the stairwell, which

I blasted open with a jet of air; I didn't want to get jumped by anyone waiting. I stepped through the door and heard the bang of a door above me.

I took the stairs two at a time until I'd cleared the three flights and reached the only door above me: the entrance to the roof.

The wind was freezing cold, and it had started to rain as I opened the door and stepped onto the roof. It contained a mass of metal pipes, air conditioning units, and a variety of electrical equipment that supplied a lot of power to the hotel. The mass of steel meant that the winds, which had been biting at ground level, had some of their sting taken out of them.

Across the large rooftop stood my target. She was glancing over the side of the hotel at a smaller building a hundred feet away, too preoccupied to hear as I crept toward her. Once within a good distance, I created six tendrils of air, which moved toward the woman until they'd wrapped silently around her ankles and calves. By the time she noticed what was happening it was too late and I'd hardened the air into a substance easily as strong as the steel that was littered all around me.

She screamed as I pulled back, causing her to drop to the ground. She slammed her hands onto the concrete roof, and I found myself falling back as the roof bucked in an attempt to get me to release my magic.

"I don't want a fight," I told her.

"Yeah, says the man who just threw magic at me."

"Point taken." Not everyone who isn't a sorcerer can identify magic when it's used against them. She'd clearly had some run-ins with magic users in the past. I released the magic and put my hands up. "Okay, I just want to talk."

The roof stopped doing its impression of a bucking bronco and allowed me to stand up.

"Talk," the woman said.

"You plan on keeping the balaclava on, or do I actually get to see your face?"

"Get on with it," she snapped.

"Who are you? And why were you in that hotel room?"

"If I'm not going to remove the balaclava, I'm not going to tell you my name. And that last part is none of your business."

Her green eyes held a determined expression, and her tone suggested that she wasn't used to having to explain herself.

"My name is Nathan Garrett," I told her, hoping that she might give me something to work with in return.

"Is that meant to mean something?" she asked after I'd paused for a second.

Apparently not, which was probably for the best. It meant she wasn't with Avalon, nor any of the major players who worked with them. "No, I was just hoping you'd return the courtesy. My friend and I were here looking for the murderers of a cop in Ottawa, a friend of mine. I'm doubting that you were involved. They were more . . . chatty."

"I'm sorry for your friend, but like you said, it had nothing to do with me."

"His name was Bill Moon," I told her and instantly noticed something in her eyes, a brief recognition.

"I'm going now."

"How did you know him?" I demanded, feeling my barely concealed anger at his murder begin to bubble up inside me.

"I don't feel like being questioned by someone who attacked me in a hotel room."

"You're going to answer my questions," I told her. "You don't want to do this the hard way."

She laughed, which was something I wasn't exactly expecting. "I've been threatened by bigger and badder people than you."

"Trust me when I say this: I doubt that very much."

She placed her hands on the three-foot wall that ran around the edge of the roof. With an almighty creak, the part she was touching extended outward, using the concrete around it to create a two-foot-wide bridge to the nearest building. It was instantaneous; I'd barely had time to register what she was doing, let alone move to stop her.

"That's very impressive," I said as the woman stood up on the roof and took the first step onto the bridge. "But it won't stop me from getting the answers I need."

"That will." She pointed to my feet, and I looked down to find that the roof had solidified over my shoes, holding me in place. I struggled as the roof exploded up, covering my arms and shoulders, dragging me down onto all fours and forcing my hands inside the concrete of the roof itself.

Before I could get myself free, she sprinted across the hundred-foot bridge, which was sucked back into the hotel the moment she stepped off of it.

Once she was out of sight, the roof moved aside, allowing me to stand up without issue just in time for Sky to come crashing through the door.

"Where the fuck is she?"

"Over here," I said as the last remains of the bridge returned to the building.

"Well, where is she?"

"She used the roof to create a bridge to that building over there and then ran across it and got away."

"You let her escape?"

"Not exactly." I explained about the roof.

"So, we have nothing."

I shook my head. "We have two things. One, she knew who Bill was, although she didn't kill him. Two, she could have killed me—I wasn't exactly on top of my game up here. But she came here for some reason or another."

"You think that dead body wasn't just a message for us?"

I nodded. "Maybe, yeah. That could mean that Bill was working with her on an investigation. It seems a bit too much of a coincidence that Bill's murderers lead us to a hotel where we meet someone who knew him."

"Or it could mean that we're being played with, the same as her, by a bunch of psychotic assholes."

"There's that. But if Bill was looking into something, and the writing of the bathroom wall suggests a link between Bill and his killers that could be very bad indeed, then I don't have a lot of choice about my next destination."

"And what does it mean?"

"That I have to go to Maine."

Sky was silent for a few heartbeats. "You know I can't go with you."

"I know."

"You'll be alone there, that's dangerous. And whoever this woman is, she's capable. She kicked your ass."

"Thanks for the reminder. You got stuck in a wall."

"Okay, we'll call that even." Sky chuckled. "My point still stands, it could be dangerous there."

"I've been alone before, and I know precious few people who aren't linked with one group or another. Shadow Falls will never allow more outsiders to go snooping around."

"Call Tommy. He's independent these days."

Tommy and I had been friends for centuries and had worked together many times. But he had a family now, and I was hesitant to fly him across the planet on the possibility that there could be trouble I couldn't handle alone. Still, if I didn't call and he found out, I'd only have to hear him complaining about it for a few centuries. "I will, although I'm not sure he'd be much help either. By the time he gets here—"

"Just do it. I guess I'm going to have to go back and tell Dad that this is no longer something we can look into."

"There's still plenty to do. You've got a dead cop who works for you, and someone gave the psychotic bastards who killed Bill my number. I'd put money that whoever it is, they're playing a dangerous game." And one I was sure Sky would take great pleasure in seeing they lose.

"I assume you don't want to fly to Portland?" Sky asked.

"Not if I can manage it, no."

"I have an acquaintance in town who'd be able to set you up with something, probably some weapons, too. For a price."

"Is this going to cost me a fortune?"

Sky's sly smile was usually reserved for the moments she thought I'd be out of my comfort zone. "Something like that, yeah."

CHAPTER 6

The sun had set just before we'd left the hotel, although that hadn't done anything to decrease the traffic. Sky phoned ahead to let the garage know we were coming and then drove us to a sizeable five-story garage on East 84th Street by the name of Full Moon Repairs. They advertised themselves as a twenty-four-hour auto repair shop. Several very expensive-looking cars were being worked on by a dozen men and a few women as Sky pulled into the garage. I wondered if they catered to a clientele that wasn't a hundred percent human.

"Try not to piss anyone off," she said as she got out of the car.

"I'll try," I called after her. I wasn't exactly sure what she thought I was going to do, but she seemed very nervous and I didn't want to add to whatever the problem was.

I got out of the car, trying not to notice the gazes that were suddenly on me as I walked over to Sky and the woman she was talking to.

"Felicia Hales," she said. "So, you must be Nate. Sky tells me you need a car?" Her voice had a hint of a southern accent. She looked me up and down and smiled. "Gonna cost ya."

"So I was told, Felicia. How much?"

"Depends what you want. Come with me, we'll see what we can do for you."

I followed her through to the rear of the shop, where she opened a door that led to a set of steps leading down.

"Where do you put all the cars?" I asked as I wondered exactly what Sky had gotten me into.

"We have a lift that can take the cars up and down. We keep most of our customers' cars above ground, it's easier. But we keep a selection of *special* cars down here to sell."

"You mean stolen," I said and Felicia stopped as we reached the bottom of the stairs, and turned back to me.

"Not always. Some are given freely, some are taken in payment. We have all of the documents for each car, so we do legally own them, no matter where they came from originally." She held my gaze. She was a beautiful woman, her long dark-red hair framed her face perfectly, and her piercing sky-blue eyes appeared to look through me. "Will this be a problem?"

I shook my head. "Just want to know where I stand."

"On thin ice," Sky whispered and slapped me around the back of the head.

Felicia smiled. "I was not offended; it's nice to have someone ask outright and not play games. I detest games." She looked me up and down again and then turned around and led us down a short corridor, which ended with a set of double doors that looked strong enough to stop a tank. She placed her hand on the palm reader and, once it beeped, inputted a five-digit code into the numerical pad above it.

"Very security conscious," I said as she held one of the doors open for Sky and me to walk through.

The room inside was cavernous and held dozens of cars, all in rows. A quick glance told me they were in make and model order. It was a mass of incredibly expensive metal and fiberglass. I wondered how long it would take Sky to start drooling.

"Oh my god," she said as she started off toward a blue 1969 Boss 302 Mustang. "Screw Nate, I'll have this for me."

"Do you need a bib?" I asked her as she saw another car she liked, a red Ferrari 458, and ran off.

"It's car porn in here," she called out to me.

"So, Mister Garrett. What car do you want?" Felicia asked.

"Seriously, I can buy any of these?"

"Of course, although Sky tells me you wish to purchase some weaponry, too." She led me past the cars to a small office at the end, where a young man sat reading a book.

"Warren, can you show Mister Garrett the weaponry?"

Warren bowed, then pushed something under the desk he was at. The wall behind Felicia slid open revealing yet another cavernous room.

"This place is like a maze," I said as Felicia led me through the wall to another corridor with half a dozen doors.

"What do you need?"

"Blades," I said.

"Of course." We stopped at the third door and she opened it with a flourish.

I stepped inside and glanced around for some useful additions. Back in England, I kept dozens of blades of a variety of sizes and shapes, but I hadn't brought any of them with me to Canada. A good sword is part of the wielder, like an extension of the person. And my *jian* had been made to be used by me and only me.

I picked up a *katana* and a dozen silver throwing knives on a leather belt that fit around my waist. I don't like to rely on weapons, but I do like to have them as backup for when I go against something that my magic can't beat.

"That everything?"

I stared at the huge claymore in the corner—it was probably overkill. "Yeah, I'm good."

Felicia closed the door behind me and took me back through to the cars, where Sky had stopped running around and was talking to Warren, who Felicia passed the weapons to.

"Now for the car," she said to me.

"Audi R8 coupe," I said. "It's fast, handles well, and has enough room in the storage space to put my stuff. Plus, it's really, really fast."

"You said that already," Warren said.

"Yeah, but it's worth mentioning twice. And besides, the people I'm after already know I'm coming. If I'm going to be a bull's-eye, I may as well be one in a really nice car."

"Do we have any in stock?" Felicia asked Warren, who picked up a tablet from a nearby table and tapped a few things on it. "Two, a red and a black FSI V10 plus."

"Black," I said.

"I believe that model had black rims too," Felicia said, approvingly. "It's a beautiful car. Warren will get it ready for you. It'll be upstairs when you're finished here."

Warren walked off into his office and vanished through the still open wall.

"And now for payment," Felicia said with a smile.

"Okay, what's this going to set me back?"

"Well, Sky is a regular customer of ours, and we were going to do a discount rate for her, but I have a better idea. The payment is you."

"Look, you're a very lovely woman, and I'm sure you can spoon with the best of them, but I'm really not interested."

Felicia laughed; it was deep and rumbled around the room. "My apologies, I probably should explain." She opened her mouth slightly and showed the two long fangs.

"You want my blood? Go fuck yourself." I was furious; blood is considered a sacred thing—you don't take blood without asking, you don't use someone else's blood, and you certainly don't give your blood to a group of people you just met. Blood can be used to do bad things. I know, because I've done some of them.

"Nate, calm down," Sky said.

"Did you know about this?"

"They don't want to take your blood away. She drinks it in front of you, here and now. My dad has done this before, as have I. Felicia is neutral, but she's still our ally."

Sorcerer blood is incredibly potent. Those species who feed on blood, such as Vampires, can gain a lot of power from it. "Did you tell her what I am?" I demanded to know from Sky.

"I already knew," Felicia answered instead. "Your name is well-known in certain circles. Rumor has it you defeated a lich. An impressive feat."

"Actually, Sky did the defeating. I mostly got my ass kicked."

"But you survived. That in itself is something very few have done. It has been a very long time, over a century, since I've tasted from your kind. Your blood contains immense power. I will be able to taste that power, to see more about you and who you are. And in exchange for your letting, I will give you the car and weapons for free, and you will be known as a friend to the New York Vampires."

The fact that both Hades and Sky trusted her went a very long way in changing my mind about allowing my blood to be used. "You're in control of them all?"

"Three hundred and six vampires. Each of them was sired by me or by one of my own. I am the master vampire for the state of New York. What you do today could aid you in many ways in the future."

"Who gets to drink?"

"Me and only me, I swear. One pint of blood."

"Okay you have a deal. One thing: if I find out you ever used my blood to hurt, or do anything that causes me to come back and find you. I will erase you and every vampire you sired from the face of the earth."

Felicia snarled—vampires don't like having their brood threatened—but I kept my gaze cool until she nodded in agreement. "I promise, I shall do nothing of the sort."

"Where do we do this?"

"I'll stay here," Sky said to me. "I'm going to make a few calls about our dead cop in a bathtub, see if I can get something on him."

"I'll be back soon," I told her.

Felecia nodded and turned to me. "Follow me." She led me back through the office and down to the final door in the corridor, which she opened and stepped through.

In movies when a vampire lord enters a room, everyone does one of two things; they either stand and bow as one, or they resume whatever sexual games they were playing. As we walked into the room, neither of those things happened. There were nineteen people in the room, a dozen of whom were women, all clothed, which was real shame as each and every one of them could have held a stadium's attention just by walking in. The men too looked like they'd just stepped out of a modeling shoot.

The room itself was covered in soft rugs and comfortable-looking couches. A huge TV sat on the wall at one end, playing a music channel, although the song itself was something I'd never heard before. The occupants had been lounging around watching TV, although a few of them had been reading or chatting amongst themselves. While it's true that vampires tend to pick the attractive humans to turn, most of them also pick people who have a modicum of intellect or interesting things to say; no one wants to be stuck with a pretty idiot for all eternity.

When Felicia stepped through the doors no one moved to bow, no one even glanced her way. Only vampire masters with self-esteem issues make their people bow to them on a regular basis.

At the end of the room, on top of a raised platform, sat a large leather chair, behind which was a full set of armor. Felicia stood in front of it and clicked her fingers, switching the TV and lights off and replacing their light with torches that had been set around the room. It was an impressive trick. Vampire masters could usually do a little magic. As one, every man and woman stood in silence.

"Today is a great day," Felicia said, her voice carrying so it sounded as if she were standing right next to me. "Today a new ally has come to us to offer himself to our great brood."

I wasn't really sure of how to respond to that, so I waved slightly, drawing a smile from Felicia as everyone turned to look at me.

"This man is Nathan Garrett," she continued, causing all nineteen heads to snap back toward her. "Let it be known that he is a friend to us all." She stepped off the platform and walked toward me as her subjects watched her move. She really was stunningly beautiful. A few inches shorter than me, but in three-inch heels she was roughly the same height. Her long billowing skirt had a slit down one side that allowed me to glimpse her slender legs with every step she made. She placed one elegant finger on my chest and brushed her mouth across my neck, allowing me to inhale her. She smelled like passion fruit. I really like passion fruit. I had to remind myself that there were twenty people in the room—and also that she could tear me in half without too many problems. Vampire masters were a level of power that was scary to anyone with two brain cells to rub together. If she'd decided to take me by force, the only way I could have stopped would have ended with one of us dead. And I wouldn't have put money on me.

"You're a very handsome man," Felicia whispered as she walked around me, running her hands over my body. "I like my men rugged, to be men. Have you ever had a vampire take blood from you before?"

"Many times," I said. "Are you sure you want to do this?"

She nodded and grinned. "How many of those did you allow?"

"Two." Both of them were to help a vampire heal.

"What did you do to those who took your blood without permission?" Felicia had made a full circuit of my body and stood in front of me.

"I turned them to ash." I had whispered the words, but they appeared to explode around the room so that everyone heard.

"And do you give yourself to me willingly?"

"Yes." My words were almost a snarl; I had no idea why, but just being near Felicia made me want to tear her clothes off.

"Then come to me."

She didn't so much as lead me as I followed without complaint until I was on top of the platform and sitting in the chair. "This won't hurt," she said and straddled my lap. Her words were normal to my ears. Whatever magic or power she was using had stopped, although I still wanted her.

My head felt clearer. "Not me it won't. Last chance to change your mind."

She kissed me hard on the mouth before breaking away and sinking her teeth into my neck.

Allowing your blood to be taken by a vampire did incredible things to both participants. It created a bond, albeit briefly, whereby just after the bite stopped, you could see into each other's lives. It was a tiny glimpse into a person, and it was how most vampires gauged whether they wanted to extend that bite into one that would turn the other person. And if the person being bitten wasn't human, then the vampire gained strength from the blood far in excess of anything they could get from a human.

The bite lasted only a few seconds, but once it broke I saw Felicia as a small girl on a ship to America. I saw her grow up, marry, have children, and then I saw it all taken away by a vampire, who left her alive to use as his own. I saw her kill him, take his brood, and move away from Georgia. Images of her throughout her life flashed through my head—men and women she'd been with, and those she'd killed—until it faded and I sat, exhausted, in the chair.

Felicia had a slightly different experience. She screamed.

It took me a few seconds to realize that she was on the ground thrashing about as whatever memories of mine ripped through her. None of her subjects leapt to help her, most appeared shocked and confused, but some were glancing at me with the intention of blaming me for what was happening to their master.

One of the men, a huge monster of a vampire, stared at me and took a step forward.

"No!" Felicia ordered. "You will stay where you are."

The man stopped in mid-step and then moved back.

"Are you okay?" I asked. I didn't bother to offer my hand; no one in a position of power would have accepted it in the circumstance.

She nodded and got back to her feet, using the chair to keep herself steady. "Who are you?"

"I did say you could back out," I told her and tried to stand up.

Felicia pushed me back into the chair and straddled me once more. "Out, all of you."

The entirety of the vampires quickly left the room.

"Now, who are you?"

"What did you see?"

"Death and power. I saw you fight that lich. I saw you kill a ghoul with magic. I heard someone call your name. Hellequin."

"Yeah, I'm Hellequin."

She kissed me so hard it took my breath away. "You are not real."

"Yes, I am. I'm just not what the stories say."

She kissed me again. "I have rarely felt power such as yours. I can feel so much of it locked inside you, but a part of it courses through me. You cannot access it all, can you?"

I shook my head. "No."

"When you can, when you have full control over what you are, promise me something?"

I wasn't sure where she was going with her words, but I was beginning to stir as she moved against my lap, making any thoughts that might be rational a good deal more difficult.

She reached down and released me from my jeans, taking the time to stroke me slowly with one hand and move her thong aside with the other. When she was ready, she positioned herself just above my tip. "Promise me that when you have all your power, you won't use it to conquer all you can see."

I would have promised to burn the moon if she'd asked at that point. She moved in circles, never quite lowering herself enough to take me inside her; her breathing quickened and her movements sped up.

"I promise," I said breathlessly and grabbed her hips, pulling her down onto me in one motion as she turned her face into my neck and cried out in pleasure.

A vampire's stamina is at the same time a scary and incredible thing. I have no idea how long we sat in that chair, or in various other places in the room, but I would have guessed a few hours. At some point, she'd bitten me again and I'd tasted some of her blood. By the end of our time together, I could still feel her energy coursing through me. I had no need for sleep or food or drink, just her. Repeatedly.

"How the hell do vampires ever get anything done?" I asked as we lay on one of the rugs, our clothes somewhere forgotten.

"Sometimes we don't," Felecia said with a sly grin. "You're going to feel it when that blood of mine wears off." She rolled off me and stood up, giving me the perfect view of a perfect body. I could have bounced coins off her stomach and ass.

"I'll manage."

"So having your blood taken wasn't such a bad thing?"

"Unexpected," I said. "Although if I get a car every time I come here, I'm going to need to buy some sort of multistory car park to keep them all in."

Felicia laughed, bent over, and kissed me on the lips. "What I said before, about the power inside you. I meant it, Nate. Please don't let it change you. I saw what you're truly capable of without those marks on your chest."

"You saw my future?"

"No, just a glimpse of your potential. I saw your past. You are a frightening man, Nathan Garrett. But a damn good fuck."

I laughed. "Ah, I bet you say that to all the men you bond with and then fuck on the floor."

She kissed me again. "You should go, I've delayed you enough."

"Did Sky tell you where I was going?"

Felicia shook her head.

"I'm off to Maine. Does your influence extend enough that you've heard anything about up there?"

Felicia picked up her top from the floor and turned to look at me. "I can ask around, but I'm not aware of anything."

It took a while for me to get dressed, mostly because I couldn't find half of my clothes, but once we were both acceptable, we left the room and made our way back through the cave of cars and upstairs.

"Fucking hell," Sky said as we walked through the door to the main garage. "You two have been hours."

"Sorry," I said. "Sort of lost track of time."

Warren walked toward me and offered me some keys. "Your car and bags are ready."

"Nate," Felicia said. "It'll be daylight soon, I'll have to go. Remember, you *always* have a friend here, and be careful." She said goodbye to Sky and then left.

"I think you made an impression," Sky said.

I exhaled. "You have no idea."

"You off to Maine now?"

"Stratford, yeah. It's a few hours' drive."

"Be careful, and we'll contact you if we get anything from that safe, or from whoever is working against us."

"Thanks. Just watch your back, Sky. Something weird is happening here."

As we walked together over to Sky's truck, she whispered, "Our people are still sifting through the house. When we find something, and we will, I'll call and let you know. So, was it worth coming here?"

I couldn't stop a grin from spreading across my lips. "You're a fucking genius, Sky. And I will never ever say that again."

Sky laughed as she climbed up into the driver's seat of her father's Range Rover. "You know, you never told me who you think is behind this. What's the House of Silent Screams?"

"It's a house that belonged to a group of people that made the Mansons look rational and normal."

"And why were you so shocked to see it written on the bathroom wall?"

"Because it doesn't exist anymore, and it hasn't for over thirty years."

CHAPTER 7

Portland, Maine. 1977.

After finding the misericorde dagger in the motel room wall, I packed up all my stuff and switched rooms. I did actually want to get some sleep at some point. Not that I thought there would be a repeat performance; they'd made their point and would have waited for me to make mine. But better to be cautious than dead.

I met up with William outside the motel just before 7 AM. He had two polystyrene cups in his hand and passed me one, which I waved away.

"You don't like coffee?" he asked; it was clearly something he'd never encountered before.

"No, it's horrid stuff. Smells nice though."

William shrugged, downed one cup and crunched it up, throwing the remains into the bin beside him before starting the second cup.

I told the detective about the visitor the night before and his expression soured.

"I promise you, only the captain and I know, and he's not going to tell anyone."

"Well, someone figured it out. Let's get this done as quickly as possible, I don't want to drag it out."

The detective drained his second cup of coffee and threw the cup away as a black BMW E12 pulled up beside us. A man wearing a suit opened the passenger door and glanced at us while he walked to the rear door and pulled it open, whereupon an older-looking man stepped out.

William immediately brought himself up to his full height. "Mayor Richards," he said and offered his hand to the immaculately dressed man.

"Bill," he said and shook his hand before turning to face me. "You must be Nathan." He didn't offer me his hand; he just stared at me, as if trying to figure me out.

"That's what people tell me," I said. "I didn't think anyone other than the detective and his captain knew I was here."

"Well, apparently I'm important enough to be told these things," Mayor Richards said. "Galahad himself sent you here; the old king would not have sent an *outsider* to deal with the problem."

"Maybe that's why he's the old king," I said as Bill's mouth dropped open in shock.

The mayor forced a smile and nodded slightly. "You should be careful here, Mister Garrett, the people you're after are dangerous. I would hate to have to explain to Galahad how you didn't complete your mission."

I noticed that the man who had opened the car door for the mayor had his hand resting on top of a pistol. I wondered how far the mayor was going to push it before he just allowed his man to use the gun. I really didn't want to have to kill a mayor and his bodyguard within twenty-four hours of arriving. It's terribly bad form to do such a thing.

"Thanks for your concern," I said with a smile of my own. "I'm sure I can find those responsible and bring them to justice before long. Galahad will be happy to hear the warm welcome your lovely town has offered me during my stay."

The mayor straightened his blue silk tie. "Yes, of course. I'm sure *the king* would be more than happy to hear how you've been treated. I look forward to telling him how your visit went." He nodded to Bill and then got back in his car. The bodyguard closed the door, and once he was also in the car, it drove off.

"You don't want to piss him off," Bill said.

"Bill or William?" I asked, ignoring his comment. I'd pissed off people in bigger positions of power than some mayor of a tiny town in the middle of nowhere. In fact, some people would say that pissing off people in power is almost a hobby of mine. "What do you prefer?"

"Bill," he said. "I mean it though, pissing off the mayor isn't a smart move. Word is he's friends with some powerful people."

"I guess we know where the leak came from. Maybe some of those friends of his aren't too keen on me being here."

"I'm telling you the captain didn't sell you out."

"Oh, I have no doubt. I'd guess someone who works for Galahad told him. Though I have no idea why at the moment. Hopefully we can get this finished before I have to find out."

The mayor's unscheduled visit had clearly left a mark on Bill, as he barely spoke while we went to the nearest clothing shop and picked me up some hiking boots and a few bits I would need. We dropped everything off at my motel room, and then he drove me over to the city morgue to see the most recent body.

We parked outside the front door of the small building and walked inside to be greeted by a middle-aged man with a bald head, scraggly dark beard, and a faded tattoo on one forearm.

"It's military," he said to me. "Got it a very long time ago just after Germany. You're probably too young to even remember WW2."

"You'd be surprised, Doctor . . . ."

"Pierce," he said and shook my hand. "Harold Pierce. I'm the coroner for this town. We don't normally get a lot of deaths, so it's usually quiet."

"Nathan Garrett," I said.

The doctor led through a reception area, where a young woman and man sat behind a desk talking; the man wore a security guard uniform. He was older than the woman, who couldn't have been much more than thirty, whereas the man must have hit fifty a few years previous. Neither of them looked up at us as we walked past.

"You're not squeamish, are you?" he asked as we scrubbed our hands and arms.

I shook my head. "Not yet, no. How bad are these bodies?"

"You'll see."

The doctor took us through a set of double doors and into an examination room. There was a body with a sheet over it in the center. Doctor Pierce folded back the sheet, exposing the battered and bruised face of a young man. The body had clearly been examined already and then stitched back up.

"Someone beat him to death," Doctor Pierce said. "I've already carried out the autopsy, but Bill said you'd want to see the body firsthand."

"Thanks. So what does the autopsy say?" I asked.

"I'll do it in layman's terms, for Bill's sake; some of these words are quite long."

"Piss off, doc," Bill said, and the mood in the room lightened slightly.

"Layman's terms are fine," I said, pulling the sheet down further to find more bruising around the clavicle, sternum, and ribs. "What the hell was he beaten with? These marks on his chest aren't from a fist."

"You know your injuries," Doctor Pierce said, sounding slightly impressed. "It was something steel . . . we found shards of the metal imbedded in his—along with the other victims'—flesh. He also has cuts and burns all over his legs and genitals. I've seen that type of torture before, in Germany. A man talks pretty fast when you start putting out cigarettes on his cock. And apart from his wounds, he hadn't eaten much prior to his death; in fact, it had been a few days since his last meal. There were no alcohol or drugs in his system." He picked up the arm beside him and showed me the victim's wrist. "It wasn't tied up recently, but at some point someone had been. These marks are from struggling. They're all over the other wrist too. It's the same for all four victims."

"So they tortured and killed these people for kicks, or revenge, or because they wanted something from them," I said more to myself than to anyone in the room. "Anything out of the ordinary, something weird in all four bodies?"

"No, unfortunately not. However, apart from the severe beatings and torture, all three of them do share a common wound."

Doctor Pierce motioned for Bill to help him roll the body onto his side, showing me the gaping hole, about the size of my closed fist, on the back of his shoulder. "There's an identical one in the other man and the older of the two women we found."

"And the fourth victim, the young woman, I assume that's Sally-Ann?"

Doctor Pierce nodded. "She's the odd one out. There are still some beating marks, but they were done after she died. And they were from someone's booted foot."

"Someone kicked her in anger after they killed her."

"I wouldn't like to say if it was done in anger or not, but the rest of what you say is correct."

"So, what was cut out of them?" Bill asked.

"I have no idea," Doctor Pierce said. "But from the size and depth of wound, I'd say they were either removing something from inside them, or there was something on them that they needed and weren't too concerned about how much flesh they took to do it. They were also inflicted postmortem."

"A tattoo?" I asked.

"It's possible. Although they could have taken a lot less flesh if they were just removing one. Oh, one final thing, the knife to do this was incredibly sharp. There's no hacking or sawing, it was just gouged out."

"How was the girl, Sally-Ann, killed?"

"Throat was cut, one slice across the carotid artery. She bled out in minutes at most. She would have been unconscious in seconds."

"So her death and the way her body was treated after death was different?" Bill said. "Could be someone using the other murders as a way to hide the body."

"That's also possible," I said. "But something tells me otherwise. I think she was a mistake. She didn't fit with the usual victims for some reason and they had to kill her anyway."

"All I can say," Pierce said as he and Bill lowered the body back onto the metal table, "is that I hope you find those responsible very soon. I don't want to keep seeing the young men and women of this state end up on my tables."

CHAPTER 8

After the morgue, Bill drove us both up to where the body of Sally-Ann had been found, just inside the forest that surrounded Mount Bigalow. We didn't talk on the journey, but it wasn't uncomfortable, merely the silence of two people who had bigger things to think about than small talk.

Bill pulled his Ford Bronco over to the side of the road and switched off the engine.

"They found her just up there," he said and pointed toward a slight hill before opening the door and stepping out into the cold.

I quickly followed. The air was jarring, but the wind would have been much worse if not for the protection of the dense forest that towered on both sides of the road. A few dozen cars passed us by as I followed Bill to the top of the hill. We stopped there and looked down a steep fifteen-foot bank. I was amazed that anyone had seen Sally-Ann's body.

"She was dropped here and pushed down the verge," Bill said. "The snow should have completely buried her, but her hand remained free."

I jumped down the embankment, using air magic to keep myself upright, and skidded along the top of the snow until I reached the bottom.

"We can't all show off with magic," Bill shouted as he made his way farther along the road to where the drop was more manageable.

I left the detective to his own devices and stepped into the forest. "Were the other three bodies found here?" I asked as I heard Bill arrive.

"The other three were found about a mile north of here. There was nothing done to hide the bodies. They were just dumped in the woods."

"Do you have a lot of predators around here?"

"We've got some lynx and the occasional black bear, maybe a few wolves; people say there're cougars here, but I've never seen one."

"Maybe they hoped the wildlife would do the job for them."

We walked deeper into the woods until we could no longer see, nor hear, the cars on the road.

"You fancy telling me where we're going?"

"I need to see someone," I said. "According to Galahad I can find him and his colony around this area of Mount Bigalow."

"A colony of what, exactly?"

I didn't answer as as we carried on walking for a few hundred yards until we reached an opening with a stream. It was maybe ten feet wide and looked deep enough to swim in when it was warm. Twigs and branches were piled up against some of the larger rocks that had been there for a lot longer than I'd been alive, deposited by the gentle current of the water as they'd been swept from farther up in the forest.

A few feet away there were two huge boulders and then a third smaller one. Someone had placed a sizeable branch between the two boulders to serve as a makeshift bridge, then piled stones and rocks beside it to make steps.

"Stay here a second," I said and climbed up onto the first boulder and walked across the branch, which as it turned out was actually a tree trunk. Someone had torn it from the ground and placed it in exactly the right spot. The roots had been ripped away—bite marks said someone had probably eaten them.

When I got to the second boulder, I saw what I was looking for. Fur. Dark brown in color and coarse to the touch, it had been snagged on a smaller branch.

"Bill, this way," I said and dropped down onto the third rock before jumping over onto the other side of the stream.

I waited for Bill to make his way across, as he was considerably more nervous than I was, although he still made the way without complaint.

"What is that, bear fur?" His eyes darted around us and his hand dropped to his gun.

"No, no bears here, this belongs to something else." I noticed movement out the corner of my eye. "I'd take your hand off your gun. And I'd do it really slowly."

Bill did as he was asked, but never stopped glancing around to see what was going on. "Are we in danger?"

"Not yet, but you'll know if we are."

"How?"

"We'll be dead." I walked into the forest once more and after a few hundred feet stopped and sat on an fallen tree.

Bill sat beside me. "We're still being watched."

I nodded. "They're trying to figure out what we're here for. Take your holster off and put it on the grass beside you. I'm going to try and get them to trust us."

"You want me to remove my gun? Are you mad?"

"Okay, you can keep your gun, I'm almost certain there's not a bullet you own that will hurt one of these. So unless you're planning on using it to shoot yourself, it's sort of useless here. Hunting is illegal, yeah?"

He nodded. "Had a few hunters out here about three years ago. Never found the bodies."

"Still think your gun is going to help?"

Bill sighed and unbuckled his holster, dropping it on the ground by his feet.

I stood up and took a deep breath. "My name is Nathan Garrett," I said, using my air magic to carry my voice deeper into the forest. "You may have heard my name, you may not. But I am not here to hurt you. I've been sent by Galahad to discover the identity of those who have been killing. Those who have been hunting on your land, those who will keep killing. They will not stop. But I will stop them. I will bring peace back to your forest. But I need your help. I need to know what you know. I need to know where these people are."

"Why?" came a booming voice from inside the woods.

Bill fell back off the branch and immediately started looking around for where it came from.

"These people only placed one body on our land. We made sure she could be found, uncovered the snow that hid her. They did not stay long enough for us to remove them."

"But you tracked them?"

There was a long pause. "Yes."

"Will you help me?"

The pause was longer, and for a second I thought I'd lost them. "Are you really Nathan Garrett?"

"Yes, why?"

"Many years ago, it's said that you saved the life of a member of another colony. Is this true?"

"He was injured . . . another sorcerer tried to kill him to use his blood in a ritual. It was in Wisconsin as I made my way back from Montana. I was in no mood for people with delusions of grandeur."

"You killed the sorcerer—one of your own kind?"

"My kind don't slaughter because they want more power. They earn it."

There was another pause, and the tree next to me seemed to move slightly before something stepped out from behind it. It was as if it had been part of the tree, the camouflage was so complete. It was nearly eight feet tall and very slender, with long powerful arms that looked a little like those of an orangutan. He had long fur, a mixture of dark browns, greens, and black. It was a little darker than the patch I'd found on the tree. What appeared to be leaves were growing out of his body, and I noticed that some of the other trolls had small flowers or a bark-like substance over their fur. His face resembled that of a gorilla, dark and hairless, although the skull wasn't quite as tall and the maw was longer, almost baboon-like. He opened his mouth and showed the razor-sharp front teeth of an apex predator.

"What is that?" Bill asked. "Is that Big—"

"No," I snapped. "Don't use that word, they really don't like it." Three more creatures had stepped out of the shadows behind Bill, none of them less than seven feet tall. All of them were slender and very strong. One of the three, a female, touched Bill's head and he jumped in shock.

The creature who had made himself known to me barked at her in a language I didn't understand and the female moved back.

"What's he saying?" Bill asked.

"No idea, but I'm guessing he told her to leave you alone."

"How do you know she's a girl?"

"White strip on the top of her head. The wider the stripe, the older they are."

"I was only wondering why you had no hair," the female said, making Bill look very nervous.

"You can all speak English?" Bill asked, ignoring the hair comment.

"Yes, of course," she said. "Some of us can speak many languages. English isn't very hard." She glanced up at me. "The one you saved was my brother. I thank you for what you did."

"It was no problem," I told her.

"How do you keep in touch?" Bill asked. "Do you have phones?"

The female laughed; it was an odd sound, sort of like a human laugh, but as if the person had swallowed a bag of nails first. "All kin share a mild telepathy."

"Umm, who are you?" Bill asked her.

"My name is Theris of the Maine Wood Troll colony. I am the alpha female. My mate, the one Nathan was talking to, is Rean. And you, human, are welcome into our homes." She stepped aside as dozens of wood trolls stepped out of the shadows.

"How did you know this place even existed?" Bill asked as we sat against a huge tree, watching the wood troll children running around. Occasionally a brave one would come toward us and ask a question, scurrying away the second we answered.

"Galahad told me to come here and find the colony."

"So, they'll help us?"

"Not sure, it's why the elders went off to talk alone. Wood trolls don't tend to get involved in events that don't concern them. If our killer was dumping a lot of bodies in their territory, they'd have been jumping at the chance. As it is, it's probably fifty-fifty. But it was worth a try."

"You think they know where the killers are?"

"If they tracked the car, then yes, they would know. It depends on how angry they were about what happened. They may not have wanted to get involved, but they're still going to want to be aware of what's out there."

"Have you dealt with wood trolls before?"

"Oh, yeah, there are a few who work in Avalon, and you can find them all over Europe and Asia."

"And they're all friendly?"

"Some are assholes, some aren't. But as a rule, they don't go out to hurt people who leave them alone."

"Are there any other types of troll?"

"Swamp, cave, and snow, although wood trolls are the most tolerant of people."

"And the other three?"

"Swamp trolls are fairly ambivalent toward everyone else as a rule. Snow trolls, or yetis, want nothing to do with anyone. In my entire life, I've seen three yetis. They're not exactly social."

"And cave trolls?"

"They're probably the closet thing to a psychopath that the troll world has. They kill for sport, for food, or because they simply have nothing better to do. They're massive beasts who would tear even another troll apart just because they can."

"You ever met one?"

"A few, yes."

"You ever kill one?"

"Once. It's not something I care to go through again."

Any further questions were cut short by the arrival of Theris and a young wood troll I hadn't met before. I stood and gestured for Bill to do the same. Theris gently pushed the youngster forward with one of her huge hands.

"My name is Thean. You have met my mother and father."

"Nice to meet you," I said and Bill nodded a hello.

"My father has given me the duty to inform you that we cannot help in this matter. We will not be dragged into a conflict with these people."

"From your tone, I guess you don't agree," I said.

"My mother and I think he is wrong. *I* think he is short-sighted. These people will get bored of hunting humans soon enough. Because I voiced my displeasure at his decision, I am duty bound to give you the news. Apparently, I have to remember my place."

"Thean," his mother said. "Your father looks out for the colony. And Nathan, I am sorry we can't help further."

"Are you serious?" Bill demanded as Rean arrived and glared at the policeman. "People are being murdered out there, and you know where these people could be, but you *won't* help?"

"Bill," I said, warning him to stand down. Trolls aren't like people, they take anger as a sign of challenge. Bill did not want to challenge a wood troll in front of his entire clan—I wasn't sure I could stop them from tearing him apart.

"No," he snapped. "I don't want to see any more bodies brought into the morgue because these people are too afraid to involve themselves."

Silence descended like a dropped anvil.

"You dare question our bravery?" Rean roared and took a few steps toward Detective Moon. The detective was a good two feet shorter than the wood troll, but he didn't back down or even blink.

"Then help us," Bill said softly. "What if it were your son we'd found? What if it were one of these kids? Wouldn't you want me to do everything in my power to find those responsible?"

"You compare our kinds, but we are not the same," Rean said, his voice full of anger. "*We* would have tracked down the killers and slaughtered them after the first body was found."

Emotions were starting to run high, and I had to drag Bill aside before he said something he'd regret. Wood trolls might be more accepting than their brethren, but they still had a limit after which they would physically retaliate. And having a human get in their face and question their decisions was going to make that limit arrive a lot sooner than anyone wanted.

"Thank you for your time," I said to Theris and Rean, the latter of which stormed off as we left the colony.

"You're a lucky idiot," I told Bill after we'd reached the stream a few minutes later. "A few more minutes of shouting and I'd have been trying to stop him tearing you in half."

"That fucking asshole knows where these people are; they're just not going to tell us because they're scared."

I took a seat on a sizeable rock. "They've been in this forest for decades, probably longer. If they got involved, there was always a chance that any peace and quiet they've managed to make for themselves would be shattered. People could die. And to a wood troll, their own people are more important than the lives of other species."

"All they had to do was take us to where they tracked the killers, and we'd have done the rest."

"But to them, that was too much. You can't push trolls; when they push back, it tends to be very final."

"So, we're back to square one?"

"Not exactly. We know that the trolls tracked the killers when they drove off, and that no wood troll I've ever heard of would have left the confines of the forest to track."

"Okay, so instead of no idea, we have a couple hundred square miles to search through. That's not a whole lot better."

"You have better than that," Rean said as he stepped out into the clearing. "I'm going to show you where they are."

I had to admit that took me by surprise, but Bill got there first. "What the hell are you playing at?"

"I'm sorry for my deception, but most of the elders do not wish for us to become involved." Rean bowed his head slightly and stared at his feet; such a gesture was to show either fear or respect. I knew for a fact that Rean wasn't scared of Bill or me. It was an apology for his actions. He soon straightened back to his full height. "However my mate and I both agree that our involvement is a necessity if we're to remain protected in this forest."

"But you had your son—" I started.

"I know, but I cannot have my son involved any more than he already is. He's young and impulsive. As we all are at his age.

I won't risk his standing with the elders by going against their wishes. I'm an elder already, the worst they can do to me is make disapproving noises."

"*More than he already is?* It was your son who tracked them, wasn't it?"

Rean nodded. "He was out with a small hunting party, they saw the body, and Thean decided to go after the killers. He came back once he established the threat against the colony was minimal. He wanted to go back and force them to leave, but I would not allow it."

"How far away are these people?"

"A few miles. I will not help you kill them, but I will not stand by while they do as they wish, either."

"Just point us in the right direction," I said. "We'll do the rest."

CHAPTER 9

The hike through the woods was long and, on more than once occasion, dangerous. Loose dirt and a lack of handholds, made climbing some of the steeper hills a treacherous proposition. I had my magic to fall back on, but Bill had nothing more than his natural skill and a bit of good luck.

Rean on the other hand, barely stopped to take a breath. He walked in a straight line, never deviating from the path, no matter how much hard work it was. He glided up hills without the use of a handhold or slipping on the surface. It was impressive to behold, as if his own weight shifted itself to ensure he remained in balance at all times.

By the time Rean stopped walking and motioned for us to crouch low, the sun was setting behind us.

We were lying prone on top of a cliff, fifty feet above the house that Rean had led us to. It gave us an excellent vantage point, and the dense bushes all around afforded us some extra protection from any wandering eyes below.

"Are you sure Sally-Ann's killers are in there?" I asked Rean.

The wood troll nodded. "This is where they were tracked to."

"How do we get in?" Bill asked. "There are only two of us, and we have no idea how many of them there are, or what weapons they have."

Bill had a good point. The house was a large two-story wooden building that had probably been constructed during the late-seventeenth or early-eighteenth century. It had been re-painted a deep brown at some point, but small patches of white showed through the side facing the cliff.

There were no windows facing us, but even without them any approach would be difficult. The driveway, clearly a new addition to the property, was made of deep red brick, with large irregular sized rocks set on the verge on either side. It curved with the land, vanishing behind some trees after a few dozen feet. The rear of the property was mostly woodland, but the trees were sparse and there was a fifty-foot gap from their edge to any side of the house.

"Rean, can you take Bill back to the car?"

Bill opened his mouth to argue, but I got there first. "We'll need backup; you have to arrest whoever is alive in there after I've gotten Simon out. Unless you plan on either marching them all into town or making them all sit in the back of your car, you're going to need more people. Besides, I need you to get hold of Galahad and get him here; I assume your captain knows a way."

"And what are you going to do?"

"I'm going to stay right here and watch," I said. "And when it's dark enough I'm going to try and find out exactly what we're dealing with."

"The cliff slopes down to the ground a short distance that way," Rean said. "You're still going to have a sizeable gap between there and the house though, so you'll need to be careful."

I thanked Rean and he began moving back from the cliff edge. "Bill, give me twelve hours, then turn up with the cavalry.

I should have Simon dealt with, and hopefully anyone else in there will go quietly."

Bill shook my hand and then followed Rean back into the forest.

Once alone, I returned my attention to the house and wondered if it were possible to get around to see the front and back of the building without giving myself away.

The rear of the building was simple enough, I just followed Rean's directions and made my way down the slope to my right, ensuring to keep far enough back that any sudden movements didn't give me away.

The back of the house contained seven windows—three on the lower floor and four above it. There were no lights on in the house itself, but a large shed sat nearby and light spilled out from the small windows.

I moved back up the slope and along to the left of where I'd started, but was unable to get all the way around to the front of the house as the cliff stopped short. The only way to move any farther was to use the huge trees. I glanced around to ensure there was no one about and took a few steps back. I started to run toward the cliff edge, but just then the house's front door opened. I managed to stop myself before I hit the point of no return and dropped to the ground, getting a mouthful of dirt and snow for my trouble.

A man, wearing an expensive long coat, stood on the front porch in the light of the open front door and looked around the forest in front of him. His collar was pulled up, obscuring his face, but a second man joined him, wearing only a dark t-shirt and jeans.

Even with air magic, there was no way I was going to be able to hear anything the men said to one another, but the conversation was short and the better dressed of the two men was clearly the one in charge. After a few minutes, the well-dressed man walked around to the side of the house, and a short time later there was the roar of an engine starting.

The second man hadn't moved from his spot in front of the house. He turned and watched as the car sped off down the drive, but didn't immediately go back inside. Instead, he glanced around the forest and removed a cigarette from his pocket, which was quickly lit.

He stayed where he was for a few minutes, the only movement was the removal of the cigarette from his lips and the exhale of the toxic smog. He turned toward me and stared at the exact spot where I was hiding. I wasn't concerned he'd spotted me; he couldn't have seen me if he were only a few feet away, much less the few hundred that separated us.

All of a sudden a scream sounded out over the quiet night and the man dropped his cigarette onto the ground, using his foot to extinguish it.

A second man walked out of the woods. He was a huge brute of a man; at least a foot taller than me and probably several stone heavier. He was dragging a young woman, her blonde hair wrapped up in his fist to ensure that escape was impossible. She flailed in his iron grasp, twisting and turning as her feet scraped along the ground behind her. I couldn't hear her words, but I could see her pained expression. Anguish and fear were obvious beneath the grime. She kicked snow up constantly from the ground, covering everything it touched. The man dragging her stopped and kicked her in the stomach once, twice, and a third time. I winced with the last strike as the fight left the young woman and she sagged, defeated. Dragging her was easier now, and he continued to perform his task with a smile.

A third man came into view, equal in size to the first, with a prone male thrown over his shoulder like a bag of flour. As they reached the light from the still-open front door, I saw the blood that had covered one side of the male victim's face. It had matted his long hair and dripped steadily onto the ground where it was swallowed up by the snow.

The first brute dropped the woman onto the house's porch, and she immediately tried to bolt, but she was grabbed once more and thrown through the front door. The second brute followed with the unconscious man, while the smaller man glanced around quickly as the woman's screams started, then joined the others in the house, closing the door behind.

The screams died with the closing of the door—the house was probably soundproofed, although I doubted there was anyone within a few miles who would have heard anything even if it wasn't.

I couldn't just leave the newcomers to the company of these brutal men, and I hesitated to think about whatever horrific end would befall them if I didn't act. But rushing in would likely end in disaster, either for me or the new victims.

I moved back a few paces and once again sprinted to the cliff edge, launching myself toward the nearest large tree and using my air magic to land on one of its thickest branches. I swung myself down onto another branch and then dropped onto the soft ground ten feet below, my air magic ensuring I'd be silent.

I used the cover of foliage to make my way around to the front of the house, where I could see the front door for the first time. It was a well-made wooden door that had been painted a deep red color. Several marks, which appeared to be from a claw of some kind, sat in the middle of the door. The window next to the door was broken, the bars on the inside clearly visible. I'd have wagered that the house was a well-fortified structure, probably not easy to break into without some serious help.

I wondered if Simon had sorcerer-proofed it—he must have been aware that someone would come for him. So, if he'd sorcerer-proofed the door with some runes, it probably wasn't worth trying. Just in case.

I'd decided that the window closest to me was probably my best place to gain entry. I'd all but made my mind up when Bill walked toward the house, with Rean behind him, occasionally pushing him forward. They reached the front door and Bill knocked twice, which was answered by the man in jeans I'd seen on the porch earlier. He spoke, but I couldn't have heard him even if I'd been standing right next to them, my anger took over. Rean had betrayed us.

"You're out there," the man said. "Nathan, I know you're out there."

Rean pointed in my direction. Apparently a wood troll's vision was even better than I'd heard about.

"Come out, come out," he said and punched Bill in the face hard enough to knock the big man to his knees. "Or do I need to start on your friend here?"

He punched Bill once again, and blood exploded from his nose and mouth as he fell to the porch's wooden floor. A second later there was a knife in the attacker's hands and it was held to Bill's throat.

I held my hands up and walked out of the forest. Magic was no use, it would have gotten Bill killed.

"Kneel," the man said and pointed to the ground. "Fingers linked and placed behind your head."

I did as I was told. The ground was cold and the snow crunched under my knees.

"My name is Simon Olson," he said. "My friend Rean here tells me you're interested in finding me. Well, congratulations."

"Why?" I asked.

"Why what?" Simon replied, a quizzical look on his face.

"Not you.' I nodded toward Rean. "Why?"

"After my son tracked them, they came to our colony and I met with them. They said they'd kill everyone in my colony if I didn't stay away from them. So I made a deal with them. They stay away from my colony in exchange for me giving them you. Simon said someone might come around trying to find him."

"The one over the many, eh?"

Rean glanced down at the ground for the briefest of moments before raising to his full height and keeping eye contact with me as he spoke, "No, just the one who isn't my colony against those who are."

Simon walked toward me, a smile spread across his bearded face. His long dark hair was tied back, and his cold black eyes held nothing but hate and anger.

I'd expected gloating, but the punch came out of nowhere, knocking me to the ground. Before I could move, the two brutes from earlier were next to me, moving much faster than their size suggested. They held me down while Simon stood above me, showing me the silver gauntlet that covered his hand like a glove. A second later it vanished, turning into several silver bracelets on his wrist.

"Do you see this?" he asked, showing me the bracelets. "Do you know how long it took for me to perfect the use of a small amount of silver to cover my entire hand? Many years. I'm a patient man, as you're going to find out over the course of your stay here. I'll show you just how much I've learned."

Before I could do anything to show him the error of his ways, he spoke again, "If you use your magic at any point in the next few minutes, your friend the cop dies." He got right next to my ear, the smell of blood overpowering whatever aftershave he'd used. "And then I go find that freak's family and make him watch while I butcher them." He jumped back up and walked over to Bill, kicking him in the ribs.

"Oh, where are my manners?" Simon said as he kicked Bill once more. He spun around and with a flourish of his hands motioned toward the house. "Welcome to my home. Welcome to the House of Silent Screams."

CHAPTER 10

Stratford, Maine. Now.

The drive from New York to Maine was long and not exactly exciting, but it was also without incident. By the time I'd reached the outskirts of the town, whatever energy I'd gained from Felicia was beginning to wane.

I figured I'd probably need to get some sleep sooner rather than later, but I also wanted to check out the house before finding a room for the duration of my stay.

I remembered the route to the house without problems, pulling up outside the old building with a little trepidation inside me. I seriously doubted that whoever had attacked me and murdered Bill was stupid enough to be staying in the first place I'd come to look. They clearly wanted me to be a part of some sort of game, and I doubted me finding them and killing them all factored into it. They might have been insane, but they didn't appear to be stupid.

I switched off the Audi R8's engine and stepped out into the cool Maine air, scanning the area around me just in case I'd been wrong about my assailants and they were indeed utterly incompetent idiots.

After making a complete circuit of the house and noting nothing of interest, I found myself looking at the imposing front door. The red paint had peeled off; like the rest of the house, it had been left in a state of disrepair. The grass was overgrown and dirt had blown all across the porch. The window next to the front door had been smashed long ago, showing one of the metal bars that had been fixed inside. They'd blocked escape and turned the old house into a prison.

I placed my hand on the door handle and twisted—it felt cold beneath my fingers—but the door was locked. The sound of a car coming up the driveway reached my ears just as I stepped off the porch. I made my way to the side of the house and waited to see who'd turned up.

I didn't have to wait long, as the police car pulled up behind my Audi and two officers got out. The driver was an older man, probably mid-forties, with an army-style haircut and alert eyes that moved slowly over everything around him.

The second man was taller and skinnier than the first, and didn't have his companion's calm demeanor. He glanced around skittishly. It was possible he'd had too much caffeine, but as he was also much younger, the likelihood was that he'd only been a cop for a short time and was still nervous.

I stepped out from the side of the house and the officer's attention was immediately centered on me.

"Hold it right there," the younger cop said, his hand resting on the butt of his gun.

I raised my hands. "Not here for any trouble. Was just looking around. I don't think the gun is necessary."

"We don't like people around here," the older cop said. "What were you looking for?"

I opened my mouth to speak, but the words came out slurred and my head felt as if full of cotton wool. Apparently when Felicia said I was going to get hit when the energy ran out, she wasn't exaggerating.

I only managed another step before my entire world started to spin like a washing machine drum and I crashed forward onto the ground.

I woke up slowly, my brain registering that I was awake well before my eyes decided to bother opening. And once they were open, I decided I'd preferred it when I was asleep.

I was lying on a small bed, in a jail cell that apart from the bed contained a toilet, a sink and a small barred window. Another identical cell sat next to mine, and three more opposite, with a short but wide corridor separating them.

"You're finally awake?" someone asked as they entered the corridor from the set of double doors at the far end.

I glanced over and saw a young woman place a folding chair in front of my cell and take a seat. She had light-green eyes and dark hair that was cut to shoulder length, part of which was pulled back and secured with what appeared to be a chopstick. She had a metal bracelet on one wrist, matching the ring on her thumb, and her trouser suit was well-tailored and expensive. Her shoes, black Adidas with a white stripe along one side, went against the rest of the image somewhat.

"I've got a few questions for you," she said as she sat down.

"Me too," I said. "I assume I'm in the Stratford police station."

"Good assumption. Your name is Nathan Garrett, yes?"

I nodded. "And yours?"

"Agent Caitlin Moore of the FBI. You should know, this isn't an *I ask a question, then you ask one* type of moment. This is a *you're in deep shit and should be telling me what I want to know* moment."

"Okay, exactly why am I in deep shit?"

"You passed out in front of two officers. They thought you were drunk or sick or something. I ran your name and came up with nothing, so I got some friends of mine at the Bureau to do me a favor. Guess what came back?"

"It said I was innocent and should be allowed to go about my business?"

"It said they didn't have clearance. Your name being searched on got them a phone call from someone much higher up the pay grade. They wanted to know why anyone was searching for you. Then I got a phone call telling me to leave it alone and forget I ever saw your name. Why would that be?"

"You don't appear to be following orders very well. I assume my mobile went off not long after?"

Caitlin nodded. "They told me I was to put you on the phone; I told them you were unconscious in a jail cell and you'd call them back when you woke up. They were less than happy."

"Was her name Olivia?"

Caitlin nodded again.

I'd put Olivia as the point of contact for anytime someone without clearance searched for my name in any government database. She gets a text telling her who has tried to gain entrance. To be honest, considering it was the first time it had been used, I was impressed it had actually worked.

"Who are you?"

"Open the cell, we'll go to breakfast—I assume it's still breakfast time—and I'll tell you what you need to know."

"You could be a dangerous criminal."

"Oh, yeah, good point. How about I promise not to kill and dismember you until I've had a cup of tea and some toast?"

"Do women often fall for your charms, Mister Garrett? Because they're not going to work on me."

"Okay, how about this? What do you actually have to hold me on? Drunk and disorderly? I'm pretty certain you have to let me go. And I'm curious, why did you get someone to run my name for such a petty crime?"

"First of all, you were up at the old house, and people in this town don't like anyone snooping around Blood Red too much. But secondly, and oh so much more importantly, I don't have to explain myself to you."

Why wasn't anyone allowed up near the house? And what the hell was Blood Red? There were questions I wasn't going to get answers for until Agent Moore actually trusted me. And I was certain that probably wasn't going to be quick. Especially considering I was going to have to blackmail her. "That's true, and I don't *have* to explain why I'm in town, either. But *you* may have to explain why you were in a New York hotel, where the body of a Toronto cop was found."

Caitlin's mouth pursed slightly. "How'd you know?"

"Well, I could say that your eyes are quite beautiful and that shade of green is very distinctive, but we've already established that my charm has no effect. Honestly, your voice is the same. It took me a moment to figure it out, because we were on top of a building and you were wearing a balaclava, but your speech pattern is definitely the same. Sort of gives it away."

Caitlin stood, removed some keys from her pocket and used them to unlock the cell door. "I've removed the weapons you had in your car, but I assume if I try and have you arrested for not having a permit, you'll magically get one. So, I'll make this clear for you. You don't start trouble in this town. If you hurt a single innocent person, I'll shoot you myself."

"Fair enough, but I'm really not the bad guy here."

Caitlin pulled the cell door open and motioned for me to step outside. "Prove it."

Once I'd reclaimed my car and found that Caitlin had been telling the truth about removing my weapons, I decided to stop off at the nearest clothes shop and purchase a few pairs of jeans, socks, underwear, some t-shirts and a jacket. I also grabbed a pair of hiking boots similar to the ones I'd purchased the last time I was there. It was obvious from the glances and occasional whisper, that the staff was curious about who I was and why I was there, but they were still friendly enough and offered to help me carry everything to my car.

Once suitably attired, I made my way to the motel, the owner of which appeared to be a much younger version of the same woman who'd given me the keys the last time I'd been. I requested the room farthest from the entrance; I didn't want too many prying eyes.

I took my bags into the room, which I was pleasantly surprised to find, had been refurnished and decorated with modern appliances; it even had wi-fi. Once I'd had a quick shower and got changed, I used Skype on my tablet to call Tommy. It didn't take long for him to answer.

"Nate," he said with a smile as his face came into view on my phone's screen. "I was wondering when you'd call. Olivia was going nuts."

Olivia, Tommy's girlfriend and the mother of his daughter, Kasey, was the director of Avalon for the south of England. For a while it was touch and go whether she'd be allowed to keep her job, but after Avalon received a few phone calls from both agents who worked with her and a certain Hades, they decided it was better, and easier, to leave her in charge.

I explained to Tommy what had happened in the last few days.

"Sorry about Bill," he said when I'd finished. "You got any ideas who's behind it?"

"Yeah, a few. Most of them involve Simon."

"You're going to have to see Galahad if you want access to him, you know that, right?"

"I'm hoping to put it off for a while. I'm going to go to the house and take a look around. Try and figure out what's happening before anyone else dies."

"You need my help?"

"I'm not sure yet; I'll call after we've check out the place. Can you apologize to Olivia for me, I hadn't expected anyone to run a check on me."

"Ah, she's just worried, she lost too many people last year, doesn't want to add to that total."

Before I'd gone to Canada to learn how to use my necromancy, I'd helped Olivia defeat a lich, an undead being of pure evil. One of her agents had been working for the enemy all along, which allowed the lich and his forces to kidnap Tommy and Kasey before attacking the LOA, or Law of Avalon, head-quarters, killing a large number of agents in the process. We re-took the building and saved a lot of lives, but the weight of her people's murder because of someone she'd trusted had rested heavily on her.

"How's Kasey doing?" She'd been twelve when she was forced to watch the lich beat Tommy almost to death. She'd also put herself between that same evil and myself, quite probably saving my life. After it was all over, she'd had some nightmares, and a few issues with trust, but she appeared to be getting better.

"She's good," Tommy said. "She has a list of questions for you to answer the next time you're back."

As the oldest person Kasey saw on a regular basis, I was inundated with questions about every part of history she could think of. Some of the answers hadn't been what she'd expected, but it hadn't slowed down her need to know.

I laughed. "Tell her that's fine, I look forward to my inquisition meeting."

We stayed online for a few more minutes—two old friends catching up—until Tommy had to go. I told Tommy I'd call him later and signed off; it would be dark in a few hours and I wanted to get some time looking around the old house.

I'd already discounted actually going into the house itself; it was locked, and even if anyone was still using it, they were clearly expecting me. So, once I'd parked the car, I set off in the direction of the woods at the rear of the house, sprinting the distance of the open ground between the two.

It wasn't especially dark once under the canopy of whatever tree leaves remained, but the constant drizzle made me glad that I'd purchased a new waterproof coat and boots. I wasn't really sure what I was going to find. Bad guys rarely leave big neon signs pointing to their direction, but from the brazen display that I'd seen from whoever wanted me in Maine, they may as well have been.

It took another fifteen minutes, and the realization that not only was the rain going to hang around for a while but that I was also being followed, before I actually found something. Several trees had claw marks, as if used by a cat to scratch on. The farther I went, the more trees I found.

"Do you ever pay any attention to authority?" Agent Moore asked as she walked toward me.

"No," I said. "They tell me what to do, and I'm not such a big fan of that."

"You need to leave this place."

"Why? So far I've seen a few scratched trees and a lot of leaves. Those marks are from a big cat. I assume you have mountain lions around here."

"Not quite. We had three hikers from town killed three days ago. We found the bodies about a hundred yards to the east of here, by an old cave, during a routine check of the area. It was only by chance—one of their phones went off. Coroner said a big cat had killed them; their wounds were matched to those of a lion As in, of the African variety."

"You have African lions in Maine? That sounds a little crazy."

"That's what I said, but I spoke to a zoologist from town and he confirmed it was likely a lion attack. He said they were probably pets who got out and killed out of desperation. The SPD had their K9 unit out here, but the dogs won't go anywhere near these woods and we couldn't find the lions. The SPD has been up here every day, and they've advised people to stay away from the woods until we find them."

"Them?"

"Maybe three or four. And they were big cats too. I know I don't want to find myself out here with them hunting me."

"Can you show me the cave? Where the bodies were found?"

"I just told you we have dangerous animals out here and you want to go spelunking?"

"Indulge me. It won't take long, I promise."

"What makes you think you can protect yourself? You couldn't stop me from melting the hotel roof over you."

I stopped walking and wondered if Caitlin was either trying to get information out of me or having fun at my expense, but decided that was a conversation for another time and so, I set off toward the caves once more.

Caitlin sighed and marched off to the east. It didn't take long to reach our destination, which had a huge opening, easily big enough for two people to walk in side by side and without stooping. I stepped into the cave and noticed that a fair bit of light still came in from outside, but as I kept walking that quickly extinguished. I used a small measure of fire magic to allow myself to see in the dark and discovered that the cave went another thirty feet before taking a steep fifty-foot drop. I had no idea where it went from there, and very little inclination to find out.

I made my way back to Caitlin, who was staring out in to the woods as the rain hammered against the ground in front of her.

"Great, now it's fucking pouring it down," she snapped. "We need to get back to the car before it gets dark."

"There aren't any bones in here. If they are lions, they're not using this place to sleep or feed. We could probably stay here for a while longer until it stops raining."

"I am not staying in a cave with you." She rested her hand on her hilt of her pistol as she stared at me. "I don't know who you are, or what you want."

"Okay, go get wet, I'm staying here where it's dry." I found some dried leaves and twigs and used a small magical flame to start a fire.

Caitlin took one look outside and placed her hand against the side of the rock wall, which groaned as it moved, shrinking the hole until it was just big enough for a full-sized man to climb through. She glanced at me, sighed and sat next to the fire.

"I didn't arrange this," I pointed out. "I'm many things, but I'm not a weather spirit."

"Okay, so who are you?"

"Seriously? You open with that? I'm a concerned citizen, who's in town to find someone."

"Who are you looking for?"

I removed some mints from my pocket and popped one into my mouth before offering one to Caitlin, who waved them away. "The person who killed Bill Moon. You knew him?"

"He's well thought of in the police department here. Some sort of big bust back in the seventies. He called about three weeks ago asking if anyone had been looking into some missing people; he suspected that a group of serial killers was involved. I'm in town for a similar reason, so I asked what he knew. We met up in New York and discussed the case."

"What did he tell you?"

"A lot of stuff about that house—they call it Blood Red because of all the bodies they found. He thought people were being murdered around here, and I tended to believe him."

"What makes you think he was right?"

Caitlin sighed.

"Okay, fine, let's go to utterly pointless questions. Why the Adidas trainers? Because no FBI agent I've ever met, at least not one who wears a suit, would get away with trainers."

"Sprained my ankle helping out with those bodies, the shoes hurt."

"Right, can I ask you things that are important now, or are you going to keep sighing? Do you know who killed my friend?"

She opened her mouth, presumably to argue, but instead shook her head. "I'm really sorry about him. He was a good cop. Why are you involved?"

"Apart from leaving Bill and his wife's bloody corpses as a message, they left me a bomb. The message took me to a hotel in New York, where they left a second one. The House of Silent Screams. So, now I'm here."

"I assume you were the person who worked with Bill during the initial investigation. He didn't mention you by name, but I got the feeling he liked you."

"I was here, yes. I thought we'd stopped it. Apparently I was wrong."

Caitlin watched me for a few moments before speaking again, "I've been in town for three months. I'm tracking a serial killer. A group of them, to be exact. I've been after them for a long time, and I have no idea why they're in town, or what they want, but the body count will increase until we stop them."

"Serial killers don't tend to travel in groups."

"Yeah, well these are special. There's no type, each person vanishes without a trace. No struggle, just gone."

"Did you think I was involved?" I asked, wondering if that was why she was so hostile toward me.

Caitlin shook her head and a smile crept onto her face. "Nope, I just thought you were an ass. Besides, no one comes up here. Even before the lions it was off limits. Someone called the station and said you were there, that's why Edward and Danny, the officers who found you, were sent."

"Who called?"

She shrugged. "No idea, probably someone in the woods. I didn't find out about it until after you were brought in. The SPD wanted me to check that you weren't one of the people I'm after. But when I saw your face, I figured it would be better to discover if you were after me."

"While you did leave quite the impression, especially on my friend, I had no idea you'd be here," I admitted. "But someone was tracking me. I was there for all of five minutes before the cops turned up. It's a twenty-minute drive from the station to the house. I know, because I've done it. Whoever called, did so before I'd even arrived. From the moment I came into town someone has been watching me, it's why I got the Audi; thank you for allowing me to get back."

"Nice car, a bit ostentatious for a small town like this one."

"Good, whoever sent me here will think that they can keep an eye on me by keeping an eye on the car. It makes me nice and public, right up until I don't want to be."

"You want to tell me about your stash of weaponry?"

"They were gifts," I said.

"If you want me to believe that you're the good guy, lying to me isn't going to help."

"Not a lie, they really were gifts ... sort of. I was given them just in case I needed something more than my magic and general all-around awesome personality."

Caitlin regarded me for a second. "In addition to the dead hikers, we've had two people go missing in the last few weeks. None of them were likely to vanish and there's no evidence of foul play. One of them was the caretaker of the Blood Red. She had the keys and made sure no one went up there to destroy anything. Her neighbor said she heard shouts the day she vanished, but there was no evidence of a struggle and her car keys were gone."

"What about the other one?"

"He was a security guard just outside of town. He left for work one morning and never turned up."

"So, you've got missing people and dead hikers. Doesn't sound like the best time to live in this town. Did you ask around?"

"I've worked with the FBI for eight years. I'm pretty certain I know what I'm doing. Yes, I spoke to the people he worked with, his friends, neighbors, family. Everyone. No one has any idea where he's gone or why."

"Is that why you were in New York? To try and figure out who's doing this?"

"It doesn't matter why I was there," she snapped.

"Okay, but it's a hell of a coincidence that you arrived at the same place and time as Sky and me."

"Change the subject."

"You've got some serious power. That trick with the roof was very impressive."

"Impressing you is hardly at the top of my list of things to do."

"Did we not just discuss that I'm not the bad guy? Because I'm pretty certain you were ready to jump on board that particular wagon."

"Yeah, well, the jury's still out on that one."

CHAPTER 11

We sat in the cave for a while longer as the rain turned into a sheet of water. Caitlin and I got as comfortable as possible, and she contacted her dispatch and told them where she was. She explained that her GPS tracking on her phone was switched on and that she'd contact them with an update every few hours.

Afterward, we'd both just remained silent as the small fire flickered beside us.

"When you find the people who killed Bill, what are you going to do?"

My initial response was to tell her I was going to kill them. It was probably the truth, even if I was certain she wouldn't like it. "I don't know."

"You *won't* murder them—I told you I don't want trouble in this town. I'm an FBI agent, I can't be part of murder and vengeance just because you decide to carry out your own brand of justice."

"I'm not going to promise anything, and if you want to argue this point, whoever killed Bill isn't human, so your laws don't apply to them in the same way."

Caitlin looked shocked. "So you'll just kill them and move on?"

I shrugged. "If they give me a choice, I'll hand them over to the relevant authorities. That won't be you, by the way. But if they push it, I'll just bury them."

"Who are the relevant authorities? I've heard of Avalon, had some dealing with them, don't know much about them though."

"Shadow Falls controls Maine."

"Who's Shadow Falls?"

"Not a who, it's a where."

"Then let's go see whoever controls *them*." A determined expression settled on her face.

"Not until I know what's going on. The king and I have . . . history."

"They have a king? Does the constitution of *this country* mean anything to anyone who isn't human?"

"Of course it does; Avalon let you write it in the first place. If they didn't want it, you'd be ruled by the British or French, or hell, maybe even the Canadians. This country was easier to break up, easier to manage, when it got its own identity."

"So, the War of Independence was a lie?"

I shook my head. "For the most part, Avalon lets human governments do as they please. They have their people in high-ranking positions, but unless it adversely affects their plans, Avalon leaves them alone. When the humans started to rebel against the British, Merlin and the rest of the council—which includes people like Hades, Ares, and various high-ranking members of different species—saw it as an opportunity to have America be its own place, but they also saw it as an opportunity to break up America into manageable chunks. Each piece governed by different groups. Unfortunately, it didn't work out that way and very little of the country is actually under the control of only one person or group. Most are controlled by a hodgepodge of different people or different species. It's why they created neutral states."

Caitlin raised an eyebrow in question and I quickly explained the concept of the neutral states.

"Are Europe and Africa and the like all the same?"

I nodded. "Very few countries or territories on Earth are ruled by only one party. Even England, which comes under Avalon, has parts that are controlled by someone else. In a weird sort of way, it keeps the peace. No one person or group has enough power to control large amounts of land, not without a fight anyway. And most form alliances with whoever else is in their territory, so fighting is the last thing on their mind. And those who do fight, spend so much effort on it, they never seem to have time to actually consolidate their power."

"So, Shadow Falls controls Maine?"

I nodded. "They're independent from any of Avalon's influence. Which, I can tell you, is pretty damn rare. But Merlin agreed to let them live separately in exchange for them forgoing all rights to have a say in how Avalon is governed. It works out quite well for the most part, although it resulted in a lot of very stupid stipulations about anyone from outside of Shadow Falls not being allowed to step foot in the state."

Caitlin was silent for a moment, probably absorbing the information she'd been given. "Merlin is in charge of Avalon, yeah?"

"He's meant to be, although there are far too many people in there who use it as an excuse to do as they wish. A lot of the more powerful members or groups, like Hades or the werewolves, have their own security and deal with internal problems in-house. But no one dares try to overthrow Avalon. There would be anarchy, for a start. And that's if Merlin and his cronies didn't incinerate anyone who tried."

"Merlin's that powerful?"

"Merlin is easily in the top ten most powerful things on the planet. And while he's nowhere near as interested in the day-to-day running of Avalon as he should be, he's not someone you cross lightly."

"And you used to work for Avalon?"

"I worked for *Merlin*."

Caitlin exhaled in surprise. "Are you meant to be telling me about this?"

There was no indication of shock at hearing the name; clearly she knew of Merlin's existence. But that didn't really tell me much. "Discovering the existence of Merlin, Avalon, and those who worked for and against them isn't illegal or met with fire and brimstone. Many people know about them, but taking that knowledge to prove to the world that they existed, that *is* illegal. Basically, it's not illegal to find out, but it's illegal to publicly tell people about it. Besides, you're not human, so I think you've earned the right to know. I'm curious, though, why haven't you ever worked for Avalon, or even know a lot more about them then you do?"

"I had to deal with members of Avalon when I worked for the FBI. They've not exactly forthcoming with details about that whole side to the world. I think I had contact with them twice."

"Didn't you tell them you were an alchemist?"

"They never asked and I didn't like people finding out. My mom told me about it when I was little—she told me never to tell anyone. I guess some things she taught me stuck."

"So, no one knows what you can do?"

Caitlin shook her head. "I thought I was alone in the world until I was sixteen and I met a sorcerer. He was a cocky little shit, but I was entranced by him. Young, stupid love, I guess."

The fact that Caitlin had never integrated herself with a whole world of people was kind of sad. I couldn't have imagined growing up with no one to share my magic. It would have been awful. "So, who taught you how to use your alchemy? Your mum?"

"My mom didn't teach me anything except how to distance myself from people. My parents are human, so I mostly taught myself."

She clearly knew what I was thinking about her parentage, because she already had an answer.

"Which, yes, means that one of my parents isn't my birth parent. My dad met my mom when she was already pregnant. I don't know the ins and outs, but he's my father as far as I'm concerned." She was very matter-of-fact about it, something she'd come to terms with a long time ago.

"Fair enough. So how did you learn about alchemy?"

"I met another alchemist, Melissa, when I was in college, and she taught me a lot. We were in the same dorm and would sneak out at night so she could show me how to control my abilities. Melissa told me about my longer life, about living for millennia, about my healing and how I could use my alchemy to affect the world around me. Probably the most fun I ever had. What was Merlin like?"

I tried to think of an answer that didn't make me angry. "That depends on the year. When I first met him, he was kind, patient, attentive. He would sit and let me ask him a million questions and he'd always answer them honestly. Over time, he became more detached, distant from everyone. But then you'd talk to him for a while and that old Merlin would come through. After a while that spark became dimmer and dimmer until it just vanished. Even then it took a long time for me to figure out something had changed. By that point I only saw or talked to Merlin when he needed something. The rest of the time, he left me to my own devices."

"So, what did you used to do?"

"All sorts of things: negotiations, peace talks, spying, anything needed." Assassinations, murder, theft, regicide, blackmail, those were the things Caitlin didn't need to be told.

We didn't speak after that for over fifteen minutes until she decided to break the silence. "I know you're a killer. The weapons in your car tell me that. But I want to know, is everyone from Avalon like that, do they value life as such an easy thing to remove?"

"No," I said honestly. "Like humans, some have trouble taking a life and some don't. I fall into the latter. I'm not psychotic or evil or anything so damn melodramatic, I just don't have the luxury of second-guessing myself. If someone is coming to attack me or the people I care about, it's them or me. Simple. If they want to push something to that degree and they threaten a life, then theirs is now forfeit. That's not to say there aren't people I've killed who stay with me, ones I regret ever having to take or being put into a situation where it's them or me."

"You sound like it's normal for you."

"It is," I said. "I was born over sixteen-hundred years ago. I killed my first man before I was a teenager. That wasn't anything out of the ordinary for the time period. If taking a life means people I care about are safe, then I don't think twice about it."

Another long silence. Apparently, Caitlin had a lot of information to think about. She fished a piece of paper out of her pocket and passed it to me. "This is why I was in New York. It was left for me at the reception desk. It's why I got changed and decided to go incognito."

I opened the folded paper and read the sentence on it: *Make them fear you, and once they're dead, you will live free.*

"What does it mean?" I asked, handing the paper back.

"The psychopaths who are murdering people, the ones I'm here for, they left that message for me in New York. They've left similar ones at the previous four crimes scenes around the country. It's why we know they're connected."

"Why no task force?"

"I'm not exactly the Bureau's favorite agent; apparently I get involved too much. I think my boss was pretty happy with assigning me the case. I have issues with playing with others."

"No shit, really?" I said with mock surprise. "Sounds like you're close to the investigation. You sure you're okay with being involved?"

She nodded, but brought her knees up to her chest and hugged them against her. She was scared, although I doubted she'd admit it. "I don't have the luxury of stopping now. They need to be caught, and I'm the only one who can. I *need* to stop them." She stood up, knocking dirt onto the fire, which flickered a few times before extinguishing. "Fuck."

I was about to restart it when I saw movement outside of the cave.

I closed my eyes and used my fire magic to change my vision, but instead of night vision, my eyes now operated as if could track a thermal image. Everything above absolute zero gives off infrared radiation, so the landscape before me was now a mass of dark blue with small dots of red, orange, and yellow where heat could be found.

There was some small movement to my right, which I quickly identified as a rabbit or other small mammal—it was difficult to say exactly what anything was when all you can see is their heat signature.

After a few seconds, I spotted what had caught my attention. A massive deer was eating something from the ground. I was about to remove my magic, when I noticed movement to the far left of the deer. Five very large objects were moving slowly through the trees toward the deer.

"What do you see?" Caitlin whispered.

"Your lions," I said. "They're hunting a deer. But something doesn't seem right."

"What?"

I didn't answer, as the mass of color from the creatures' heat was immediately replaced with my night vision. The lions were maybe a hundred feet away from us and I could see them clearly, three females and two males.

"They're too big," I whispered.

The lions went from crouched to sprinting forward in an instant. The deer never knew what was happening until one of the females landed on its back and drove it to the ground, grabbing it around the throat and holding on as the deer struggled against the overwhelming power of its attacker.

As the deer died, three more lions appeared from the darkness; apparently my thermal vision had a distance limit. Six of the eight lions moved away from the carcass and watched as a male and female, clearly the pride alphas, padded toward it and tore open its stomach, spilling the contents onto the leafy earth.

The sounds of their eating filled the night, and once the two alphas had finished the rest of the pride was allowed to have their fill.

"What do you mean, they're too big?" Caitlin asked, her voice barely above a whisper.

"Barbary lions," I told her. "They're extinct in the wild, and you have eight of them running around a forest in Maine."

"How is that possible?"

"It isn't." And it didn't leave a whole lot of good answers either.

"So, what are they?"

"Very bad news."

I was about to say more when Caitlin's phone started to ring, and even though she managed to switch it off before it played music for long, a few notes managed to escape.

One of the lions, a big male, turned toward our cave and took a few steps forward. He was quickly followed by a few more lions, all of whom had dark red maws where they'd been feeding. "We need to get out of here, now."

"No lion is going to get through solid rock," Caitlin said. "I think we're safe."

The alpha male lion was slowly moving toward us, the alpha female at his side, and for the briefest of moments, I saw her smile.

"They're not lions, and they'll tear through that rock wall like it was made of paper."

"Okay, so what do we do?"

"Create a thicker wall," I said. "It'll give us time to go farther into the cave and find another way out."

"Can't you fight these things?"

"It's dark, raining, and there are eight of them. I'd probably take out three or maybe four, but then I'm just as dead as anything else. And I definitely couldn't give you odds for your survival. Now make the damn wall."

Caitlin placed her hand against the cave and once again the rock groaned. The lions must have sensed that something was wrong, because they set off in a flat sprint the second the noise went out into the night.

They hit the outer wall in seconds, just as Caitlin had finished creating a second wall by turning the rock into a layer of interlocking rock spikes that would certainly give our would-be attackers something to think about.

The lions thundered into the front of the cave like a freight train, knocking pieces of rock loose with an explosion of deafening sound that bounced around the interior.

I grabbed Caitlin's hand and led her to the rear of the cave. "There's a drop here, can you make stairs?"

"No, I can't see a damn thing. If I start moving rock around blind, I could cause a cave in."

"Okay, then you hold onto me and we'll drop down."

Caitlin stared down into the dark abyss beyond. "That isn't any less insane."

"There are a lot of jagged rocks, but I should be able to avoid them." The sound of crumbling rocks and the low growl of lions told me we didn't have long and I grabbed Caitlin around the waist and jumped.

CHAPTER 12

You know when people say that the landing is always worse than the fall? Well those people are idiots, because the fall is just as awful.

I couldn't avoid all of the stalactites or stalagmites, whichever one it was that I crashed into and sliced a huge gash in my arm, but I managed to use my air magic to avoid or destroy most of them as Caitlin screamed bloody murder into my ear hole for the entire fifty-foot fall. It only took a few seconds until we hit the hard rock bottom, but it felt like a hell of a lot longer.

We both rolled along the cold, wet cave floor as the roar of angry lions filled every inch of space around us. "Run, little rabbits," a man's voice called out. "I'll see you soon enough."

"I'm blind down here," Caitlin said.

I created a small ball of fire in my hand and tossed it into the air, using more magic to keep it floating a few feet above Caitlin's head. It wasn't a huge amount of light, and I still used my night vision, but it gave off enough light that Caitlin could see a few feet in front of her. Unfortunately, it also allowed the lions high above us to see more easily too.

"We should get moving. That fall won't stop them for long."

Caitlin nodded and we followed the only direction that wasn't solid rock. The ground was wet and slimy and occasionally I saw bats flying, high up in the cave ceiling above us.

"We're walking on bat shit, aren't we?" Caitlin said as the sounds of the lions faded behind us.

"Yep, bat shit and bug guts. They're not exactly the cleanest animals on earth."

"Nor do they smell very good."

She was right, the stench of bat permeated the very essence of everything around us, but occasionally there was another smell fighting for space. A rank odor that I couldn't quite place, but one that sent a chill up my spine.

The cave walls shrunk for several yards, causing us to walk hunched over and in single file for a hundred feet or so, until it began to open out again.

We stopped walking and took our bearings in a huge open area with several man-sized pathways that had been carved into it through quite probably millions of years. I jumped over a small stream that moved down the center of the room and investigated a few of the pathways, but quickly found that they became too short or narrow to navigate without chopping off my head or arms, neither of which was a very good solution.

Caitlin offered to move the rock around to create an exit, but it's easier to use one that already exists than make one that would have taken us who-knew-where. An alchemist can move around and shape nonorganic matter with ease, but the matter they move has to come from somewhere, so moving a large rock around was easy, but moving the walls of the cave, would leave a huge hole in the cave.

The more advanced alchemists can shape several types of matter into one form, or collapse an item into its base components, but I doubted that Caitlin was anywhere near old enough to manage either of those.

"We're stuck," Caitlin said as she exited from one of the holes. "All I've found were bugs. Oh, and a gigantic fucking spider that I'm hoping wasn't the last of its species as it's now a large stain, after I dropped part of the cave on it."

"Did you feel better after doing it?"

"I did after moving the rock around a bit to make sure it was good and paste-like."

I couldn't help but smile. "After you're done ridding the world of arachnids, you want to help me consider which of these tunnels to go down. There's no way of knowing where they actually go. We may get really lost."

"Well there are three left, which one should we choose? And if any of them have that damn spider out of *Lord of the Rings* down there, I'm going to be really pissed off."

"No promises," I said. "But I don't think it's likely."

"New species are found all the time, who's to say a large spider isn't amongst them."

I suddenly had an itch on the back of my neck. "Yeah, great. Thanks for that. Can you close that entrance we came in here from? I'd like to give those lions a hard time to catch up, if possible."

She placed her hand against the cave and the entrance was squeezed shut until it appeared as if it never existed. "I can't make it permanent," she said. "But it should last a few hours before moving back."

Using alchemy to make changes permanent is a skill learned through experience; the lack of contact with other alchemists had left her abilities much less powerful than they should have been for her age.

I knocked something with my foot and bent down to retrieve the item that dislodged. It turned out to be partially submerged bone that had been in the mud and grime, and I washed it off in the small stream. "If we're still here in a few hours, we'll have more than lions to worry about. This is a human thigh bone."

I passed the bone to Caitlin, who squinted in the light of the fireball as she examined it. "Did the lions do this? There are teeth marks."

"No idea." A small gust of air moved more of the grime and exposed several more bones. "But whatever stripped the flesh from these bones is not something I want to meet down here."

"We should keep moving then."

I wiped my hands on my jeans and picked the furthest right of the three remaining tunnels, primarily because water trickled from it into the stream. Caitlin and I trekked down the claustrophobic tunnel for what felt like miles, but was probably only a few hundred yards, until we arrived at a second chamber.

It was smaller than the one we'd left several minutes earlier, but full of huge boulders that I wouldn't have been able to lift with or without magic. The smell of the bats had long since gone, and was replaced with the stench that had done its best to override the bat smell. It was a strong odor, a mixture of feces, urine and blood. A lot of blood.

"I'm going to extinguish the flame," I told Caitlin in hushed tones.

Her eyes widened in fear. "Are you fucking around?"

"Can you smell that? There's something down here." I moved the ball of flame so that it hovered a few inches over the ground and saw the dozens of bones that were littered across its surface. Some of them human in size.

"Holy shit!" Caitlin managed to whisper.

"Stay here, don't move. I'll be back in a second."

She nodded and I removed the small ball of flame, plunging our surroundings into pitch darkness. I squeezed Caitlin's hand and then set off to scout our next path, my magic-enhanced night vision the only magic I dared use. Even though my glyphs only light up on the initial use of magic, and the fact that I was wearing a coat that covered by arms and chest, I still had to watch my step; I didn't want to accidentally step on a fragile bone and alert whatever was there to my presence.

There were two paths that left the chamber, and I decided to try the one that was partially hidden by a huge bolder. I took two steps inside and froze. I concentrated for a second and allowed my necromancy to activate, and I was astounded as dozens of spirits all drifted into view. I tried to reach out to any of them, but couldn't, so stopped using it and continued on.

The path was short, but I was never going to finish going through it. On the other side lay a cave troll. It was easily fifteen feet tall and weighed as much as a truck. I moved back very slowly, making sure that I put my feet down in the lightest way possible.

It took me a lot longer to get back to Caitlin than it had to get to the troll—fear makes you extra careful. And make no mistake, I was afraid. Fighting a cave troll in an enclosed space, such as an underground tunnel, was suicide. There was no way to get space between you and the thing that would easily tear you in half and feast on your remains.

"Did you find anything?" Caitlin asked as I returned to her and made sure she knew it was me.

I told her about the cave troll.

"What the hell is a cave troll?"

"Big, pissed off, people eater. We'd better hurry, I don't like the idea of facing one in his own cave."

"Can you put the light on?"

"Too risky. You're going to have to be piggy-backed."

To her credit she didn't argue; instead, she allowed me to move her into position and then up onto my back. Her arms were wrapped around my chest and her legs around my waist.

I took two steps when an almighty roar came out from somewhere in the cave. The werelions were somewhere behind us— they'd probably found the blocked path—but the noise sounded as if it were happening right next to me.

I didn't wait, I just sprinted toward the second path, ignoring the sounds of the bones as they splintered and broke beneath my feet. But as we reached the tunnel there was another sound. It was something I'd heard out in the open many years ago, and even then it was a terror-inducing noise. But underground, in an enclosed space, with no obvious place to hide or escape ... Well, right then I was pretty sure I knew how Jack had felt the first time he'd heard the giant. Although in my case it was much worse than a giant. The cave troll had woken. And as they always are, it was very, very hungry.

CHAPTER 13

I grabbed Caitlin and ran with her through the nearest tunnel, re-igniting the ball of flame so we could move quickly without the need for me to carry her. It didn't matter if the troll saw the light, it was going to be able to smell that we were inside its territory. It couldn't have pinpointed exactly where by smell alone, but it wouldn't have taken long to find us; a cave troll can see in absolute darkness better than they can in the daylight.

The winding tunnel ended in yet another boulder-infested large cavern, but there was no obvious way to go any further. Fortunately, the tunnel was too narrow for a cave troll to easily fit down it.

"So, what do we do now?" Caitlin asked.

I looked around and pointed toward another tunnel about forty-five feet above the ground, at the far end of the cavern. I could have probably climbed up there with my magic, but it would have been impossible to carry Caitlin too.

"How are we meant to get up there?" she asked.

"You're going to create some steps for us."

We jogged over to the far side of the cavern. "There's a lot of rock to shift around," she said after examining the area. "If I pull too much out of the rock here, it could cause it to collapse somewhere else."

"Is there a better way?"

"Pulling it from the ground would be easier, but again, I have no idea how far beneath us this rock goes. If there's a giant cave under us, I could cause a few extra problems, like us falling through it. Alchemy isn't easy when you can't see exactly what you're working with."

"How about one of those boulders?"

She walked over to the ten-foot boulder and examined it. "Yeah, I could use this. I'd have to collapse the boulder here, spread it across the ground, and then re-shape it near the tunnel. It'd be a strain, but certainly possible."

"You have a few minutes to move several tons of rock then."

"How far behind us is the troll?"

As if on cue, a huge roar sounded out from somewhere in the darkness that we'd just left. The troll was now coming for us, but hopefully it wouldn't get through until Caitlin and I managed to escape.

Several tons of rock screeched and groaned as Caitlin went to work collapsing the boulder and moving it slowly across the cavern floor.

While Caitlin worked, I searched the rest of the cavern and found several more piles of bones. From the look of it, the troll had been underground for years. I found several pieces of clothing and a few rucksacks that had been torn apart.

I searched through them, but found no IDs, which was strange. It was unlikely that the troll would have eaten the wallet if it had taken the time to remove any clothing before feasting on its victims. I searched for a few more seconds, but found nothing to tell me who any of the people were.

"There are a lot more victims here," I told a heavily sweating Caitlin, who had managed to move half of the bolder across the cavern.

"Anything more than bones?"

"Trolls eat everything except for the bones, so no, nothing to go on. It's weird that there are so many bones here, though. It can't be easy for the troll to get in here, not through that tunnel."

"Is there another way in?" Caitlin said, her nerves showing even through gritted teeth.

"I'll take a look." The idea that we were vulnerable once again made hairs on the back of my neck stand up and I immediately set about searching for any entrances big enough for a troll to come through.

I walked the entire circumference of the cavern, but found no obvious way in which a cave troll could get to us. It gave me a measure of ease, but didn't answer why there were so many bones. I concluded that the troll had probably eaten them when he was younger and could fit through the tunnel with ease.

Another roar of anger sounded throughout the cavern, and the rock groaned as huge fists pounded against the inside of the tunnel.

"Can you hurry up?" I asked. "I don't think the troll is keen on waiting for his lunch."

"Nate," Caitlin said.

I turned around to find a large lion standing in the mouth of what was meant to be our exit. It dropped down to the cavern floor with barely a sound and changed from lion to a werelion beast form, in two steps. At well over seven-feet tall, it towered above both Caitlin and myself.

"I guess I found my rabbits," it said. The beast form of a werelion is similar in appearance to any other were's beast form: long muscular arms, with razor sharp claws on the end of each elongated finger, their faces still resembling a lion's, but it's a horror version of a lion, with an exaggerated mouth and nose that's much larger than a normal lion, and teeth that could carve through flesh like it was a Sunday roast chicken.

"You're in our way," I said as Caitlin moved back from the nearly finished boulder and rejoined me. "I think you should move."

"*I think* I'm going to skin you both and hand you to the troll."

"You've been dumping the bodies down here, haven't you?"

The werelion's brown, rage-filled eyes fixed firmly on me. "We throw them down, and then they get to wait. And wait. And hope that they can reach the ledge. And then the troll comes through and we hear them scream."

"So, what happens when that troll comes through and finds you in here?"

"I won't be here."

He made a grab for Caitlin, but she was too far back and managed to avoid his attack. I used his off balance to slam him in the chest with a blast of air, which took him off his feet and threw him toward the rear of the cavern.

"Get the exit finished," I told Caitlin. "I'll deal with our feline friend."

Caitlin ran off to finish her alchemy while the werelion found his feet and stood up to his full height.

"That meant to be imposing?" I asked. "Because I have a list of things that have impressed me. It's pretty short and you're nowhere near it."

Unfortunately, letting loose with my magic would have meant removing the ball of flame that hovered around Caitlin, bathing her in darkness and prolonging our escape.

The lion darted forward, swiping wildly, trying to catch me with his claws. There was no skill to it, just power. I dodged aside for a few seconds, while the lion continued to throw punch after punch, trying and catch me with its strength or claws. After half a minute, the werelion was beginning to anger and the small measure of patience he'd portrayed during the first attack had vanished. He charged forward, closing the distance between us and meeting my fist wrapped in dense air, which I used to slam into his temple. The werelion went down to one knee, and a second punch sent him onto his back.

He kicked out, catching me in the ribs, sending me flying back several feet. I landed on some sharp rocks, slicing open my arm once again.

The werelion got back to a standing position and smelled the air, taking a long deep sniff.

"Caitlin," I called out. "Don't move."

I extinguished the flame and a second later sent out a torrent of fire magic, which rushed over the werelion, causing damage and pain to every part of it. The lion screamed out as the fire ignited its fur, and it dropped to the ground, rolling around to try and put the flames out as I reignited the small ball of flame and moved it back over to Caitlin.

"Well that was quick," I said and remade the ball of fire that hovered around Caitlin. "You're new to this whole werelion thing, I assume? You fight like a human, not using your speed or strength and just wildly throwing punches."

"And you only pay attention to what's in front of you," the werelion said with an approximate sneer as its flesh began to heal.

The roar from behind me was deafening and accompanied by a crash as part of the cavern fell from the wall onto the ground and exploded, peppering me with small shards of razor-sharp rock.

At the far end of the cave was a huge boulder, something I had originally decided was immoveable without dynamite. The cave troll rolled it aside with the effort of a starving animal getting to a meal, revealing a second path beyond. But the troll wasn't starving, it just liked to kill and feed, and if it wasn't hungry, it would kill for fun. As the beast turned its head to look at Caitlin and then me, it grinned. To the troll, our deaths would supply food, but it was going to enjoy itself.

The troll darted toward Caitlin, its speed unnatural for a being of its size. Caitlin unloaded her gun into its chest and it stopped running, not because of gunshot wounds, the bullet holes had barely bothered it, but because of the explosion of sound that bounced around the inside of the cavern as if it were directly in my head. The troll clamped its enormous hands over its ears and roared in pain.

I gathered all of the rock shrapnel up in a whirl of air and threw it at the troll's face; some of it sunk into the inside of its mouth. It didn't do much damage, but it did take its attention from Caitlin to me. Which suddenly felt like a very stupid thing as it turned on me and charged.

I rolled behind a nearby boulder and the troll tried to turn, but while it was fast in a straight line, it also was about as maneuverable as a moon. It crashed into a nearby stalagmite, adding yet another noise to the never-ending cascade of sound.

"How long?" I shouted, using my magic to ensure that the words met Caitlin's ears.

"Few seconds and we're done."

The troll brushed itself off and stood up to its full height, its murderous eyes boring directly into me.

"We don't have that long," I said and slowly moved so that I was stood between the troll and the werelion, who was just beginning to get back to a sitting position, its seared flesh quickly healing itself.

The troll stalked forward slowly, ensuring I wasn't going to escape behind another boulder at the last second, and when it was certain I couldn't move aside, it dove for me. I used air magic to push myself back behind the werelion, which was in the way of what the troll wanted to tear in half.

The troll slammed into the werelion as if he were a toy, grabbing his leg and tossing him up into the air before smashing him back down onto the rock, removing the werelion's leg from the knee down. Blood poured out of the wound, spraying all over the troll, who stopped moving and licked the stump of the leg, while the werelion screamed for help.

I ignored his pleas and darted back to Caitlin, who was starting to climb up the steps she'd made. "Nate, are you going to help that guy?"

I turned to watch as the troll grabbed the werelion, who screamed and pleaded for help. The troll placed one hand on his pelvis and one on his chest and tore him in half with a sickening sound.

"Oh my God," Caitlin said.

"Vomit later, let's go." I almost had to pick her up and carry her up the newly made stairs. Once at the top I made Caitlin look at me, while a draft of fresh air made its way down the tunnel. "You need to drop all of the steps. We can't have a cave troll getting out."

Caitlin glanced over toward the sounds of the troll feasting on the remains of the werelion.

"Blood drives it nuts," I said. "It'll be transfixed for a while, but once it's finished, it'll look for another meal. And if it can get out of here, it's going to find a whole town full of them."

Caitlin nodded and knelt down, placing her hands against the top of the steps. The rock groaned and then collapsed all at once. "It's easier to remove something than make it," Caitlin said and slumped against me.

The noise gained the troll's attention and it dropped the fleshy remains of the werelion and darted toward us, roaring with anger the entire time. But we were too high up and all it could do was impotently rage at us.

I picked up Caitlin and carried her up the tunnel, and the second we stepped outside and into the darkness of night, I placed her on the soft grass, where she rolled over and threw up.

I couldn't leave the tunnel open, I couldn't risk anyone else getting in there, so I created a sphere of air magic in my hand, spinning it over and over again, pouring in more and more magic, until it was a powerful blur. And then I sunk it into the rock around the face of the tunnel and released the magic. The result was spectacular as the entire tunnel imploded, collapsing in on itself and burying the exit under several tons of earth.

"You okay?" I asked as I sunk to my knees and took in a deep breath. I'd first used the sphere just over a year ago and it almost tore a werewolf apart. It was incredibly powerful, but also took a lot out of me.

"It ate him, ripped him to shreds."

"I'm sorry you had to see that."

I used the newly formed rockslide to get myself back to my feet and then walked to the edge of the cliff. It was the same cliff I'd been standing on as I watched Simon talk to the man in the suit. The house sat silently beneath me.

I changed my vision back to thermal once more and looked all around, and picked up the four shapes of werelions watching me from the tree line.

"They're here," I said as the four massive lions left their shelter and padded across the open ground. Not one of them took their attention away from me.

Caitlin was beside me a moment later, gun in hand. "Can we take them?"

"Do you have silver bullets?"

She shook her head.

"Then probably not, no."

One of the lions, the female I'd seen arrive at the deer kill with the large male, took a step forward, sniffed the air, and then turned back to her pride. A second later and they were all bounding off into the woods, my thermal vision tracking them for as long as it was possible.

"They're gone," I said.

"It was weird that they left like that, they must have known we couldn't have taken them all."

"Don't know, all I know is the lions are gone, and we need to be too. We need to find out who they are and where they came from. I need to go to Washington."

"D.C.?"

I nodded. "I have a friend there who should be able to help; I want as much information as possible before I go to Shadow Falls."

Caitlin glanced behind her at the cave. "First, we need to get the hell out of here."

The roar of a lion sounded out from somewhere in the distance. "I couldn't agree more."

I felt a slight tinge of relief when I discovered that neither Caitlin's truck nor my Audi had been tampered with. Apparently, the lions had decided that the troll was more than enough to make sure we didn't leave alive.

Caitlin followed me back to my hotel, where I parked, went inside, and immediately removed the sword and knives from the bag I'd stashed in the cupboard, placing both it and the weapons on the bed.

"You're going to wear those around town?" Caitlin asked, pointing to the sword.

"You going to stop me?"

Caitlin shook her head. "Probably not wise to take it with you to D.C. though, they tend to frown at people arriving heavily armed." Caitlin's smile vanished and sat on the edge of the bed. "We could have died tonight."

"Pretty much," I said and replaced the sword in the cupboard, although I kept some of the daggers on me. Caitlin had a point about traveling around the country heavily armed, but being armed was probably a smart decision. "But we didn't. And that's all that we need to focus on."

"Do you think some of those missing people are down there with that troll?"

I nodded. "I think those werelions used the troll to dispose of evidence. After that bomb got detonated back in Canada, the werewolves who went to smell around got the scent of a troll. I think I know where it came from."

"They lost one of theirs though."

"They're going to lose a lot more than that by the time we're through." I passed her one of the daggers. "Keep this on you, it'll kill a werelion pretty quickly in the right place, and ruin their day even if you get it in the wrong place."

She took the blade and turned it over in her hands. "Thanks. You know, I've been thinking. It's like a ten- or twelve-hour car ride to Washington. How do we get there quick enough?"

"Leave that to me. I'm going for a shower. You going home to change first?"

"I'll wait here until you're done. Then we'll go to my house and I can get changed while you wait. I don't really want to be home alone at the moment."

I understood perfectly and took a very quick shower, using my fire magic to dry myself instantly. I threw my clothes in the bin inside the bathroom and replaced them with a clean pair of green fatigues, a blue t-shirt, and a black hoodie. Considering who I wanted to see in D.C. I should probably have worn a suit, but it wasn't like I had a lot of options to shop at eleven at night.

I followed Caitlin to her place, a two-bedroom apartment a few minutes drive from the police station. I waited in the car while she ran in to get a shower and changed. I told her she had five minutes before I came in to get her.

Being alone in the car gave me the opportunity to make the first call I was going to need. It got picked up on the second ring.

"Nate," Felicia said with more than a little purr in her voice. "How happy to hear from you."

"I'm sorry it's not under more pleasant circumstances, but you know when you said you'd help if I ever needed it?"

"I don't think I phrased it quite like that."

"Yeah, well, I need your help."

"What do you need and will it break any laws?"

I explained what had happened with the werelions and that I needed to go to Washington.

"And how does you needing to get to the capital mean you need my aid?"

"Do you happen to have a jet we could borrow?"

"A jet? Why do you assume I have a jet?"

I could hear her smile, even if I couldn't see it. "Because for some reason vampire masters own jets. Maybe it's because you really like to push your luck by flying too close to the sun. I have no idea. But if you have access to one, it would really help."

"We do like to push our luck. Did you push yours with the energy I gave you?"

"I passed out in front of two cops."

Felicia's laugh was incredibly sexy, and a little annoying considering what I was asking her for. "I felt the energy leave me—now you know how we vampires feel if we don't feed for a few days."

I had to admit I had no idea that vampires who don't feed would have that kind of reaction. No wonder they're always on the lookout for the next meal.

"I do have a jet," Felicia said, her voice suddenly serious. "How long do you need it?"

"Forty-eight hours, if possible."

"Upon touchdown in D.C. the jet will develop mechanical issues that will take it several hours to fix. You have two days, any longer than that and I'll have questions of my own to answer. I may be the vampire master to New York, but D.C. has its own vampires, and they will not like my arrival for too long."

"Deal. Thank you, Felicia."

"I'll text you the address. And yes, you will owe me one. Or three or four, depending on how long you last the next time we meet under pleasant circumstances. I look forward to it, Nate."

She hung up before I could reply, although I was pretty certain the memory of what she'd done to me last time was more than enough for me to agree pretty quickly. So long as there were no law enforcement around when I passed out.

My next call was to Tommy, who answered on the first ring, despite it being nearly 5 a.m. where he was. "What's wrong?" he asked.

"Don't come to Maine. There are werelions here."

Tommy exhaled in one breath. "Fuck."

"Yeah, that was my response too. That and 'oh shit they have a cave troll.'"

"Look, Nate, if you need me there, you know I'll have no issues pushing my luck. But if any of those lions has links to those in charge . . . ."

"I know, war."

"I'm happy fighting a war with you, but not starting one. I lived through it once . . . I don't like a lot of people's chances for doing it again."

"Stay in England. I've got help, and while I don't think these lions want to start a war, I can't risk it."

"Keep in touch. And stay safe."

"You too." I ended the call and placed the phone in my pocket. Tommy really would have risked war to come help me, but he had a family and I really wanted to avoid a global conflict.

Caitlin returned after four minutes and thirty-one seconds wearing jeans and a hoodie along with another pair of trainers. She opened my passenger car door and got in. "We'll take yours, I've contacted my office and told them that I'll be out of Stratford for a few days chasing a lead. To say my boss wasn't enthusiastic to hear from me is an understatement. But I don't think he's all that bothered about where I am or what I'm doing, so long as it's not bringing the Bureau into disrepute."

"Excellent, we've got our transport sorted out. Just have to get to New York."

"So, who are we talking to in D.C.?"

"Not we, me, and he may not even talk to me."

"*Why*, how'd you piss him off?"

"Oh, I'm sort of asking for something illegal from him."

"So, he could lose his job?"

I started the car's engine. "No, his life."

CHAPTER 14

Stratford, Maine. 1977.

I don't think I passed out from the first five punches—I vaguely remember Simon still talking to me, still gloating about something or other. Simon had his cronies drag me into the house and I blacked out for a moment, waking up inside a cage. I said something, no idea what, but it was enough to piss off someone who kicked me in the head like it was made of leather and usually used to kick around a field.

"Nathan?" Bill shouted. "You okay?"

I raised a hand in what I hope was a thumbs up, but considering I couldn't actually figure out where my hands were, I wasn't a hundred percent certain.

I rubbed at my eyes and tried to get some of the fog to leave my brain, but I felt wetness when I touched my head. Someone had busted me open.

After what felt like hours, but was probably only a few seconds, I figured out where I was. Inside the same cage from earlier. My new home was six foot square, meaning I could lie down flat and not have to curl up. But it was only three feet high, so anything that required sitting level was out of the question.

I placed one hand against the bars and tried to heat them up, but it wouldn't give.

"What's wrong?" Bill called out, from what I noticed was the cage two over from mine.

"These are silver plated. I could probably break out using my magic, but the amount involved would incinerate the cage and pretty much anything else in this room. Not the best start to an escape attempt."

"How's your head? That Simon asshole hit you with something, some sort of glove I think."

"Silver gauntlet, yeah I saw it. Several times in the face."

"Rean betrayed us? Goddamn troll bastard."

"Got to admit, I didn't see that one coming. Did they let him go?"

Bill nodded, and for the first time I noticed his swollen eye and split lip.

"How are you feeling?"

"I'm okay," he said with an approximation of a grin that made him wince. "Apparently being lippy doesn't hold a lot of ground with these assholes."

With my head no longer feeling like a space shuttle was using it as a launch pad, I took in my surroundings. We were held in some kind of basement or cellar, stairs led up at the far end of the room, although there was no way of knowing where to. There were nine cages in all, including mine and Bill's, each cage the same size, and all of them were occupied. Of the seven remaining, five were occupied by young women, and two by young men. None of them had to have been older than thirty, and all of them carried marks of torture, cuts, and bruises. They were all scared and watched me with a mixture of fear and trepidation.

I could tell who had been there the shortest, their eyes still held hope of rescue.

The cage between mine and Bill's held a woman with short brown hair. She wore dirty blue jeans and a t-shirt that was covered in cigarette burns, as were her arms and neck. She hugged herself tightly and sat as far back from the front of the cage as possible.

"My name's Nathan," I told her softly. "Yours?"

"Her name is Fern," the young man in the other cage next to mine said.

I turned around, bumping my head on the thick bars twice. The man was probably a few years older than Fern, although the beard and disheveled appearance didn't exactly help in guessing his age. He had similar burn marks on his black t-shirt, although I didn't see any on his heavily tattooed arms or neck.

"And you are?" I asked.

"Glen," he said.

"Have you both been here long?"

"Fern was here when they grabbed me. Which was maybe … three weeks ago. It's hard to tell. You only ever see a clock or calendar when they take you upstairs. And then they just … they hurt you."

I wasn't sure I wanted an answer to my next question, "What do they do?"

"They cut you, beat you, put out cigarettes on you. It's always that Simon guy who does the asking, and when he's tired of you, or thinks you're lying, he hands you over to one of his friends so that they can have their fun. Those brothers upstairs, the big guys, they always take the girls. They usually don't come back."

I filed the information away, for when I could devote all of my attention to the brothers and their crimes. "What do they ask you?"

"About the town, about the people in it and who I know. They ask about my tattoos. That seems to be the common theme. All of us have them, although they're in different places. Simon only seems interested in where we got ours done, or how long ago."

"Does he ask about a specific tattoo?"

Glen shook his head. "No, just about where we had them done. And about people we know in town with tattoos. No idea why."

"Me neither," I said mostly to myself. "What about the rest of the people down here? How are they faring?"

"Most are so out of it I don't even think they know what day it is. And those that do just sleep or scream. You don't want to sleep, but they put something in the water. So you die of thirst or you pass out. That's when they come for you, when you can't fight. This one girl refused to drink anything. She died about three days ago. I heard the two bastards talking about throwing the body into a cave for some troll or something." Something caught Glen's attention. "Didn't you say you know a troll? Are they the same? Are trolls real? I thought it was a metaphor or something. I heard you mention magic too."

"Hope you don't have to find out." I pointed to the grate behind Glen's head. "So, anyone tried to escape?"

"One guy managed to pick the cage lock and even got an arm out there, screaming his head off the whole time, but no one came. No one ever comes around here, except for that man in the suit. They have two rooms on the top floor, they're sound proofed. It's where they ask the questions."

"Who was he, the man in the suit, I mean?"

Glen shrugged. "He doesn't hurt anyone, just comes and pokes us and asks questions, the same ones as Simon. Then he leaves. Fern pleaded with him to let her go, but he just laughed at her. Since then she's been really quiet."

I glanced over to Fern who was picking at a freckle on her forearm.

"They broke her. They like that, they're always really giddy when they finally break one of us."

"How many upstairs?"

"Not sure, I've only seen Simon, the two big brutes and another three. Two of them are women. They're almost as bad as the men. My dad, he used to tell me that when he was in Germany he could see the people who just lost it and were killing for fun. Those women up there, that's how I imagine the soldiers my dad was talking about appeared. Just cold and emotionless, unless they're killing. Then they're smiling and joking and laughing. You can hear it, among all the screaming and pleading. Laughter." Glen shook his head and wiped his eyes.

"We're gonna get out of here, somehow."

"Everyone new says that. The last guy managed three days before they killed him just to shut up his constant begging."

"Yeah, well I'm a terrible beggar, but I'm an even worse prisoner."

"So, do you have a plan?" Bill asked.

"Sort of," I admitted. "I need everyone to make as much noise as possible. I need whoever is upstairs to come for us."

"You're asking people to put their lives on the line," Bill said.

I nodded. "I know, but it's our only chance, and if we don't do it, we're as good as dead anyway."

"And once we get those psychos down here, what do we do?" Fern asked, having woken from her stupor.

I stared at her for a moment and felt the anger radiating off her in waves.

"Well, I plan on getting out and killing the whole fucking lot of them," I told her.

Fern stared back, and for a second I thought she was going to glance away. "Make it hurt," she said and started screaming.

At some point Fern's screams encouraged the other captives to join in, creating a cacophony of noise that was sure to gain the attention of anyone in the house above. In fact, it only took a few seconds for the door to be flung open and light to bathe the steps.

"What the fucking hell are you lot doing?" shouted a gruff voice, which as he descended the steps I soon discovered belonged to one of the two brutes who'd held me down while Simon had gone to work.

No one stopped screaming or yelling, and the Brute made his way to the bottom of the stairs and walked over to Fern's cage. "You want me to give you something to scream about again?" He smiled and turned to me. "She bucks and fights like a trooper. But damn is she ever sweet once she calms down."

"I'm going to kill you," I told him.

He laughed. It wasn't the reaction I'd expected.

"You want me to open the cage and let you out? I'm not a fucking idiot."

"Stupid enough to leave me with my magic." I threw a whip of air through the bars and wrapped it around his neck, yanking him forward off his feet. He slammed onto the top of my cage, causing it to rock violently.

"Fucking little—" he started as I reached through the bars and held the back of his head in place, pushing his face into the bars.

"The key, where is it?"

"Fuck you."

I removed one my hands from the back of his head and created a blade of fire. He tried to escape, but tendrils of hardened air magic kept him in place. "Last chance," I told him and pushed the tip of the blade into his ribs.

He screamed in pain as the smell of cooked flesh filled the cage. A second later the keys had fallen out of his pocket and into my hand. Another blast of air against his chest, sending him tumbling away and giving me time to unlock the cage.

I stepped out and took a second to stretch, while the Brute tried to get back to his feet.

"I let you hold me down because Simon threatened to kill people if I fought back. Well, Simon isn't here now." I kicked him in the ribs hard enough to feel them break. The Brute rolled onto his back and yelled out. I grabbed his leg and dragged him over to Fern, kicking him in the ribs twice on the way when he tried to struggle.

After unlocking Fern's cage, I took hold of the Brute's head and pulled it up, causing him to wince. "You're going to answer my questions and you're going to say sorry to the girl here. How many upstairs?"

I didn't have long to wait at all.

"Twelve—me, my brother, Simon, five more guys and four women. And they're going to tear you in—"

I smashed his head against the cage.

"Don't try to make yourself sound big, it'll end badly. What are you doing here?"

He smiled at Fern. "Killing bitches."

I cracked his skull again. "Why are you doing this?"

The Brute spat blood onto the floor, his nose was pretty badly broken and his lip was pissing blood. "Because it's fun, because Simon wants us to. Because we are The Vanguard."

I was surprised enough by the Brute's words, that I took a step back, giving Fern enough distance to grab the keys from the lock of the cage and plunge them into the Brute's neck. She stabbed him over and over, maybe a half dozen times before I managed to grab her and pull her away without hurting her. I didn't care how hurt he was. He'd deserved it.

By the time Fern was off him, she was covered in his blood and shaking. I tossed the keys to Glen and told him to unlock everyone else, while I went to see to the Brute, who was trying to stem the flow of blood that was squirting from the hole in his throat.

"Normally I'd end it quickly for you," I told him softly. "But you got off lucky. So, you can bleed to death on the floor here, silently."

He tried to say something, but no words left his mouth.

"Your brother isn't going to be as lucky. I'll be killing him myself." I left him to die as I helped Glen unlock the other cages.

Bill stretched as he was freed and glanced over at the now dead Brute. "He deserved worse," he told Fern as she wouldn't stop staring at the body.

She nodded, but remained transfixed.

"Stay here until I come get you," I said to Glen. "No one comes out of this cellar. No one tries to escape. When we get up there people are going to get hurt, if anyone of you are there I can't guarantee your safety."

"They took two girls up there earlier," he said. "Before you got dragged in here, if you find them, help them. Please."

I told him I would and set off up the stairs. When I reached the top I placed a hand on the cold, wooden door and allowed my air magic to reach out into the house beyond. It worked a bit like sonar, my air magic moving invisibly sending back a ping of feedback when it found something alive.

"There's one to the right of the door, about ten feet down," I told Bill.

"I may be unarmed, but I'm not exactly defenseless."

"They're all yours."

I turned the handle and opened the door slowly. The man was standing by the front door, having a cigarette. His back was toward us as we crept out of the cellar, and I moved aside, allowing Bill to move slowly toward him. When he was just a few feet behind, he moved with deadly force, grabbing the man around the neck and dragging him to the ground with a crunch as his neck snapped. He dragged the dead body over to a small utility room, which once opened showed to be full of coats, assorted umbrellas, and shoes. Bill pushed the body inside, closing the door behind him.

"I'm going to clear out the rear of the house," I told Bill. "Stay guard here, I won't be long."

Bill had taken a long silver dagger from the dead body and was weighing it in his hand as he nodded.

I left him alone and crept toward the rear of the building, passed a large empty room and set of stairs. I heard grunts and groans of pain upstairs, but I forced myself to keep going. Whoever was up there was going to have to hold out for just a few more minutes.

As I moved closer to the kitchen, I overheard two men speaking and moved into the shadows next to a large chest of drawers, giving me a good view of the occupants. The first man was short, stocky, with a shaved head and several tattoos along the back of his neck. He was digging the point of a dagger into the softwood around the doorframe. His friend was well over six- feet tall, but was just as broad as his smaller comrade. His arms were bare, except for a few scars that looked a lot like bullet holes. He was sitting at a kitchen table a few feet away from his friend.

"Who's that new guy? The one Simon wants left alone?" the shorter man asked as I moved toward them.

"No idea, but he's freaking out about it. I think the government has finally sent someone to deal with us."

"Then why aren't we dealing with him first? Sending those fucks a message."

The larger man sighed; clearly he'd heard his friend's words before. "Because we're not finished here yet. And because we don't want a long drawn out battle with the Feds."

"So, what about that cop? Moon?"

"Well that little piggy is going on a spit. Son-of-a-bitch once took me in for assault."

"Who'd you hit?"

"Some bitch who didn't know when she was allowed to open her mouth."

"Never, am I right?"

Both men laughed as I entered the kitchen and silently made my way toward them. The larger man was still laughing when I slit his throat with a blade of fire. He made a bubbling noise as he died, which caught the attention of his shorter friend, who died a second later as the same dagger severed his spine.

"What the fuck?" a woman shouted as she entered the kitchen from the opposite side. She turned to shout once more, but I threw the stocky man's dagger at her. The blade entered her skull and killed her before she'd hit the linoleum floor.

I made a circuit of the remaining rooms, but found no one else until I reached Bill. "Three down," I told Bill. "The exit's free now, take everyone from downstairs out through the kitchen. I'll go deal with whoever is up there."

"You need a hand?"

"Get them outside first, take them to the tree line. Then go get Galahad. Call a bar in Portland, the Mill. They'll sort it out."

"Be careful," he said, and within a few seconds I was watching him lead a half dozen people safely out of the house.

When I was certain enough time had passed for them to get away, I walked toward the staircase. The noises I'd heard from before had ended, and I really hoped that whoever they had up there was still alive.

I crept slowly up the staircase and peered through the wooden banister onto the empty landing above. Once at the top of the stairs, I opened the nearest door, but although it held several single beds, it was devoid of life. I re-closed the door and heard muffled voices coming from the far right of the floor.

It took me a few minutes as I continued to open every door I came to in an effort to not be surprised by any would-be attackers. As I got closer to the voices, I made out a woman laughing. I stopped at the door for the briefest of moments before bursting through in one motion. The explosion of sound as the door slammed open startled the two women inside. They each held a carved dagger and straddled the bodies of a young man and woman, both tied to old wooden chairs, each drenched with blood.

The first woman never even moved before a torrent of air slammed into her and flung her through the window at the rear of the room, her screams echoing in the night as she fell the thirty feet to a soft thud and then silence. The second woman flung her dagger at me, which I easily avoided and then set her legs on fire before she could try to get away through a nearby door. She screamed in pain, rolling around trying to put out the magical flames as they leapt onto her arms with seemingly a mind of their own.

I left her to scream as I checked the man and woman tied to a chair and found them both dead. Their tops had been torn off, exposing the three tattoos on their backs, one on each shoulder and one on the base of their necks. They had dozens of knife wounds, and both had been dead for a few hours. The voices I'd heard earlier hadn't belonged to either of them.

I clicked my fingers and the fire vanished, leaving the murderess moaning in pain.

"Why?" I asked her.

"Fun," she said and smiled through the pain.

I grabbed her by her hair and dragged her toward the unbroken window. "Where's Simon?"

"No idea. He lets us enjoy ourselves. He doesn't own us."

I glanced outside at the lawn below, to the body of her friend who was lying at an impossible angle. "You may live from this high up, but it wouldn't be a good life. Why did your brute of a friend say you were the Vanguard?"

She followed my gaze, her eyes wide open at the sight of her friend. "Because we are Vanguard. We will rid the world of the lesser souls."

"Lesser souls?"

"Anyone we deem to be beneath us. Simon picks them and once he's done questioning them, he leaves their punishment to us."

"You're human, all of you. In the eyes of any true Vanguard, *you'd* be the lesser species."

She appeared confused for a second. "I don't understand. *We* are the true Vanguard."

I shook my head. "No, you're psychotic cannon-fodder."

The gunshot exploded inside the room as bullets came pouring through the nearest wall. One of the bullets hit the woman in the temple, spinning her to the ground as I managed to throw myself behind the two deceased victims.

Once the shooter had finished, there were well over a dozen bullet holes in the wall and the door that led to the hallway. The door opened slowly, showing the framed image of Brute Two in the gap, an uzi in one hand.

A quick blast of air threw his gun arm up toward the ceiling, something he couldn't do anything about in time to stop me barreling into him and out into the hallway. His gun skittered away into the room as I landed blow after blow on his face and chest using my fists and forearms to remove any fight that might have been in him. When finished, his features were a bloody mess and he was wheezing badly.

"Where's Simon?" I asked.

"Out," he said and started to cough up blood onto the floor.

I dragged him to his feet and marched him down the corridor, searching the remaining rooms on the floor until I found another woman. I pushed the brute onto the floor and checked on her. She'd been tied to a bed with cable-ties, which had cut into her wrists and ankles, drawing blood. I checked her pulse, but there was nothing there. She'd died while I was downstairs helping everyone escape. One more life lost so that others could live. Unfortunately for the brute, that didn't make me feel any better.

I dragged the injured murderer out into the hallway once more and toward the large window that looked out over the front of the house. He struggled a few times, but it's amazing what a well-aimed punch to the kidneys will do to get someone to co-operate.

I smashed the back of his head against the window, leaving a bloody print in the now spider-webbed glass.

"Where's the rest of your people?" I demanded.

"They'll find you. My brother—"

"Your brother has a large hole in his neck where his jugular used to be, he probably won't be doing much."

"Bastard!" he reared up at me, gaining a kick to his knee, which popped, and a right-hook to his jaw.

I glanced out of the window and saw Simon walking toward the house. I dragged Brute Two to his feet and held him steady. "There's good news and bad. Good news, you won't be going to jail."

"And bad?"

"This is going to hurt like a fucking son-of-a-bitch." I kept hold of him as I took a few steps back and then ran at the window, using the Brute's own body to drive through the glass.

I kept hold of him until we were free of the house and then I released him to fall alone, using my air magic to drop softly to the ground as the Brute landed with a sickening crunch on the porch behind me.

I took a step toward Simon, with what I was sure a murderous glint in my eyes, but he dropped to his knees, placed his hands on his head and said, "I surrender."

It wasn't enough and I took another step, but before I could do more, Galahad and his forces exploded out from the trees around us, screaming orders at Simon to lie down.

"You okay?" Galahad asked.

I had an urge to wipe the grin from Simon's face, but pushed it aside. "There are a lot of scared people in the trees behind here. Most of them will need a doctor."

"I'll ensure it's done. You did good work here."

"How'd you get here so quickly?"

Galahad shook his head. "Rean found me. He knew who to contact in town."

"Rean?" I didn't even bother trying to hide my surprise. "He betrayed us to Simon. He wanted to save his family and clan."

"Well, he must have had a change of heart," he said dismissively.

One of Galahad's men—a lanky, grizzled man with a scruffy beard—marched Simon over toward us, forcing him to his knees before Galahad.

"I only kneel to my king," Simon said.

Galahad kicked him in the face, sending him sprawling to the ground. "Get him to the jail, I want around-the-clock guard. And I want runes on the cell, if this piece of shit touches anything resembling metal, I want his fucking arms to catch fire."

"I want to talk to him," I said.

"Yeah, not a problem."

I thanked my old friend and went off to find Bill and the survivors, all the while wondering why, for a tiny fraction of a second, I thought I saw concern on Galahad's face when I asked to speak to his prisoner.

CHAPTER 15

Simon Olson was a fairly unassuming man. It was a decision I came to while watching Galahad's forces march him through the police station to his little cell at the far end of the row of four. The other cells were empty, although I doubted Simon would have cared one way or the other. Aside from his bland exterior, there was something not right about him. It coiled under his skin, like a great white shark just under the surface of glassy water. Danger just waiting to be released to devastating effect. He looked at people in two ways. Either as someone who was beneath him, or as prey. I apparently fell into the second category. Lucky me.

"Do you think these bars will keep you safe?" he asked me once Galahad's people left us alone. Simon had immediately lain down on the single bed, trying to look as disinterested in his current predicament as possible.

I tapped one of the steel bars with my finger. It made a satisfying noise. "Pretty much. There are runes drawn all over these bars, you could rub them off, but doing so would make it go boom if you do it in the wrong order. That will turn you into a paste."

"You too."

"Nope, the focus of the blast is directed toward you. Me, I'll just get a bit of a jolt and try to avoid flying parts of psychopath."

Simon's eyes narrowed. "You're a smug little prick, aren't you?"

"Well I'm not in jail. So, yes, yes I am."

"Where do you think Galahad is going to put me? He'll take me to Shadow Falls and put me far away from any living thing."

"I don't give a shit if he puts you in a Siberian Gulag. In fact if I had my way, I'd probably send half of you to one place and half somewhere else. Just to make my point."

"This isn't over."

"Oh really? Are some of your human friends running around the place? What are they going to do?"

"You'll see. I don't play the short game."

"Good for you. Do you play the dodge-the-large-man-who-wants-to-make-you-his-bitch game? Because on the off chance that Galahad keeps you in a human jail, you're gonna have to get really good at it. A whole life of sweaty man love and sorcerer's bands. Never to use your alchemy. That would be a very long life for you, I think."

Simon's eyes narrowed again. "Why are you here?"

"Why kill those people? What did you get out of it apart from just the act of murder?"

"Isn't that enough?"

"You're not an idiot, you tortured those people and removed parts of them. I'm guessing tattoos. So, why the interest in people's ink?"

"I like collecting tattoos. They're pretty."

"That's an awful lot of work just to get some tattoos. And why have those fucking idiots you were working with think they're Vanguard? Because we both know they're about as far removed from Vanguard as you are from President of Algeria."

"What do you know about Vanguard?"

"Well, I know they're never human. That they want to destroy Shadow Falls and anyone else who has left Avalon and that they're full of insane idiots. So I guess you got the last one right."

"What makes you think I want to tell you anything?"

"Because you're itching to. You want to tell everyone how smart you were, and how easy it was to string all those people along."

"Fine, you're right. I told them they were Vanguard to give them a purpose. Make them think they were doing something they consider worthwhile. They were a band of misfits and murderers when I came along, it didn't take much to convince them that the world's ills stemmed from the people I wanted dead."

"So, why did you want those people dead?"

"Ah, that's for me to know. Let me ask you something, why did Galahad get you to bring me in? Why not do it himself?" He glanced around as if checking for anyone who may overhear us. "Why ask *Merlin's Assassin* to come get me?"

I stared at Simon as a thought popped into my head. "Have we met before?"

"Oh, yes, although it took me a little while to remember you. The last time we met you were trying to kill me."

"Clearly I didn't do the best of jobs."

"Milan, 1709. You remember it now? Do you remember those dead kids?"

Reality dawned on me as the memory of dead teenagers found in snowy woods flashed in my brain. "You were the assassin."

Simon nodded, apparently proud of his work. "You almost had me. Almost."

"So, who do you work for? Did you work for Shadow Falls back then?"

"No, I was freelance. I came under the notice of the old king of Shadow Falls a century ago. He made me very rich. And will continue to do so again when the impostor who stole his crown is removed."

"So, all of these murders was to, what? Make Galahad look bad?"

"I think we're done talking now. If you stick around town you'll find out exactly what I have planned."

I stood and looked down at Simon who had closed his eyes.

"Please do close the door behind you. I'm sure Galahad's men will be in here shortly to rough me up; I'd like a nap before then."

"Make sure we don't meet again, Simon," I told him.

Simon opened one eye and stared at me. "Oh, we'll meet again. And next time, I don't plan on letting you win."

I found Galahad outside the police station talking to the mayor, who scowled and walked off the second he saw me. "That man is a weasely little bastard," Galahad said before taking a drink of what smelled like coffee.

"Why'd you hire me?" I asked. "No more bullshit. Why have me go after him? He's clearly working for the ex-king. So, what is he really doing here?"

Galahad drank his coffee and dropped the polystyrene cup into the bin next to him. "I have no idea. I'm hoping our interrogators will be able to figure it out. But know this, Simon never does anything for the fun of it. If he is working for Charles Whitehorn, the ex-king, and I'm certain he is, there's a game plan here."

"Why not go to Charles and threaten him off?"

"There's a rumor that he's about to run for Senator."

"As in a United States Senator?"

"Unfortunately, yes. If we go after him and there's any link back to Shadow Falls, it could cause problems for us. Avalon certainly wouldn't be happy that we're threatening people who are in the neutral territory of D.C. My position isn't solidified enough that I can risk it. Besides, Simon was killing on my own doorstep—that was more important than threatening someone and maybe creating more support for him in the long run."

"How was everyone from the house?"

"We took the three remaining members of Simon's gang to a nearby cabin. Once Simon's been taken back to Shadow Falls, they'll be given over to the SPD to do with as they see fit. Bill and the rest of the inhabitants of the house are at a nearby hospital. They're mostly suffering from shock and minor injuries. The psychological impact is going to be the big thing for them."

"Simon was asking about tattoos," I said. "Is there a parlor in town?"

Galahad shook his head. "What type of tattoos?"

"No idea, he wouldn't say. But he only grabbed people with tattoos. It's why Sally-Ann was disposed of; she didn't have any. But then, why did they think she might have?"

I walked back into the station and made my way to Simon, who was still alone. "Why'd you grab Sally-Ann?" I asked.

"Who?" Simon asked without opening his eyes.

"The girl you threw out of a car?"

"She fit my type."

"Bullshit. You wanted tattoos, why her? She didn't have any."

Simon sighed. "Two of my boys grabbed her before I could stop them. I checked her for marks and discarded her. Then I killed one of the boys to make sure we didn't have any more stupid errors. Is she why you're here?"

"She was the daughter of a friend of Avalon's."

Simon sat bolt upright. "Are you fucking kidding me? You're here because of some bitch my idiot group grabbed because they couldn't keep their shit together?"

"You're in here because you murdered someone important to an Avalon official. You very much killed the wrong girl."

"Those fucking idiots!" Simon screamed and launched himself at the bars, which ignited his hands as he touched them, causing him to scream in pain and drop to the floor. "It's a good thing you killed them."

"Looks like you picked the wrong people to trust."

Simon seethed silently for a few seconds. "Speaking of trust. You see that miserable fucking wood troll who set me up, tell him I'm going to make him watch as I butcher his clan. I promised him what would happen. And now I plan to follow through."

"Well, good luck with getting out of there without cooking yourself. I'm sure he'll be up all night concerned that the mighty Simon Olson, char-grilled to perfection, is going to come for him."

"Go fuck yourself."

The door opened and two large men stepped inside. One was pushing a table, the contents of which were covered by a black sheet. "I think you've got bigger problems," I told him and left him alone with his newfound friends.

CHAPTER 16

The fact that Simon had been removing tattoos, and only taking those sporting them, was something that was still bouncing around my brain when I finally managed to fall asleep later that night. Galahad had assured me that he would get to the bottom of whatever Simon was after, and it was no longer my job to worry. But even so, something bothered me and at the time of 2:34 AM, I decided to go for a walk to clear my head.

Apparently I wasn't the only one, as I bumped into Bill only a few minutes later.

"Couldn't sleep?" he asked and sat on a park bench.

I shook my head and sat beside him. "Something is bothering me about all of this. I can't figure out what it is. But it was all too easy."

"That Simon bastard surrendered without a fight. Does that seem normal to you?"

I shook my head. "Apparently we met in Milan a few hundred years ago. He didn't go without a fight then. In fact, he escaped the first chance he got."

"So, why give up now? Why would anyone want to be captured and taken somewhere where they can have the shit kicked out of them by people looking for answers?"

"That's a good question."

I stood up and started walking toward the police station, with Bill beside me.

"What's going on?" he asked.

"When was the last time you spoke to someone in the station?"

"A few hours ago, why?"

I didn't answer; instead, I went into a flat out sprint, leaving Bill far behind as my magic made me much faster than any human could hope to be.

I reached the police station's front door and gave it a push. Locked. A second push was accompanied with a magical blast, which removed not only the lock, but most of one door, which then swung open.

"You armed?" I asked Bill, who'd caught me up.

He drew his revolver and I stepped into the police station. The desk sergeant had been pulled over the desk, where a metal rod had been stabbed through the back of his head, pinning him to the now-red floor. Behind him, three more bodies sat, each of them covered in blood.

I motioned for Bill to open the door to the cells, which we found were also devoid of life. One of the two men I'd seen enter the cells earlier in the day was hanging from one of the cages, metal bars wrapped tightly around his throat while several more had been inserted into his chest and then pulled out of his back. Blood was everywhere, covering every part of the cell.

I turned to talk to Bill, but he'd already ran out of the cell and back through the door to the front of the police station. I followed and found him in the main part of the police station, where we'd first met. Three more bodies lay on the floor, one with gun in hand.

"I'm sorry," I said.

"These were good people, why'd he do this? Why not just leave?"

"He wants to make a point."

"But—"

"Oh, shit," I whispered. "Bill, get Galahad and his people up to where we met the wood trolls. Get them there now."

"Where are you going?" Bill asked as I grabbed some car keys from the desk beside me.

"Where are the cars kept?"

"It'll be parked outside. Where are you going?"

"The woods. Simon told me he was going to go kill Rean's clan. I'm going to go stop him."

"And if it's too late, like it was here?"

I didn't have time to answer, as I was already running back toward the front exit, and a few seconds later I'd found the right police cruiser and had set off toward the woods.

I parked the car where Bill and I had stopped the previous day and began running through the woods, using my night vision to avoid branches and trip hazards. I didn't find anything wrong until I reached the stream. There were bodies, half in the water, and another two on the boulders, which were covered in dozens of sharp, foot-long rock blades. I stopped by the three bodies in the water and found that they were a mother and two of the adolescent wood trolls. They'd probably been ambushed by Simon.

I crossed the stream and continued to run in the direction of the muffled cries I heard from further in the woods. It didn't take log before I found more dead wood trolls. Two men were crouched over one of them, laughing as they stabbed the troll over and over. I didn't even stop sprinting as I buried a blade of fire in the neck of the man closest to me. The second man turned toward me and caught the same blade between his eyes, almost cutting off the top of his head. I left them both to die and continued toward the cries, which had turned into louder and louder screams with every step.

As I entered the clearing where Rean and his colony had welcomed Bill and me, all I could see were the bodies of trolls. Most had been torn apart by a bladed weapon, and it didn't take long for me to find what was responsible.

Simon was crouched in front of Rean, who had been tied to a tree, forced to watch as the psychotic madman in front of him butchered his colony. While I couldn't see the front of him, I could tell that Simon was wearing a gauntlet with a long blade protruding from one end. It was covered in blood, and as I walked toward him I noticed that Rean's mate and son were already dead.

I stepped on a branch, which broke, causing Simon's head to snap toward me. He smiled.

"You're a bit late," he said and stood, showing me the almost entirely red gauntlet, which stretched up to his elbow. "I took some silver from the police station to make this, it's quite effective."

I glanced past him at Rean, whose eyes were glazed over, seemingly unable to focus on anything.

"I guess it's surrendering time." Simon removed the gauntlet and threw it onto the ground before placing his hands on his head and kneeling on the blood-soaked earth.

"No," I said and ran at him.

He tried to move, but it was too late. I kicked him hard enough in the chest to dump him on his back. He tried to push me away, to get distance between us, but I locked his elbow tight and broke his wrist before snapping his arm. I wrapped air around my fists and kept on punching him, over and over again, tearing his face apart from the impact from each blow.

I dragged him to his feet and smashed his face into the nearest tree, punching him in the kidneys, and he cried out through ruined lips. A hand against his ribs created enough pressure to crush the bones, and when he tried to move away, I snapped his knee for good measure.

Every time he tried to move or get away, I broke a bone. I was more than ready to beat him to death, but I wanted him to suffer, to feel some measure of the pain he'd inflicted on so many.

"Nate," someone behind me said, and I felt arms around my waist, dragging me away from Simon. I pulled my head forward and shot back, bringing the back of my skull against their nose. They released their grip and I dove on Simon, who was trying to crawl away, kicking and punching him with a rage that didn't want to leave. It wasn't until more hands grabbed me, that I finally calmed down and allowed myself to be removed. I noticed that the man I'd head butted was Bill, who was holding his now bleeding nose. A ping of guilt went through me.

"I'm sorry, Bill," I said.

He waved my apology away. "Don't grab you when you're in the middle of killing someone, I'll keep that in mind."

Galahad appeared in front of me and motioned for someone to see to Bill.

"He killed so many people," I said. "Innocent people. Children."

"I know. But we need him alive."

"Fuck you, Galahad. He deserves to die like a fucking rabid dog."

"Yes, he does, but it's not about what he deserves. It's not about what any of these people deserve. It's about what's best for my people. And his brain if full of information that we need."

"How'd he escape?"

"One of the men I sent to interrogate him was working against me. Simon used him to get free and then killed him."

"Good, saves me the job."

"You son-of-a-bitch!" Rean screamed at Galahad as his hands were freed and he fell forward, holding the lifeless body of his mate against him. "I did everything you asked."

"Rean, not now," Galahad said softly.

"Go to hell," Rean snarled, his bloody and beaten appearance made him look even more enraged. "When my son found those men, I told you what happened. You told me you'd protect my family. You promised."

"I'm sorry—"

"Fuck you and your apologies. They're dead and it's your fault."

"What's happening?" I asked.

"Shadow Falls business," Galahad snapped and someone tried to drag Rean away, but I put myself between him and the wood troll.

"Anyone touches Rean until he says his piece answers to me. After what I just did to that puddle of crap on the floor, is there anyone here who wants to see what else I can do?"

No one moved.

"My son found the body of that girl," Rean said to me. "He tracked Simon and his men down to that house. So I went to

Galahad and told him. He told me that if I took you there, if I got you inside the house, he could make sure my clan remained safe from Simon and his people."

"That's why you betrayed us?" I asked.

"I'm sorry about that, it was the quickest way to get you in. And Galahad told me I was to mention nothing about it to you. So once you were in the house I got Galahad here to oversee the arrest." Rean laid his wife's head back onto the ground and rounded on Galahad. "You promised me they'd be safe."

"I did all I could. I had no idea the mayor was going to help Simon escape."

"But you knew that some people in this town were working against you. Surely the mayor must have been on your list?" I snapped.

"He was but we assumed . . . I assumed there was time.'

"Did you know Rean planned for me and Bill to be taken by Simon?"

"It was my idea, yes," Galahad said. "I knew you'd make it out. I just needed you to subdue Simon and his people."

"Rean, I'm sorry for your colony," I said without taking my eyes off Galahad.

"We found some survivors," one of Galahad's men said as he entered the clearing.

Rean dragged himself upright and walked toward the newcomer, stopping by Galahad to wipe his wife's blood on the clean white shirt of the king. "Her blood is your fault," the wood troll said before refusing help and leaving the clearing.

Galahad glanced down at the blood and closed his eyes.

"The mayor is responsible for this?" I asked.

Galahad nodded. "He works for the old king. We have eye-witness accounts of the mayor meeting with Simon once he left the police station."

Simon was having a sorcerer's band—a small bracelet that was designed to negate the abilities of the wearer—placed on him. He'd still be able to heal quicker than a human, but his alchemy would be lost to him while he wore it. Simon smiled, showing missing teeth, and spat blood onto the leaves around him.

"If I ever see him again, he dies," I told Galahad, who nodded. "And me and you are going to have a conversation about your lies and using me to get to Simon. But it'll be later, when my anger no longer blinds my judgment."

I walked passed Galahad to the edge of the clearing.

"Where are you going?" Galahad called after me.

"I'm going to go and make sure you have no further problems in this town."

CHAPTER 17

En Route to Washington, D.C. Now.

Felicia arranged everything exactly as she said she would, and once Caitlin and I arrived at the airport in New York, we were quickly placed on Felicia's Learjet and soon in the sky.

Caitlin managed to fall asleep almost immediately, leaving me to make a phone call to try and pre-empt what I was going to have to do once we'd landed. I managed to get a hold of his assistant and spent several minutes trying to convince her to give my contact a message for me, something it was clear she was less than interested in doing.

"Just tell him Nathan Garrett called," I told her eventually. "Tell him I'll meet him at the Lincoln Memorial at noon."

She told me she would and hung up.

Before I could curse her silently for being a miserable pain in the ass, my phone rang again. "Sky," I said.

"Nate, I figured you'd be missing me. How goes Maine?"

I told her about the cave troll and werelions.

"You don't get involved in half-assed shit, do you? Would it be possible for you to go somewhere and not have things try to kill you?"

"What's the point in that? Life would be all boring and stagnant."

"Well, if it helps, I have some information that may tell you *why* people are trying to kill you."

"Thanks, so what did you find?"

"We were searching Bill's house and found a safe. It took a while, but we finally managed to get it open without destroying what was inside."

Sky very quickly had every ounce of my attention. I didn't even notice my nerves at flying. "What did you find?"

"Files. Eleven of them. Each of them is a missing person from around the country. All of them, six men and five women, vanished without a trace in the past three years. Three have officially gone missing from Stratford in the last few weeks. There are police reports for each of them. No signs of a struggle, all three were well liked and respected. Three hikers were killed a few days ago too and the other five are from all over the place."

"Anything else?"

"He left notes detailing what he believed was a link between these murders and disappearances and what happened in Maine in 1977. The older victims were all people who escaped the house with you and Bill. That information isn't in any of the files though, he wrote it separately himself. There are also three more files with names—Patricia, Joshua, and Bianca. There are grainy CCTV images of them, but nothing else. He must have thought they were the killers."

"Send me everything you have. I'll ask Caitlin when she wakes up; maybe she's seen their pictures before. The names of the victims who escaped were left out of any police reports.

No one but people who were around at the time would know that they're linked, but we still don't know what they're killing *for*."

"There could be more bodies. The fact that none of the recent victims have been found tends to make me believe they were very good at making people stay gone."

I flashed back to the cave troll and piles of bones. "I found them," I said. "I'm pretty certain that they were taken to Stratford and fed to a cave troll."

"Oh, shit," Sky almost whispered. "That would explain not being able to find them. But why take people across country just to feed them to a monster?"

"No idea, and oddly enough the hikers weren't fed to anything. They were found mauled to death. I'm on my way to Washington to see if I can find out more about the werelion prides in the area. The werelions in Stratford are Barbary lions. That can't be too common."

"Well, they probably are in some parts, but it's doubtful that Maine is an overly large source of extinct lions."

"Of those victims, any of them have tattoos?"

I waited while she flicked through something, the sound of paper rustling in my ear. "Six. Although no more details than that. Why?"

"Simon was murdering people and removing their tattoos back in the seventies. No one ever found out why he was doing it, but it must have been important."

"You could go ask Simon himself."

"I don't think that's a very good idea at the moment. Although it may well turn into one if this trip doesn't prove fruitful."

"You think Simon's old friends are killing again?"

"I think someone who knows him is finishing off his dirty work. No idea what they're doing, though. They're not killing randomly, and they're being very quiet about it. But other than that, I've got nothing to go on."

"I'm still looking into who might have been helping these people get your phone number. We checked into the dead cop, Jerry, and he had some large deposits in his bank account, but he had no way of getting hold of your phone number. Dad's not exactly thrilled about a breach of security, so I'm trying to hold him off from hoisting everyone into the air by their ankles until they say something. He's already moved on from thumbscrews, so I think the staff are safe for another day."

"How's your mum doing?"

"Angry. Probably angrier than Dad. Dad expects this shit once in a while, but Mom treats everyone like family. So to her, this is a huge betrayal. She wanted Dad to drag Jerry's spirit back from wherever it is so he can question him. Dad refused, saying it was like searching for a needle in a country-size needle stack. Mom didn't exactly take his sarcasm well. I believe he's sleeping in the den. Or the floor. Whichever she decided was going to be the least comfortable."

Persephone had a mean temper when someone angered her. And she held a grudge for just long enough to be able to gain some measure of revenge at some point. She wasn't cruel or vindictive, but she could be a very dangerous adversary when she'd been offended. As Hades knew all too well.

I told Sky to give her family my best and she said she'd stay in touch.

Caitlin woke just as I ended the call. She rubbed her eyes and stretched. "Did you miss me?" she asked.

"I kept busy," I said and explained about the phone calls.

"So, who is this mystery person we're...sorry, you're meeting."

"A four-star general by the name of Roberto Cortez."

"Why is he so important to what's happening?"

"For years the werelions and werewolves were at war with one another. It was mostly a cold war; occasionally there were skirmishes, but nothing of huge note. That changed a thousand years ago. No one is really sure what started it—whether it was wolves killing lions or lions killing wolves, but it changed everything into a full-blown conflict. There were plenty of attempts at solving it, at trying to make peace, but nothing ever took for more than a few months. Eventually peace was reached, but it was decided that someone had to figure out exactly how many lions and wolves there were. Roberto got to personally track every single werelion in North America. If anyone can tell us who they might be, or who turned them originally, it's Roberto."

"What if this lion isn't originally from here?"

"Then we're going to have to try a different tactic, but I'm hoping he has an idea of who might have turned them. From there we could find out who they are."

"But if he gets found out?"

"By asking for his help, I'm sort of breaking a few rules. I should go through proper channels, but that would take too long."

"Will he do it?"

"Depends on whether he still considers owing me."

I used my phone to open the email I'd been sent and downloaded the file. I passed Caitlin my phone and she flicked through the various documents. "Bill Moon had files on these people?"

"These are the victims from across the country."

I took my phone back and downloaded the information about the three potential killers. "What about these three?"

"Not sure," she said a little quicker than I'd expected. "We don't have any images of the killers, so these are possibilities."

"The names Patricia, Bianca or Joshua mean anything to you?"

"No."

I told her my theory about them being dragged across the country to kill in Maine.

"That's a lot of extra work," she said when I'd finished. "Dangerous, too."

"I don't suppose that when Bill spoke to you he mentioned anything about the survivors of what happened in '77? I'm not great at recognizing faces." I flicked through the pictures on my phone. "Some of these people look familiar, if a lot older than I remember. I'd guess that they were the '77 survivors."

"He said there were no files, that most of them moved away from the town. But no one kept tabs on them, so I can't tell you if those people were the survivors of back then."

"Can you check if a Glen or Fern live in town? They're the only two names I remember who aren't in these files."

She made a quick phone call and relayed the information. "There's no one in town by those names," she said, sounding deflated. "You think those lions got to them?"

"No idea. There could be more missing people, there were a lot of bones in that cave. But that leaves the question of why allow the hikers to be found? Did any of them have markings, tattoos on them?"

"Big chunks of their flesh were missing—it's possible they had tattoos, but there wasn't enough of them to find out. As for why they were left to be discovered, maybe someone interrupted them."

"Hopefully we'll get answers. Didn't you say your dad works in D.C.?"

"Yeah, I did. Although, I'm not exactly relishing the fact of meeting him."

"You two don't get on?"

"No, it's not that. It's just ever since my mom and brother vanished, he's always been distant toward me." Caitlin was quiet for a moment. "I'm not saying he doesn't love me, or that he was mean or anything like that. It's just we grew apart. He threw himself into his work and whenever I see him there's usually an argument about one case or another I'm working on. He says I get too close to things, that I should back off. Doesn't matter what the case is, I'm always too close according to him. Okay, that must sound nuts."

"Not at all," I said. "I don't know who my dad is. Nor my mum, for that matter. I grew up in Camelot and the closest thing I had to a father was probably Merlin, although that changed when he decided to start training me. Then I was his pupil and nothing more. I always got the impression there were things he wanted to tell me, but after a while that vanished and I never knew if there really was something or if it were all in my mind."

"So, do you ever wonder about who your parents really are?"

I opened my mouth to say that it wasn't something I dwelled on anymore, that it had been a long time since I'd even thought about it, but the captain announced that we'd soon be landing.

"Another time," I told her as the jet made its final approach toward a city containing both unbridled power and corruption.

CHAPTER 18

Now, I'm not saying that I hate Washington, D.C., certainly no more than any other capital city. But due to the fact that D.C. was also a neutral city, there tended to be a lot more people vying for whatever scraps of power they could find.

To be fair, there were a lot of scraps lying around, but once someone had a taste they always wanted more. Avalon also had a large interest in the city, which made everyone else feel slightly uneasy, as if Avalon could just take over the whole place and remove those with whom they didn't agree.

To the outside human looking in, it would have appeared crazy with very little actually getting done, but all the little deals and handshakes that were carried out were usually in place for a long-term plan. On top of all the dealing, there were people who just looked out for themselves. Making everyone else's job a thousand times harder.

So, I tended to stay away from the city. I was never sure who exactly knew what and where people's allegiances lay, and so long as they didn't interfere in my life, I was quite happy to live in ignorant bliss.

We left the airport and grabbed a taxi, and after dropping Caitlin off outside her father's office, I got the driver to drop me off near the Lincoln Memorial.

As per every single time I'd visited the impressive structure, the entire area was full of tourists, both domestic and foreign. Yet it didn't feel busy. People sat on the steps chatting or looking out over the reflecting pool. Others took photos of the building and its surroundings. It was quite a peaceful place, even during the day.

"Did you ever meet him?" Roberto asked me as I stopped at the spot where Doctor King gave his speech.

I turned around and shook my friend's hand. Roberto looked, contrary to the laws of time, younger than when I'd last seen him almost thirty years earlier. One of the benefits of being a shapeshifter who can control how he looks. "Who, Lincoln or King?"

"Either?"

"Lincoln, once. He was an interesting man, and very clever. I never had the pleasure of meeting King, though. I wasn't even in America when he gave his speech here. Did you meet them?"

"I met Doctor King a few times. I was here the day of his speech. We'd been given information that some enemies of Avalon wanted to cause trouble here to make a point. We didn't allow that to happen."

"And Lincoln?"

"I was assigned to give him his First Meeting."

The First Meeting was an old tradition that went back to the formation of the first monarchy of England. When someone was elected or crowned, either as a head of state, or a government, an agent of Avalon was sent to let the new person in charge know exactly where they were in the pecking order. Some didn't take the meeting well and refused to play along. They tended to be removed fairly quickly. Usually on a permanent basis.

"How did that go?"

"I was probably more nervous than he was. He just sat and listened and at the end shook my hand and told me he had a job to do. Only other man I had an issue meeting was Teddy Roosevelt, I thought he was going to shoot me."

I laughed. "I met him, twice. He was a hell of a force. If he hadn't been human, he'd have changed the world."

"You're not kidding. Did you ever get nervous about any First Meetings?"

"A few," I admitted. "Henry VII was a difficult one for me. I tried very hard not to kill him within the first few seconds."

"Why?"

"I liked Richard III, he didn't deserve the death or reputation he got. Henry was a big part of making sure Richard was vilified. Charles II was an interesting one—I'm pretty sure he was either drunk or stoned for the entire meeting. I met George Washington, too. Merlin wanted me to be the first thing the new country saw. To know exactly where they stood. I'd met him a few times before the war, so he already knew the score, but it was still a big deal. It didn't help that I actually admired him. To take on King George and win, was something I was sure the king was never going to let go."

"Didn't Merlin tell King George that America was off limits?"

I nodded. "He wanted to send every soldier he had to take back this land. He was told very nicely to mind his own business and stay out of it or he'd be removed from power."

We walked down the stairs and toward the Reflecting Pool, passing a large group of tourists and their guide as we went.

"You know," Roberto said when we were out of earshot, "the number of times you've asked for a favor since we've known each other is zero. My assistant wasn't very happy to give me a message to meet someone she hadn't vetted."

"I'm not exactly flush with time on this one. Send her some flowers from me, if it'll make your life easier."

We stopped beside the pool and Roberto took a deep breath. "Why are you here, Nate?"

"I was in Maine and was attacked by a pride of werelions. Werelions who appear to be continuing Simon Olson's work."

Roberto's expression darkened and he cracked his knuckles. "Are you sure?"

I nodded. "Pretty sure. I need your help trying to figure out who they are."

"There are three thousand or so werelions in North America. They may be a lot fewer in number than werewolves, but that doesn't mean I can just tell you who goes where. I don't have a list of names, just population numbers, and even that's about ten years out of date. And I'm not even mentioning how much trouble I could get in for giving you this information."

"They were Barbary lions," I told him. "And I know you could get into trouble. I'm asking for the name of one lion who could have turned them. Someone involved with either Simon or the old king of Shadow Falls. If these lions are continuing Simon's mission, then they would have met with people in a position of enough power to tell them what to do."

"Do you have any evidence?"

I shook my head. "They went after the old victims who lived through what happened. Then they waited around for two years before killing again. Someone fed them that information, maybe the same person who turned them."

Roberto rubbed the back of his neck. "If I do this for you, it didn't come from me. I like it here, I like my job. I enjoy working with the people around me. It takes a huge amount of work to ensure that I look like a younger version of myself every few decades. I do not wish to throw away all my hard work because it got out that I gave you classified information."

"I promise you, it stays between us."

He removed a card from his pocket and passed it to me. "I'll call in one hour with that name. My phone is clean, so there are no worries about people listening in. I'll find out who this werelion is. If there are people out there taking up Simon's insanity, they need to be stopped."

Roberto actually called after an hour and seventeen minutes. I knew because it interrupted the game of Picross I'd started on my phone just after he'd left. I stood up from the memorial steps and walked off to an emptier area.

"Can I assume you've found something?" I asked.

"What I'm about to tell you goes no further."

"I'll try not to post it online."

"I'm serious, Nate. I have a family. If this gets out …."

An image of Rean holding his dead son in his arms shot into my mind like a bullet. "It goes no further, I promise."

"Before I tell you who I found, you need to know that this is some serious shit you've uncovered. If you follow through with whatever plan you have, which I only assume will involve pissing these people off, you're going to bring a hornet's nest down on yourself."

"Won't be the first time," I said. "Nor the last, I imagine."

"Well, I warned you. There are four Barbary lions in North America. Only one lives on the East Coast. His name is Karl Steiner."

"Why does that name sound familiar?"

"Because he's the senior aide to Senator Charles Whitehorn."

"Ah, shit, how the hell did the ex-king of Shadow Falls manage to get a job as a senator, anyway?"

"If you believe certain rumors in the city, it's because he purchased the win from the good people of his constituency. A journalist started looking into his dealings a few years back, when he was first running. That journalist very quickly shelved the story and moved to another state."

"What do you know about this Karl Steiner guy?"

"He's ambitious, dangerous, and pretty much operates as Charles Whitehorn's shadow. He's not a man you want to get angry. He's got a temper. Rumor had it, he once got his body-guards to put some student in the hospital for bad-mouthing him in a bar. They waited until he left for the night and jumped him. There's no concrete proof, just whispers. The kid wouldn't press charges and refused to give details. Other than that there are also rumors that he's killed people for his boss."

"Anything that isn't rumor or conjecture?"

"I've met him twice and I wanted a shower straight after both meetings. He's not all there, and he's certainly not above doing what it takes to get the job done. He's also devoted to his boss. Utterly devoted."

"Any sort of relationship there that can be exploited?"

"They're not romantically involved, if that's what you're asking. Karl likes his women paid for. That much is well known."

"Any of them willing to talk?"

"Publicly, not a hope in hell. In private, we've found a few things. He hates Galahad—they found it weird that he mentions someone from mythology."

"So, they're not exactly clued in on Avalon. Karl can bitch and moan and they don't know what the hell he's talking about. Any idea why the hate?"

"Nope, he just hates him with a passion. Apparently he has a plan to get back at Galahad for some unknown slight. One girl told us it was all he would talk about for hours at a time. Also, he sees himself as taking over from Charles at some point. The phrase he used was a plan of succession. Apparently Karl's the one who arranges everything. Charles just reaps whatever rewards come his way."

"Okay, so they're both assholes. You sure Charles is not in charge of what's happening here?"

"That's possible, but the more likely scenario is that Karl's in charge of the operation, and letting his boss take the glory, so to speak. You think they're trying to humiliate Galahad by killing people in his territory?"

"If that's the case, why make the bodies vanish? You'd nail the corpses to the walls of town hall, set them on fire, and sit down to wait for Galahad to turn up. No, this isn't about humiliation, although it could be about revenge. If Karl hates him that much, he could be using these werelions to kill people for him."

"You think that's what's happening?"

I nodded. "It sounds that way, although the why's still elude me. I wonder how Karl will react when I tell him I know about his little pride in Maine?"

"Badly, I'm going to guess."

"Do you know what Simon's plan was? Because I haven't spoken to him or Galahad in over thirty years, and it's too much of a coincidence that people are dying in the same place he was killing."

"No idea, although I wouldn't have thought the king of Shadow Falls would have been keen on telling me anything."

"Good point. Do you have any contact details for Karl?"

"You're going to call and tell him what? That you know what he's up to? They have no idea who you are, and will send people after you until you're dead or they are. We both know *you're* not going down without a fight. You're going to turn this town into a war zone."

"Will you please have some trust in me, Roberto? I'm not going to start a war, but I do need to confirm that he's the one involved. And if he is, he can tell me who the lions in Maine are. It would make life a lot easier if I had their names. It means no more being hunted in the woods. I'd be the one with the advantage."

"What about your friend?"

"What friend?" I asked innocently.

"Caitlin Moore, she's in town with you."

"She's here to visit her dad."

"She came with you to this city so she can have a family reunion?"

"People are being murdered in Stratford. I think she'd quite like to stop them. I told her she could come, I figured maybe some of her contacts might be of help if you didn't come through."

"Thanks for that."

"Hey, I was asking a lot. And I'm thankful you came through with what I asked, but even so it pays to have a backup. But it doesn't matter, you came through. And on the plus side, it also means I don't have to ask her to do anything she might not want to."

"You're okay asking me, though."

"I figured you could take it, Roberto. We've known each other a long time, and like you said earlier, I've never asked you for a favor before. After you dumped that crap back in Stratford on me, I figured you owed me. Where can I find Karl tonight?"

"If you *really* want to find Karl he'll be at a club on New York Avenue, about a ten-minute cab from here; it's called Ray Ray's. There are a lot of very rich people spending far too much money on stuff that doesn't matter. Karl is there pretty much every other night. He'll have at least five people with him, all human, but armed."

"Why human?"

"Karl isn't scared of humans. He knows he can kill one if they betray him. And there are very few in D.C. who aren't human, and who would dare cross him."

"Anything else?"

"You won't get in unless you're dressed for it. Having a pretty woman on your arm will help. That place is loud and crowded, but Karl will sit in the VIP area on the second floor, there's a balcony overlooking the dance floor below."

"That it?"

"Yeah, the guards carry silver bullets. I had the cops pull over a few the other week to check them out. They didn't shout and scream about it, Nate. They didn't even curse. They just nodded and agreed, because they knew that they were going to get out of whatever trouble they were in. These guys don't rule Washington, but damn it, they certainly think they come close."

"Any ideas on how to get close to Karl without causing a fight?"

"If you're set on committing suicide, I'd say you have some weapons to sell. He seems to be dabbling in buying swords and daggers. No guns, just blades."

"Do you have this guy's office bugged or something?"

Roberto put on his automated response voice, "I can neither confirm nor deny the existence of any bugs or bug-related paraphernalia that may or may not be in Charles Whitehorn's office, car, and possibly home."

"Right, so why the interest in the guy?"

"Because he's bad news and this is my goddamn town. I put up with human crime, I'm not putting up with jumped-up little pricks thinking they can bully and corral people into doing their bidding because they have delusions of grandeur."

I waited for a second to see if he'd finished. "What did he do? To you, I mean."

"Nothing."

"Roberto, you've gone to a lot of effort for nothing. Both of these men were on your radar long before I turned up. So why have they caught the attention of a four-star general?"

"My job is to keep an ear out for people who might upset the status quo and report back to Avalon. But on occasion, I make a special effort to look into people. And considering Charles's association with that evil little bastard Simon, it didn't take long for me to start searching for something. I would go to his office and let him see me; I wanted him to know that he couldn't just get away with doing whatever he wanted. And then one day, my daughter was out with her friends and someone stopped them. They beat one of the boys in front of them and told my daughter that the next time her father made a nuisance of himself, they'd make her watch as they killed her family."

"Threatening your family, very classy."

"Yeah, well it worked. I stopped digging, at least in public. But I'm not about to let someone like them push me around, so we do everything covertly now. They think the message worked, and I know once they step out of line within Avalon law, I'll have the lot of them executed. My wife doesn't know I'm still keeping tabs—she'd probably leave me if she found out. But I can't let that go, Nate. But neither can I risk my family. To suggest it's been hard keeping up the lie is an understatement; every time my girl goes out I worry. But it's not in me to quit."

"Your family will be safe. Karl Steiner and his friends, well probably not so much."

"You can't kill the senior aide to a U.S. Senator, Nate, not without attracting a lot of attention to yourself."

"I'm not going to kill him, Roberto. I learned long ago that apart from some rare occasions, you can only truly kill a man once. But if you ruin everything he is, he gets to live with that shit over and over again for the rest of his very long life."

CHAPTER 19

I finished on the phone with Roberto and immediately called Caitlin. "How'd it go with your dad?" I asked.

"Next question," she said without much enthusiasm.

"Okay, so how'd you like to go to a club?"

The sigh was not encouraging. "Are you serious? I thought we were here to find out who made those werelions, not go dancing until the morning sun."

"Well, they're sort of tied together." I explained what Roberto had told me.

"They threatened his family?" Caitlin said after listening silently to the new information I gave her, her voice oozing anger.

"Feel like pissing off some really powerful and dangerous people?"

"What's your plan?"

"Oh, now, where would the fun be if I told you that? But we need some clothes, and expensive ones, too. We're also going to need somewhere to get changed."

"My dad's house will be empty. He'll be working all day and night and probably forever more." Her tone suggested there was a lot more to her meeting with her dad than she was ready to discuss. I really hoped whatever issues she was having weren't going to spill over into the evening and cause problems.

"You know the city better, where do you buy expensive clothes?"

"Do you have a budget?"

I removed my credit card from my wallet and was surprised to see there was no dust on it. "Nope, no limit at all."

"Then I know exactly where to go. Penn Quarter has the kind of places we need."

"Excellent, just don't expect me to do any actual dancing while we're there. Clubbing isn't something I'm good at. I know, I've been inside nightclubs before."

"Is it the loud music? Does it hurt your sensitive hearing?"

"You're a very witty woman. When I was eighteen, clubbing literally meant hitting someone with a very large club."

Caitlin snorted with laughter. "Well, no clubs tonight."

"Well, let's not count that out just yet. Maybe a good clubbing is exactly what the place needs."

Finding the right clothes for the job wasn't all that difficult. For me it consisted of a nice dark suit, a light blue shirt, and some black shoes, and for Caitlin . . . well, I have no idea. I'm pretty certain I dozed off at one point while she wandered the store in search of an outfit. But when we'd finally picked up everything we needed and gone back to her dad's house to change, it was beginning to get late.

"Look, for you Ray Ray's is just a sharp-dressed suit," Caitlin said as she opened the front door and switched off the alarm next to the staircase. "For me, I have to look like I just stepped out of a model shoot. And that's not exactly something I'm used to."

The clock on the wall said it was 8 p.m. "Shouldn't we be going soon?"

"We've got plenty of time, Nate. If this guy really is the big shot he thinks he is, he'll want to make an entrance in front of as many people as possible. Just walk in, no line. He'll enjoy that. Did you leave your daggers here?"

I moved my jacket to show the thin belt of silver blades against my back. "Okay, I'll go find the kitchen and eat something."

Caitlin pointed toward the rear of the house. "Kitchen's down there."

I found the room easily enough and grabbed a bottle of juice from the huge fridge that I was pretty certain was larger than some people's entire kitchens. The whole place was immaculate, and I was concerned that if I actually did eat anything and crumbs fell onto the floor, that a maid would burst out of hiding with a broom and start shouting at me. So, I grabbed an apple from the fruit bowl and went in search of somewhere to sit and wait.

The main living room had a huge TV on the wall and a leather couch pointed at it, next to a recliner chair that really was as comfortable as it appeared. Several remotes were arranged in size order on a side table next to the chair. I thought about touching one, but decided against it. I didn't want to put them in the wrong order or out of alignment and cause someone to have a meltdown.

Fortunately I didn't have to wait in silence for long, as Caitlin appeared after a few minutes. She looked utterly stunning in a green top and blue mini-skirt that showed off her athletic legs. A pair of sexy four-inch heels helped to complete the picture.

"Wow," I said. "You look incredible."

Caitlin ran her fingers through her now-curly hair. "Yeah, I scrub up okay. And this should be good enough to get us in."

"Remind me again why you don't have a boyfriend?"

"I never said I didn't have a boyfriend," she said with a coy smile.

"Then allow me to tell you that he is one lucky bastard and I hope you remind him of that on a regular basis."

"I remember telling you that your flattery and charm will get you nowhere."

"At one point, you also told me you were going to shoot me."

"The night is young, Mister Garrett, the night is young."

I stood up and straightened my jacket, tossing the apple core into a nearby bin. "Your dad is a neat freak."

"Yeah, he likes everything in an ordered way. He can be a little OCD about it." She glanced at the remote controls. "And sometimes he can be a lot. He's usually doing it when he's nervous. Probably work stuff."

I held out my arm. "So, are you ready? I really wish I'd brought my Audi; it would have completed the picture."

"Oh, I think we can do better than that."

Caitlin took my arm and we walked through the huge house into the garage.

"How does a federal judge afford all of this?"

"Ah, my grandparents were loaded. And I mean, *loaded*. They left me and my dad pretty much everything, so I got to grow up in a beautiful house in Wisconsin. We lived there after Mom left until I went to college. And then Dad sold up and moved here." She walked over to a car that was covered with a drape, pulling it away to reveal a dark-red Mustang Boss 429.

"Holy crap, I haven't seen one of those in years," I said with more than a little bit of excitement.

"I think it'll make enough of an entrance to turn heads. Might even help get us in." She grabbed a pair of keys from a well-organized key rack and threw them over to me.

A few seconds later the car's engine was roaring with joy as a smile broke my face. Caitlin took a garage door opener from her tiny purse and clicked it open as she got into the car next to me.

"Do you feel all manly?" she asked.

"I'm so goddamn manly, you better make sure you don't get pregnant just by being in my proximity."

Caitlin's laughter echoed into the night as we drove out of the house and off toward a destination that I doubted was going to be anywhere near as pleasant as the journey.

Going out to a place where crowds of drunken people congregate would not make it onto any list of things I like to do. When you get so many people in the same place with lowered inhibitions and increased levels of self-importance, you tend you get trouble. Something I was hoping to avoid, at least to begin with. I didn't want Karl spooked and running off before I'd had the chance to talk to him.

We drove past the huge line, which snaked around the corner of the building, turning more than a few heads as the roar of the engine, and Caitlin's presence, stole their attention.

I parked the car in the lot opposite the club and climbed out.

"You think that did the trick?" I asked.

"One way to find out," Caitlin said as she sauntered around the car and placed her hand in mine, almost hugging my arm as we began to walk toward Ray Ray's. "Need to make this look good. You're meant to be a rich playboy who's here on business, and I'm your paid date for the evening, remember that."

I smiled. "I think I can make that role work."

The pair of us walked straight up to the bouncer on the door and stood in front of him, as if waiting for the door to be opened.

"And you are?" the bouncer asked before glancing behind me at the Mustang. "A hot girl and a nice car aren't enough for you to get in here."

I removed a hundred dollar bill from my pocket. "Is this enough?"

"Please, I've been offered ten times that for someone to jump the queue."

"Okay, how about this?" I leaned closer to whisper in his ear. "I have business with Mister Steiner, you know the man, yes?"

A nod confirmed that he did.

"Excellent, now, let me ask you this, if he discovers that you stood between him and several million dollars of merchandise, what do you think he would do to you?"

The bouncer swallowed hard.

"So, you have two choices, you could go get Mister Steiner and tell him that there is someone waiting for him. That is a bad plan, you would be interrupting his night and I doubt he would enjoy that. Or, the second choice is you accept my hundred dollars and you open the fucking door. Because if my date and I have to wait out in this shitty line for another second, I'm going to cut your fucking balls off, have them bronzed, and give them to Karl as a gift."

I stepped back from the bouncer, the hundred note still in my hand. He took the note, opened the door and wished us a good evening.

"Right choice," I told him and stepped inside the building.

"What did you say to him?" Caitlin whispered in my ear.

I told her.

"That could have backfired."

"I took a chance that Karl doesn't like to be disturbed for unimportant things. He may not own this club, but I'm guessing he has more than enough clout to deal in his own personal way, with people who annoy him. Besides, we're in."

We walked down some steps and opened a set of double doors, where the sound from within washed over me like a tsunami.

To say the music was loud did a disservice to the word. Dozens of people were dancing or gathered at the bar sitting at the far end of the room. A set of stairs snaked to an upper level beside the bar, and I guided Caitlin towards it.

A bouncer stood at the bottom of the staircase and another at the top, both nodded to us as we passed them and opened the door. The music was different than what was blasted out on the floor below, but no less loud. If anything, there were even more people on the dance floor and I wondered how I was going to be heard by Karl, let alone have a conversation with him.

Caitlin nodded toward the VIP area, the balcony of which overlooked the dance floor. Two men stood either side of a couch, which was occupied by a third man and two young women who spent just as much time kissing each other as they did him.

"Okay, so how do we get up there?" I had to almost shout in her ear.

Caitlin grabbed my hand and led me across the dance floor, stopping every few feet to dance a little until we reached the far side. For my part, it was much easier to pretend she was dancing for me and just stand and watch with a smile on my face.

By the time we were out of the throng of people, I discovered I wasn't the only one who had been watching Caitlin dance. Along with several men and women who were sitting on the couches that surrounded the floor, Karl was standing against the railing of the baloney, watching Catlin as she moved up against me and kissed me on the cheek.

"I think that might have done the trick," she whispered.

"Yeah, one of the bodyguards has left the balcony, I imagine he'll be out here in a few seconds to talk to you."

Like clockwork, the bodyguard did indeed make an appearance a few moments later, walking over toward us, the gun in his holster evident to anyone who knew what they were looking for.

"Mister Steiner would like to meet with you," he said to Caitlin, who glanced over to me and shook her head.

"I'm sorry, I'm otherwise engaged tonight."

The bouncer glanced at me and I could tell he was mentally deciding how much of a problem I was going to be. "Bring him with you, I'm sure Mister Steiner would like to chat with him too."

I let the bodyguard lead the way as Caitlin once again took hold of my hand and held my arm close to her.

We stayed that way until we reached Karl Steiner, who clearly wasn't impressed to see that I'd tagged along, but even so, he asked that we talk for a moment. One of the bouncers searched me, removing my knives. "You never know who you'll bump into," I said with a smile, and told Caitlin to go get a drink from the small bar and took a seat next to Karl.

Karl was a good few inches taller than me, but lacked my broad shoulders. He was clean shaven and looked more pampered than most of the women who flocked around him. He was, in short, a bit of a pretty boy, the kind of person who looks great on camera, but has all the vapid qualities of glass. Something about the way he looked at me made me think it was all for show, that deep down inside of him was a repressed monster that he liked to let out to scare folk and show how tough he was.

"I love this place," he said as he looked out on the dance floor. It was nice that he could speak without the need to shout. The acoustics on the balcony allowed just enough sound to travel that you could still have a conversation without the need to use sign language or semaphore to get your point across.

"It's a nice club, I heard good things about it." I took a moment to glance around the sizeable VIP area, where at least two dozen people sat drinking and talking. There was no lighting against the walls and it was fairly obvious that some of the inhabitants were taking advantage of the darkness it offered.

"Where from?" he asked.

"Sorry?" I said and took a seat next to a beautiful young woman, whose eyes were ever so slightly glazed over.

"Who told you about this club? Who told you to come see me with a business deal? I heard what you said to the bouncer, they wear microphones and the owner came and informed me of your arrival."

One of the large bodyguards stood behind me and placed a hand on my shoulder. Karl sat next to me and shooed the two women away. "Who are you and what are you doing in this club?" He glanced behind him at Caitlin. "And if you don't tell me the truth, I'm going to have you gutted. Then, as you bleed out, I'm going to take your woman and fuck her all night long. In fact I'm pretty certain that last part is going to happen no matter what you say."

"She's not my woman, she's my date," I told him without moving my gaze from his. "I paid for her for the night, and she'll be leaving with me. Now, as for who I am? My name is Nathanial Carpenter, I'm here because a friend of yours and mine, Vadim, told me you were interested in purchasing some equipment."

Before I'd finished on the phone with Roberto, I'd gotten more information on Karl's dealings for bladed weapons. Roberto told me who the dealer was, a nasty little Ukrainian man by the name of Vadim. He was well regarded for not sharing information on his clients. Even under torture.

"Why not just call?" Karl asked.

"Because Vadim didn't want to give me your phone number. He said that you didn't like people calling out of the blue. I was coming to D.C. anyway and thought I'd drop by and test the waters for a future business offer."

Karl waved the bodyguard away and the grip on my shoulder was released. "What's the offer?"

"He tells me you're interested in blades. I can get you a thousand swords, daggers, halberds, pole arms, and any other blade you can think of. All of them fine quality, and all of them with a silver coated blade. Six hundred each, or half a million for the lot."

"That's a lot of money."

"It's a lot of cargo. And these are expertly made. There are no dull or brittle blades. Also, I can guarantee you that there will be no interest from customs or the feds."

"I don't care about either of those. But the deal intrigues me. Throw in the woman and you've got a deal."

"Like I said, I paid her for the night. I was very much looking forward to getting my money's worth, which was, just so you know, *a lot* of money."

He waved Caitlin over and as soon as she was sitting beside me he asked, "Where did you find her?"

"I work out of Chicago," she said.

"I wasn't asking you," Karl snapped. "I asked the man who owns you for the night."

"Chicago," I said with a little weariness in my voice. "I have some friends there and one of them arranged it all. I don't know what agency she's from, I didn't have contact with them myself."

"She could be a cop."

"If she is, she takes her work *very* seriously. Besides, I trust the person who arranged it all."

Karl stared at Caitlin, looking her up and down as she did her best to keep smiling. Eventually his phone rang and he walked off to have a conversation in private.

"That man is all kinds of fucked up," Caitlin whispered. "I certainly wouldn't want to be left alone with him."

"Well, right now I'm going to make him an offer that I hope you don't find too offensive."

"If you actually send me off with him, I will most definitely have to shoot you."

"Let's put the shooting me part to one side for the moment and focus on the part that he's coming back over. Smiling."

He sat next to me again and I noticed his bodyguards all walk away. Hopefully that was a good sign.

"I agree to your terms," he said. "But I want the woman."

"How about this?" I asked after a moment's thought. "The weapons are yours for three hundred thousand, and after tonight, I will pay for you to keep the woman for one week."

"And what do you get from such an interesting deal?"

"I have some men who are simply ... not tough enough. I've heard that you are a werelion, a beast of incredible power. I wish for you to turn them into werelions."

"You do realize that not all of them may survive?"

"Of course, but enough will that I will increase in power. Having my own werelion guards will ensure that people think more than once about crossing me."

Karl's laugh was deep and full of menace. "I have a counter proposal."

Caitlin made a noise behind me and I turned to find one of Karl's bodyguards holding a knife of mine to her throat. "What is the meaning of this?" I demanded.

"Mister Garrett, did you really think that you and your agent friend here would fool me? Did you assume for one second that Roberto would actually be looking into our operation without us knowing? Of course we know. We just wanted to make a point. So we threatened his family and he backed off from being a public nuisance. He can spy on us or tape our calls all day long for all I care, he can't do a damn thing with the information. Avalon aren't going to storm this city to bring us down, not unless they want a war on their hands. So all he can do is listen and watch from the shadows while we live our lives as we see fit."

"Let her go," I said, my voice hard and cold.

Karl waved his hand and the bodyguard took a few steps back as the rest of the VIP area began to clear out. "You are a stupid little man for coming here. And before you get any idea of doing anything, take a look down there."

He pointed to the dance floor, where the customers of the club were enjoying themselves oblivious to the danger I saw. Five of Karl's bodyguards stood around the room, each next to a group of people.

"One word from me and they open fire. They'll kill maybe twenty people, but I would put money on at least twice that number dying in the stampede on the way out. So, here's what's going to happen. You're going to walk out of here with my associate behind you, you're going to get into a car outside and you're going to be taken to a nice secluded place outside of town. Then someone is going to shoot you in the head and bury you in an unmarked grave. If you deviate from this plan, if you try to escape at any point, I will know about it and will order my remaining men to kill those innocent people. You do care about innocent people I take it?"

I nodded, feeling slightly detached from the sudden turn for the worse. "I'll make you a counter offer."

Karl laughed again. "There's no counter offer, you leave and die, or dozens of others do."

"There's always another option," I said and jabbed my hand into his throat.

Karl gagged and choked as I grabbed him around the neck and drove him onto the floor, placing one of my knees on his chest to make sure he stayed still. "I know you're a werelion," I said and pulled my final silver dagger from the holster around my ankle, holding the blade against his throat. "But if you change, I'm going to push this up into your brain and you'll be dead."

A crash behind me signaled that Caitlin had removed the threat of the bodyguard. "He's not getting back up," she said.

"Now, here's how my way is going to work." Orange glyphs burned brightly on my arms. Karl stared at them as the realization of what I was dawned on him. "You ready?"

He nodded slightly, not wishing to push the sharp knife into his neck.

"Good, my plan has three steps. Get through them all and you live. Don't and you and your people all die tonight. Step one: tell your people to eject whatever ammo is in those guns, walk to the bar and, one at a time, place their guns and ammo behind there. And then I want to see all of them walk into the men's toilets down there." I released the grip I had on Karl's throat a little.

"Empty the guns, then put them down behind the bar, all of you. Then go to the men's room and await further instructions. The first one to question me dies."

I watched the men all enter the toilet in single file and then I ripped out the earpiece that Karl was wearing, tossing it behind me where a crunch signified that Caitlin had ended its usefulness.

"So, on to part two. This is a simple part—you're going to walk out of this club with me and Caitlin. You're going to do it without fuss. Or you die. I know you're a big strong werelion and you're faster and stronger than me, in fact I know that it's taking a lot for you not to just throw me over this balcony and jump down to tear me in half. I appreciate the restraint, but if that ever stops, I'm just going to remove your head from your shoulders and see how good you are at healing yourself. You understand step two?"

"Yes. What's step three?"

"Oh, yes, that's an easy one. Tell the DJ to stop playing this god-awful shit and put something fun on. Maybe a bit of Kenny Loggins, you can't go wrong with *Footloose*. Everyone likes Kevin Bacon."

Karl's eyes widened in shock. "Are you insane?"

"Hey, Kenny isn't that bad. Yeah it's a bit cheesy, but it's a good fun song." I stared at Karl for a heartbeat. "Oh, you meant in general. No, I just really fucking hate dance music."

"I'm going to find you for this, you have to know that."

I dragged Karl to his feet and moved the dagger so that the point was touching his groin. "Wanna threaten me again and see what happens, or would you like to follow the plan?"

"Nate?" Caitlin said.

I looked out over the balcony and saw the bodyguards leave the bathroom and then stand and stare up at us.

"You might kill me, but I'm certain they're going to kill you before you get out of this club."

The glint of sliver blades appeared in the hands of the body-guards. "Yeah, okay, this is going to be hard work. So, slight change of plan. Caitlin, make us some stairs."

Caitlin stepped in front of us and placed her hands on the balcony, which started to shake and then suddenly it collapsed into a staircase.

"Are you going to behave yourself?" I asked Karl who laughed. "Okay, your call." I stabbed him in the femoral artery and left the dagger in before kicking him back over the sofa, where he lay screaming.

"Will that kill him?" Caitlin asked.

"If he leaves the knife in and gets checked out, no. He's no longer a problem we have to deal with right now."

Those who had seen Caitlin create a staircase from nothing had one of two reactions, panic and running like mad, or awe. Most people fell into the first category, and once some people start screaming and running, everyone else does it out of a sense of self-preservation. I'd tried to ensure that there wasn't a stampede, and from what I saw, no one was trampled. So thank heavens for small mercies. The sudden evacuation meant that as we descended the stairs, the bodyguards could spread out in preparation. It also meant that the DJ had given up and gone home, so it wasn't all bad news.

The first I saw of Caitlin was when she threw her shoes at the nearest guard and then dove at him, driving her fist into his nose and kicking him in the balls with enough force to lift a rocket. I left her to her clearly enjoyable hobby and walked down the rest of the steps slowly, watching the four guards who were waiting for me.

"You guys must be nervous, I've just made your boss bleed all over the nice carpet up there and now you're wondering what's going to happen to you. Well, I won't lie, it's not going to be fun for you."

I made it to the bottom and saw that all four men held daggers. I would have put money that they knew how to use them too. Karl didn't strike me as the kind of person who took failure well and would employ in competent people.

The first guard darted toward me knife out. I side-stepped him and smashed my elbow into his throat, using my momentum to bounce off into the path of the second guard who I hit with a blast of air that send him spinning back into the bar in the center of the room, pulling several shelves of alcohol and glasses on top of himself.

The third guard kicked out at me, hoping to catch me unaware, but I kicked out at the other leg and broke his knee. He collapsed to the floor like a felled tree, writhing in pain until I kicked him the head. The last guard had clearly stayed back out of some sense of not getting the shit kicked out of him, but now there were no friends left and it was fight or flight time.

He picked wrong and charged at me. I knocked the blade away with the back of my forearm and slammed my free arm into his face. He staggered slightly as blood streamed from his ruined nose and waved wildly with his knife. I ended it quickly with a blast of air to his head, which rendered him unconscious before he knew what had happened.

As soon as he dropped to the floor, two more men I recognized as bouncers ran onto the floor and started firing in my direction. I dove behind of the bar and found Caitlin next to me a moment later.

"Plan?" she asked.

"Stay here, back in a second."

I stood up and threw a column of air at the two men, knocking them to the ground. The second the guns were pointed away I hardened the air around their legs and pulled them toward me. I jumped over the bar and grabbed the first by the throat, cracking his head against the hard wood of the bar, as the second tried to scramble away. He got a few feet before I surrounded him in a circle of enraged flame. He turned onto his back and aimed his gun at me again, which he quickly dropped when I threw a ball of fire at it.

I strode toward him and as I reached down and grabbed him around the throat, lifting him from the ground, he pissed himself.

I lowered him so his feet no longer dangled in the air and then head-butted him hard on the nose.

"You fucking little idiot," I said. "You came up here and started firing wildly. It's lucky there was no one here or you'd have killed someone." A blade of molten hot fire appeared from my hand.

"Please don't kill me. I just took the job because it was a cool place to work. I just thought I'd get to hang out with cool people and get laid a lot."

"How old are you?"

"Twenty-two."

"Go home, never come back here. People will be keeping an eye on you." I brought him closer to me, until our noses were almost touching. "Do not disappoint me. I do not give third chances." I removed the fire and watched as he sprinted off toward the exit.

"You really going to have someone watch him?"

"No, but he doesn't know that."

"I thought you were going to kill him for a moment there."

"For a moment there, I was." I noticed two more groaning men next to the one that Caitlin had kicked. "You've been busy."

"Worked out some aggression."

She retrieved her shoes and carried them with her as we made our way down the stairs and onto the ground floor. Five bouncers stood together by the far wall and all of them showed us their hands as we walked toward them, wanting us to know they were no threat. One of them was the guy from the front door, who glanced down at the ground as our gazes briefly met. Dozens of people were huddled under tables and behind the bar, all aware of what had happened above them.

Once outside, we discovered that the line had vanished, no one really wanted to hang around when they heard gunfire, although there were a lot of people just milling around as sirens sounded in the distance.

Caitlin and I hurried to the car. I put the key in the lock only to be struck in the head from behind, knocking me against the car. My attacker clamped a large hand on my shoulder and spun me around, hitting me again, this time in the stomach. It was like being hit by a car, and I dropped to the concrete as the air rushed out of my lungs.

I glanced over and saw that a young, thick man held Caitlin's arms behind her, ensuring she couldn't use her alchemy.

"Caitlin, Caitlin, Caitlin," a woman said as she strode toward us from the shadows. The huge slab of mountain that had been hitting me stepped back and crossed his massive arms.

"You're such a disappointment, little Caitlin," the woman said again as the streetlights illuminated her face. Although she appeared to be in her late forties, I got the impression she was much older. "Hanging around with rough sorcerers will get you killed."

Caitlin's face was forcibly turned toward the newcomer and her mouth dropped open in shock.

"Do you remember us, Caitlin?" the woman asked and tapped the mountain man on the arm.

"Joshua?" Caitlin asked. "Is that you?"

The mountain man smiled, showing his razor sharp canines. "Big sister."

"Sister?" I asked and stared at the woman. "That would make you . . . ."

"Patricia Moore," Caitlin whispered. "Mom."

CHAPTER 20

I sat against the car door, for several minutes, while a still restrained Caitlin chatted to Patricia, her mum. Chatted was probably the wrong word to be fair, it mostly consisted of Caitlin swearing at her mum, who seemed to ignore her daughter by continuing to list her disappointments.

After only a few moments, it became clear that it wasn't going to be the most productive meeting of all time, but Joshua never stopped staring at me with murderous intent. I was pretty certain that getting away without any serious injuries to Caitlin or myself had left me a very limited set of options.

So, I sat and listened and tried very hard not to tell everyone to fuck off and set them on fire.

After what I was sure was several days of sitting still, I got fed up with the whole thing and was just about to interject myself into the conversation, when Caitlin decided to calm down. "What do you actually want?" she asked.

Patricia glanced down at me before turning around as some-one caught her attention. A slender young woman with a face that wouldn't take looked out of place on a modeling agency's books stepped out of a nearby car, her shoulder-length brown hair was tied back and she flashed her bare long legs as she walked confi-dently toward us.

"Ah, I remember you from Canada," I said, remembering the picture of her in Bill's file. He'd done some good work. It was a shame he'd never get to see it through. At the thought of my friend and his wife, butchered in their own home, my anger began to rise inside me. "I didn't get your name though."

"My name's Bianca, did you miss me?" she cooed. "I said we'd meet again, and I can't begin to tell you how excited I am about our time together." She crouched in front of me and ran a finger across my temple, showing me the blood before putting the digit into her mouth and sucking on it.

"Yeah," I said, managing to put as much sarcasm in one word as possible. "I do miss the crazy."

Bianca's expression changed in an instant to anger and she slapped me across the face. "You should be nice. The things I don't like anymore tend to get broken."

"I'll keep that in mind," I told her as she stood and ran a hand along the chest of Joshua who grinned like a schoolboy who'd seen his first naked girl.

"When I saw you on top of that cliff in Maine, I was so relieved," Patricia said with genuine emotion in her voice. "I had no idea it was you inside that cave, and to see you'd escaped from the troll gave me hope that you'd join us in our quest. And then I saw *him*." She pointed at me and her voice filled with hate. "The murdering bastard who was with you."

"You mean the people inside the house back in the seventies?" I asked.

She glanced down at me. "You slaughtered my friends, people I cared about. You and that pig friend of yours. But we taught him what it means to cross us. He thought he was clever, investigating us and calling Stratford PD to let them know what he found, but we have friends who work there, friends who let us know what he knew. The surprise on his face when we arrived. And the horror it held when he realized what we were going to do to him and that wife of his." She crouched down in front of me and grabbed my jaw, forcing me to look at her. "I will cherish that moment for the rest of my life. Cherish his screams, his pleas to let his wife go. It was ... well worth the wait."

"You killed Bill and his wife," I said, seething with anger.

"Yes, and then we killed that cop who had helped us find the little piggy. We left you that message because I wanted you here, you remember the House of Silent Screams. I wanted you to find us so that I can kill you last. Slowly, painfully as you realize that Simon's plan, the Vanguard's plan, is fulfilled, and there's nothing you can do to stop it."

"You feel like telling me what Simon's plan is?" I asked.

Her grin told me that chat time was over.

"How about Karl?" I asked, hoping to draw her back into revealing something. "I assume he's the one who turned you all. You do realize he works for the ex-king of Shadow Falls, a place the Vanguard want to destroy. Doesn't working with him go against your plans?"

"He's realized his mistakes. He's making up for it by helping us eliminate that place."

"Well he's currently bleeding to death on the top floor of that club, so his help is probably going to be limited now."

Caitlin's mum motioned for Joshua and the crazy girl to go check out what I'd said, leaving me relieved the moment they both left.

"Why are you even here?" I asked. "You couldn't have known we were around."

"After I saw you both in the forest, I called Karl and told him. He asked for the pack to come to D.C. to discuss our next plan. It was dumb luck that we were already here when you pulled up. Once you were inside, I let him know who you both were. I was told to wait, that his men would bring you out."

"His men are mostly unconscious or moaning in pain," I said. "You do realize, I'm going to kill you for what you did to Bill and his wife, amongst other things."

"You'll be dead by the morning," she said with a chuckle.

"Hey Caitlin, that guy holding your arms back, is he a relation of yours?"

"No," Caitlin said. "Never met him before."

"Good to know." I hit Caitlin's mum with a blast of air that took her off her feet and threw her with enough force into the side of a nearby van and through the metal. I quickly turned to Caitlin and caught her captor in the neck with a whip of fire, opening his throat. He let go of Caitlin and tried to hold the wound closed as blood poured out of it. "In the car," I told Caitlin, who didn't need to be told twice, and sprinted around the bonnet and got into the Mustang.

I ignored the injured werelion as the sound of metal tearing behind us convinced me that getting out of there as quickly as possible was a much better idea.

I didn't stop driving until I was certain I'd put as much distance between us as possible. Werelions are, by their very nature, excellent trackers, but I doubted even they could track one specific car over several miles.

I pulled into a car park and switched off the engine. Caitlin took the opportunity to open the car door and dash over to some trees, vomiting the second she reached them. I watched for a few seconds to make sure she was okay before her shoulders began to shake from the unmistakable sobs that left her.

I exited the car and started walking over to her. "You want someone to talk to?" I asked.

She shook her head.

"I'll be by the car."

"That was my brother and mom," she said, more to herself than anything else. "I always knew my mom was fucked up, but my brother too. He was such a sweet kid. She's turned him into some sort of monster."

I finally decided to say my piece. "So, the reason you seemed so close to that serial killer case is because the ones doing it are your own family? You saw them in the pictures on the jet, why didn't you say something?"

"Because I wasn't really sure what you'd do once you found out. I wasn't really sure what I'd do." Caitlin rubbed her eyes and placed a hand over her mouth. "They are *my* duty to stop."

"That's why your boss isn't a big fan of you? You're too invested in this case."

She nodded. "He's allowing me to investigate because I threatened to quit if he didn't let me. Because of my dad he can't just fire me, so he's washed his hands of me instead."

"You should have told me, Caitlin."

She shook her head. "Couldn't. My mom took Joshua away at a young age. She spent a lot of time turning him from the sweet kid that I remember into something more like the man he is today. I had to be involved, had to try and find out if there was anything of him left." She turned to me. "Do you think there's anything of him left?"

I thought back to looking into Joshua's face, staring into his cold, empty eyes. I'd seen eyes like that on a very select group of people who had killed people and enjoyed it. "No, there's nothing left of him now, but rage and hate."

Caitlin burst into tears, using the tree to keep her upright. I removed my jacket and put it around her shoulders, she spun toward me and buried her face in my chest. Her sobs were deep and raw. I held her in place for an unknown amount of time until those awful sobs turned into mute anguish and I felt her body slump against me.

"I'm sorry, Caitlin," I whispered. "I'm truly sorry."

"So am I," she said. "I always thought my mom would have changed him, would have made him cold and hard. But a murderer, someone who hunts people and hurts them? I never thought he would be taken that far."

"It probably happened over years. She probably pushed him to do something he didn't want, so she'd compromise, moving his moral compass slightly. Do it often enough and at some point, the thing you'd never do originally suddenly doesn't sound so bad.

"It takes a lot of patience to do it, but after a while you've got yourself someone whose moral outlook is exactly where you want it to be. Do you think your mum has that kind of patience? And I'm talking about months and years of molding someone into the kind of person she needs to help her."

Caitlin didn't even need to think about it. "Yeah, she's more than capable of doing it." She took a seat on the bench next to us. "It started when I was maybe four or five. When my dad was working, she'd take me hunting. We didn't kill anything, just tracking animals and occasionally people. Over the years she took it up one step at a time, we moved from tracking to her killing the animal and leaving me to skin and cook it. From there, I killed the animal myself.

"Over the next few years she taught me self-defense and how to watch people for signs of strength or weakness. We'd sit on a bench, like this one, and just watch the people passing by. She'd ask what their ailment was or get me to pick the weakest member of the group."

"She was training you to hunt people," I said.

"I was about six when I got into a fight at school and broke a boy's arm. The school called my mom who told me off for getting caught. I had to watch her burn my favorite stuffed bear for that one. Every time I did wrong, I was made to watch as she destroyed something of mine. When I was eight, just coming up to my ninth birthday, I disappointed her. So, the night of my ninth birthday, she came and told me that lovely little message that she put in the dead cop's mouth, you remember the one? Well, she also killed my rabbit and left it in my room."

"How did you disappoint her?"

"There was another boy in my class, a real bully. He would terrorize the kids in the neighborhood and get away with it because his dad was a high-priced lawyer. So Mom wanted me to teach him a lesson. I was meant to break into his house at night, make my way to his room, and then cut him bad enough to leave a scar on his face.

"I refused. So, she changed it to giving me an option. I either scarred the boy or killed the parents. I refused again. She beat me so badly I couldn't walk for two days. I could barely move through pain. I still have the marks where she used a piece of tree as a whip to draw blood." Tears began to fall once more.

"We're going to stop her. We have to."

"Yes, we will," she said with determination. "Do you have a plan?"

"They're following Simon's old plan, it's time we found out what it was. That means going to Shadow Falls. Before that, I'm going to call Roberto and say sorry for starting a small war and then we're going to go see your dad."

"Fucking hell, no, not right now."

"He's a federal judge, whose wife is back in town to murder his daughter. He deserves to be made aware of the danger *he's* in, let alone you. Besides he may know some things about Karl and his boss that Roberto didn't."

"He's not going to be happy that we took his car. And he's not going to like the fact that anything Avalon-related is involved. That's going to cause an argument."

"Would he be happier if we'd both been killed by his wife?"

"Ex-wife, he applied for a divorce, but the point still stands." She stood and took a few steps before glancing back at me. "My mom, she really hates you, doesn't she?"

I nodded. "I killed a lot of her friends, although it's interesting that she wasn't there at the time. Makes me wonder where she was."

"And what she was doing," Caitlin finished for me.

CHAPTER 21

She may not have felt up to it, but Caitlin didn't complain as we pulled up to her father's front door and switched off the engine. She opened the car door with a flurry and hurried up the steps to the large entrance, where she didn't bother knocking, just walked straight in.

I allowed Caitlin to have some alone time with her dad, while I called Roberto.

"What part of, don't start a war, did you not understand?" he said as he answered the phone.

"Technically, I didn't start it, I sort of ended it. I left you a bunch of human thugs alive, you should be able to question them and get some info on Karl and his boss."

"They might have been alive when you left, but they aren't now. Someone tore their throats out. It's a huge fucking mess."

"The werelions."

"They killed everyone still on the second floor. Twelve people in all. No sign of Karl either. There's a shitload of blood in the VIP area, though, I assume that was down to you."

"Karl wasn't a very accommodating host. In fact, I'd say he was an utter prick. The werelions must have taken him with them. I assume it's too much to hope he's dead."

"He could be, but I wouldn't bet on the little cockroach dying without someone tearing his head off."

"I'll remember that for later. They know you're watching them by the way, bragged about it in fact. They don't seem to care too much though."

"I sort of assumed they knew something. Damn, I'd say we'd have to try a different tactic, but we tried to contact Charles Whitehorn and he's had to leave town on urgent business."

"Any ideas where they might go?"

"No, but you certainly spooked them enough to run. I'd be careful once you leave D.C., they may try to get a measure of revenge."

"Because attacking me worked so well last time."

"Oh it won't be a direct assault, they'll go through that agent you're with."

"It's probably a good idea if she stays with me then. I'm going to take her to Shadow Falls. I need to speak to Simon to try and get something from him."

"That'll mean talking to Galahad."

"I'll come to that when I get there, but these werelions are following Simon's old plan. They confirmed it. Now I need to know what the hell that plan was."

"Good luck, Nate. And if it happens that neither Karl nor Charles make it back to D.C., no one is going to miss them."

"Take care, Roberto," I said and hung up.

I followed Caitlin a few moments later, walking in on an argument that had erupted between father and daughter. The fight stopped as Mr. Moore caught sight of me.

"Who the fuck do you think you are, getting my daughter caught up in your Avalon bullshit?" he snapped, pointing a bony finger at me.

Mr. Moore was a tall, skinny man, with thick gray hair. "I asked you a question, boy!" he snapped again, taking a step toward me.

"Dad, if you could just listen for one second," Caitlin said, trying to get the attention of her irate father. "Nate doesn't work for Avalon, I said he used to work for them."

Mr. Moore turned on his daughter. "Used to? They always fucking say they used to, but that never seems to stop them from pissing around with the laws of this country. And you, young lady, what kind of insane trouble have you gotten into that you're working with some goddamn spook from who-knows-where?"

"Dad, you never listen, you only hear what you want to. I'm trying to tell you what's happening and you're just talking over me."

"I haven't seen you in over a year. And you come here in the middle of the night with one of them." He waved in my direction. "What the hell am I meant to think?"

"You're supposed to trust me."

Norman's expression softened, but I could still see the angry fire in his eyes. "Oh, Caitlin. You're a Federal officer, running around with Avalon. That's not exactly displaying good judgment."

I was never going to get them to calm down and actually talk while they were arguing, so I opened the door and slammed it shut. With a little air magic to carry the sound all around the room, it resembled a gunshot more than a door slam.

The fighting stopped immediately and both Moores turned to look at me with fire in their eyes.

"We're here to talk to you about your wife."

"Boy, I don't know who you think you are but—"

"Shut up," I interrupted. "Just so you know, if you call me boy again, I'm going to punch you in the jaw. Now, let your daughter talk. You're not angry at her, you're angry that some *Avalon spook* is in your home."

"My *ex-wife*," he stated, "is of no concern to me." He turned to his daughter. "Please tell me you're not investigating that woman. Please tell me you've given up, Caitlin. Going after her is only going to cause you trouble. I've seen agents get too close, allowing their emotions to compromise the job, if you do that it'll get you hurt."

"It's a bit late for that, Dad," she snapped. "Nate is helping me."

"This charlatan is using you. And he just threatened a federal judge."

I had to laugh. "Add it to the list of people I've pissed off tonight. Besides, considering your *ex-wife* just tried to kill your daughter and me, I'm thinking you may want to make her your concern."

Mr. Moore turned to his daughter, any anger or resentment in his face evaporated. "Is this true, did she hurt you?"

Caitlin shook her head. "I'm fine, just a little shaken. She had Joshua with her."

Mr. Moore's hand shot to his open mouth. "My boy," he whispered. "She has my boy."

"He's not a boy anymore, Dad," Caitlin told her father with a pained expression. "He's a monster."

"No, no, not. Not my boy."

"You've seen the eyes of a killer," I told him. "Someone who enjoys it, considers it a sport or a fun way to spend the evening. Your son now has those eyes. There's no boy left. I'm sorry."

Mr. Moore's face crumpled and Caitlin rushed to him, both of them holding one another in a moment of tender need for the comfort of another. I left them to their pain and walked to the kitchen, getting myself a drink of water while I waited for the inevitable conversation once Caitlin and her father calmed down.

"So you *used* to work for Avalon?" Mr. Moore said as he walked into the kitchen alone.

"Where's your daughter?"

"Gone to freshen up. She's had a crappy day. You going to answer my question?"

I finished my drink of water and placed the glass in the sink. Normally, I would have answered him first, but since he'd been rude to me, he could bloody well wait. "Yes, I used to," I said. "I don't work for Avalon now."

"I deal with Avalon a bit in my job, all federal judges do. I'm not a big fan of their secrecy and the fact that they seem to think the law doesn't apply to them."

"Yeah, you mentioned that during the finger-pointing and shouting. Not to cause another row, but it doesn't apply to us," I pointed out. "Well, not all of it anyway."

"If I had my way, Avalon and the whole lot of you would be outed to the world. Having sorcerers and monsters running around the place, waging war, innocent people get hurt."

"That's precisely why we're not outed to the world. If that ever happens *a lot* of innocent people will get hurt. You know full-well that anyone can discover things about our world without consequence, but if someone tried to make a public spectacle, so that everyone was left with no doubt over what we are, that person would vanish before they could ever achieve their plan. Anyway, it's a moot point, because your daughter isn't human. So, outing us all would hurt her just as much."

Mr. Moore paused for a second and regarded me with a slightly less than friendly expression on his face. "I don't trust you."

"Wait till you get to know me, we'll get along famously."

"Making flippant comments won't change my opinion."

"Being rude to me and dismissing your daughter because of the company she keeps isn't going to make me think you're anything other than an ass, but here we are."

Mr. Moore sucked on his lower lip—either frustration or a nervous habit, it was hard to tell. "That was out of line, what I said earlier to Caitlin. I do trust her. She's a damn good agent and an even better daughter. But she has blinkers on when it comes to her mom."

"So would I if my mum was a raving psychopath."

"My daughter tells me that I can trust you. That you're a good guy. Is that true?"

"That depends on your definition of good guy," I said. "I try to do the right thing. That doesn't always work out, though."

"If you hurt her, I'll make it my mission in life to destroy you." He held my eye while he spoke. If nothing else, Mr. Moore had some balls of steel.

"Dad, I don't think that's necessary," Caitlin said as she re-entered the room.

"I'm just letting him know." He walked over to a drinks cabinet and opened it, picking up a bottle of bourbon. "Nate, you can call me Norman. Do you want a drink?"

"Whatever you're having is fine," I told him.

He filled two glasses, each with a large measure of alcohol and brought them back, passing me one before he took a seat on the chair next to me.

"Can I ask you a personal question?" I enquired.

Norman motioned for me to continue.

"Caitlin told me that you're not her birth father. Any chance whoever that is, is helping your ex-wife? Do you know who he is?" I paused. "I know that was more than one question, but your ex-wife is involved in some serious shit, I'd take any help you can give."

"I'm not Caitlin's *biological* father." He turned to his daughter and took her hand in his before looking back at me. "I raised this girl into a fine, upstanding woman. A woman who deserves more than a dad who works all hours and a mom who, in your own words, is a raving psychopath."

"You did a good job," I told him and Caitlin mouthed a thank you.

"There are some things you should know about Patricia. Things I haven't told anyone."

"Caitlin, you sure you want to be here for this bit?"

Despite the shocked look on his daughter's face, I was pretty certain Norman would have had to use explosives to get her to move.

"Caitlin was two months old when I met her mother, Patricia," Norman began. "I have no idea who her father is, although clearly he's an alchemist, so that should narrow it down. I also don't know why he wasn't around, but when I first met Patricia, it was like walking into a tornado. She was passionate and loving and caring. Our relationship started to sour after the first two or three years. Patricia would go away for days or weeks at a time and never tell me where she was or what she was doing. She would turn violent and angry at the drop of a hat. More than once I caught her hitting or screaming at Caitlin, and every time I tried to involve myself, she'd turn that rage on me.

"One day, when Caitlin was about four, I decided enough was enough and filed for divorce. She responded by running off for two weeks. During that time, I went out for a drink and met a young lady. We ended up sleeping together. Two days later I received a letter with photos of our encounter. The letter was unsigned. It said that from now on I was to do as I was told and recant the divorce papers. I was certain that Patricia had set the whole thing up just to blackmail me; she'd hired the woman, a prostitute, to seduce me. And I fell for it like a fucking idiot."

"You had an affair? Surely that wouldn't end your career."

"Probably not on its own, no. Though it certainly wouldn't do me a lot of good. But what sealed it for me was the fact that the woman's body was found a week later. Her throat had been cut with a dagger. A photo was sent to me. It was my dagger, a present from my wife when we got married. There was a note with the photos, *behave or your family is next.* I couldn't believe that Patricia was involved in the murder, not at the time anyway. And I couldn't go to the police, not with my dagger being the murder weapon."

"This is getting worse," I said with a sigh and drank the rest of my whisky, which Norman immediately refilled.

"I confronted her when she came home and she swore it wasn't her. But for the next few years, I lived in a sort of limbo. Scared to put a foot wrong and not really trusting her. For her part, she didn't even act like it had happened and eventually I started to believe that it was someone else. It helped that she spent less and less time away from here, I started to think that there was no way our marriage was anything other than perfect. She'd gotten better with Caitlin; I never saw the anger or violence anymore. Then one day we had a party and both of us got very drunk and ended up sleeping together and she got pregnant from it.

"I know what you're thinking, was I sure the baby was mine? And the answer is no, I have no idea. But once Joshua was born, I didn't care. I trusted Patricia and we were a family. But soon after, I started to notice that Caitlin was always scared when Patricia would take her out for the day. She wanted to spend as little time as possible with her mother, I saw the fear on my daughter's face and I started to think that I'd been wrong. That was when Patricia started leaving again, taking Joshua with her for days at a time."

"She left for good when Caitlin was nine, yes?"

"Patricia came back for Caitlin's birthday and then vanished with Joshua. She told me we were done and she had more important things to do, that Caitlin was a disappointment to her, but that she'd come and find her when or if she needed to. She told me she'd cheated on me over and over again, with dozens of men and that she'd sent those letters blackmailing me. She'd murdered the prostitute too. She dropped my dagger on the sofa beside me and told me that if I ever went to the police, she'd come and make Caitlin watch as she skinned me alive. And then she left and we never saw either of them again. Although when I filed for a divorce and it was made official on Caitlin's sixteenth birthday, I heard from her. She sent me a letter with photos of her having sex with a variety of different men. But there was a letter. It said that if I ever took Caitlin away from her, she would find

Caitlin and me and kill us both. It's why I didn't move until after Caitlin finished college and went to the FBI."

Caitlin hugged her father tightly. "Why didn't you tell me any of this?"

"Because I know you, I know how angry she makes you. Telling you about her threats would have done little, other than made you even more determined to find her. And I didn't want you within a hundred miles of her. It's not your job to protect me, it's mine to protect you."

"But, Dad, you should have told me. All these years you've kept that to yourself. Is that why you kept turning down the job in Washington, because of her threats?"

"I couldn't risk it, couldn't risk having to look over my shoulder for the rest of my life."

"So, you don't think she'd come after you anymore?" I asked.

"She has no reason to, although I've no idea what her warped mind thought at the best of times."

Caitlin stood and took her phone out. "I'm getting some protection here."

"Caitlin, no," Norman argued. "I won't be kept here like some prisoner. Besides do you really want to explain why the serial killer you're after is your mom?"

"Call Roberto and ask him for help," I said, throwing my phone to Caitlin. "Last call on there. Tell him I'll owe him."

Caitlin nodded and walked off to make the call.

"This is unnecessary," Normal protested again.

"You know what, Norman. I've lived for a very long time, and in that time I've seen people like Patricia lash out at those who used to love them. If she thinks she can get to you, she will.

I promise you that. Do you think you could kill her, or your boy, if they came calling?"

Norman's expression told me he couldn't.

"Just let Caitlin do what's best. In the meantime, I have a few more questions. Did Patricia ever mention a Simon or a plan in Maine?"

"Simon, yeah. Not until we'd been together a few years, though. She was in love with him. That was obvious. She said he was her ex from many years ago. The rest, no."

"So, you didn't want to see anything was wrong, and by the time it was obvious, it was also too late."

"Maybe you're not quite as stupid as you first appeared."

"And maybe you're not quite a crotchety old asshole," I said with a smile. "Maybe."

"You think you can stop Patricia and her people?"

I nodded. "I have to, because otherwise a lot of people are going to die. You and your daughter included."

I went for a walk on the grounds of the lavish house when Caitlin returned, allowing her some time with Norman. She found me after an hour or so as I sat by a sizeable pond watching the fish swim around without a care in the world. Lucky buggers.

"I think your calling as a ninja is pretty much shot," I called out to her as she made more noise than a stampeding rhino as she approached me.

"Well that's a terrible shame," Caitlin said and sat beside me.

"So, how are you holding up?"

"Well, I just found out that my mom, who I already think very little of, blackmailed my father and threatened both him and me. Although, none of it really surprises me." She exhaled deeply before speaking again. "I'm sorry I didn't tell you about my mom and her . . . pride, I guess. I should have done it sooner."

"Yes, you should. But you didn't and we've moved on. Your dad likes me."

Caitlin laughed. "Yeah, he said you were a cocky son-of-a-bitch. I think that's about as high praise as you're going to get from him."

"You know if you come with me, it's going to result in you crashing into them both again."

Caitlin nodded, sadly. "I figured that out. We have to stop them from hurting anyone else. Something big is happening here. Karl, the senator, and my mom are all working together. They've killed multiple people, including your friend Bill and those who survived Simon's original attack over thirty years ago, and no one goes to that much trouble for anything small."

"Okay, so what do you think is going on?"

"I think my mom, brother, and the rest of the werelions are being used as muscle. If anything goes wrong they're the ones in the firing line. My mom said that they were Vanguard. What's that?"

"The Vanguard are a group of terrorists who exist to cause problems for Shadow Falls. They see the place as an affront to Avalon. They're insane, but they're also highly trained and don't employ people as far gone as your mum and brother. Someone helping Simon said the same thing back in '77."

"So, Karl, and before him Simon, was using the Vanguard name as a way to get people to hurt Shadow Falls?"

"Simon told me he'd let them believe it to give them purpose. You make people think you're fighting against an aggressor, make them believe there's a cause at stake and they can be pretty damn motivated. Doesn't explain why your mum is involved though. I mean specifically, why her?"

Caitlin shrugged. "No idea. But this is all looking like a trip to Shadow Falls is in order."

"Unfortunately, you're right, it does."

Caitlin stood and walked back toward the house before stopping and turning back toward me. "Nate, you can't hold back if we go up against them. You have to do whatever you can to stop them."

"I promise, if they give me no choice, I'll stop them. But you need to be able to do the same, and I'm not sure you can."

"This isn't about my mom and me. This is about stopping a serial killer from causing more harm. I need to do my job and bring her to justice."

"You know she won't go to a human prison. Not in a million years."

"Then we'll find a great big pit and throw her in it. But she will pay for her crimes."

The way she said that final sentence made me wonder if she meant the murders Patricia had committed, or the crimes perpetrated against Caitlin's family.

CHAPTER 22

Roberto's agents, a man and woman, arrived after about an hour and confirmed that both Charles Whitehorn and Karl had vanished from Washington, which certainly didn't make me feel any better about whatever they had planned.

A taxi took us to the airport, where true to Felicia's words, the jet still sat. Whatever fault they had told the staff was with the jet was suddenly solved and a few hours later we were in the air. The pilot told us that he was taking us to Portland, where my Audi would be waiting. Apparently, Felicia liked to make sure her friends were well taken care of. That and she probably liked the idea of me owing her a favor.

Once at Portland we took my car and a short time later were sat opposite the Mill.

"So, this is the entrance to Shadow Falls," Caitlin said, sounding about as impressed as if I'd just taken her to the dump-it site.

"Yep, it's in that bar," I told her and glanced around the neighborhood. A lot had changed in over thirty years. The Mill was much bigger for one, maybe twice the length it had been. Dozens of new builds had been built-up around it, most of them what appeared to be a mixture of bars and restaurants.

"So, do you feel like telling me what Shadow Falls actually is?"

"It's one of the Hidden Realms."

Silence hung inside the car. "Yeah, I'm going to need more than that," Caitlin eventually said.

"Okay, imagine a large white board. The kind of things you see in school. That board is our current realm, realm A, Earth, or whatever the hell you want to call it. Now imagine that board is covered in post-it notes, hundreds of them. Each one of those notes represents one of the Hidden Realms."

"So, you can only get to the Hidden Realms through this realm?"

"Not exactly," I said trying to figure out how to explain it. "Some are linked to one another. The only constant is that every single realm is linked to this one via a gateway, which serve as both the entrance and exit."

Caitlin sat back in the seat and rubbed the side of her neck. "What are the realms themselves?"

"Each realm is its own, self-contained world. They all have their own species, weather, plants, day/night cycle, and a host of other things. You've heard of many of the realms before, just without knowing that they were in fact real: Tartarus, Olympus, Valhalla, Albion, and countless others, all exist as realms."

"So," she said slowly, obviously turning the idea over in her head. "If you're a criminal, you could just hide in one of these places and jump from realm to realm never getting caught?"

"It's happened more than once." Mordred had done it for centuries; it was why I'd never managed to track him down for any real length of time. "It's an incredibly difficult thing to do though. The problem is that to go from one realm to another, without coming back to this one, means you need to know where the gateways are. Very few maps of the realms exist; usually whoever lives in one realm maps it out, but then keeps the map in the realm. Most people who try to evade capture usually get stuck in one realm. Then it's just a matter of sitting outside the gate and waiting, or going in and getting them."

"Can you tell me about these realms?" she asked. "Do they look like earth?"

"Some do, some don't. I know that's not exactly the most scientific of answers, but it's true. Shadow Falls, for example, can't use electricity. At least not in the way we can; they have gas lamps in the street."

"Why is it called Shadow Falls?"

"There's a huge mountain range called Shadow's Peak," I continued. "Once a day it casts a huge shadow that stretches all across the rest of the realm. The people who first found the place probably thought the name was more original several hundred years ago."

"And the entrance to Shadow Falls is in a bar in Portland?"

"Well, under it, but yeah, essentially."

"What's stopping everyone from walking through the gateway, then?"

"The guardians of the realm. Or guardians, for short. They're the only ones who can activate the gate. Each gate has between four and six guardians, who can only activate the gate by touch. They're basically immortal, so long as they stay within a mile or two of the gate. Once outside that cordon, they're just as easy to kill as any other human."

"So, what happens if the guardian is away from the gate and someone wants in?"

"If anyone touches the gate who isn't a guardian, those linked to that realm will be alerted. Doesn't always mean someone's going to come let you through."

"How do they become guardians? Are they born like that?"

I opened my mouth to answer and realized that I didn't have one. "No, at least I don't think so. I vaguely remember being told that they used to be human. In fact I think only humans can become guardians. To be honest, there is a lot about them I don't know. They're a secretive bunch, and beyond knowing that their power is based on proximity to a gateway, I don't know much else. Oh, they're linked to a gateway. One gateway per person. But my knowledge of guardians is now exhausted."

"Anything else I should know?"

"Your phone won't work, leave your gun in the car, and try really, really hard not to tell anyone that you're FBI. Plenty of humans live there though, so it shouldn't be something to concern yourself about."

"How many people are we talking about?" Caitlin asked as we both got out of the car.

"Including humans and all the species who live there? About a million," I said and walked off toward the bar, aware that Caitlin was still staring at me from the car.

"I'd like to see Rebecca Dean," I told a young waitress who came toward us and asked if we'd like a table.

The young woman glanced around, ever so slightly nervous, but the smile on her face never wavered. "Miss Dean is currently in a meeting. Is she expecting you?"

I shook my head. "I doubt it very much."

"In that case, I can't disturb her," she told me, clearly unimpressed that she'd pulled the short straw of coming to talk to me.

"What's your name?"

"Anna," she told me.

"Well, Anna, how about this? You go tell Rebecca that Nate Garrett is downstairs in her bar having a scotch. She'll probably yell a bit, so you may want to make a hasty retreat then."

"Mister Garrett, she's in a meeting and can't be disturbed."

I leaned in closer so I could whisper. "Ask her if she'd prefer to be disturbed or get to bury her king?"

Anna swallowed and then walked off. I did feel a little bad about getting her to tell Rebecca I was here, and the bury-her-king part was probably overkill, but considering Rebecca arrived under a minute later, I guess it worked.

"Get the fuck out of my bar," she snapped as she stamped her way toward me.

Several people who were eating stopped and glanced at the curvaceous woman who was bearing down on me like a force of nature.

"No," I told her.

Rebecca hadn't aged a day in the over thirty years since I'd last seen her, but her eyes were harder than they'd been and I wondered what had happened to cause it.

"You can leave, or I'm going to throw you head first through that window."

"Is everyone you used to know like this when you turn up?" Caitlin asked as Rebecca grabbed me by my jacket and slammed me up against the wall.

The air rushed out of me, and my head bounced off the hard brick, making me momentarily dizzy. "Nice to see you, too," I said.

"I heard what you did. I told you back then that you weren't going to put your hands on him."

"To answer your question, Caitlin, it usually depends on how much I've pissed them off." I met the eyes of the woman who held me against the wall with ease. Guardians were strong as hell, and if she'd wanted to she could have really hurt me. But the same was true of me. And I really didn't want it to get that far. "In your case, Rebecca, that was probably a lot.

You can either let me go and I'll tell you why I'm here, or I'll make you let me go and still tell you. I've been shot at, attacked, and generally had a shitty night. I'm not in the mood to piss around."

Rebecca released me and took a step back. "You have thirty seconds; come into my office."

She turned and walked away, leaving some shocked diners to stare in disbelief at what had happened. I noticed the skull shaped hole in the plaster and rubbed the back of my head, ignoring the customers as I followed Rebecca upstairs to the office. Apart from a different paint job and some modern appliances, it appeared to be identical to the one I'd been in over thirty years earlier.

I almost bumped into Rebecca when she spun abruptly, and with Caitlin directly behind me I couldn't step away in time to avoid the punch to my stomach. I dropped to my knees and sucked in air, while I tried not to cough up my lungs.

Caitlin quickly stood between me and my assailant. "That's enough! You've made your point, now let him tell you why we're here."

Rebecca smiled. It wasn't pleasant. "He deserved that."

"Probably," Caitlin agreed. "Hell, I've wanted to do it myself more than I can remember and I've only known him a few days. But this is important, and we don't have time for childish shit. Too many people are already dead. I don't want to stand around while that tally increases."

Rebecca leaned up against the desk at the far end of the room. "Thirty seconds."

"I need to go see Galahad," I said as I stood, the pain in my gut finally subsiding.

"I think we can end it there," Rebecca said.

I told her about the werelions and how they were working to Simon's plan. It probably took longer than thirty seconds, but the second I mentioned Simon's name and got a reaction, I knew she wasn't about to kick Caitlin and me out.

"When they brought Simon here," Rebecca said, "he winked at me. I thought nothing of it at the time, until I was told that he would only speak to Galahad with me present. So, for one day a month, every month, I used to travel to Shadow Falls and sit with Galahad. We did that for the first ten years."

"And how'd that work out for you?" I asked.

"Simon never said anything of value. He talked about the people he'd murdered or told me how much he liked seeing me. Never anything about what happened in Stratford. He's a cruel, vile, little man. But he's also locked up in a dungeon and there's no way he's had any visitors."

"Well he might not be giving the orders, but he knows what they are. Galahad needs to be made aware of what's happening."

"You're right, he does," Rebecca agreed. "Although I'm unsure why you have to be the person to tell him."

"Because despite whatever might have happened, we were friends. I'm hoping I can get him to allow me to see Simon and try and figure out what the hell is going on here, because if we don't, a lot more people *will* die."

Rebecca remained quiet for a short time until she picked up the phone on her desk and pressed a button on the base unit. "Get the gateway ready; I think we're going to have to send two people through it."

"Thank you," I said when she'd replaced the handset.

"I didn't do it for you, Nate. I don't give a shit if you go through or not, but if I can stop Simon or those who are working with him once and for all, I will do it."

"Even so, thank you."

Rebecca went and opened the office door, grabbing my arm as I walked passed her. "One thing, Nate. If you hurt my king ever again, if you lay your little finger on him in anger, I will gut you like a fish." She released me and walked off without a word, expecting Caitlin and me to follow.

"What the fucking hell did you do back then?" Caitlin whispered.

"Oh, you know. The usual."

CHAPTER 23

Stratford, Maine. 1977.

Whatever rage and hate I felt as I left Galahad and the forest, both marked with the blood of Rean's wife and son, remained with me for the entire journey back into Stratford.

I drove through the town, stopping off at the motel to pick up the misericorde dagger and put it in the car. I had a feeling it was going to come in handy. While in the motel, I asked the owner for directions to my target before setting off once again.

The mayor's house was on the opposite side of town, so it took me a short time to drive through the deserted streets. I drove past the property twice before pulling up to the guarded front entrance.

The house itself was huge, certainly more of a mansion than what I'd been expecting. The street itself was full of half-built houses, all looking slightly smaller than the mayor's and all utterly abandoned in the darkness.

I walked across the street, the dagger in hand, and gave it to one of the two guards, who stared at it in confusion.

"Someone from here put this in my bedroom," I told him. "It had to be one of you, because if Simon or his cronies had done it, I'd have found it nailed to a dead rabbit or something much less subtle."

"Fuck off," the guard said and moved to shove me back.

I pushed his hand aside and struck him in the throat. He dropped to the ground, trying desperately to breathe, as a blast of air took out the second guard and threw him into the small hut that they'd been using as shelter while on duty. He crashed inside and didn't move again, as I walked into the hut and pushed the button to open the gates.

"Where's your boss?" I asked the first guard, who was just beginning to catch his breath again.

He pointed toward the house.

"Yeah, I got that. Whereabouts in there?"

"Not sure," he said, his voice raspy.

I removed the air from his lungs and allowed him to crash unconscious to the floor, as cries sounded out from more guards who were spilling out of the mansion's front door.

I cracked my knuckles and walked toward the four men who called out warnings, while one of them aimed a gun at me.

"We will shoot," the nearest one told me.

A blast of air knocked the first man over into his friend behind him, the sound of the gun going off filled the night as I turned my attention to the two guards who remained upright.

They ran toward me with batons out, erroneously confident. I wasn't really sure what they hoped to achieve. The closer of the two reached me and missed with his first strike. I snapped his arm and drove my knee into his ribs, pushing him into the path of his friend. He tried to avoid the injured guard, but walked into a kick from me that snapped his head around and sent him unconscious to the driveway.

The first two guards had finally managed to untangle themselves just as I caught one of them with a vicious elbow shot to the back of the head instantly knocking him out. His friend tried to get away, but I grabbed the back of his shirt and spun him around, throwing him over the bonnet of the nearest car.

"Where's the mayor?" I asked as I picked him up and repeated the process of throwing him onto the car, this time his head struck the windscreen, cracking the glass.

He slid down the bonnet, leaving a streak of red on the white car. I helped him on his way and pulled him off the car, punching him in the stomach as he moved.

"Don't make me ask again."

"Inside," he said as he crumpled to his knees. "Ground floor, at the back."

I hit him in the head, sending him to join his comrades in the land of unconscious assholes, before walking into the house.

I'd only taken a step into the large hallway, before another guard came out of a room beside me with a shotgun. I grabbed the gun with one hand and forced it up toward the ceiling, twisting as I moved to claim it from the guard. I jabbed him in the face with the shotgun's butt then blasted him into the wall several feet away with a gust of air, knocking him and several pictures to the floor with a loud crash.

After emptying the shells onto the floor, I tossed the gun outside and closed the door. The rest of the lengthy hallway remained problem free, allowing me to get to the final door without having to hurt anyone else.

I pushed the door open, just long enough for me to see the mayor and three more guards, at the end of the kitchen. Bullets filled the air, and I dove through the doorway behind the nearest counter.

The second I heard the click of an empty gun, I surrounded my enemies with a wave of air then ignited it, instantly engulfing the three guards. Their screams of fear soon turned into ones of anguish as the fire did its job.

I sat motionless and counted to ten before extinguishing the flames. The cries had vanished, replaced with the soft whimpers of semi-conscious bodyguards. I glanced around and only saw three men, all lying on the tiled floor, but the mayor was nowhere to be seen.

"You can't hide forever," I said, slightly surprised that the mayor had managed to escape the flames. If we'd been outside I would have used a lot more magic, but in an enclosed kitchen, I didn't want to risk igniting a gas main, or killing the mayor before I'd talked to him.

"Fuck you," he snapped and fired randomly, achieving nothing but giving away his position behind a door at the side of the kitchen.

I crept around the counter until I was opposite the door, then I stood, took the extra two steps to the door itself and kicked it with everything I had. It tore off the hinges and collided with Mayor Richardson, who was standing behind it. His gun, a small revolver, fell to the floor as I pushed the door aside and grabbed my prey, throwing him back into the kitchen and over the counter.

He landed on one of the guards, who was badly burned, his face already blistering. I'd tried not to kill any of the guards, they were only doing their jobs for the most part, but using semi-automatic machine guns to kill me was going above and beyond, and needed to be dealt with accordingly. The three in the kitchen would probably live, but they'd remember this day for a very, very long time.

I dragged the mayor upright and punched him in the solar plexus, standing him back upright. He dropped to his knees.

"You arranged for Simon to get out," I told him.

He opened his mouth to speak.

"Don't deny it, you'll only make me angrier. You did it, we both know that. I just want to know what you got out of it. What did you get from having him murder wood trolls, or police officers?"

"You have no idea what's going on, do you? You stupid little man."

"Enlighten me."

"Why do you think Galahad had you do all this? Because he wants me dead. Because with me dead, that's one less person who's loyal to King Whitehorn. He's using you, he set you up."

"Are you saying that Galahad is working with Simon? Because I find that hard to believe."

"You're a fucking idiot."

I placed a foot on his knee and pushed down hard, causing him to cry out. "Keep talking, but do it nicely, I'm in no mood for rudeness."

I removed my foot and he rubbed his knee. "Galahad and Simon aren't working together. But Galahad is keeping things from you, and you know that. Simon knew about the deal between Galahad and the trolls before you turned up; he allowed himself to be captured. And then allowed himself to be freed so he could kill them."

"Why?"

"Because Simon was making a point, to show everyone that Galahad can't protect his people. That he's weak. The murder of that Sally-Ann girl moved everyone's plan around. After her death you got involved, although until you told Simon that she was friends with Avalon, no one knew why she was so fucking important."

"That doesn't explain why you think Galahad set me up, or why you're spilling your guts."

"Because I got set up too. Galahad sent you after me. I bet he told you I released Simon from prison. But I didn't, he was already free. He knew the first thing you'd do is come running here and try to kill me."

"You were going to release him anyway, so you're just playing semantics."

"Maybe, but I didn't want him to massacre a colony of wood trolls. I'm many things, but murdering women and children is a little above what I'm willing do to."

"And the cops? They would have had to die anyway, no matter who released him."

"Collateral damage."

The ease at which he described the murder of people who were there only to protect the public was sickening, but hardly surprising. "Why do you hate Galahad so much? What did he do to you?"

"He sent me *here*," he snapped. "I used to be a human advisor to King Whitehorn, and after he was overthrown, Galahad decided to remove me from that post and stick me in the middle of fucking nowhere to be the mayor of a shithole of a town. No one even knows where Whitehorn is, no one but Simon. I've heard rumors that Whitehorn plans to run for some political office in Washington, but hell if I know how accurate that is. Simon was in charge of this whole operation, I don't even think the old king even knows about it."

"Then why go to all this trouble?"

"Because Simon has a fucking hard-on for getting back at Galahad for Whitehorn and him being kicked out of the realm. When Simon turns up and tells you about your obligation to help him put Whitehorn on the throne, you do as your fucking told, or he skins you in front of the town hall." Mayor Richardson sighed. "I don't care about these people, or this town, I just want out. I want to move back to Shadow Falls, and Galahad isn't going to make that happen. So, I hitched my wagon to Simon and Whitehorn. I just want my fucking life back."

"So, all of this death that you were quite willing to help cause is because of some petty attempt at a temper-tantrum."

"Simon came to me with a need. To be able to kill and take people without any police interference, so I helped facilitate that. In return, I was to be given my old life back and I would have gotten to be there when Galahad finally lost his head and it was stuck on a pike for all to see."

"Petty vengeance for a small man. All because Galahad demoted you, which it turns out was probably a good thing considering you were in league with his enemies."

"You call it petty vengeance, I call it justice. Righting a wrong against a man who committed harm against me and my life."

"Harm?" I said. "I'll tell you what, you tell me all about what Simon wants from this town and I'll pass you over to Galahad unharmed."

"I don't know a damn thing," he pleaded.

"You are partly responsible for everything that has happened here, for all the death and terror that Simon and his friends spread. You thought you could do all of this and get away free. I'd planned to come here and kill you, but I'm not going to do that. Galahad wants you dead, and I'm not playing his game anymore. So, if you want to lie there and tell me you don't know anything about what's happening in your town, that's fine with me." I removed a paring knife from a nearby knife block. "In fact, that's exactly what I was hoping you'd say."

It didn't take long for me to discover that Mayor Richards knew nothing more, so by the time I'd finished and dragged his bloody and broken body through the house, Galahad had arrived with five of his guard in tow.

I dropped the mayor at Galahad's feet. "Surprised to see him alive?" I asked.

Galahad glanced down at the human and then up at me. "Yes, to be honest. I figured you'd kill him."

I dragged the mayor to his feet and shoved him into the arms of the nearest guard, a young woman who spun the mayor so he was facing away from her, and then slit his throat. She pushed his body to the ground to let it bleed out on the driveway.

"He needed to die," Galahad said, turning his attention back to me.

"You set me up," I said, barely able to keep my temper in check. "You got me here to find Simon, and you knew that he was going to escape. You planned for it."

"Nate, do you really want …."

"Yes, I fucking want to talk about it. Right here, right now. You knew someone would free Simon from his cell, didn't you?"

Galahad nodded. "We were pretty certain of it, yes. Like I told you back in Portland, I didn't know whom I could trust here. We needed Simon alive to hopefully identify those he was working with. We were sure the mayor was in on it, but weren't certain if he was acting alone. Unfortunately, I didn't realize that members of my own guard were working with them. Those who betrayed me have been dealt with."

"You told me the mayor had set Simon free, so I'd come storming over here and kill everyone."

"Yes, I'd hoped you'd make so much noise that anyone looking here would realize what happens to people who cross me. That it might bring some peace to my reign."

I punched Galahad in the mouth, drawing blood and knocking him to the ground, as his five guards all reached for their weapons.

"No," Galahad shouted at them. They stepped back, but kept watching me, a tense readiness in their stances.

"I'm not your personal assassin. I don't kill for your political career. You came up with this plan to get me to kill for you, but it backfired and now there are two dozen dead. Today you're responsible for the murder of innocent people. If you'd been honest with me, if you'd actually protected the people you were sworn to keep safe, Rean's family might still be alive. You played at being this manipulator and, let's be honest, you're just not that good at it."

"You think I like knowing that because I fucked up people died?" Galahad said as he got back to his feet. "It was meant to show that we would protect people. Simon escapes and we get to him in time. You kill the mayor for helping and I get to tell everyone that there's no one untouchable. That even if my people can't do it, I have those outside of Avalon or Shadow Falls who will do it for me."

"Your plan was horseshit from the start," I snapped. "All you had to do was be honest with me. That was it. I never would have left Simon alone if I'd known that you'd planned for his escape. I never would have left those wood trolls unprotected."

"Wood trolls can take care of themselves," Galahad said. "They're not weak."

"Yeah, those children were great at protecting themselves, especially from an attack in the middle of the night. By the time anyone knew what was happening, those who could have fought back were dead. Simon's not a fucking idiot, he knew how to attack the colony to create the most fear and get the most dead."

"Like you would have done, you mean?"

"I'm well aware of the innocent people I've killed or hurt. We've both lived a long time and killed many, many people. But I never thought you were the kind of person who would allow such a plan to go through."

"I had to show people I was strong."

"Yeah, well now you not only look weak, but you look like you can't even protect your own people. Good fucking job there, your kingship. Are you going to mention in the story how you slit the throat of the mayor or how...?" I noticed the misericorde dagger on the ground; I must have dropped it when I was fighting the mayor's bodyguards. I walked over and picked it up, throwing it at Galahad's feet. "You had someone put this in my room. You wanted me angry, focused. You gave me a reason to really hate these people, as if all the murder and pain they'd caused wasn't enough."

"I was advised."

"Fuck your advisors," I screamed. "You've known me since we were children, we grew up together. You could have just come to me and said 'I have a problem, I need your help.' Instead, you tried to make me your own personal killer."

"You've killed for worse reasons in the past."

"Watch your fucking tongue, Galahad."

"Go fuck yourself, you arrogant asshole. You think you're above all of this, that there are no innocent deaths on your hands. I remember that battle with the Saxons. I remember you burying an axe in that soldier's chest, finding out he was only twelve. I saw you sit with him until he died as a battle raged about you. Was he the first? How many innocent people followed him?"

I charged toward Galahad, picking him off his feet and dumping him on the ground, with me straddling his chest with a blade of fire in my hand. "You fucking cunt," I snapped.

"No, stop," Galahad called out to his guard. "He will kill you." He returned his attention to me. "Isn't that so, Nathan? That's all you are, a killer. Are you going to kill me too?"

"You would use that boy's death against me, you dare compare the heat of battle to your wretched attempt at manipulation? To your ability to follow a plan that you must have known would fail? You placed your secrets and lies above our friendship."

"I'm a king," he seethed. "I had no choice. Unlike you."

"What the fuck does that mean?"

"You're like a nuclear missile, you're dropped somewhere and cause devastation all around. You've always been that way. And I figured you'd come here and just fucking destroy everything that stood against me, like you do all the time. I wanted to tell you, I really did, but I couldn't. I couldn't risk you saying no, to the whole plan going out the window."

I got off Galahad, who adjusted his suit, but didn't bother getting back to his feet.

"Do you even know what Simon was here for?"

"No, although we will. A few years in a dungeon will loosen his tongue a little."

"I never thought you'd be on the receiving end of my anger," I said softly. "I always thought you'd be honest with me. That you knew how I felt after leaving Merlin, leaving behind the lies and manipulations. But I was wrong. You're just shittier at it than he was."

"I have more important things to do than lament whatever has broken in our friendship," he said, anger leaking from every syllable. "I think you should leave this city and this state."

"You're having me kicked out?"

Galahad shook his head. "I'll be putting Bill Moon in charge of the investigation into what happened here. We'll make things more palatable for the humans living here, and then we'll be taking Simon back to Shadow Falls."

"And Rean?"

"He has refused my aid and vanished with his remaining colony into the woods. Nine out of twenty-two died today, I doubt he wishes to involve himself with the affairs of anyone other than his colony."

"You lost two allies in space of a day and damaged your reputation as a ruler who takes care of his own. Congrats. You must be very proud."

"I think we're done here," he said and got back to his feet once more.

I took a step toward him and I noticed something in his expression. Fear. But not fear of me, Galahad would never have been scared of me, but maybe the fear of what had been lost between us, and my anger evaporated, replaced with sadness. "Galahad, you should know something," I said, gaining his attention as he walked off toward the house.

He stopped at the open door and glanced back at me. "What is it?"

"I'm not a nuclear bomb, I'm a scalpel. I cut away the tumors and diseased flesh that threatens to consume everything. So, you need to be very careful that during your reign, you don't become something that requires *my* utmost attention." And with that, I turned and walked away.

CHAPTER 24

Portland, Maine. Now.

On the journey from the top-floor office to the basement of the Mill, I managed to fill Caitlin in on what had happened between Galahad and me through whispers and the occasional hand gesture. Rebecca walked several paces in front of us, so didn't hear us. Which was good, because I was pretty certain that if she had, it would have just started another row. And I had precious few desires to get punched again.

Once we reached the basement, where the number of very tough-looking restaurant staff increased exponentially, Rebecca led us to the far end and placed her hand on the palm reader before entering a five-digit code into the numerical pad next to it. Runes were etched into the door along the top and bottom; I didn't want to find out what they did, but I was certain it wasn't good for anyone forcing the door open. The door clicked loudly and moved aside. Rebecca took one step inside and the whole place lit up immediately, showing the lengthy staircase that spiraled down several dozen feet.

"Have you been here before?" Caitlin asked. "To Shadow Falls, I mean?"

"Once, about a hundred years ago. The security here has been upgraded a lot since then."

"The old security was insufficient," Rebecca said. "Anyone could come and go."

I assumed that meant me, but let it go. I'd punched her king and humiliated his guard by preventing them from interfering. If circumstances were swapped, I'd be pretty pissed off too.

After descending the fifty or so steps, and walking down a short hallway, we ended up at a second door, which Rebecca opened, motioning for Caitlin and me to enter.

"No security on that door?" I asked.

"If anyone has managed to get past the guard upstairs and then through the door without killing themselves and everyone else with them, I think any security measures we have left would be sort of moot."

The room inside turned out to be a long corridor, about half the length of a football pitch, although nowhere near as wide. A dozen or so doors led of each side, most off which I discovered were closed as we made our way along the marble-floored hall.

"This hall is probably worth tens of millions of dollars," I said as I recognized some of the incredible art that adorned the walls in between each door.

"What happens down here?" Caitlin asked, which was just as well as my curiosity was hitting fever pitch, and I doubted Rebecca would have told me.

"We have rooms for those who have made a long journey to get here. Most people like to be rested either before or after the trip, there are beds on the other side too, if you feel the need to take some time." She glanced at me. "Although some people may not be offered them as easily as others."

"Yeah, we get it, you're all pissed off at me," I snapped. "Galahad was the one I hit, not you guys. So, let's all move on, shall we?"

Rebecca took a step toward me. Part of the floor moved up her body to her hands, where it became a very sharp looking dagger. "You have no idea what you did that day? Do you even care? You made my king's guard seem impotent. Worthless. The king told them not to touch you, that you would kill them without a thought. The king's fear of your actions forced them to stand by while you spoke to him as if he were a common traitor. As if he were nothing. It is not something we can just 'move on' from, as you eloquently said, it's something that we have spent thirty years ensuring never happens again."

"I'm not going to attack Galahad," I said. "You do know that he hired me, yes? That he set *me* up and tried to manipulate events so that I'd *murder* people for him. You are aware of that, yes?"

"Yes, I know exactly what happened. I'm one of the very few who do. I may not disagree with your reasons for striking him, but he's my king. Your reasons don't make it any better that it was *allowed* to happen." She dropped the dagger, which vanished into the floor, before turning and striding off.

At the end of the corridor, Rebecca opened the door and ushered us both inside. There were half a dozen people inside, all of whom were seated at computers, typing away. Another five stood next to the door, all of them in uniforms of blue and black and carrying rifles.

"Why the rifles?" I asked.

After a few moments of awkward silence, when it became clear that I was certainly not welcome in the room, one of the guards spoke up. "Sometimes unfriendly people come through the gate," he said. "And sometimes they come this way. We're here to make sure nothing bad happens on either end and silver bullets do that job pretty well."

"Thanks," I said to him, receiving a curt nod in reply.

"What the hell is that?" Caitlin said and walked to the far end of the sizeable room, staring at the huge archway in front of her. It sat about twelve feet away from anyone else in the room and was nowhere near any walls or doors.

"It's a realm gate," I told her.

All realm gates are the same in terms of composition: a mixture of wood and rock and metal, although no one really knows how they're created or where they came from. They're all different shapes and sizes; the one before us was about fifteen feet tall and ten feet wide. Each gate has runes carved on its surface that give the gate its color. In the case of Shadow Falls it's a dull purple glow.

"It's beautiful," Caitlin said.

"I remember the first time I saw one," Rebecca told Caitlin. "I was mesmerized. Even after all these years, it's hard to believe that such a simple-looking structure is a gateway to the closest thing to heaven many of us will ever see."

"So, Shadow Falls is a paradise now?" I asked. "Looks like Galahad did good."

"You'll see," Rebecca said with a sly smirk.

"How does it work?" Caitlin asked.

Rebecca nodded to one of the other people in the room who walked up to the realm gate and placed his hand on the gate. The runes on the side of the realm gate exploded to life, the dull purple glow now bathing the whole structure in light. The blank space that had occupied the middle of the gate changed, becoming a mass of swirling colors. The man touched the runes on the opposite side of the gate and the swirling colors changed to a picture of a room. Several people were inside, all of them wore leather armor and had swords at the ready. They saw Rebecca and relaxed.

A huge man appeared in the image, his long almost orange hair tied back. "Rebecca, I was not aware of anyone coming here today."

"I'm sorry, Harrison," Rebecca said, "but these people must speak to the king."

"And, who are *these* people?"

Caitlin waved at the large man, but he saw me and reacted as if he'd been struck. "*Him! He* will not come through."

"Harrison, he must speak to the king. It's urgent. And, no, you can't do it for him. It has to be Nathan. I'm not happy either, but his case is solid. Simon is killing again."

Harrison laughed. "Simon is in a cell."

"That hasn't stopped him," I said. "I just need to figure out how."

"If you step out of line, I will kill you."

You'll try, I managed to bite down. "I'm not here to start trouble, just stop people dying."

Harrison spoke in whispers to his colleagues around him. "We will arrange transport to the king," he said. "He will not leave our sight."

"I need to go to see someone else first."

"Who?" Harrison snapped.

"The person who built the prison."

Harrison smiled. "That won't be a problem. Maybe one of his inventions will blow up and we'll be spared your existence."

"So, can they come through?" Rebecca asked over Harrison and his friends' laughter.

"Yes, send them over. We'll get them to where they want to go. They have twenty-four hours, after that I'm opening the gateway and throwing them back, job done or otherwise."

"Deal," I said.

"Are you both ready?" Rebecca asked us.

I nodded.

"If you have weapons, you must leave them here."

Caitlin and I shook our heads, but the guard still patted us down. I assumed it was nothing personal, but the man who decided to check me for weapons was a little more aggressive about it than necessary.

After the checks had been completed Caitlin and I walked up to the gateway as Harrison stared at me from the other side.

"Nervous?" I asked.

Caitlin nodded.

"Don't be, it's just a tear in reality."

We both stepped through together. The trip was instantaneous, although Caitlin tripped once in Shadow Falls, falling to the ground.

As one of the guards helped her to back to an upright position, Harrison towered over me. "If you step out of line, I will kill you."

I waited until the guardian had switched the gate off before replying, it would take time for them to recharge and be able to open it again. "Anyone ever told you, you're a colossal dick?"

Harrison appeared flustered, but then bent toward me, so his face was only an inch from mine. "I really hope you step out of line."

I smiled. "Take us where we want to go, or get out of the way. But every second you stand there and flex your muscles at me is time I could be doing something much more important."

Harrison almost growled, but stepped aside, allowing Caitlin and me to walk out of the gigantic temple where the realm gate was kept and into the vast city beyond.

CHAPTER 25

Standing outside the temple and looking down at Shadow Falls is an incredible experience. It stretches for miles and miles in all directions. At one time the city was tiny, just a few hundred people lived there, but over the centuries it grew and grew as more people decided that Avalon rule wasn't for them.

"So, if the realm is called Shadow Falls, what's the city called?"

"This," I said with a gesture, "is the city of Solomon."

"Solomon, as in the Bible?"

I nodded. "Originally this place was to be the paradise for the wise and righteous. The original founders wanted it to an enlightened place, and one of them said Solomon and it stuck."

"Didn't he have, like, seven-hundred wives or something?"

"Yeah, I think that part's optional."

Caitlin laughed. "So, where's the king?"

I pointed to the far end of the city, there was no way to see the castle without binoculars, though. "There's a stream that starts on the mountains, by the time it gets to the city, it's a river. When the city was first made, it was used as a moat to protect the people who lived here. But as the city grew, it became a river that separates the king and his council from the rest of the people who live here."

"So, are different parts of the city doing different things?"

"See the aqueducts?" I asked. "They not only supply water to the city, they also divide the city up. The west is mostly agriculture and farming, the east is industrial. You have to pass check points to get through them."

"What do the people who live here use to get around?"

"Trams," I said and motioned toward one of the three coach vehicles that moved along a structure next to the aqueducts. "They were designed by the man we're going to go meet, the same person who did the blueprints for the prison."

When we'd walked out of the temple, the sun was high in the sky, with barely a cloud in sight, but after a few minutes of walking down the steps to the nearest tram station, the sun had moved until it was behind Shadow's Peak, the mountain range to the east, casting a huge swathe of darkness across the city.

"It happens every day," I told Caitlin as the lights began to ignite, bathing everything in a blue hue. "That's different," I said to the guards who had been accompanying us.

"They were changed a few years back, the gas ones were unreliable," he said.

A twinge of guilt hit me as I realized that I'd never visited Galahad in Shadow Falls since he'd become king. After what had happened in Maine, I'd made a conscious effort to stay as far away from the place as possible. But I began to wonder if maybe that had been the wrong decision, to allow the anger of that day to build up, maybe it had done more harm than good. I pushed the thought aside. It was not the time for second guesses.

We followed the three guards and Harrison to the closest tram station, a small hut next to the line.

"What do the trams run on?" Caitlin asked.

I shrugged. "At one point it had been gas power, but with the removal of the lamps, I don't know anymore."

As one of the trams stopped at the station, I realized that they were completely different from how they used to look. Gone was the blocky design, replaced with something sleek and elegant, almost bullet-train-like.

Harrison motioned for the passengers to disembark before allowing Caitlin and me to get on. "You will have two guards accompanying you at all times until you reach the king's district. There are more than enough armed soldiers there to keep an eye on you. Me and my men have better things to do than babysit the two of you, but if you step out of line . . . ."

"Yeah, they'll kill us," I said. "You've mentioned it before."

Harrison stared at me. "Just give them a reason. They'd enjoy it almost as much as I would."

I took a seat on the tram and watched Harrison, who didn't move as we pulled away, high above the rest of the city.

As much as I didn't want to feel like a tourist, I couldn't help but look out of the windows at the hustle and bustle of the city a hundred feet below. The tram moved up and down with the aqueduct, stopping every few minutes, although the guards ensured that no one else got into our coach. I wasn't sure if that was because they thought I might attack someone, or because they were worried that someone might recognize me and attack. I doubted it was the latter, but it had been thirty years and a lot could have happened in that time.

The shadow continued to move across the city, eventually catching the tram in its snare. As the shadow engulfed us, the interior lights sprung to life and I began to wonder what the hell had replaced the gas lamps of old.

The view below regained my attention as it changed from dense housing to open fields and farmland, and then a few minutes later we arrived at the stop just inside of the king's district. When I'd last been in the city the tram had stopped on the opposite side of the river; it had been deemed unsafe for the tram to go further, but apparently things had changed.

The four of us got off the tram as a stampede of passengers made their way inside. The guard took us along the tram platform and down some steps where the grand splendor of the king's district shone through. The houses were bigger, many with ornate paintings or mosaics on the street-side external wall. The street itself was different; the pavement was made with tarmac and concrete, while the rest of the city had to contend with brick.

"How far do we have to walk?" Caitlin asked.

"Not too far now," one of the guards said.

The inhabitants of Shadow Falls wore a mixture of modern clothing, such as jeans, and older-style Victorian outfits. The result was a bit of a mishmash, but Caitlin and I could walk around without looking like we didn't belong.

We made our way to the far side of the king's district, under an aqueduct arch and into a large field with only one house in the middle.

"This is it," the guard said and both of them turned and walked back up to the main part of the district.

"We should go say hello," I told Caitlin, who took a step and then froze as an explosion rocked the ground.

"You're probably safe," I said. "From him anyway."

Although clearly uncertain, she followed me to the sizeable two-story house where I used an easel-shaped brass knocker.

The door was opened almost immediately by a large young man who appeared to be in his early twenties, although I knew he was at least two hundred.

"Antonio," I said with a smile.

"Nathanial," he bellowed and picked me up in a massive bear hug.

"Nate," I squeaked. "Call me Nate. And also, put me down."

Antonio laughed, a deep bellow that would have probably woken the dead. "And you've brought a lady friend."

"Emphasis on the friend part," Caitlin said as Antonio took her hand in his and kissed it lightly.

"Any friend of Nate's is welcome in this home," he told her. "I assume you wish to see the idiot working out back."

"Idiot?" I asked as we stepped into the house. While the first room we stepped in was neat and tidy, the further back into the house we went the more and more drawings and sketches sat on every surface. Any spare space was taken up with small models or the occasional bust.

"He's found a new toy," Antonio said. "And by toy, I mean something that's going to blow him up if he's not careful. But you know him, he can't stay away once his mind starts tinkering with things. I swear he has the attention span of cheese sometimes."

I laughed and caught Caitlin looking at some of the sketches that hung on a nearby wall.

"These are incredible. What are they?"

"No idea," Antonio said. "He has ideas, sketches them out and works on them for about a day, and then something else catches his attention. A few weeks later, he'll come back to this and do some more. You can try to tell him to calm down, but that's just not him. Since he found those damn crystals he's even worse than he ever was. It's like they charge his mind."

"Crystals?" I asked.

"He'll explain better than I could."

Antonio opened a window and shouted, "You have guests."

A few seconds later a door opened and closed, followed by footsteps heading toward us.

"If it's one of Galahad's men, they can come back when I'm not busy; the king has commissioned me for enough projects," said a male voice from a nearby room.

"Then why aren't you doing any of them?" Antonio barked back.

"Because this is more interesting," the second man said as he stepped into the room, noticed me and gave me a hug that rivaled Antonio's.

"Nathanial, it's been so very long."

"Leonardo," I said as he placed me back on my feet. "It *has* been too long. How are you?"

"Good, good," he said with a dismissive wave of his hand. "Now, who is this delightful lady?"

"Caitlin, Leonardo," I introduced. "Caitlin's an FBI agent, we're working together."

Leonardo spoke in hushed Italian and kissed her on both cheeks.

"What did he just say?" she asked when the greeting was over.

"That you were a sight that he thought only the heavens themselves could create," I said.

Caitlin made a noise that sounded like she approved. "So, his name is Leonardo? And he's Italian? Oh shit, not *the* Leonardo?"

Leonardo beamed a smile that I'd seen used to melt frosty hearts.

"It's less impressive when you get to know him," I said, receiving a hearty laugh from Antonio.

Leonardo clasped his hands to his chest in mock outrage. "You wound me, old friend. Wound me deeply."

"Stop flirting then," I said with a smile as Leonardo continued to ham it up.

"I assume you're here for something important," Leonardo said, running one hand over his lengthy beard.

"Wait a second," Caitlin said. "I've seen a self-portrait of you as an old man. There are first hand records of people meeting an elderly man, but you don't look anything over thirty-five."

"Ah, that was simple. Prosthetics. I'm an alchemist; I can create most things through sheer willpower, so remodeling some items to make me look like an old man wasn't difficult. I couldn't just leave Italy when there were so many people there I cared for, so I aged myself as if I were human. Then I moved across Europe to live and work in Avalon. Turns out I was just swapping one dictatorship for another. Shadow Falls is a place that suits me perfectly. Galahad allows me the freedom to do as I wish in exchange for working on things for the city."

"Like the trams?" I asked.

"Yes, they were unreliable for a long time, but they were also the best we could manage on the technology that's available here. Then we found those crystals and everything changed."

"Antonio mentioned them," I told him. "What are they?"

"Oh, you're going to be very excited." A thought seemed to stop Leonardo from saying more. "Am I still a turtle?"

Caitlin and I glanced at once another in confusion.

"Ah, I should explain," Leonardo eventually said. "The last time I was in your world, I found that television had moved on, there was a cartoon about four turtles. One was named after me. I assume that's a beloved program still. Leonardo was the leader. That impressed me, although I always thought that the fact that I wasn't the inventor of the group put me in a bad light."

"It's still on," Caitlin said. "My neighbor's kids watch it."

"Ah, good. I did so enjoy what I saw. Michelangelo would have hated it. He was such a melancholy man."

"He was human?" Caitlin asked.

Leonardo nodded sadly. "Yes, unfortunately. I often wondered what we would have achieved if we'd both still been around. But then, I didn't get to meet Einstein either, so there are many opportunities lost to times gone by." For a moment Leonardo appeared to lose himself in his memories, before grinning a moment later. "We can neither live in the past, nor in the opportunities lost to us. So, why are you both here? I assume you and Galahad still aren't on talking terms, Nate?"

"I haven't seen him in thirty years, although I get the impression everyone knows what happened."

"The guard who came back told people, who told more people. They said you killed the mayor and then attacked Galahad because of a disagreement. I knew there was more to it than that, but rumor has a way of becoming fact if enough people believe it."

I explained what had actually happened.

"They used you," Leonardo said. "I can understand your anger. And I understand why you wouldn't want people to think you had killed someone you'd left alive. But I also understand why Galahad's guard told people it was you. People can't think that Galahad will kill those who go against him; he doesn't want to show himself as a tyrant. But the fact that you killed someone who had been responsible for the murders of many of Galahad's subjects, that's more palatable to the people here. They would have wanted a trial. Galahad couldn't risk that, so he kept you in the dark. A new king, new rules. He was in over his head back then, although I'm glad to say he's improved with time."

"You seem to know a lot about it."

"Well, I was an advisor when the plan was delivered to him. I advised him to ignore it and go a different route. He went with them. Political pressure I imagine, the advisor who had devised the plan had a lot of clout with the elite in the city. Although that vanished when it came out that his plan had failed and innocent people had died because of it. Galahad fired him the second he was back in the city and the advisor fled the city after that. Unfortunately, I can't remember his name." Leonardo tapped the side of his head and smiled. "Too full of more important things."

"Well, whoever he was, he was an asshole," I said.

"No argument from me," Leonardo agreed. "He had too much power and nowhere near enough talent to use it."

CHAPTER

Leonardo was an easy man to talk to, so the conversation carried on for a while. Eventually, after Antonio asked if anyone would like tea, I managed to get Leonardo back onto the reason for our visit.

"Simon Olson," I said, which stopped any frivolity or laughter that had built up during our chat.

"An evil man," Leonardo said. "I had to design a whole wing of the prison to house him. It's covered in runes and is, if I say so myself, escape proof. Are you here to see him?"

I nodded and then explained about what was happening in Stratford. Leonardo listened intently, taking in every ounce of information and never once asking a question or fidgeting.

When I'd finished he turned to Antonio and said, "Make sure Galahad knows that Nathan is coming. We don't want any surprises and I'm going to guess that the guard will still try and stop him on sight, with or without Harrison's proclamation that he be allowed to see the king without trouble."

Antonio nodded and picked up a coat and told us to wait until his return before going to see the king.

"So, you believe that Simon is still issuing orders?" Leonardo said.

"He is somehow, yes," I said. "Does he have visitors?"

"That's something you'd have to ask Galahad. All I can tell you is that he cannot get messages to anyone without help. He can't escape his cell, let alone the prison itself. The runes won't let him."

"What do they do?" Caitlin asked.

"They link him directly to the cell he's in. So if he walks more than about an inch outside of the cell, the runes ignite. Leaving him a messy stain on the floor. The same thing happens if he uses his alchemy on any part of the cell."

"Why not just put a sorcerer's band on him?" I asked.

"Oh, of course you don't know, you've never been involved in trouble while you're here," Leonardo said. "Sorcerer's bands don't work here. Never have. We like to make people think they work just fine, but in reality we use runes to keep people's abilities in check."

I was a little surprised at that revelation, and at the extreme measures that Galahad had employed to keep Simon in prison, something that Leonardo picked up on.

"He murdered dozens, Nate. There was call for his death from a lot of people, but Galahad wanted him made into an example not a martyr. We alchemists live as long as sorcerers. Having to live that life in a ten by ten cell with no hope to use his abilities—that's a harsh punishment for anyone. But in his case, a deserved one."

"People supported the old king?" Caitlin asked. "Even after what he'd allowed Simon to do?"

"People believe what they want to. We still see the occasional flyer or poster in support of Whitehorn."

"It's a good thing you don't have the Internet, then," Caitlin said. "Actually I haven't seen any electrical appliances. You have candles and gas lamps in here and those crystal things outside."

"Electricity can't be created here," I said.

"Actually that's incorrect," Leonardo said with a glint in his eye. "Electricity can be created anywhere. We have thunderstorms here, just like in your realm. We can create man-made electricity without issues. In fact, the palace has something that's based on the Tesla coil that it can deploy as a weapon. I modified it to use solar rays to charge the system until it's ready for use. But you've got maybe five minutes of use and then it's all gone. The problem is keeping that charge going for long enough, at a steady level, to be useful. We can't use the electricity we create for any real length of time, certainly not to actually power something like a house or street lights. We tried and blew out every lamp for twenty square miles. It's why we eventually settled on gas, which was collected from the mountains.

"It's something that's baffled me from the moment I arrived here, how to create a sustainable energy that doesn't pollute. Unfortunately finding an answer made the act of gas drilling redundant. It made some people very unhappy."

"Costing people money usually does, no matter what realm they live in," I pointed out.

"Yes, well, jobs were found, for all the men who wanted them, in the collection of the crystals you no doubt saw on your way here."

"I was going to ask you about that," I said. "What are they?"

"Ah, come with me and I'll show you."

Leonardo led us through the house and out into the back garden, which was both expansive and immaculate. Stunning flowers that I'd never seen before, a mixture of reds and blues, adorned one side. We followed a short footpath to a large building with two huge doors, which Leonardo pushed to either side, opening the front up.

"Welcome to my study," he said with obvious pride.

"What the hell is that?" I asked walking over to the sleek, black item that appeared to be a motorbike.

"It's a motorbike," Leonardo said with a dismissive wave of his hand. "Or will be if I ever get it to work properly."

"How *does* it work?" I asked, walking around the stunning bike and finding no kind of combustion engine that I could see.

"Ah, that's where these come in," he said and picked up one of the many crystals that adorned a large table along one side.

He tossed it to Caitlin, who caught it with a shocked expression, as if it might explode.

"They're safe," Leonardo told her, but she didn't appear convinced.

"What are they?" she asked.

Leonardo threw me a second crystal and I noticed it held the same blue light that I'd seen when first arriving in Shadow Falls.

"I'm no closer to an answer," I pointed out.

"Okay, first you need to know something I've figured out. Magic is alive."

"I know," I said. "I've always known. Everyone knows that."

"Yes, but not in the way you or your brethren think. You see, I think magic is dormant right up until it's placed inside a living thing. Then it becomes alive, feeding off its host, needing to be used. Sorcerers have a special affinity for the stuff; it's why you're born with the innate ability to use it in the first place. But before all of that, it's just an element like any other.

"Have you ever heard of the Norse dwarfs? They used magic in their creation of items; they were the greatest alchemists ever. It's a skill no other alchemists have. And when they vanished, whatever secrets they had vanished too. This is one such secret." He picked the crystal from my hand and held it in front of me. "This is magic."

"It's a rock," I said. "A pretty colored one, but I don't feel any magic from it."

"Because it's dormant and needs a trigger."

"Like what?" Caitlin asked.

"Leonardo, how about you start from the beginning?" I said as I pulled two stools from under a nearby bench and offered one to Caitlin who sat beside me as if we were in school.

Leonardo took a deep breath. "Okay, magic. The reason you can't use your magic properly is because this whole place is full of the stuff. Dormant, tiny particles, smaller than atoms, of magic. You use your magic and it's like igniting kindling. It's uncontrollable and impossible to wield, because those little pieces of dormant magic become little pieces of very active magic."

"You're saying there's magic in the air?"

Leonardo nodded. "Yes, exactly. It's in the air we breathe, don't worry it's harmless and evaporates on contact with anything, making it very difficult to study, but it's definitely there."

"So the crystals create magic?" Caitlin asked.

"No, they *are* magic." Leonardo picked up a lighter and clicked it on, holding the crystal above the flame. The crystal immediately lit up brightly.

"This is what the dwarfs knew about?" I asked.

Leonardo's smile would have been seen from space. "That's my theory, yes. There are no alchemists who can use these crystals to work with. Any who try get a nasty shock when the crystals blow up, as you may have heard earlier. But if you apply even the slightest energy source to them for more than a few seconds, they ignite. It burns up all the magic in the area. In theory that would mean wherever these are burning, your magic would be normal."

"So the lamps all have little fires in them?" Caitlin asked, although she didn't exactly sound convinced by what she was saying.

"Nope, you see as well as activating when they're heated, they also have another trick." Leonardo grabbed a thick blanket and wrapped it around the crystal, which started to glow brighter and brighter. "Without any sunlight on them, they light up. We had no idea until someone removed some from the cave and as they walked back from the mountain it got dark and the whole batch lit up."

"Are you telling me your street lights are solar powered?" I asked.

"Well, not exactly, they absorb energy and release it when it's dark, but it doesn't change that energy into electricity. But as soon as it gets dark outside, well, dusk really, the crystal activates automatically. It's incredibly impressive. I'm currently trying to get them to power items, like the motorbike. It's one thing to produce light, but can it produce a more potent form of safe energy? Oh and one last thing, they don't run out of power. Ever."

"Seriously?" I asked.

"So far, no. We replaced every lamp ten years ago. Not a single crystal has required renewing since. We've been working on an idea to place them in every house, but it's taking a lot of planning before we can get that far."

"Wait a second," Caitlin interjected. "You said Nate can't use his magic, why?"

"Well, technically he *can* use it, but it's not advisable."

"Because of the magic in the air?" Caitlin asked.

Leonardo nodded.

"I can switch my magic on okay," I said. "But instead of a small flame, it would be an inferno. One I can't shut off without a lot of effort. While I'm trying to shut it off, my magic is just flowing out of me, destroying everything. Magic here is a dozen times more potent, but it's also a dozen times more difficult to wield. Even experts, the true masters of sorcery, would have a hard time. It's one of the reasons Avalon allows this place to remain; they'd lose any conflict because any magic used would hurt their own men as well as the enemy."

"But aren't alchemists using magic?" Caitlin asked.

Leonardo glanced at me with a look of shock on his face.

"No one taught her," I said.

"Oh, I'm so sorry. To answer your question, alchemy isn't magic, at least not in the same sense that Nate has. Whereas Nate's magic is from an internal source, we use our alchemy as a sort of catalyst to change the world around us. So long as we're touching the object we want to change, we can shape and create whatever non-organic matter we see fit. I can touch that wall there and make a doorway, or a staff or any of a hundred things. I can take the components of an object, say glass, and so long as they're all touching, I can make those components into a beautiful vase, or a mirror. There's very little limit on alchemy's use, beyond our own exhaustion and being unable to change living matter. As our alchemy isn't magic-based, we don't ignite the magic in the air. It means, we don't have the same concerns with our powers being overly charged within Shadow Falls."

"So these crystals have given Shadow Falls a near limitless supply of energy that, under the right conditions could also be used as a weapon?" I said.

"A weapon?" Caitlin asked.

"They blow up when alchemy is used on them," I explained. "I'd say that probably counts as a weapon, even if it's an unreliable one. Who outside of Shadow Falls knows about this?"

"No one," Leonardo said. "Only half a dozen people know what the crystals actually do. Most assume they require an external power source to work, if they think about them at all."

"Are these crystals in other realms?" Caitlin asked.

I shrugged. "No idea, I've never seen them before, but then I've never started digging in mountains either."

"This is the first realm I've found them," Leonardo said. "Although it does raise interesting possibilities. And very dangerous ones."

"Can they be used in our realm?" I asked.

I'd known Leonardo long enough to recognize when he didn't want to answer a question. "I'm not sure," he said eventually. "My guess is yes, but I don't really want to find out. The fewer people who know how they really work the better."

A terrible thought occurred to me. "If someone like Avalon, or maybe Charles Whitehorn found out about them . . . ."

"They will eventually take them if we don't give them up," Leonardo finished for me.

"Who knows about them exactly?" Caitlin asked.

Leonardo looked taken aback. "Me, Antonio, Galahad, and a few of his advisors. The men and women who mine them only know they're crystals, and we no longer ship them during the night just in case someone figures out how they work."

"You think that's what all of this is about?" I asked. "Finding a way in here to get the crystals?"

Caitlin nodded. "As much as revenge is always a good motivator, money is a better one. I'm sure selling an infinite power source would make them more than a little money, and probably a lot of power to go along with it. I hope I'm wrong, but it fits."

"How do they get in here?" Leonardo asked. "They'd need an army to get through Rebecca's."

"Yeah, I don't get that either," Caitlin said. "We're missing something."

The idea was a grave one, and everyone took a moment to pause until Caitlin asked, "And how are they used to power the bike? Is there any way they could be smuggled out in it?"

"Ah, that's the problem. These crystals can only be used to power something of very low capacity. A bike, well that's a lot more complicated. I can get the crystals to power it, but I can't get them to switch off. Once you remove the light they come on and don't go off." Leonardo walked over to the bike and ran his hand over the sleek chassis. "I've been trying to come up with a way to have a retractable array of panels covering the crystal, but then you can't select how fast you go, you just go. And you don't stop until the crystal is exposed to light. I've been working on it for a few months; if I can crack it, I can revolutionize the way we travel in the city."

"But can they be used to smuggle?"

"Only if you want to ride a really big bomb. There's one crystal in here and that goes bang with enough force to eject the rider.

You put any more than that and you're going to make a crater with you smeared in the middle."

"What about the trams?" Caitlin asked. "Don't they work on crystal power?"

"Yes, but the trams have go and stop. They can't change their level of power or speed—it's all or nothing. It's a conundrum I haven't quite figured out. I thought I had it, apply a small amount of external power to the crystal, albeit not directly, but you probably heard the explosion before you arrived. And as for smuggling on them, they'd need to get through Harrison and his men. They search everyone coming in and out."

I nodded as I remembered both the rough searching and the explosion I'd heard just before we'd entered Leonardo's house. We discussed more ideas, but didn't really get anywhere and started to get frustrated at our lack of progress, so Leonardo went to get us some drinks.

He returned to find me standing by the bike. "Where did the idea for a bike come from?" I asked.

Leonardo nodded as he returned with a tray of cold drinks. "Antonio went to your realm and brought me back a few dozen books on bikes and engines. They were very interesting, although ultimately I think I've grown past them. I picked a design I liked based on aerodynamics and practicality. I'm quite proud of it, although I'll be much happier once I can actually get it to work without killing anyone who rides it."

"I didn't realize you were into bikes," I said with a smile as I took my glass and drank the refreshing water.

"Yes, well, I may have ridden one or two the last time I was visiting your realm. They're quite liberating."

"Well, when it's ready, I'm happy to come test it for you."

"Thank you, Nate, although I think you may have to pry Antonio away from it first. The man took to a motorbike like a duck to water. He's told me he'd like to perform an endo on the bike, unfortunately he won't tell me what that is."

"It's where you lift the back wheel off the ground and ride only on the front one," Caitlin told him. "I liked the occasional bad boy back in the day," she told me when she noticed the expression on my face.

Leonardo's expression was even easier to decipher. "He will not be doing anything of the sort on this bike. Not after the time and effort it took me to make it in the first place."

Leonardo walked off back toward the house, ranting the whole time about finding an assistant who would respect his work, while Caitlin and I stayed in his study.

"Is he coming back?" Caitlin asked.

I nodded. "He's probably gone to make a note about yelling at Antonio before he forgets and starts work again."

"Does he go through a lot of assistants?"

"He had three or four last time I was here, but Antonio is his main one. They've worked together for a few hundred years I think. Sometimes Leonardo needs to be reminded of work he's agreed to do for someone, especially when he gets caught up in a bit of a pet project, like this bike and those crystals."

She picked up one of the crystals from the table and turned it over in her hand. "These would revolutionize the energy over the world. Free sustainable fuel for everyone."

"Yeah, except it doesn't work like that. If any of these crystals became common knowledge on earth, there would be wars fought over them. And with them from the sound of things."

"Wouldn't Avalon try to stop that sort of thing? Isn't it in their best interest to do so?"

"Probably not, although they'd make sure the people they wanted to win, did so. No matter the cost. Everyone would want these, and no one in any sort of position of power would allow free energy. They have to stay here. Besides, who knows what happens when they go through the gateway. We don't have particles of magic in the air, they'd have been found by now. These things might detonate the second you step into our realm. It's just too dangerous."

"It's a shame though," she said and replaced the crystal.

"Nate is correct," Leonardo said as he returned. "Avalon would try and control this place. Or there would be an influx of people here and we simply don't have the ability to take on millions, or even thousands, of extra people. The first option would result in a war, the second in a devastation of the way of life of the people who live here. Neither would be acceptable."

"What happened to your other assistants?" I asked. "You didn't blow them up, did you?"

Leonardo laughed. "No, I still have three others. They're all away today, I need one day a week to myself. I think I've gone through four or five sets since you were last here."

"Where do they go?" Caitlin asked. "I mean, once they finish here, what do they do?"

"Most go to work in the palace as advisors or engineers. I think in the last hundred years, since Nate's previous visit, I've only had a real problem with one person. A young woman, she stole from me about thirty years ago, just after the plans for the prison were finalized. Such a shame, she was well-liked by many, including the king."

Antonio arrived as Leonardo mumbled names to himself. "The king will see you," he said. "No guard will try to stop you, although I'd advise not picking a fight. They're on edge with your arrival. They see what happened last time as a slight against them all, and guards hold grudges."

"Thanks, Antonio," I said and shook his hand. I was itching to get an audience and arrange a visit with Simon. As nice as it was to see Leonardo again, and as useful as the visit had been, it was time to get going.

"Antonio?" Leonardo asked. "What was the name of that girl I had to fire? The one who stole from me?"

"Patricia," he said with a slightly angry tone. "Human girl who betrayed us all and fled the realm before we could stop her."

The name made both Caitlin and I glance at each other. "Was she short, long dark hair? Utterly nuts?" I asked.

"Not sure about the last part," Leonardo admitted. "But the rest is accurate. Do you know her?"

"Yeah, she's my mom," Caitlin said. "She's also the one currently killing people and working with Simon."

"I'm sorry to hear that," Antonio said. "Although it does shed new light on what happened."

"What was it?" I asked.

"She tried to steal the blueprints for Simon's cell, and when she was caught, she killed a guard and escaped."

Caitlin and I aimed a barrage of questions at both Antonio and Leonardo for the next few minutes. They appeared infuriatingly calm the whole time we made our way back into the house where Antonio prepared tea.

"Did she take anything else?" I asked. "Maybe information about the crystals?"

"No, we didn't even know about them back then. She was obviously trying to figure out how to break Simon from jail, but her plan went awry."

"Did you find anything else out about her?" Caitlin asked.

Leonardo shook his head. "The king would know more, he had an investigation conducted. Humans were only allowed to arrive here in limited capacity for a while after that." He glanced behind him at a sizeable grandfather clock. "Speaking of which, that's a meeting you need to attend soon. The guard will be getting anxious that you haven't turned up, and I'm sure Galahad will be keen to see you both."

I stood and embraced Leonardo and Antonio. "Don't be strangers," the latter said as he allowed me to be removed from another bear hug.

"I hope you stop these people," Leonardo said. "If their aim is to free Simon, then I will talk to Harrison about strengthening the guard at the realm entrance. He'll be only too happy to gain extra help up there."

"Thank you," I said.

"No need to thank me. That man is not someone I want running around again." He turned to Caitlin. "I'm sorry about your mother, but rest assured, your parents do not define who you are. If at any point, you think that maybe because she's turned out a certain way, that you might too, you need only remember that you, and you alone, are the master of your own destiny. That takes people far too long to realize, and even longer to do something about."

Caitlin nodded thanks and gave Leonardo a hug.

"Nate, take care of this one." He grasped my hand in his. "And of yourself. Charles Whitehorn and his minions are involved in this and they will not hesitate to kill those in their way. You have always been a survivor, and I am not a man of war, despite some of my inventions being designed for such. But if you need to, end them. All of them. Ensure there is no third time lucky for these people."

CHAPTER 27

I found Caitlin outside, leaning against the wall of Leonardo's house. She had a piece of steel in her hand and was using her alchemy to change its shape.

"Nervous habit?" I asked.

She glanced up, but continued transforming the steel until it became a thin blade. "Leonardo told you to kill my mom, didn't he?"

I considered lying to her, but she deserved the truth. "Not in so many words, he told me to deal with what was happening. Whitehorn was king here for twelve years. During that time, the cells were full and people were not allowed to cross between our realm and this one without his written permission. He stole from the city and had people killed who crossed him. He was, in short, a very bad man. If he gets back in power, a lot of people will die."

She dropped the steel onto the ground, where it changed back into a small disc. "Let's go see the king." Caitlin pushed herself off the wall and started walking toward the palace.

It took ten minutes to walk to the foot of the steps, which led to the palace high above the rest of the district.

"We have to walk up those?" Caitlin asked, staring up at the several hundred steps.

I'd noticed several guards watching us since we'd arrived in the king's district, but there were larger numbers of them the closer one got to the palace. "Yeah, it was meant to be a defense mechanism. Very few invaders are still in peak physical condition once they've made their way here and then have to run up a few hundred steps."

"And Leonardo couldn't have just built a lift or something?"

"We could go back and ask him, if you'd like?"

Caitlin started up the stairs, and three hundred and twelve later we reached the courtyard to the palace.

"That's pretty damn impressive," she said.

The building was a mixture of old stone that gave it a medieval appearance. Ramparts with guards patrolling them sat high above the dozens of windows and several balconies that were on the front of the building.

The guard stared at me for a short time before moving aside. We made the rest of the way to the palace's imposing front door and inside, without anyone else trying to tell me how much they disliked me, although I could still feel their stares on me every step I took.

The first room inside the palace was a massive reception room, with an incredible staircase that led up to a landing. Several people were walking around, either tidying and cleaning, or chatting amongst themselves, and no one really paid us much attention as Caitlin and I stood there and waited for Galahad or one of his people to turn up and talk to us.

The massive, thirty-foot, floor-to-ceiling windows down one side of the room allowed in a huge amount of light and showed the opulent garden that must have taken a fleet of people to keep in good shape.

"How does someone live here?" Caitlin asked. "There are so many people."

"The king's own chambers are near the rear of the house; very few people get to go in there."

"So, how do you know about it?"

"Ah, well, one of the older kings, a few hundred years ago now, used to have a weakness for sleeping with women who weren't his wife. Avalon wanted leverage and I was tasked with making sure that happened."

"You watched him having sex with people?"

I shook my head. "No, just took a few objects to let him know how easy it would have been for me to find out whatever I wanted. Fortunately, the plan backfired and he resigned instead of becoming Merlin's puppet. That was the last time Merlin tried to get leverage over anyone here. At least as far as I know."

"It was the last time," Galahad said from the balcony above us. "Wait there."

I wasn't entirely sure where he thought we were going to go, considering the shit I'd put up with to get here in the first place. But I did as I was asked and waited, while he walked down the staircase, wearing an expensive dark suit.

Galahad wore his kingship a lot easier than when I'd last seen him; he was smiling and showed none of the stress that I was expecting to see. It suddenly dawned on me that I hadn't asked anyone how Galahad was, not as a king or ruler of his kingdom, but as a man. I hadn't asked how my old friend was doing, and I felt more than a little regret and anger at myself for being so selfish.

Galahad stood before me, ignoring everyone in the room who had bowed as he passed by, and smiled at Caitlin. "Good to see you, welcome to Shadow Falls and my palace."

"Thank you, it's beautiful," she said.

"You do me a great honor for saying so. Some people call this palace The Shadow's Break. Apparently the red brick was meant to symbolize the sun. It's a little ostentatious for my liking, and I grew up in a castle, but even if we're alchemists, we can hardly knock it down and start again just because the new ruler doesn't like something."

Galahad turned to me and breathed out through his nose. "Nathan."

"Nate," I corrected. "You can call me Nate."

Galahad nodded. "Nate," he said, as if trying it on. "It suits you."

"I hope so. We're here to talk about Simon." I explained what had been happening in Stratford and Washington. There was no point in hiding anything from him. I wanted his help.

When I'd finished, he nodded, more to himself than anything else. "I will arrange for Simon to be interviewed tomorrow morning; even a king cannot move mountains. Metaphorically, anyway."

"Thank you," I said.

"In the meantime, Caitlin and Nate, I will have someone take you to your rooms for the evening. Feel free to explore my home and ask for whatever refreshments you wish."

A moment later a young woman arrived and walked off with Caitlin, talking as if she'd known her her whole life. "I assume Harrison threatened to have you forcibly ejected?" Galahad asked me.

"He may have mentioned something."

"I will talk to him and arrange a twenty-four hour cease-fire. I won't have you followed while you're in my home, Nate, I promise you that." He smiled and then immediately sighed.

"Thank you," I said. "Your majesty." The second I saw the hurt in his face from not using his name, something I would do for every friend I had, I knew I'd said the wrong thing.

I watched Galahad walk away and as a butler arrived to show me to my room, I just knew it was going to be a really long night.

While the room itself was stunning, I needed to stretch my legs and left the room to wander around the palace. True to Galahad's word, there were no guards following me at discreet distances, I even received a few nods of hello from the staff. Hopefully Galahad had told people that I was neither the bogyman, nor some sort of assassin sent to kill everyone.

After a few minutes I opened a door to what turned out to be, an expansive balcony. The sole occupant was Galahad, who turned to look at me, cup of tea in hand.

"Sorry," I said and went to close the door.

"Stay, Nate," Galahad said, placing his cup on the table beside him. "Would you like a cup? I think we have some things we need to discuss, and as there is no one around who may listen in or interject, this is probably as good a time and place as any."

I stepped onto the balcony and closed the door.

"Earl Gray okay with you?" Galahad asked, pouring the boiling liquid from a teapot into a second cup. "Lemon, honey, sugar?"

"Lemon would be fine," I said and took the cup from him once he'd placed a slice into the boiling drink.

He took a drink of his tea and sighed a little. "I think I'm the only person in the city who drinks this stuff, apart from Leonardo. I guess that makes him my dealer."

I smiled and savored the hot drink. "You don't get back to our realm often, then?"

Galahad shook his head. "About once a year, I make sure to go back. The guard usually has a bit of a mental breakdown at the same time. Apparently I'm incapable of taking care of myself since I became king."

"You wear the role well. Better than when we . . . ." I paused, unsure how to finish that sentence without saying something stupid or offending him without meaning to.

"When we last met," he finished. "Is this how our friendship ends? With awkward silences and small talk?"

"I don't know," I said honestly.

"That's not good enough, Nate. Do you remember when we were young, we'd go to a tavern and drink and gamble and pick up wenches?"

I wondered where he was going with his walk down memory lane, but it was a good memory, so I didn't mind. "Ah, the wenches," I said with a smile. "I do remember them. The drink was, in hindsight, fucking horrible though."

Galahad's smile was genuine. "It tasted like piss, I remember that much. But do you remember that time you stopped me from doing something stupid?"

"Which of the many, many times are you referring to?"

"The girl and her betrothed. She was all over me, and then her bloke turned up and challenged me to a duel. You stopped me."

"You'd have killed him and he wasn't in the wrong."

"Yes, that's the one. You were always the one who didn't get as drunk as the rest of us. It sometimes felt like your job to look out for us all."

It was, I thought. "Someone had to."

"I wish I'd listened better thirty years ago, Nate. I wish I hadn't allowed people in my council to push their way to get what they wanted. I cleaned house when I returned, got rid of the old council and started anew." He paused. "What I'm trying to say is, I'm sorry. I'm sorry I put you in a position you shouldn't have been in, I'm sorry I lied to you, and I'm sorry I tried to manipulate you into doing something I knew you'd hate. But I'm most sorry for what I said outside the mayor's house, I was so full of anger and disappointment at myself and what I'd allowed to happen, that when given a target to aim at, I did with ferocity."

As Galahad's words sunk in, I stood still and watched the beautiful landscape before me: rolling hills and forests, a dream place for many. "I'm sorry too," I said eventually. "I treated you like a friend in front of your subjects, I should have treated you like a king. I didn't give you the respect that you deserved. And I shouldn't have punched you either. Thanks for not taking my head off after that, because we both know you could have."

We both remained in silence for a few moments. "Have we just become women?" Galahad asked.

"I do think our man cards may need to be returned," I said with a chuckle.

"You don't want to kiss and make up, do you? Because I think that might end badly for us both."

I placed a hand on Galahad's shoulder. "If it's all the same with you, I'd really rather not. But don't take that as a knock against your manliness, it's me not you."

"So that's it? I say sorry, you say sorry, and we both move on?" Galahad's laugh was enough to force him to sit down. "It's a good thing we're almost immortal, or the last thirty years would have felt like a really stupid waste of time."

I smiled. "Yeah, lucky us, we have longer to realize that we were both idiots."

"Ah, but I'm royalty. So I'm a better breed of idiot than you."

"You were elected," I pointed out.

"Doesn't matter. I have a crown and a palace. That just makes me better than you."

I finished my tea and placed the cup on the table. "Nice to see it hasn't gone to your head."

"Before we don't talk about what happened back then, ever again, I just want to say something. I know you're probably annoyed that we told everyone that you killed the mayor . . . ."

I put up my hand to stop him. "I get it, I really do. All I ever wanted was an apology for what happened and the chance to do the same."

Galahad poured us both another cup of tea. "Okay, onto something more current. I had a nice chat with Caitlin. She's an amazing woman. She told me that her mum was a lady by the name of Patricia, someone who is now hell-bent on murdering her way through Stratford. She asked if I'd known her when she lived here, before she ran off after killing one of my guards."

"Leonardo tells me you had an investigation conducted. What did you find?"

"Well, she vanished totally after getting out of this realm. We know she was working with Simon—we had sightings of her in Stratford. It's assumed that she went to the house to try and find her friends."

"That would be why she called me a murderer then," I said. "Why was she here in the first place?"

"To kill me," he said flippantly. "That much we did discover. She was meant to slit my throat, but then Simon got caught and that all went to shit. Besides she had plenty of opportunities to kill me and never did."

"You were sleeping with her, weren't you?"

"Often. I was most upset when she decided to betray us and flee. Apparently she was able to conceal her psychotic tendencies from me and Leonardo. He hired her based on a recommendation from one of my advisors at the time. Since she escaped, it's much tougher to get in and out of the realm now. Something I'm not hugely proud of, but it is necessary. Oh, and you want to know the really good bit of info I think I've discovered?"

"That you're Caitlin's dad?"

Galahad's face dropped. "Yes, although you clearly knew the surprise before I did. How long have you known?"

"About thirty seconds. Are you sure she's yours?"

"Maybe Patricia was sleeping with other people, I don't know. But, before she ran, Patricia said she needed to talk to me. To tell me something important. The dates match up; I'm pretty sure Caitlin is my daughter." Galahad took hold of a spoon and changed it until it became a small knife. "I could cut myself and if you take the blood, we could find out if we're a match. You can do that sort of thing with Blood magic, yes?"

"Yes," I said and managed to stop him before he actually did cut himself. "But I can't do it. I don't have access to my Blood magic anymore."

It took a while to explain what had happened. From Mordred taking my memory, to him returning them along with the side effect of removing the marks on my torso. I told Galahad about the necromancy and how I still didn't know fully how mine worked.

By the time I'd finished, Galahad clearly had something he wanted to share. "And Hades couldn't help you figure out what type you are?"

"Apparently necromancers just have to figure that bit out for themselves. Every spirit I've taken has been angry, full of fire, but that's all I've got. The places are always different, so are the times of day and any other variable you care to mention. Hades told me that necromancy is hard to learn, that at some point it'll just click and I'll understand the type I have. I wish it would hurry up."

"Have you been practicing with it?"

I used my necromancy to reach out around me to try and find something. I could see the spirits, almost touch them, but it was like they were ignoring me. "Nothing," I said. "I'm not sure if it's me or if there's something wrong, but I haven't felt like this since Merlin tried to get me to light those hundred candles in the castle."

"It'll come to you," Galahad said and patted me on the shoulder as he walked past me, to the balcony edge. "Merlin might have been an evil old bastard, but he had a way of getting the best out of people. And hopefully this time you won't set fire to a large portion of our home."

"It wasn't large." The memory of the flames shot to my mind. Of Merlin removing them with a wave of his hand. "Okay it was a little large, but Merlin managed to teach me in the end," I said with a slight edge to my voice. As he got older, many of Merlin's "teachings" had been something I'd wouldn't have wished on my worst enemy. "Leonardo told me about the crystals."

"I assumed he would; he's very proud of what he's discovered."

"Yeah, but Caitlin and I think Charles Whitehorn is trying to get hold of them. Either that or his assistant, Karl."

"So he's moved from trying to take my throne to just destroying my kingdom. There really is nothing he won't do for money and power."

"It's just a theory, but it makes sense. What doesn't make sense is why Simon was killing people in Stratford, of all places. It seems fairly pointless. Like an afterthought to another plan, but considering the trouble they went through then and now, there's got to be something."

"Anyone around from back when we took Simon?"

I shook my head. "Most of the current victims have been the survivors. I can't find two of them. Apparently they vanished. Whether they're victims too remains to be seen. Something tells me what Simon is doing is the key to everything, but I can't get my head around it."

"We'll see him tomorrow, maybe he'll let something slip."

"Or I'll kill him."

"I'd rather you didn't. But if you're going to have temper issues, let me know now."

I knew that when I saw Simon, I was going to want to kill him. It was as sure as the knowledge that the sun would rise. And I knew that he was going to try and get me to fluster and attack him. I had to remain detached, cold. But then I thought of Rean, of his family who died at Simon's hands, and any detachment vanished. It was going to take a lot for me not to throttle Simon the second I laid eyes on him. But I had to do it. Otherwise there was no point in even going. "I'll be fine. The little rat-bastard isn't worth the time it would take to clean the blood off me."

We drank more tea together for a few minutes until Galahad absentmindedly said, "So, I have a daughter."

"Congrats," I said, grateful for the change in conversation. "You're the proud papa of a thirty-something-year-old woman. At least you don't have to worry about night feeds or puberty."

"Very bloody funny. How do I tell her? What am I meant to say? 'Sorry I haven't been there the last thirty years, but I didn't know you existed and your mum is fucking insane?'"

"Well, maybe you don't want to phrase it quite that way, even if it is accurate. I don't think there's a right way to do this, so long as you don't do it through interpretive dance or something."

Galahad rubbed his eyes. "I'll think of something. Probably not involving dance. Any idea how she'll react?"

"No, not even a little bit."

"You and she aren't ...." He made a gesture that I really hoped was meant to mean sex.

"No," I told him with a laugh. "I don't think you have that to worry about."

"Okay, I can do this, I can tell her and then be a dad. I'm a king for crying out loud, how much harder can it be?"

I stood and placed a hand on his shoulder. "My friend, you're well and truly screwed. You need to tell her soon—the longer she realizes you know and she doesn't, the worse it's going to get."

"Thanks for the chat," he said dryly. "Very helpful."

"No problem." I walked off toward the balcony door. "So, Galahad. Good luck with that."

CHAPTER 28

"**S**o, my dad's an actual king?" Caitlin said to me as I left the palace the following morning.

It took me a few seconds for my mouth and brain to catch up. "I don't think you can go around calling yourself Princess Caitlin or anything, but it appears that way. We'll have to use Blood magic to confirm, but I'm pretty certain you're a match. How'd it go?"

Caitlin smiled. "I didn't think I'd care when, or if, I ever found out who my real dad was, but it was actually really nice."

Galahad arrived a second later, along with a dozen guards, who were all trying very hard to act like they weren't watching me with every fiber of their being.

"They're still nervous about you, Nate," Galahad whispered. "But they no longer think you're going to kill me."

"Well, baby steps," I said with a smile.

As we walked through the district, I noticed the reception that Galahad received from his subjects. He was genuinely loved, and many people came up to him to ask how he was or thank him for doing a good job. On occasion he stopped and would talk to someone at a shop or outside a house and would ask about their family or store.

It was the sort of thing that Arthur used to do in Camelot, he knew everyone's name and story and the people loved him for it. I was happy to see that Galahad had taken a similar approach, using his charm and likeability to good effect. Like Arthur, Galahad was genuinely interested in those he spoke to, treating them as if their lives or problems were the most important things on his mind.

Caitlin and I remained a few yards back from him when he spoke to his subjects, but occasionally he would point to me or her and say something. After the fifth person he'd done this to, I caught up to him.

"Why do you keep pointing at me?" I asked.

Galahad smiled. "Just telling the people that you're here to help, a few of them recognize you. News of your arrival has spread pretty quickly and, without blowing my own horn, people like me in one piece."

"You're telling them we're friends again, aren't you?"

"Yes, although I'm making it sound a little less like we're both five-year-old girls."

I laughed and coughed and couldn't catch my breath for a few seconds, while Galahad walked on cheerfully. The bastard.

It didn't take too long to reach the prison; we took the tram for several more stops, getting off by some dense woodland. Five minutes later, we'd walked into the woods and up to a huge clearing that contained the prison.

The building itself was made with dark brick and concrete, and there were no fences keeping the inmates in; they would have been pointless to stop an alchemist from escaping. Instead, the bottom floor of the prison was a guard's barracks, and the only floor where the windows weren't blacked out.

Runes were clearly evident on the exterior walls, many of them etched right into the concrete or brick.

"Do you have a lot of people in there?" I asked.

"Hundred and nineteen at last count," Galahad said immediately. "Only six or seven are for serious crimes."

"Is Simon in there?" Caitlin asked.

"No," Galahad told her, his voice suddenly hard. He pointed to a large tower at the side of the prison. It was at least seventy yards tall, with large windows every few yards. "He's in there on the top floor of seven. The rest are occupied by guards and supplies."

I'd been watching the guards as they patrolled the prison and Simon's tower and counted sixteen people, with everyone in sight of someone else, at any point. It was a good system.

Galahad told his guard to stay outside and took Caitlin and me up to the tower, which I noticed was almost smooth to the touch. There was nowhere you could gain purchase to escape without falling to the ground. Simon might have been able to survive the fall, but he definitely wouldn't be doing anything for sometime after landing.

As Galahad pushed the tower's door open, I was surprised to find that it wasn't locked or guarded; clearly Galahad and his people thought that they'd placed enough security measures. They had a good point; if Simon could escape to the front door, he wasn't about to let a lock or some guards stop him.

As if able to read my thoughts, Galahad said, "There's no chance of Simon getting this far down without his runes going off. And in case he does, I had the enchanter put runes inside the door itself. If Simon steps through that door without permission, he probably won't be doing much more stepping anytime soon."

The ground level of the tower was empty, consisting of nothing more than a set of steps at the far end of the lengthy floor, that wasn't far off the same size as the palace's reception room. You could have easily fit a few houses, at least in terms of square footage, if not height, into it.

We ascended the stairs and found ourselves in a kitchen, a few dozen men all sat around a long table eating a meal. They stood and bowed as Galahad approached, which he waved off, insisting they continue with their food.

The next stairs were at the far end of the room, forcing any visitors to walk through an area that I assumed was usually populated by guards or cooks.

From the second set of stairs, it was a straight walk until we reached the fifth floor, where Galahad opened a door and motioned for us to go in.

"The floors between two and here are all barracks," Galahad told us. "Each guard has his own room."

"Considering it's a prison, it's quite light in here," I said, motioning toward the large windows that allowed light to stream into the tower.

"A lot of people work in here. I don't want to make this somewhere they don't want to go. There's already enough of that just because it's a prison."

The fifth floor consisted of a straight corridor toward a door on the opposite side. Four doors on either side of the corridor led to a variety of office-like rooms, most of which were occupied by people Galahad appeared to know by name. They all offered to take us to the floor above, but Galahad refused, telling them he didn't want to interfere before moving us further along the floor at a hurried pace.

The sixth floor consisted of several single-person cells down one side, although none of them were occupied, and two large rooms opposite, also empty.

"This is where we do our questioning," Galahad said. "We used to bring Simon down here and talk to him in either one of the two rooms."

"Used to?" Caitlin asked.

"We decided it was far too much work to bring him down here, just to have him ignore us, so we had one of the rooms up there converted into an interrogation center."

"You mean torture?" I asked.

Galahad stopped walking and turned back to face me. "No. As much as I'd like to have pulled various parts of him off, while roasting him over a large fire, we would have gotten nothing out of it. And I would have been the one left feeling dirty about what we'd done. I'm not going to sacrifice my morals ever again. Especially not just because it's the easy solution."

My friend's words gave me a newfound respect for his position. I was almost certain that I wouldn't have been able to keep my patience in check during thirty years of asking the same questions and getting nothing in return. But then I've never been known for having the greatest of patience at the best of times.

The final floor of the tower was different to everything else I'd seen. There was no cell. At least none I could see. As soon as we walked through the door—the first one with an alchemy-based lock that required Galahad to use his abilities to shift the door aside—we were greeted by a young-looking, thin man with a large mop of dark hair, who with four guards stood in a size-able room.

"Martin," Galahad said and shook the man's hand. "Nate, Caitlin, this is our enchanter. He's one of three who works here."

Martin offered me his hand, which I took. "I've heard a lot about you," he said to me after shaking Caitlin's hand.

"That's probably not a good thing," I said.

"Oh, no, it's not from the king or his guard. From Simon. You're the only person he asks about."

That was a bit of a surprise and I turned to Galahad ready to ask why he hadn't said anything.

"Because I knew how you'd react," Galahad told me. "You'd have stormed in here, ready to see him last night, full of anger and righteous indignation. You couldn't come here full of fire, Nate. You'd have gotten yourself or someone else hurt."

I opened my mouth to argue and immediately closed it again. There was no point, when Galahad was right.

"So, what does he ask about?" I enquired instead.

"Where you are, what you're doing," Martin told me. "The usual idea is to tell me how he's going to find and hurt you. He really doesn't like you very much."

"He can join a very long queue," I told him. "So, where is the psychotic little prick?"

"Back there," Galahad said and pointed to a wall that had no obvious door, but did have a huge silver sheet attached to it. A small window with a flap on it sat to one side.

"Okay, how do I get in there?"

One of the guards walked over to the sheet and placed his hands on it. The silver slid aside like liquid, revealing the solid brick wall behind, which also began to move, creating an archway.

"What's the silver for?" I asked.

"Show them," Galahad said and the guard nodded before continuing his demonstration. The silver slid up onto the ceiling, where it transformed into dozens of deadly spikes.

"If the guard takes his hand from that wall, those spikes come down," Matthew said. "It doesn't have to be spikes, but it's an interesting version of a dead man's switch and a little extra protection when the guards have to bring Simon his food and water."

"I want to go alone," I said, while the guard moved the silver back onto the wall, where it stayed. "And before anyone argues, clearly he's got some vested interest in me. Let's just see if I can't push his buttons."

"You okay with that?" Galahad asked Caitlin who nodded.

"Don't kill him," she said to me.

"We have very specialized runes in this office that are linked to the cell," Martin said. "We'll be able to hear everything you say, but not vice versa. He has no weapons, but that's not going to mean he won't try. He killed two guards the first year and has maimed another three in the years since. He's dangerous."

"Nate, get what you need and leave," Galahad said. "Every second you spend in there is more time he's in control. He's different than when he went in, more unpredictable. He's had a long time to work on using his mouth to hurt you. He'll relish the chance to get you to lose control and attack him."

"Just remember, his runes will ignite if any part of him leaves that cell," Martin told me. "It would be bad for you if that happened while he was holding you."

"Is that how he killed one of the guards?" I asked.

Martin nodded. "Gave himself burns over sixty percent of his body, and we had to increase the runes' power by several times to ensure it didn't happen again."

"I get it," I told him. "Dangerous psycho in a cell, willing to hurt himself to hurt others."

Galahad nodded to one of the guards, who unlocked the cell by using alchemy to push the lock to the middle of the door and turn it ninety degrees before pushing the door open.

I stepped through the door and into the crystal-lit corridor beyond. There were small windows, just large enough to get an arm through, every few yards, but the amount of light they let in was minimal at best. The guard led me down the corridor and around the corner before stopping outside the only cell. He used alchemy to push the metal bars aside, creating an entrance. "Good luck," he whispered before moving away as quickly as possible without running.

Simon sat behind a metal table, staring at his hands. He glanced up at me, his hair long enough to cover his face. The shadow in the room did its best to cover any part that was visible. He wore a sleeveless shirt and had put on a serious amount of muscle in the thirty years since I'd last seen him.

He leaned forward, allowing the blue light to do its job and I saw the beard, probably several months old.

"You look good," he said, his voice low and full of menace.

"You look like a hobo," I told him and removed the chair from opposite him, sitting down as I tried to ignore the fact that he could have easily pounced at me. Killing him in his cell wouldn't do me any favors.

"I don't get to shave very often. They don't like to give me sharp things. Apparently it makes them nervous." He leaned further into the light and pushed his hair back over his shoulders, showing me the scar that ran from under one eye to just above his mouth. But it was his eyes that caught my attention. They were devoid of anything even resembling a spark of humanity. Any ideas of threatening him vanished in that second; there was nothing I could do to hurt him that he hadn't already stopped caring about.

"I've been waiting for you to come say hello," he said and clicked his fingers, turning the lights off. "Welcome to the party."

CHAPTER 29

When the lights returned, after about ten seconds of darkness, I held Simon by the throat, pinning him to the ground.

"Were you nervous?" he asked with a slight grin.

"How'd you manage that?" I asked, letting go of him and stepping back.

"The lights go out every few hours. I'm guessing the runes interfere with the crystals."

I picked my chair up from the ground and sat back on it opposite Simon, who moved slowly, making me want to wait.

"How'd you know about the crystals?" I asked.

"Ah, is that still confidential?" Simon replied as he finally sat down. "I have a lot of spare time on my hands these days, the sheep out there probably don't sit and stare at one of them for hours on end. I'll have to ask Galahad to bring the Italian here so I can find out how they work. Maybe I'll ask him myself when I get out."

"You don't think you're ever getting out, do you?"

"What's Galahad going to do, keep me here for thousands of years? His options are kill me or eventually let me out. Unless I escape first, of course, but clearly that's impossible."

The way he said that final sentence was a lot smugger than I'd have expected.

"You have a plan to escape then."

"I have a thousand plans. Sometimes I think, I'll just run out of the cell and take my chances. And then I think of you, so I stay and wait."

"You think of me? That's very sweet of you."

"I'm going to carve my name in your face," he said softly. "That's the memory that sends me to sleep every single night."

"A soft pillow and the love of a good woman does the same for me. But since you've got neither of those, I guess you take what you can get."

"You didn't come here to trade witty insults." Simon leaned back in his chair and laced his fingers behind his head. "I assume you want to know what King Whitehorn is doing."

"Actually I just want to know why Patricia is killing people back in Stratford."

"Ah, you figured out who it was. Congrats. Have you met Joshua yet? I assume he's a true monster by now; the last I heard he was cutting heads off cats. He would have been six or seven at the time."

"So, people do still get you messages. Good to know."

"Of course they do, not often, but enough to keep me up-to-date. Unfortunately, Galahad started changing the guard every few years, and that made it more difficult. Still, I get the info I need."

"Whitehorn wants to take back his throne. I assume you getting released is part of that plan. How does Karl Steiner feel about you taking his job back?"

"No one has told me either of those things. And I don't give a shit what Karl thinks, I have no opinion of him whatsoever. I've never even met him. If *my king* is happy with his performance, than I won't question it."

"Don't pretend you give a shit about Whitehorn or his throne; you worked for him because he paid well and indulged your ... baser needs. You were his fixer, his little Rottweiler, sent after anyone who dared cross him."

"Like you were to Merlin."

I couldn't help but laugh. "Yeah, it's exactly the same. You murdered people for fun, innocent people who spoke out. I killed people who had committed the kind of crimes that you would have *thought* fun. I basically spent fifteen hundred years killing people just like you, over and over again. Removing one little stain at a time."

"And yet the world is still full of people like me."

I had a terrible urge to punch him in his smug little face.

"I heard you asked about me," I said, hoping to change the subject. "You feel like confessing your sins or something?"

"You never figured out why I wanted those tattoos, did you? Did that always bug you?"

I stared at the evil bastard in front of me for a second. "Yeah," I eventually told him. "That did bother me. I still don't know why it was so important."

Simon started laughing. "By the time you find out, it'll be too late."

I was about to come back with an obviously witty retort, when a guard's footsteps sounded behind me. I turned slightly, keeping one eye on Simon as the man who had taken me into the cell re-appeared.

"Sir, King Galahad wishes to speak to you," he told me before turning and leaving.

I glanced over at Simon, who appeared to be annoyed at the interruption. "I'll be back in a moment," I told him and walked after the guard before Simon could say anything to me.

"What's wrong?" I asked as Galahad, Martin, and Caitlin were all waiting for me.

"The tattoos," Galahad said. "What tattoos are these?"

"The victims back in the seventies were all tattooed, apart from Sally-Ann. How do you not know this?"

"That wasn't in the file, Nate," he said. "Not any that I ever saw."

"Someone removed it," Caitlin said.

"The mayor," I said immediately. "If there was anyone back then who could have doctored the report, it was him."

"But why didn't they want anyone to know?" Caitlin asked. "What's so important about tattoos?"

"The guardians have tattoos," Martin said, almost to himself before realizing we were all staring at him. "Ummm... it's how they operate the gates. They have to go through a bonding process and then have someone put the tattoo on them. It links one guardian to one gate."

"How do you know this?" Galahad asked.

"I spent some time with them while we were devising the runes for this prison."

"So, Simon was looking for a guardian?" I questioned.

Martin shrugged. "No idea, but if he wanted someone with tattoos, then that's a possibility."

I turned and walked back into the cell with a little song in my heart.

"That was quick," Simon said. "Did Galahad tell you to start torturing me?"

"Why were you trying to find a guardian?"

Simon's smug expression melted from his face.

"Oh, I'm sorry, was that a big secret?" I asked, with a slight smile, which I knew annoyed him.

Simon shrugged. "Does it matter? You know I wanted to find a guardian, but you don't know why, and you never will."

A memory of a conversation I had with one of the other captives back in seventy-seven flickered in my mind. "You're not after a guardian," I said. "At least, that wasn't your final aim. You were torturing those people to find out where they'd gotten their tattoos done. Finding a guardian would have led you to whoever did the tattoo. You were after a tattooist, not the wearer."

For a second I thought Simon was going to launch himself at me, but instead he took a deep breath and laid back in the chair, as if nothing I'd said had bothered him.

"What was it? You wanted to create your own guardians? Was that the plan? To attack the realm gate and install Whitehorn's own people there before you move through to Shadow Falls?"

Simon looked up at the ceiling as if bored with what I was asking him.

"But why Stratford? That's miles away from Portland; surely it would have been easier to look in Portland for a tattooist? And why is the tattooist so important? Couldn't you have just gotten anyone to do the tattoo once you found the guardian and realized what their ink looked like? Why go to all that trouble for a specific person?"

Simon continued to stare at the ceiling.

"Is this it?" I mocked with a wave of my hands. "This is the man who wanted to talk to me, who scares the people meant to be guarding him. He gets found out and decides to start sulking like a petulant teenager. You're pathetic."

"I'm going to kill you," Simon said softly. "I'm going to get out of here and then I'm going to hunt you down and kill you. And in the years after you're gone, I'll have forgotten all about you. You'll be nothing but a tiny blip on my life. I wanted to see you to tell you that. I wanted to make you understand how much horror I'm going to put you through. Not because you caught me, I always knew that was going to happen, but because you beat me. You humiliated me and then, instead of killing me and being done with it, you left me broken and bloody on that forest floor and then forgot I ever existed. So I'm going to show you the exact same respect. Then I'm going to kill Galahad and everyone you've ever been friends with."

I laughed. I couldn't help it. "Is that really the best you can do? Sit and threaten me or the people I care about? What am I meant to do, cower in fear? Beg you to leave them alone? Is that meant to scare me? Do you have any idea how many small insignificant people have threatened to kill me? Would you like to take a wild guess at how well that's worked out for them? About as well as you did back in that forest. So, you can sit there and threaten me all fucking day long, but at the end of the day, you can't do shit. I'm going to stop Whitehorn and his friends and I'm going to make sure you all rot. You're a pathetic little man, and if you ever do get out of here, I will kill you. And then I'll forget you ever existed."

Simon leaned closer, his hands resting on the table. "When I get out, I'm first going to pay a visit to that girl who used to come here every month. Rebecca. I told Galahad that I'd only speak to him and her, but that's not really why I asked for her. Do you know why I ask for her? Because when I'm alone at night, I like to think about flaying her. It's been such a long time since I've seen her, but it's soothing."

"I'm pretty certain whatever shock value you think you have, is lost on me."

"I heard your friend, Tommy, had himself a pup. Maybe, when I do get out, I should pay her a visit?"

I didn't even pause, I jumped over the table, grabbing Simon by the throat and slamming his head into the concrete floor. "How do you know about her?" I demanded.

"I know all kinds of things. Things about you, about your friends, and their children. I know whatever I need to know to get the job done. And that got under your skin, didn't it? Made you think that your friends aren't as safe as you think they are."

"They're safer than you are right now," I told him. "I could just kill you, here and now, screw Galahad's plans for you. Screw whatever information you were never going to give up anyway. The world would be better off with you no longer a part of it. What could you possibly know that would change my mind?"

"I know that we're just a cog in a machine, that you can kill me or King Whitehorn and that won't change a thing. The machine will keep working, keep going toward our destination."

"Which is?"

"I have no idea."

I squeezed his neck tighter, making his eyes bulge slightly.

"No idea," he wheezed and I released his throat a little. "But when it's time, you and yours are going to burn. And I'll be there to piss on the ashes."

"Burn you say?" I asked and dragged the struggling Simon to within a few inches of the cell's boundary. "You did say I didn't leave an impression last time, should we rectify that mistake?"

I released his throat and then head butted him, hard on the nose as the door open and Galahad came running around the corner. "Don't," he shouted.

I stood up and stepped away from Simon, whose hatred of me was written all over his face. "No one to stop me next time," I said and walked past Galahad and his newly arrived guard to the room beyond.

I was furious with myself as I stormed out of the seventh floor and began the long walk back to get outside. I needed some air. I needed to be away from Simon and the massive temptation to tear him in half.

"Well that could have gone worse," Galahad said after he found me sitting under a tree, twenty minutes after I'd left the tower.

"I could have killed him," I said. "I know you didn't want me to do that. But the temptation ...."

Galahad sat beside me on the soft grass. "Hard, isn't it? I've wanted to kill him every single time I've visited. And I know Rebecca did too. I couldn't keep bringing her along to his insane ramblings."

"He only wants to get someone there he knows he can make uncomfortable."

"I know, but she insisted anyway."

"I need to go talk to her about why the tattooist is so damn important," I said.

"You think my mom is still looking for someone who does that?" Caitlin asked as she joined us. "None of the victims were professional tattooists."

"It's still worth looking into. Maybe one of them was part time, or was starting an apprenticeship with a studio."

"I'll make some calls once we're back," Caitlin said.

"That man deserved to die up there," I said. "I really wanted to kill him. Unfortunately, I remembered that I wasn't meant to be killing your prisoners, so I decided not to."

"And I thank you for it," Galahad said. "I'll come with you to the realm gate and talk to Rebecca. She'll tell you anything you need to know about guardians and their tattoos."

"Did you all hear what Simon said about the machine still being in motion? You think he meant Whitehorn's plan?" Caitlin asked.

"I don't know," I said. "The idea that this whole thing is just a smaller part in a larger plan is, quite frankly, worrisome. But we can only fight what we know for certain. Maybe we'll get more out of it, or maybe Simon is bullshitting us just to try and wind us up. It's certainly not something I'd be surprised about."

"Agreed," Galahad said. "Let's fight one thing at a time. Hey, you remember what you said to me on the balcony? About Karl? It didn't jog at the time, but you mentioned him again up there. I know the name Karl Steiner."

"You sure?" I asked.

"Look, I know we poor alchemists don't have a sorcerer's memory with details, but that doesn't mean I forget easily either. And I don't forget names."

"So where do you know him from?"

Galahad was quiet for a few seconds. "Oh fucking hell," he said in what was barely a whisper. "I know the name because Karl Steiner was the man whose plan I followed when we took Simon the first time. I fired him after I got back, not because his plan failed, but because he said the murders of the wood trolls were not something we should bother ourselves with. His opinion was that his plan had succeeded."

I stared at Galahad for a few seconds. "So Karl used to work for you?" I eventually managed to get out. "That would be why he hates you so much."

"So, you think this is just about revenge, now?" Galahad asked.

I shook my head. "This is about money and power. But fucking you over, well, that's the icing on the cake."

CHAPTER 30

We hurried over to the realm gate as fast as possible, which with Galahad in tow, turned out to be very quick indeed. It's amazing how fast people will move out of your way when the king of their nation is with you.

Not even Harrison offered a word of dissent as Galahad demanded that the portal be opened and then explained to Rebecca that we needed to know everything she could tell us about guardians and their tattoos.

"Take care, Nate," Galahad said.

"I will," I promised and stepped through the realm gate, leaving Caitlin and her newly discovered father to have a few moments to themselves while I filled Rebecca in on all the questions she had about what had happened.

Once Caitlin was back with us, Rebecca took us up to her office, where she told us to sit on one of the couches available and offered us a drink.

"Beer," Caitlin said immediately.

"Something cold," I told her. "With no alcohol."

She brought back something that turned out to be cloudy lemonade, which, in my opinion, is the only way to ever drink lemonade.

"So, where do you want me to begin?" Rebecca asked, after she sat opposite me, a glass of red wine in one hand.

"Guardians have tattoos," I started. "What's the relevance of them?"

"They bind us to a realm gate," Rebecca said, clearly a little uncomfortable about the conversation.

"Look," I told her. "I know Galahad has told you to help us, and I thank you for that, but I'm not asking questions because I want the inside story of how to make my own guardians. We need to know because it could be the only way to stop more people from getting hurt."

"I know," she said. "But the things I'm telling you about, these are not easy things to discuss. These secrets have kept realms safe, if this information became common knowledge . . . ."

"It won't," I told her with complete conviction.

Rebecca glanced between Caitlin and me and then downed her wine in one, pouring another, much larger, measure. "The tattoos bind us to one gate, and only one gate, so each tattoo is different for each gate. It's also slightly different for each person."

"Can we see yours?" Caitlin asked.

Rebecca unbuttoned her blouse without pause, turning around to show the two fist-sized tattoos on her back, one just below each shoulder. "There are two because it means I can open the gate from either side," she told us, anticipating my first question.

"Sorry for this, I'm not being weird," I told her as I walked over and examined the tattoos more closely. Both were a single word in a language I'd only seen a handful of times in the past, I certainly didn't know what they meant.

"Do you know what they mean?" Caitlin asked Rebecca, as if reading my thoughts.

Rebecca shook her head, making her hair cascade down her back, partially covering one of the tattoos. She hastily grabbed her hair and pulled it over one shoulder. "No, none of the guardians do, but then we don't really discuss it with anyone outside of our own."

"You should," I told her. "The one for this realm could well be dwarven. Can't tell you what the words mean, but I've seen some of the writing before in Merlin's books. They believed that words had a very literal power, so their language was a type of old runes. It's why they wrote so little down, they didn't want anyone to have access to their power. The one for the other realm. I have no idea what that is, it's not something I've ever even seen before."

Rebecca pulled her blouse back on and started to button it. "I had no idea they were so old."

"It does lead to the question of how you know about the words."

"We don't. That's the job of the tattooist."

"How would they know?" Caitlin asked. "Do they have a book or something?"

"When a guardian performs the ritual to bond themselves with a realm gate, they don't go alone. All rituals are performed by two people. The guardian is the one who is bonded, but the second person sees a vision of the mark they need to make. That vision is so powerful, that they can draw that mark from memory for days after."

"So, why not use any old tattooist?"

"Only the child of a guardian can complete the ritual," Rebecca said. "Only they have the ability to see the mark. Most never take part in any ritual, but some choose to learn how to tattoo. It used to be almost exclusively males doing it, but over the years, more and more women are taking part."

"So, if Simon had his hands on the guardian, he could, in theory, find out who did the tattoo and get that person to tattoo people of his choosing?" I asked.

Rebecca nodded. "Yeah, the guardian can be any human willing to bond themselves with a realm gate, the artist has to be a guardian's child. They're much rarer and easily the most important component to the whole ritual. The bonding ritual that gives us our power makes us infertile for decades after. And while we stay in the zone around our gate, we are incapable of having children."

"Has anyone here had kids?"

Rebecca shook her head. "We have six guardians, none of them have children, and none are interested in doing so."

"So, if you want kids, you need to walk away from being a guardian."

"If you're a man, no, you can leave, get someone pregnant, and return. But if a woman returned, the baby would die. Most who decide to start a family do so after decades, if not centuries of service. And once they have left the zone, few ever return."

"What's stopping a guardian from just working for whomever pays them enough to open the gate?"

"Why would any of them do that?" Rebecca asked, sounding as if my suggestion was the most alien thing she'd ever heard. "They're loyal to the realm."

"But some psycho could become bonded and start letting in an army, for example?"

"It's possible," she conceded. "But no guardian would ever do such a thing, it would be . . . unheard of. Guardians and artists are loyal to the realm itself. The guardian has to swear an allegiance to always do what's best for the realm. It's a blood oath, and if they're lying, the ritual won't work."

"What if they were forced to open the gate? I know guardians are impervious to death, but their families might not be. In fact can you still feel pain?"

"Well, yes they could, and yes, we can feel pain. Although it doesn't last long."

"And what's stopping one of these artists from being forced to tattoo someone? Can the ritual tell if someone is being coerced?"

"No, and artists don't have to take the same bond. Any artist can tattoo anyone for any realm gate. They're not permanent positions either, they can choose who they tattoo and when."

"Which means once Simon has his artist, he can just force her to tattoo people for him. Hell, if they believe they're doing something for the good of the realm, even if they're not, then the ritual would go ahead as planned."

Rebecca nodded. "They just have to believe that they're . . . ." Her hand shot to her mouth. "Oh, my God, is that what they're doing? Simon's trying to find an artist to make guardians for him."

"But what guardian would ever give up the child of one of their own?" Caitlin asked. "Surely that's insane."

"With enough leverage, be that pain, threats, pleasure, or anything else you can think of, you'd be surprised what people are capable of forcing others to do," I said, feeling a glare from both the ladies. "I never said I'd lived a life of goodness and virtue. Sometimes you have to do bad things to make sure the worse things don't happen."

Everyone was silent for a moment, which was probably my fault. The discussion of torture is a pretty good way to stop a conversation.

"You think my mom is trying a similar tack?" Caitlin asked.

"Have you lost any guardians?" I asked Rebecca. "Any gone missing or no longer around as much anymore?"

Rebecca shook her head.

"Then, yes," I said. "She's hunting people in Stratford for a reason, the same as Simon. So, what the hell is in Stratford that is important enough to try and find not only a guardian there, but also the child of one."

"There can't be any guardians in Stratford?" Rebecca asked. "Not unless they're from another part of the world. There's no realm gate in Maine, outside of the one downstairs."

"You sure?" I asked.

Rebecca looked me right in the eye. "Yes, we would have found it years ago if there were. It would have been used, and the second it's activated, every guardian in here would know about it. I'll say again, there are only the six of us. We work in shifts of three on, three off, and if any of us leave the zone, the others would know about it. Those who are all working on the same realm gate can sense where each of us are."

"Could the realm gate be hidden?" Caitlin asked.

"That would be like trying to hide a jumbo jet on a football field during the Super Bowl. The second it was activated, we'd know about it."

"Are you thinking as a rational person, or as someone who really doesn't want there to be a second gate?" I asked. "Because yours is in a cave; why can't the other one be hidden somewhere out of sight?"

"Technically, it's possible. But realm gates don't just spring up; they've always been there. And the likelihood that no one has ever used it is, like I said, slim to none. Some of the guardians down there have been here centuries. Once you've activated a gate, you can't switch it off. We would all know it had been used, we would feel any gates that were connected to the same realm as ours."

A thought made its way into my head. "You ever heard of a girl by the name of Sally-Ann Beaumont? She was murdered back in seventy-seven."

"I knew a Philip Beaumont," she said. "He was a guardian. He died in a car crash just outside of the zone. If he had been inside, he'd have lived. He used to work for King Whitehorn, but quit when the guard changed. He decided he'd had enough and left the zone to raise a family. After a while, a guardian outside of the realm gate's influence will need to be replaced, if they come back into that area, they'll still have some of their powers, but they'll be greatly diminished. It would have been enough to save him though. It's a real shame. He was a good guy."

"That son-of-a-bitch," I seethed, almost to myself.

"You okay?" Caitlin asked as Rebecca raised an eyebrow in question.

"Yeah, I just need to go make a quick phone call. There's someone I need to shout at for a considerable period of time and then punch in the face the next time I see him."

"You complete and utter fucking idiot," I shouted down the phone, drawing a few curious glances from passers-by.

"Nice to speak to you too, Nate," Roberto said.

"Fuck being nice, you lied to me."

"I'm pretty certain I've never lied to you, but what exactly did I lie about?"

"Sally-Ann."

Roberto paused. "Tread very carefully, Nate. Her father was a good friend of mine, and if you start flinging around any sort of stupid accusations, we may just fall out."

"Her father was a guardian, wasn't he?" Before Roberto could answer, I continued, "One of Galahad's people just confirmed it. That would make Sally-Ann a bit more special than just a college girl in the wrong place at the wrong time."

"I have no idea what you're talking about. Phillip was a doorman, I told you that. He'd done some guard work for the previous king, but had left some time ago. Sally-Ann was murdered and I needed someone to do something about it. If I'd known he was a guardian, I'd have mentioned it. Sally-Ann was in the wrong place at the wrong time."

"Actually, I think she was exactly where she was meant to be. How much do you know about the children of guardians?"

"About as much as anyone else who isn't a guardian. What's your point?"

"Sally-Ann studied art; was she into tattoos?"

"How'd you know that? She was training as an apprentice. Her grandparents didn't approve, but she loved it. She was going to wait until she'd graduated before getting her first tattoo; she was really looking forward to it."

"Well the lack of tattoos got her killed," I said. "Or at least killed quicker." Pieces started to fall into place as I spoke to Roberto. Simon was looking for guardians to try and find the tattooists that did the work. Sally-Ann, as the daughter of a guardian, was the only person who could have been doing it. Which meant she was on her way to Stratford for a reason before she got grabbed.

"Simon was searching for guardians in the town," I continued. "Which means he knew that at least one lived there. He had no idea that Sally-Ann, the child of a guardian and a tattooist, was on her way there to meet friends. And even less of an idea that she was the very person he was looking for."

"Oh, shit," Roberto said. "So, if I'd known that Sally-Ann was the daughter of a guardian, it would have helped?"

I might have thought that I would have known what I was looking for. I would have been able to ask Galahad for information on guardians. I may have even been able to stop anyone else dying. But I didn't want to make it worse for Roberto. He genuinely hadn't known about Sally-Ann or her father. So, instead, I said, "No, probably not."

"So," Roberto said, his voice betraying the guilt he felt at not knowing important information. "You think Sally-Ann was going to Stratford to tattoo someone, why?"

"I can't tell you," I said. "I promised a guardian that I wouldn't reveal their secrets. All you need to know is that it looks like she was tattooing people. When Simon grabbed her, he had actually grabbed the very person he was after. He was just too impatient to find out."

Roberto sighed. "That doesn't make me feel any better, Nate."

"Wasn't meant to, but it does mean that Sally-Ann either knew that guardians were in Stratford or she was making some. I'm going with both."

"Why?"

"Well, Simon knew that guardians were there; he's not the type of person to go to all that effort for a hunch. If Sally-Ann was making more, then she must have known that some already exist. Simon's goons grabbed her, Simon thought they'd fucked up and killed her to cover his tracks. But in reality, they'd grabbed the right person. Simon was just insistent on those taken having tattoos."

"So, where do you go from here?"

"Stratford. Someone there knows something. I plan on finding who that is."

"Keep me in touch. And for what it's worth, I'm sorry I didn't know more."

"Thanks, I'll keep you informed. And for what it's worth, I shouldn't have accused you of withholding information." I hung up, feeling crappy. The fact of the matter was that I fucked up. I got so caught up in getting Simon back in '77 that I never asked myself who would want a young girl killed. I never checked into her background. I focused on my anger at the situation and not at trying to solve her murder. I owed Sally-Ann some long overdue justice, and I aimed to deliver on that.

I turned to walk back into the bar, when my phone rang.

"Fucking hell, Nate, you been hiding under a rock?" Sky asked, her voice high and full of energy.

"Have you been drinking far too much Red Bull?"

"Shut up, smart ass. I found something you need to hear. You know those victims who got away from Simon and his insane idea of house guests?"

"I vaguely remember, yeah."

"What did I just say about being a smart ass?"

"Okay, fine, you made your point, what about the survivors?"

"Well, I could find nearly all of them, except two. Greg and Fern. They're not anywhere after '82."

"Did they die?"

"More re-born. Glen is now Father Patterson; he's the town priest."

"And Fern?"

"She still vanished, but I managed to dig up something interesting. Her father was a guardian from back west."

"So, Simon killed one artist, but had another in his fucking basement. Another day or so and he'd have gotten everything he wanted." I told her about what had happened with Galahad, Shadow Falls, and the guardians.

"Well, then maybe Glen can help," Sky said, full of enthusiasm. "Priests know everyone in a town, or at least know all the rumors. And if Fern is alive and well, she's someone Karl and his friends are going to want to find, because it didn't take long for me to track down her parentage. So it won't take them long either."

"It's a start."

"Yeah, well maybe you can get your new FBI friend to help talk to him. Someone in that town knows something; you just need to shake some trees. And if there's one thing Maine isn't short of, it's trees."

CHAPTER 31

The trip didn't take long, especially considering our speed. Caitlin tried to appear very calm and collected, but occasionally flinched when I took a corner faster than she would have liked.

I'd told both her and Rebecca about the priest and Caitlin had immediately called the precinct and asked for a confirmation of Glen's location. It took half an hour until we'd received a call back from one of the officers who'd been sent to the church, but we were already on the way by then, and I think Caitlin was grateful for something to take her mind off my driving.

I slowed down once we reached Stratford and pulled up outside the church. The building was in the center of the town. It was a sizeable structure with stained glass windows and a small, well-kept garden out front. An unmanned police cruiser was parked nearby, which automatically made me pause. Had Patricia and her insane friends gotten to the priest first? All I could do was hope not and walk toward the church with Caitlin, who had also noticed the car and drawn her gun.

The door was open and as we crept inside, walking past the empty pews and pulpit, I heard voices coming from the chamber beyond. We wasted no time in rushing in, only to find Glen—Father Patterson—sitting behind a desk and talking to two uniformed officers who were drinking cups of coffee and eating biscuits.

"Ummm," I managed as Caitlin hastily put away her gun and pretended it was never there in the first place.

The two cops almost launched themselves out of their chairs, but managed not to spill their coffee all over the nice rug.

"Ma'am," the younger of the two said, his cheeks red from shame.

"You're the two who arrested me back outside the house," I said.

"Oh, yes, you," the same cop said, his shame turning to anger, presumably because he'd been caught while I was there.

"Give it a rest," the older of the two policemen said and offered me his hand. "Danny," he said as we shook.

"Nice to meet you," I told him.

"The young streak of piss," Danny said, "is called Edward." He then quickly turned to Glen. "Excuse me, Father." Glen just smiled.

"Why are you both here?" Caitlin asked.

"We were told to come check out Father Patterson. We found him in here, he offered us some coffee until you arrived."

"It's good to see you again, Nathan," Father Patterson said with a deep smile.

"You too, Father, it's been far too long. I think we need to have a chat about old times and catch up."

"You two know each other?" Edward asked. "That's weird."

"I wasn't always a priest," Father Patterson said.

While his hair was now long and gray, and his beard was fuller, the man behind it had a face that had hardly aged, since I'd last seen him in '77. Something had definitely happened to him, and I was going to find out what. But having two cops, human or otherwise, hanging around wasn't going to make that easy.

"Can you excuse us for a moment?" Father Patterson asked the two officers, completely blowing my theory out of the water.

They both nodded and left the room, taking their coffee with them. Edward kept a close eye on me as he closed the door on his way out.

"He really doesn't like me," I said, mostly to myself.

"He's nervous of you," Father Patterson said. "You were arrested and now you're working with Agent Moore. He wants to know why."

"Did he tell you that?" Caitlin asked.

Father Patterson nodded. "People can tell me things that maybe they'd have trouble telling others. It's one of the main benefits of my position in the town."

"Hearing gossip?" I asked.

Father Patterson chuckled. "No, although that does happen fairly regularly. Some people seem to think that I am here to tell rumors to. But I meant helping people. Being here to listen and not judge." He stood and walked out of a nearby door, where I heard a click and then the bubbling of a kettle.

"Do either of you want a drink?" he asked as he popped his head back around the door.

"No, thanks, Glen," I said. "We need to talk."

Father Patterson sat back behind his desk. "I never had the chance to thank you for all you did for me and many others that night. You saved a lot of lives."

"I'm just sorry I couldn't save more."

Father Patterson nodded sadly. "I assume you have a few questions for me regarding what happened since we last met."

"You've only aged about ten years," I said. "You feel like telling me how?"

"You saved my life, so I guess that gives you some leeway with my trust. But how do I know you're not a different man?"

"You don't. Except, I'm trying to stop people from getting hurt. I hope you see that. I hope you realize that I have no interest in jeopardizing the life you have here. But others won't care. And they're coming for you. And for Fern too, if she's around."

"I'm a guardian," he said without hesitation before turning around and adjusting his top to show us the tattoo. "And Fern is safe."

"Are you the only guardian here?" I asked.

Father Patterson nodded.

"You're aware that these people Nate mentioned, that they're dangerous and they're looking for you?" Caitlin said.

"Yes, I'm aware. The three hikers who were found in the woods were friends of mine. They aided Fern and me in staying safe. Those who committed the act are trying to find the child of a guardian. They want someone to be turned into a guardian so that they can pass through the gate into Shadow Falls."

"How do you know that?" I asked.

"The guardian who died figured it out, he left me a voice message before they killed him. Told me to stay hidden and not to trust anyone new in town."

"So, why haven't you taken his advice?"

"Because they don't know that I'm a guardian. It's not something I run around telling people. Besides I'm safer here than anywhere else."

"There's a second gate, isn't there?" I said.

"What?" Caitlin almost shouted. "Rebecca said it wasn't possible for a second gate to exist and the guardians in Portland not know about it."

"It's never been activated," Father Patterson told us. "But the guardians have always been here to keep it safe."

"You're close to the realm gate," I said. "That's why you haven't run, because they can't really do much to you."

"We need to get Fern away," Caitlin said. "You might be invulnerable here, but I'm betting she's not."

"Like I said, Fern is safe," he said softly. "I'm sorry, but telling you more would put that person in even greater danger."

"Okay, can you answer this then?" I asked. "You knew what Simon was after, back then, didn't you?"

Father Patterson sighed. "This gate, it's a secret. It was discovered a thousand years ago, just after Shadow Falls was settled. It was decided that a group of guardians would stay here at all time, but that the gate must never be used except in an emergency. Over the years, those in charge of Shadow Falls forgot about the gate, but the guardians never did. They all swore an oath to keep the gate secret from everyone, until the king came asking for its use. Simon discovered it somehow and knew it was the best way to get back into Shadow Falls.

"Sally-Ann was coming to Stratford to see me and Fern. We all knew about the guardians, but nearly all of the people Simon took were human, with no affiliation with realm gates or guardians. They were just unlucky enough to have tattoos and get spotted by one of his thugs. Four of the victims were guardians; that's why they were taken beyond the realm gates' influence. We assumed that Simon was killing guardians to make them tell him where the gate was and then force them to open it for him. We were wrong."

Father Patterson rubbed his closed eyes and leaned back in his chair. "He was after their children, one who would create a new guardian of his choice. But Sally-Ann never made it in time. Sally-Ann was the child of a guardian and had performed the ritual a few times during the previous year. So, we reached out to her and arranged for her to come and turn me into a guardian, hopefully bolstering their numbers enough that they could protect the gate. We figured that if we had all six guardians again, that it didn't matter what Simon did, he couldn't make more. That would keep any artists safe from his clutches."

"What happened after?" I asked. "When Simon was caught."

"I managed to convince Fern to participate in the ritual before completing my tattoo."

That's why they're killing the old survivors," Caitlin said. "They were told to find another artist and figured that they'd start with the people Simon originally picked up. When they didn't get anything, they started searching in Stratford again."

"So, where is the second realm gate?" I asked.

"I can't tell you. I'm sorry, but like I said if you know and anyone takes hold of you, they could tear that information from you. It would threaten everyone."

"Okay, so what are we meant to do, Glen?" I asked. "We can't let you stay here, it isn't safe. So, we either turn this place into the Alamo, or we get out of here and hide."

"I won't see violence done here," Father Patterson said.

"As nice as that sentiment is, I doubt very much the people after you give a shit where you are."

Father Patterson looked to Caitlin for support.

"Sorry, Father, but Nate's right. They'll come through here whether you want this place to see violence, or not. We need to get you somewhere."

"And where would that be? There is nowhere safer than this that I can go."

"Once they realize that you're a guardian, they'll come for you," I told him. "They'll try to get out of you who the tattooist is. Your best option is to leave the state, get as far away as possible. Hell, leave the country. It's the only way to be sure."

"I won't run from these people, Nathan. I'm not a coward."

"It's not cowardly, it's survival. Let's say they figure out where the gate is, they can torture you for years if they feel like it. You can't die in this place, but that's not going to stop them inflicting pain on you. To them it'll be like Christmas came early. I don't think you understand how bad that could be."

Father Patterson's eyes turned hard. "They held me once, don't tell me how bad it'll be."

"That'll be nothing compared to what they can do to a person who can't die. You still feel pain, they could parade people in front of you and execute them just to watch you cry." I felt bad for telling him that, but he needed to understand the mindset of the people he was dealing with.

"I will not run from these people," he stated again.

There was a commotion outside of the office and Caitlin left the room to find out what was happening.

"Glen, where's Fern?" I asked when we were alone.

"Hidden. I won't take you to her."

"Nate," Caitlin said as she opened the door. "We have a serious problem."

I left the office and followed Caitlin toward some windows at the front of the church.

It had gotten dark since we'd arrived, but the lights on the front lawn illuminated seven people, all of them watching the church with evil intent.

"Well, that's fucking shit," I said to Caitlin as I noticed that Patricia and her people had used their truck and mini-van to block both the Audi and the squad car.

"It took me a while to stop Edward from going out there to arrest everyone."

"Yeah, he probably wants to not do that," I said and continued to study the group outside.

Patricia and Joshua stood side-by-side, next to the crazy woman who'd blown me up, along with the man who'd held Caitlin during our first encounter with her mother back in Washington. I had no idea who the other three were, but I doubted I needed a first-hand account to know they were dangerous.

"Well, it looks like leaving is no longer an option," Father Patterson said as he joined us.

"Oh, no we're still going to leave," I said. "I just need a new way of doing it. I assume there are no other exits?"

"There's another exit at the side of the building, but going out that way would only put us in sight of the very people we want to avoid."

"Can't we just arrest them?" Edward asked. "I don't understand what's happening."

"I'd like to second that last feeling," Danny agreed.

"Okay, short version. Very bad people out there have us outnumbered. Leaving the church without a plan will result in death. They've blocked in the cars too, so we need to figure a way out without using them. Any ideas?"

"I have my truck," Father Patterson said. "It's parked out back. It's easily big enough for us all."

"So, we run for it?" Danny said.

"Those people will be waiting for it. They're faster than us and a lot more dangerous as a group. They could have disabled the truck too. So, first thing is to figure out if the truck is disabled. And that means someone going outside."

"You feel like telling everyone how?" Caitlin asked, the nerves in her voice easy for everyone to hear.

"I need to check something first," I said and turned to Father Patterson. "Can to take me to a window upstairs that overlooks the car?"

Father Patterson nodded and took me through the church and up a set of stairs to a hallway. At one end, a large window overlooked the graveyard behind the church. I spotted the two men pacing up and down in the shadows without much effort.

"Okay, this is going to be slightly more difficult than I'd expected," I told Glen. "If Fern is on the property, go get her and anyone else here and get them downstairs."

Father Patterson nodded and ran off toward the opposite end of the hallway, knocking once on a door and then vanishing inside the room, while I continued to watch the truck. I saw no signs of disturbance, although that didn't mean anything conclusive; it was slightly more heartening than seeing a giant hole in the truck's bonnet.

I stood up to walk away and noticed the runes on the windowsill. They were old, but as I touched them, I felt the power they contained.

Father Patterson returned with Fern, who looked much older than the last time I'd seen her, but still had the fire in her eyes that I remembered.

"What do the runes do?" I asked as we walked away from the window.

"Keeps people out," Father Patterson said. "They were put on the property well before I moved in. Someone tried to break in about three years ago, they threw a rock at the window, which blew back with enough force to take the would-be thief off his feet and knock him out cold."

"It's good to know they work," I said.

"What happens if I use my alchemy to move the church wall to give us some cover to the truck?"

"No one knows until you try," I said. "But either nothing, or we'll be buried under several tons of church."

"So, runes make alchemy not work?"

I shook my head. "No, it still works, but if you start moving around what the rune's attached to, even if you don't touch the rune, it may have a failsafe and they tend to be big and messy."

"Okay, so alchemy is out," Caitlin said, slightly annoyed. "Hi Fern, how're you?"

"Too old for the continuous crap that I have to go through because of Simon and his evil friends."

"Well, let's see if we can make sure this is the last time," I said.

"I've heard that before," Fern said as we rejoined everyone else. "It never seems to last very long before someone dies."

"You have something we want," shouted Patricia from outside.

I opened the window slightly so I didn't have to start shouting myself. "Fuck off," I said, retaining my winning streak on witty comebacks.

"If we have to, we will come in and get you," Joshua bellowed.

"No," I said. "You won't. The runes on this place would bounce you out of the state. You're gonna sit right there, and we're gonna sit right here. I hope you're comfy."

"Nate's right," Father Patterson said. "While those runes hold, we're safe. So long as they don't try to break through the walls or something."

"Can someone tell me what the hell a rune is?" Danny asked.

"Magic writing," I said. "It's complicated. Basically we're safe so long as we stay in here."

That appeared to mollify Danny, as he went back to glancing out of the window on the opposite side of the door, while I walked off to talk to the others.

"Are we really safe in here?" Caitlin asked.

"For now, yeah. Though I don't like the idea of staying here too long. They're going to get impatient and do something stupid at some point. And stupid things get people killed."

"Oh fucking hell," Danny said to me and Caitlin. "You need to see this."

I walked back over to the window and looked out as four people were led out of the back of the mini-van and forced to kneel on the ground. Each of them had their hands tied behind their backs and wore a hood to conceal their faces.

Bianca removed the first hood, revealing a young brunette, with a bloody nose. The woman glanced to those beside her, but was shoved roughly to the ground as the second person's hood was removed. It revealed a man who was bleeding from the nose, like the woman, although he also had a swollen eye and a nasty cut on his cheek. He glanced down at the woman as the third hood was removed.

There was a sharp intake of breath next to me as a young boy, no older than ten, was shoved to the ground.

"Don't you touch him," the man said, trying to get back to his feet, but it was a short-lived effort as he was quickly punched in the jaw, snapping his head around viciously. He collapsed to the ground as the boy cried out for his father and both Joshua and Bianca laughed.

"Caitlin," I said softly, trying not to show the rage that was building up inside me.

"I know, Nate." Her tone was soft, resigned to what needed to be done. "He's not my brother now. He's just a wild animal that needs stopping."

"So long as we understand each other," I told her as Patricia removed the final person's hood with a flourish, exposing the battered and bloody face of Norman Moore, Caitlin's father.

"Come say hi to Daddy," Patricia taunted.

"Dad," Caitlin whispered. "Don't you hurt him," she shouted out. "He's done nothing to you."

"He's done everything," Patricia snapped. "He had an affair, he didn't stop you from becoming a pig. You should have joined me in my fight. You should have been by my side, not holed up in some shitty church, cowering at my words. This man, this useless fucking bag of flesh turned you against me. We had to kill a few guards to get to him, we lost two of our own doing it." She kicked Norman in the stomach, knocking him to the ground, where she continued her assault.

"Stop it," Caitlin cried out, tears in her eyes. "Please, stop it."

The man, woman, and young boy had been left alone long enough to huddle together in a vain attempt at safety. Patricia glanced over at them and motioned toward Joshua, who grabbed the boy and dragged him away by his hair, head-butting the father who tried to stop him.

"Should I hurt this one?" Patricia said. Her hand had transformed into one of a werelion, her nails now razor sharp claws. She held one against the boy's neck. "Should I take this one's life? Or should I make him watch as his family dies?"

"Stop," Caitlin called out. "What do you want?"

"The guardian. Send him out and everyone goes free. He's all we're here for. You have ten minutes."

"I'll go," Father Patterson said immediately.

I stood in his way and placed a hand against his chest as he walked toward the door. "No, you go out there and everyone dies. They'll make you watch as they kill the boy and his family. I know this feels wrong, to do nothing, but the second you step out there, a lot more people die."

"Do you have a plan?" he asked.

I turned back to the window and watched as the boy was thrown back toward his parents.

The werelion who had held Caitlin in Washington dragged Norman roughly to his feet, which Norman countered by head-butting the younger man with everything he had. The werelion took a step back, touched his now bloody nose, and then tore out Norman's throat, shoving Caitlin's dying father down onto the ground, where he remained motionless.

Caitlin's face became a mask of shock and horror as I walked to the church's front door and opened it, stepping outside before anyone could stop me.

"Ah, the sorcerer," Patricia said. "I don't think you'll find it as easy to throw me around this time."

"When you see him, say hello to your husband for me," I told Patricia, who appeared confused right up until the moment the blast of air knocked both Joshua and Bianca off their feet. They flew back into the two werelions whose names I hadn't bothered to learn. It wouldn't matter; I would make sure they were dead before long.

All four of them fell backward awkwardly as a second blast of air took Patricia's legs out from under her, planting her face first on the concrete path.

The werelion who had murdered Norman ran past the hostages right at me, turning into his werebeast form as he moved. I ran forward, driving two blades of white-hot fire into his chest. "Into the church," I told the family, who didn't need a second invitation and sprinted past me, as the werelion struggled to breathe with two punctured lungs.

Once I heard the sound of the door slamming shut, I ended the werelion's problem by tearing the blades out of him, cutting him in half and covering everything around him, including me, in red gore.

Patricia got back to her feet and told the two nameless werelions to kill me, as she dragged Joshua and Bianca away, escaping in the mini-van.

The two lions charged together. I sidestepped one and drove a blade of fire into his thigh, removing his leg in one swipe, and then decapitating him before he touched the ground. The second lion grabbed hold of me, lifting me off my feet, and drove me back.

I twisted in his iron grip, smashing my forearm into his nose over and over again, until his strength waned and he released me. "Where are they hiding?" I asked.

He said something that I could barely understand, so I repeated the question.

"Go to hell, you piece of—"

I cut his throat before he'd finished, removing a three-inch silver pendant from his neck and driving it into his ear. He died before he hit the ground, leaving me surrounded by, and covered in, blood and gore, while my anger burned brightly inside me.

"We need to go," I said as the two werelions who had been patrolling the rear of the church ran around the corner and saw me covered in the remains of their friends. A second later, and they too were running off, a problem for another day.

The church door opened and Caitlin stepped outside. "You need to get changed."

"No time," I said. "Get everyone into the truck and let's go."

"Nate," she said and touched me on the chest getting blood on her fingers. "There's a frightened boy in there; you going in covered in blood is not going to make that better."

I opened my mouth to say we didn't have time, but she was right. "Get everyone in the truck and go," I said instead. "I'll take my car."

"Where are we going to meet?" Father Patterson asked. "I have clothes upstairs for you. The boy and his family are with Fern in my office. You have time. We're not going without you."

"We could go to the old mall," Edward said before seeing the blood and turning to throw up.

"That's not a bad idea," Caitlin agreed. "There's a lot of open space, and no one in their right mind is going to think that we've run there. It should be enough to hold up while someone goes and informs the Portland guardians. Galahad needs to get here, now."

"Agreed," I said. "I'll go change and then we'll go as one. How is the family holding up?"

"Not great," Fern confirmed as I stepped back inside the church. "They've been through an ordeal."

"We'll drop them off at the police station," I said. "It would be safer for them if their involvement ended here."

"That's probably true of all of us," Danny pointed out.

"Yeah, but we don't have a choice," I told him and went off to get changed and remove the bits of werelion that were on me.

CHAPTER 32

I showered and changed into the clothes that Father Patterson had found for me. They were a little baggy, he was taller than me, but they were better than the blood-soaked ones I'd removed. "We've run them off, but they'll be back."

"Agreed," he said, surprising me. "As Edward suggested, the mall is the safest destination for us. That would also take us far away from the realm gate."

"Even better," I said. "I know you'll no longer be invulnerable, but at least that gives us some space until reinforcements can arrive." I glanced around the room. "Where's Caitlin?"

"Outside," Fern said.

I left the church and avoided the remains of the three werelions on my way to Caitlin, who was crouched beside her father, almost oblivious to the blood that saturated the ground and her hands.

"Hey," I said softly.

She glanced up at me, her eyes puffy and tear-filled. "I can't leave him here, like this. He deserves better."

"Yes, you're right. But at this moment, we can't do better. We don't have time to do the right thing. I'm sorry for that."

"I understand," she said. "I'm going to make sure my mom spends eternity in a deep, dark hole."

"I have no doubt you'll get your chance."

"Can you feel my dad's spirit?" she asked. "Can you tell me if he's okay?"

I closed my eyes for the briefest moments and reached out around me, trying to find what I needed. It took less than a second to discover the spirit, Norman Moore's spirit. It was full of rage and hate, but more than that, there was a fire burning inside it.

"He's pretty pissed off," I said while the power I'd absorbed began to course through me.

"He was always the tough guy," Caitlin said, more to herself than me. "Even at the end, he still went down fighting."

As I opened my eyes and completed drawing his spirit into me, I instinctively knew why I could find him and not other spirits. Like Hades had said, it was as if a light switch had been turned on, bathing me in the knowledge that had been absent for so long. The spirits I could use had to have died fighting. And Norman, even in death, was one hell of a fighter.

"They need to go down guns blazing," I said.

"What?"

"The spirits I absorb, with my necromancy, they need to have died fighting."

"You figured it out? Is he okay?"

I shrugged. "I don't know. I know his name, I know details of his life, but I can't tell you how he feels right now beyond the fury at being murdered. I can't communicate with him. I just use the energy that he provides to make myself stronger."

"Use that to stop the people who did this." Caitlin placed a hand against my chest, leaving a bloody handprint on my clean t-shirt when she removed it.

"You feel up to a road trip?" I asked. "The family needs to be taken somewhere safe. And then Galahad needs to be informed about what's happening. You'll have better luck getting Rebecca and company to listen than I probably would."

"Yeah, I need to do something, I can't stay here."

We walked back into the church together, where we were met by the rest of the group.

"Thank you for what you did," the man said. "For saving us."

"We're not safe just yet," I told him. "Caitlin, Agent Moore, is going to take you and your family to the police station. Then she's going to make a call, but she'll stay with you until backup arrives, which will probably be a few hours. You'll be surrounded by cops, but the bigger part of it is you'll be somewhere that those people don't care about."

"They broke into our house," the woman said. "I don't understand why they took us."

"They needed hostages," I told her. "They won't be taking you anywhere, ever again. I swear."

"Five minutes, people," I said to everyone. "Make sure you're all ready to go, because we won't be back here for some time. If you have any weapons, Father, I'd advise you to get them."

He vanished back into his office, returning with a shotgun. "When I heard they were hunting me again, I invested. I've never even used it, but I wasn't about to leave myself or Fern defenseless."

"Good choice," I told him. "You ready?"

He threw the truck keys to Caitlin, which she caught in one hand. "Caitlin, you take the family in the truck, the good Father, Fern, and I will take my Audi, and the officers can take their squad car." We left the church through the front door in one group.

I watched Caitlin and the family walk off around the side of the building, while I made my way toward my car.

"See you soon," I called after Caitlin, who gave me a thumbs up in response. I hoped she was going to be okay, that maybe protecting the innocent people in her care would give her something more to focus on than what had happened to her father.

As I reached my Audi, an almighty roar came from the back of the church.

"What the hell is that?" Danny asked.

"Get in the car, now," I said. "Take Father Patterson and Fern and get them to the mall. Go!" I shouted when no one moved.

I didn't stay around to watch as I sprinted toward the noise, the sounds of the squad car's engine starting behind me.

I ran around the side of the church, just as a cave troll walked into view. It noticed Caitlin and the family, who were just getting into the truck and roared once more.

"Get in and go."

"What are you going to do?" Caitlin shouted.

"Give you time," I snapped. "Get these people safe." I walked past the truck as the engine started.

The troll took a few steps toward me and paused, sniffing the air. It glanced back at me and resumed its slow run, which quickly turned into a juggernaut-like sprint.

The truck reversed and began to drive off, but slammed to a stop when the trees at the side of the church exploded and a wood troll burst out of the tree line and ran towards the cave troll. Recognizing this new danger, the cave troll tried to slow down and turn towards the incoming threat, but the wood troll was far too quick and slammed into its opponent with a deafening crack, taking the larger troll off its feet and dumping it head first through the nearest wall, which exploded outward as the runes became ignited.

The distraction gave me time to sprint to the truck, which had stopped for me at the edge of the church.

"Nate, get in," Caitlin shouted as the cave troll climbed out of the rubble and kicked his assailant back a dozen feet to land in a tangle heap.

"I can't," I said. "The wood troll is going to die if I leave. Go, I'll be fine."

Caitlin didn't need to be told twice and slammed the truck into gear, driving away as quickly as possible.

I ran toward the cave troll, which had grabbed the wood troll by his head and was repeatedly punching him in the face. I unleashed a column of fire at its knee, and the cave troll screamed out in pain, then threw the wood troll towards me. We collided, both of us hitting the ground hard. I managed to roll away and get back to my feet, resting my hand on an old tombstone, as the cave troll continued to yell about his burned leg.

"You okay?" I asked the wood troll, who had finally started to move.

"No," he said softly. "I did not expect the wall to explode onto me. That hurt."

"Thanks for your help."

"Don't mention it," he told me and for the first time I got a look at his face.

"Rean?" I asked. "Is that you?"

"Nathan," he said and spat blood onto the grass. "It's been a long time, but maybe we should leave the reunion until the monster over there is no longer a problem."

"Sure, do you have a plan?"

"No, I was hoping you did."

"Excellent, this should be fun then."

The cave troll roared once again and stalked toward us, ignoring the tombstones in its way as it crushed anything that could have been considered an obstacle.

"Ready when you are," I said and darted forward, throwing balls of flame at the troll, which didn't hurt it badly, but it did take its attention away from Rean, who got close enough to it to punch it in the jaw.

The troll's head snapped around and it staggered back a few paces, but didn't fall. It struck out with an open hand, catching Rean in the chest and sending him flying. I used the opportunity to blast air at its legs in the hope that I might topple the beast, but it did nothing more than piss it off. It charged at me, and I tried to avoid it, but it grabbed my leg and flung me back toward the nearest tombstone. I managed to put up a shield of air in time, but the dust that covered me after was enough to blind me for a few seconds.

The cave troll didn't wait to take advantage, and while I was momentarily blinded, it grabbed me by the neck and lifted me above the ground, slamming me back down time and time again. Any air in my lungs vanished after the second impact and my vision began to go dark at the edges. I lost count of how many times I was used as a hammer and lashed out instinctively, throwing a continuous torrent of white-hot flame into its face. The troll roared in pain and anger, and threw me once more.

I didn't have time to use any magic to stop myself from crashing through the church wall, my body screaming as I hit the floor and bounced, slamming into several pews and coming to rest a few dozen feet away from the gap in the wall.

I groaned in pain, my ribs and back on fire with pain. I desperately wanted to use my Blood magic, to help heal myself, but that was no longer an option. I'd only used my necromancy to heal myself once before and that was under much easier circumstances, but if I couldn't heal, I couldn't fight effectively. Which would mean that the cave troll would kill me and Rean. And that was an unacceptable outcome.

With a deep sigh, I channeled my necromancy to feed my healing ability, using the energy from Norman's spirit to knit my broken bones back together. It hurt like a son-of-a-bitch, but once it was done, I felt like a new man. I got back to my feet as the sounds of battle outside carried into the church. I ran toward the hole and jumped back outside. The cave troll was clearly winning the battle, but Rean, despite the blood that was pouring down his face, refused to give up.

The cave troll noticed me and roared once again.

"Go fuck yourself," I said and charged toward the monster, ducking at the last moment and using a blast of air to push me past him. I turned my hands and with another blast of air, propelled myself into the air, behind the troll, whose attention was refocused on Rean. As I fell, I created a blade of fire, with the aim to drive it into the back of the troll's neck, killing it. Unfortunately, the troll moved his head aside at the last moment, and the blade caught the side of its face, removing a large portion of its bottom jaw in one motion.

I hit the ground with a roll and scrambled away, while the troll went insane, tearing up tombstones and flinging them in all directions.

"I think you may have made him angry," Rean said, although his words were slightly slurred, due to some damage to his face.

"I think I know how to end this," I told him. "But you need to get inside the church."

"I'm not leaving you to fight it alone."

"You can come fight it once I'm done, I just need space. I haven't exactly tried this before."

The cave troll flung a large piece of rock in our direction, which we easily avoided, but told Rean to hurry. The cave troll would remember who hurt it soon enough. Once Rean was safely inside the church, I placed one hand on a tombstone and concentrated, allowing my air magic to flow out of me into a large sphere.

As it increased in size, the circle of air picked up pieces of debris and furiously whipped them around me. The longer I kept this up, the more and more necromancy I had to channel. When the circle hit ten feet in diameter, my vision began to darken and pain began to rack my arms and chest. In the past, without the necromancy, I'd managed to create a sphere only about 4 feet in diameter, and a wind speed nowhere near as intense as this one.

I kept my concentration up, even as my hands began to slip from the tops of the tombstones and my body felt like it was being crushed under its own weight. The magic I was expelling was more than my body was accustomed to using, and the longer I kept the spinning up, the stronger it became and the more dangerous it was to me.

"Hey," I called out, my voice puncturing through the maelstrom. It was loud enough to reach the troll, who immediately turned in my direction, murderous intent in its eyes. "Come get me, you big sack of shit."

The cave troll didn't need to be told twice and bounded toward me at a terrifying pace. When it was close enough,

I unleashed the debris-filled sphere. The troll was ripped off its feet and thrown through the air as if it were shot out of a cannon. It connected with a statue twenty feet away and tried to move, but all of the rock and junk that had been carried along with it, suddenly reached its target. It was as if a hundred objects, all moving at the speed of a cannon ball, hit a target a few feet wide. They tore huge chunks out of the troll, covering both it and the surrounding ground in thick blood.

I tried to stand, but my body was drained, my necromancy depleted, and I fell forward with only the tombstone to keep me from collapsing onto the ground in what would have been the least heroic end to a fight ever.

I took deep breaths as Rean walked over to the motionless cave troll and plunged the steel, four-foot-long church windcock into the back of its neck, killing it instantly.

I tried to stand again, but Rean caught me as I slumped forward. "You okay?" he asked.

I nodded. "Never used that much necromancy at one time. It sort of took it out of me. My magic says I should be fine, but my spirit is exhausted. I don't think I'm quite used to it, yet." I glanced behind Rean. "The big bad troll dead?"

He nodded. "You're lucky I spotted the big bastard and decided to track it."

"I'd have been okay without you," I said. "Probably."

Rean laughed, I got the feeling it wasn't something he did much of. "It's good to see you again. I never apologized for how it was left last time."

"I'm sorry about your family. If I'd known...."

"You have nothing to be sorry for. Galahad has atoned for his mistake, and while we will never be friends, I can forgive him."

"That's very big of you," I said and allowed Rean to help me upright.

"Yes, I thought so too. I left my colony soon after; I've been living alone since."

"Why?"

"Because I needed time away from every reminder of what I'd lost. And by the time I'd grieved, it was apparent that I was no longer the troll I used to be, and certainly no longer the troll my colony needed. So, I live out here, helping people who need it. When I came across those werelions killing three hikers, I managed to scare them off with a few well-placed throws from some boulders, but I couldn't save the men."

"Well, I for one thank you for saving my incredibly lucky ass."

Rean placed one arm around me and helped me stay upright. "You can just owe—" he started to say, but suddenly he fell back, his arm dragging me down to the ground.

"Rean," I shouted. "Rean, you okay?" I managed to get to a kneeling position and saw the hole from a bullet wound in his chest.

I glanced around, trying to figure out where we could hide, and I noticed Edward and Danny making their way toward me. Danny appeared to be limping. Something must have happened, there was no way they could have made it to the mall and back in the time it took the cave troll to die.

"Sniper," I almost shouted, but they either couldn't hear me or weren't listening. I couldn't use my magic to protect them—I was still too weak.

They got close enough for me to see Danny's mouth was sewn shut, and I knew that we'd been betrayed. Edward winked at me, pulled out a gun and put a bullet in the back of his partner's head, removing a good chunk of his skull as it exited.

I was horrified at what had happened, but before I could say or do anything, Edward smiled at me and said, "Made you look."

I turned around only to be caught in the jaw with a punch from Joshua that sent me unconscious to the ground.

CHAPTER 33

I woke up with my arms above me tied at the wrists, with some sort of metallic pole keeping me high enough off the floor that my feet didn't touch it. I managed to open my eyes, although they hurt, and found that I was also blindfolded. That was probably not good.

"Rean," I shouted. I didn't really care who knew I was awake; if my captives came in they'd more than likely remove the blindfold, so at least my predicament would improve. But instead, there was only silence.

I stayed motionless for exactly 481 seconds; when you're blindfolded and unsure where you are, counting the seconds is a good way to keep your brain active and not allow yourself to start imagining the worst. After that a nearby door opened and I heard the unmistakable sound of high-heeled shoes walking toward me across a hard floor.

The blindfold was removed a few seconds later, after my captor had traced her fingers up and down my bare chest and stomach. I blinked to make my eyes adjust and noticed that I was, one again, inside the House of Silent Screams. Although this time, I was held in one of the upstairs rooms. Bianca stood before me, next to a pool of old dried blood that had stained the bare wooden floorboards.

"You should really give the place a clean," I said. "It's fucking depressing in here."

Bianca punched me in the stomach so hard that I thought my spine would snap.

"Now behave," she said. "What do you think of the silver-plated tube?"

I glanced up and saw that my hands were bound to either side of a circular tube that ran the length of the room, attached to each end with what appeared to be a dozen screws.

"You made yourself a torture chamber," I said. "How enterprising."

"I'm going to keep you here as my new pet," she said with glee. "I assure you, it'll be fun. And then you'll die, as all my pets do. Normally Joshua gets jealous and tears their head off, but for that brief moment, I get to enjoy myself. We'll start with the name tags."

A horrific image flashed through my mind. "You're going to carve my name into my chest, aren't you?"

"Oh, you know this game; that'll take a lot of fun out of it, but I can live with that. Normally those I keep here think it's okay, then I show them the knives and they start crying. You can start crying whenever you like."

"I'm not going to cry, Bianca. I'm going to be ever so quiet."

She punched me in my thigh, making my leg go dead. "Now, that's not nice. It's no fun if you're quiet. One man screamed so much, I had to tear his tongue out, just to shut him up. I lost interest soon after and told Joshua that I'd fucked my pet while he hung from this ceiling. I'm not sure what Joshua did, but I know it made the pet scream ... well as much as he could."

"I'm going to get free, I'm going to kill you. And when I'm done, and you and your boyfriend are remains under my feet, I'm going to burn this fucking house to the ground."

I tensed for another punch, but instead she started to laugh. "You're handcuffed, with silver, to a pipe that you can't get free from. Your hands are positioned in such a way, that if you use magic you'll only give me enough time to gut you like a fish. I like fish ... I like to play with it once I've sliced it open. It's fun. I wonder, would I enjoy it so much if I played with your entrails?"

She picked up a knife from a tray that had been hidden behind me and drew the silver blade across my stomach, just enough to draw blood and cause me to tense up with pain.

"Oh, you didn't yell. What did I tell you about the yelling?" She pushed the knife into my stomach, only about an inch, but it was enough to make me yell out. "That's much better," she said and clasped her hands together before licking the knife clean of my blood.

"Glad I could help."

"You taste good," she eventually said after staring at me for several seconds. "Maybe you'll last longer than the others and I can taste you every night."

"Are you done already?"

Bianca's smile was part sweet and part crazy lunatic, but her eyes were all the latter. She walked over and grabbed the back of my head, forcing it forward until our mouths touched. Her kiss was full of animal need, and for a second I thought she was going to try and bite my lip off, but she pulled back and sighed. "More," she said and kissed me again.

She used her hands, one on either side of my head to hold me in place. I ignored the pain in my arms and wrapped tendrils of air around her, keeping her against me as I increased the temperature of the breath inside my lungs until it was super-heated. I snapped the tendrils closed in one quick motion, making her unable to move as I breathed the heated air into her body, causing her to scream in agony against my mouth.

When the use of magic became too much, I pushed her away and she collapsed onto the floor. I shuffled along the tube until I was against the far wall and pushed up with everything I had, tearing the pipes out of the wall with an almighty shriek.

Bianca crawled away from me as I walked over and searched for the key to the silver cuffs. Once they were off, I tossed them out of the window behind me and rubbed my slightly burned wrists.

"How?" she managed, her body's healing ability already working to fix the massive damage I'd done to her throat and lungs.

"Sorcerers don't have to use their hands to create magic, it's just easier that way." A quick flick from a whip of fire removed her head from her shoulders.

I left the torture chamber and made my way down the staircase, walking slowly to keep an ear out for anyone who might want to ambush me on the way. Instead, I was left alone and soon found myself outside of the basement door, opening it slightly to the sounds of someone whistling.

I stepped inside the basement and closed the door with barely a click, but it was enough to gain the attention of Edward, who was hunched over a prone Rean. "Hello, Nathan," Edward said and stepped aside to show the machete he held against Rean's throat.

"You're human," I said, taking every effort not to use my magic to crush his body like a bread stick. "You're helping these murderers, why?"

"I wish to see the glory of Karl Steiner take his rightful place."

"Steiner? You're not working for Charles Whitehorn?"

"No, of course not. Charles doesn't want to retake Shadow Falls. He's more interested in his power in this realm. No, Charles just wants the crystals. Karl will be given Shadow Falls as his gift for years of service."

"Why do you even care? What did they offer you, money?"

"My father served Karl when he worked for Galahad. When Karl was banished, my father took his own life. But before then he made me promise that I would aid Karl in any way I could. If that meant working with these ... feral beasts, then so be it. Once the throne has been regained, we'll execute them and I can take my place in King Steiner's inner circle, as my father wanted. It's unfortunate, we had to accept some of the ... lesser members of society, people whose love of inflicting pain and damage on people far outweighed their ability to have any sort of respectable IQ."

"You're a fucking idiot who betrayed and murdered his friends. Where's Caitlin, Fern, and the family?"

"I have no idea about the agent, nor the family she took with her. Fern is enjoying my lord's hospitality."

"Where are they?" I took a step closer.

Edward pointed at the machete. "If you come closer, I will kill him."

"How do I know Rean's still alive?"

Edward poked the wood troll with his fingertip and Rean moaned slightly. "Looks like there's some life in him yet. I'm surprised that bullet Patricia put in him didn't finish the job. I don't see why you care though."

"His condition will determine how long I'm going to take to kill you."

Edward laughed. "Really? I can see the knife wound still hasn't healed. Did Bianca do that? How do you think you're going to beat me without your friend dying too?"

A smirk spread across my lips. "Do you guys all share the same threats? Do you write them down to use later? Bianca told me she was going to make me cry and beg. Now she's a good foot shorter than when she woke up this morning."

"Bianca was insane," Edward said and glanced over at Rean. "His wounds will kill him without intervention. The cuts are deep and many. I was going to drain his blood like a pig and send his corpse to my king as a gift. I guess once you're dead, I'll be spoilt for choice. There is nothing you can do—"

I blasted him in the chest with a jet of air, making sure to knock the blade away from my friend, which clattered to the floor several feet away from Edward, who was sprawled on his back.

I walked over and grabbed his shirt, dragging him upright. I head-butted him, destroying his nose. He dropped to the ground as blood streamed down onto his shirt.

"Don't say that," I told him. "I'll take it as a personal challenge, and believe me there's a shitload I can do to you to make you talk. Where is Fern?"

"Fern is back at the church," he said.

I smashed my knee into his face, ruining whatever wasn't already covered in blood. "You are a weasel-like piece of shit, but I don't have time to correct your behavior. Is there anyone else in the house?"

Edward's eyes had trouble focusing on me, so I pulled him upright again and slapped him. Hard. "No, all alone now."

I slapped him again, knocking out a tooth. "You really shouldn't have involved yourself with all of this. It wasn't your fight, and if you'd stayed out of it, you wouldn't be a problem I have to deal with."

"I am ready to die and be taken to heaven a martyr and hero to those who stand by my king."

I shook my head sadly. "You're going to die alone and no one will mourn you. Your name will vanish from the lips of everyone you knew or thought was interested in what happened to you. And soon, you'll barely register as a memory. All because you picked the wrong side." I plunged a blade of fire into Edward's heart, killing him instantly. "What a fucking waste," I said to myself as his body crumpled to the ground.

I wanted nothing more than to lie on the ground and let my injuries heal. My ribs were more than enough to slow me down, but I ignored it as best I could and went to Rean.

He heard me walk toward him and opened one eye; the other was swollen shut. "Nathan," he said weakly. "Is he dead?"

"Edward? Yeah. He won't be hurting anyone else ever again. Bianca's dead too."

"So much death, and now mine to follow."

"Whoa, don't talk like that. You'll be fine." I knew he wouldn't, the blood loss was too much and the wounds too deep. I was amazed he'd lasted as long as he had, but something inside me screamed I should have hope. It was enough to cling onto.

"We both know I won't be fine." He coughed several times, bringing up more blood. "I was too stubborn to die from the bullet in the graveyard. What kind of wood troll would I be to die from being shot? It's lunacy. But I went fighting, Nate, and that's all I can ask for. It's all any of us can ask for. He drove that knife into me, and I never once gave him the satisfaction of crying out. Not once. I spat and cursed and struck out until my strength was gone."

I placed my hand in his. Rean's grip was loose, weak. "You're a good troll, and I feel honored to call you my friend."

"The friend of Hellequin. That's quite the honor in itself."

"You knew?"

He nodded. "I found out after it all happened, although it took a long time. Very few people want to talk about those who scare the monsters. I wanted to try and find you, but then you vanished."

"Long story," I said.

"Will you kill them all?"

"Yes," I said honestly. "Every single one of the bastards involved in this deserves to die."

"Maybe killing isn't the answer. Maybe you need to show force a different way?"

"How?"

Rean shook his head and smiled. "I have no idea, I just don't want to think about you having so many souls on your conscience."

"My conscience is clear," I assured him. "I won't give these people a second thought."

"In that case, I have a request. Make Simon suffer, make him wish he'd never been born. He took my mate and my boy. He made me watch as he ended them. Made me beg for them."

Tears fell down Rean's bloody cheeks. "I get to see them again, Nathan. I get to see my boy and the woman I love. It's been so long. I've missed them so much, every day I dream of her. And when I wake, she's not there. I never understood the human term, heartbreak, but that's how I felt. A part of me died that day and I get to have it back."

I placed a hand against his face. "You hug them for me, and you tell them I'm sorry I couldn't save them. Tell them I wish that you'd grown old together."

"My friend, I will hold them so close they will never be able to leave. I will tell them how you saved me back then, and how you came back for me now. When I go to my resting place, where we dance and sing of our life's exploits, your name will forever be remembered."

"Is there anything I can do?" I asked.

"You mean end it? I don't want to give those bastards the satisfaction of me dying because of them. I want to go out a warrior, Nate. Can you let me do that? Are you able to afford me the privilege of one last battle?"

I nodded, but couldn't look at Rean as I helped him to his feet and retrieved the machete from the floor, almost having to force it into his hand, but eventually he found some strength and held it firm.

I took a few steps away and, pain or no, I created a blade of fire as brilliant as I'd ever managed.

I turned to Rean, who raised his blade to his face. "You do me this deep honor, my friend."

I copied his pose, bringing my blade down to my side. "The honor is all mine," I told him as I finally managed to find my voice.

Rean screamed a battle cry and darted toward me. His final act was to try and sever my head from my shoulders, but he was too weak, and I was too fast. As the blade of fire entered his chest and the machete clattered to the ground, part of me wished that he'd made the blow connect.

"Thank you, for allowing me to go on my terms," Rean said softly into my ear. "I will never forget your friendship."

"Go see your family," I told him as he closed his eyes.

I softly lowered Rean to the ground, where moments later he died in my arms.

CHAPTER 34

I left the house full of anger and sorrow that I couldn't afford the time to bury my friend. Leaving his body in that shithole of a building hurt, but there were very few other choices.

I staggered outside, my body screaming at me to slow down and let my magic heal me, but I didn't have time for that either, so I pushed on until I found a truck around to the side of the house, which had probably been used to transport Rean and me. I opened the glove box and found a mobile phone that still had some battery life and dialed Caitlin from inside the truck's cab.

"Hi Caitlin," I said as she answered it.

"Where the fucking hell have you been?" she snapped. "I dropped that family off at the police station and called Rebecca, who, by the way, was a patronizing ass about the whole thing and tried to tell me that it was impossible for there to be a second realm gate. I was going to drive down there and slap her, but then I figured you'd like to watch. That was over two hours ago."

I explained what happened, about the troll and Edward, about how I'd escaped and Rean's death. "They're at the church," I finished. "They've got Fern. They're going to make her tattoo a new guardian."

"I'll come get you," she said urgently. "Are you okay?"

"Banged up and bloody, but mostly fine. I'm in a truck, come wake me up when you get here." I ended the call and, as I could do nothing else, let my body rest and heal.

The sound of Caitlin's car pulling up outside the house woke me up. The clock on the phone said I'd been asleep for a half-hour, which had been enough to heal the pain in my stomach, although the wound was still raw and unpleasant, and would be for several hours due to the silver. More importantly, I no longer felt like I was about to collapse, and I got out of the truck to meet Caitlin.

"Glen—sorry—Father Patterson and Fern are at the church."

"Who is going to be the one who opens the gate? Tattoos take time to create, and even longer to heal."

"I don't think healing is going to be an issue, they just need that gate open. And if they have Glen, maybe they can force him to do it while Fern does her work."

"You think Glen would do it?"

"After witnessing their hospitality first hand, yeah, I think they'd get him to do whatever they wanted."

"You know you're covered in blood and topless, right?"

"Yeah, I'd noticed. Do you happen to have clothes on you that might fit me?"

Caitlin shook her head.

"Then I'm going to have to go for the crazed lunatic look for a little while longer." I opened the door to her own truck and got in. "We need to go to the church."

"Are you okay?" she asked as she started the engine. "You lost someone a little while ago."

"How are you coping with it?" I asked her as we set off. "How are you coping with losing your dad?"

Caitlin was silent for a long time, and I settled into the seat as the truck's speed increased. "I'm going to bring my mom to justice. I don't care what happens to the others."

"Well, Bianca's very dead. And it wasn't a good death."

"So, what about you?"

"I'm going to find Karl and Charles and every other fucker who arranged all of this, and they're going to pay for it. And once they're dealt with, I'm going to get Simon. I'm going to take him somewhere quiet and remote, and I'm going to make him famous. By the time I'm finished, I'm going to show the world exactly what happens when you fuck with me."

Caitlin pulled up outside the church, which was cloaked in an eerie darkness, with the remnants of the battle hours earlier still strung across the area.

"Did you do this?" she asked as we exited the car, her gun drawn and ready.

"Some of it," I said as I stepped over a headstone. "Okay, quite a bit of it."

We walked the short distance to the church doors in silence before moving around to the side of the building and using the huge hole to gain entry, but there was no one inside. We moved from room to room, taking the ground floor and then searching upstairs, but we found no one.

"The realm gate is around here," I said. "It has to be. Father Patterson stayed close to it."

"Within a mile of this place is a lot of area to search."

"No, it's closer than that. Easy to get to, and easy to defend. Does this place have a cellar?"

Caitlin shrugged. "No idea. I didn't build it."

I made another circuit of the ground floor, pulling up rugs, opening cupboards in my search for anything that might turn out to be a set of stairs.

"Nate," Caitlin called out.

I followed her voice and found her beside the pulpit, looking down at the floor.

"There are some weird marks here," she said. "Scrapings."

"The pulpit moves," I said and went to the opposite side and started to push, but nothing happened.

Caitlin climbed the pulpit. "There's a switch up here, it looks like an ornamental thing, but it's different than the others." She pushed it and something beneath us clicked.

I gave the pulpit a second shove and it moved, scraping along the ground. A set of steps led down into a hole lit up by dozens of torches.

"You think they heard us?" I asked and began walking down the steps, where I noticed the lever used to close the entrance.

"We have no way of knowing what's waiting for us," she pointed out and re-drew her gun.

The steps sloped down for several hundred yards, twisting and turning until we reached a huge metal door. Caitlin and I pushed it open and stepped into the room to find the realm gate directly in front of us.

It had been activated; hundreds of people were visible through the gate, all lined up in formations as they readied for battle. Fern was being dragged through the gate by Karl, who joined Charles Whitehorn in Shadow Falls.

"Stop," Caitlin shouted, raising her gun. "I will shoot."

Charles turned toward us with a smile on his face. He wore a long flowing red cloak and an actual crown upon his head. He opened his mouth to speak but an arm holding a knife snaked around his throat slitting it from ear to ear. Blood poured from the wound and the king fell forward to reveal Karl with knife in one hand and Fern's hair wrapped in the other.

"I think you may not like what happens next," I said, fully expecting Whitehorn's soldiers to attack Karl on sight. Instead, they started cheering.

"These are not his people," Karl said. "They're mine. I placed people, alchemists, and creatures of power in Stratford to wait for the day I would need them. Whitehorn was an idiot, a fool who thought only in terms of Shadow Falls and how he could make money from them. I don't want money, I want power." He released Fern and picked up a crystal from a nearby table. "Leonardo discovered these, and I'm going to take them and use them to make me the most powerful man not only in Shadow Falls, but everywhere. Avalon and everyone who works for them will bow down before me when I'm done."

"I thought this was about revenge? You and a hundred and fifty people against Galahad and his men? You're going to get slaughtered."

"It was about revenge originally; all I cared about was helping Whitehorn kill that bastard. But then I found out about the crystals and a better plan formed in my mind. As for the hundred and fifty. There are over a million people in this city, if only 1 percent of them are mine, that means ten thousand people all taking up arms for me. All of them killing their

STEVE McHUGH

neighbors in our name. This is a revolution and the blood of our enemies will flow through these streets."

"Does Patricia know this? That you're not destroying Shadow Falls?"

"I sent her on first, she and her insane friends. They've gone to do whatever they feel the need to do. Once we're done, we'll kill them as a threat to us all. I'll be a damn hero."

"Hey, I recognize a lot of those people behind Karl," Caitlin whispered. "They live in town; hell, some of them say hello to me in the morning."

"The humans who work for you, that's who you're going to make into guardians," I said.

"You have no idea how easy it was to get humans to join me. Money and immortality. That's all I had to offer them. Sad little creatures. Some of them don't want to be here, though we thought it a good idea to have some leverage."

"I'm going to find you, Karl," I told him.

"Not through this gate you're not." He walked over and dragged Fern back toward him. "If this gate activates, I kill her. Yes, it'll be a big waste, but I can always find more kids who have guardians as parents. I'm sure over the years I'll be able to get a few to help me. I've discovered that fear for those you love is a great motivator."

Someone walked over to Karl and whispered in his ear and I got a glimpse of a rundown hut not far behind them. "Well, I have to go, people to kill and empires to start. When we're done here, I'll come find you, Nate. I think I'd enjoy paying you back for what you did in the club."

"I'll see you before then," I told him. "And next time I won't let things end quite so happily for you."

"Shut this down," Karl demanded and the realm gate immediately died.

There was a cough from the side of the gate, which turned out to be Father Patterson, sitting against the wall, his face badly beaten.

"You okay?" Caitlin asked as she put her gun away and rushed over to him.

Father Patterson nodded. "They didn't seem to understand the idea of me being unable to die while near the gate. Then they threatened several people from the town unless I helped them. Turns out some of those people are actually working for Karl. Even so, they have innocent hostages with them. I couldn't let them kill people."

"It's okay," I said. "We'll stop them, although we're going to have to go to Portland to do it. Is there anyway they can open the portal from their end?"

Father Patterson glanced at me. "You appear to be covered in blood. And you're shirtless."

"Yes, it's been pointed out. Although most of the blood isn't mine. So, the portal, can they open it at their end?"

"Not at the moment, no. But soon enough, they'll have people who can. You have maybe six hours before the rituals are done and the tattoos on the first guardians are healed enough to use the portal."

"She's the only tattooist they have," Caitlin said. "They're not going to work her to death; they're going to threaten her, but not hurt her. They can't risk it."

"Those innocents they have are the leverage for her to work, just as they were for you to open the gate."

"Your arrival changed their plans," Father Patterson said. "They were going to find Fern and get her to perform the ritual before opening the gate, making me useless, but you started killing off their friends. Karl kept ranting about how the timetable had to change because you turned up in Washington."

"I'm glad I could piss off some more people; it appears to be a hidden piece of magic of mine. This realm gate gets you through to the mountains. I saw the area around them. They've got a few hours before they reach the city. We've got to get to Portland and let them know what's happening. If Karl's being honest, there are ten thousand people about to turn on their neighbors and friends. Shadow Falls is going to turn into a war-zone, but first there's going to be a massacre."

CHAPTER 35

Glen stayed behind at the church, but we gave him a revolver from Caitlin's truck and enough ammo to keep shooting until his enemies stopped coming. I hoped he didn't have to use it; he was a priest not a killer. Being so close to the realm gate would heal him up pretty quickly, and he appeared determined to stop anyone that would do more harm to his town. I admired him for that. Even so, I expected a lot of leg and arm wounds if anyone tried to attack him.

As the Audi was still outside the church, Caitlin and I thought it best to take it and get to Portland as quickly as possible. The decision was even easier to make when we realized that we couldn't get through to the Mill or Rebecca.

I grabbed a clean t-shirt from the boot of my car and quickly threw it on before setting off at blistering speed toward Portland, and not once did Caitlin look concerned at my driving.

We pulled up outside the Mill and ran inside, where we found the entire restaurant and bar empty. "Rebecca," I shouted, unwilling to bump into her or her people and start some sort of incident, which was also the reason I put a t-shirt on. A half-naked, blood-covered man does not say, please listen to me, I'm not trying to kill you.

"Rebecca," Caitlin and I called out as we made our way toward the basement.

As we reached the door, it opened and Rebecca darted out. "What the hell are you doing here?"

"We have a problem," I said.

"No shit, the phone's out and so's the power. And we all felt a second gate open."

"Karl Steiner took an army of people through it, they're on their way to Shadow Falls where another *ten thousand* people are about to start hacking their friends to death. We need to get through to Shadow Falls, right now."

Rebecca stared at me and then nodded. "I wouldn't have believed you if that second gate hadn't opened," she said as we walked through the basement. "I'm sorry for being a bitch to you," she told Caitlin.

"Let's just get people to safety," she said, and the remaining walk was done in silence.

The main room was a hive of activity, as emergency lighting illuminated everyone trying desperately to figure out the problem.

"Why can't you open the gate?" I asked.

"We can, but I deemed it safe to leave it closed until we'd determined what caused the power failure," Rebecca said and waved to the same person who opened the gate for us on our initial visit.

He walked over to the gate and the runes lit up once more, the image in the center showing us Shadow Falls.

It also showed us carnage. There were several bodies inside the temple and even more people were fighting for their lives. Harrison was transforming the temple itself into weapons, using it to crush his opponents. Apparently the order to turn traitor had already been given.

"I'm going to help," I told Rebecca, whose mouth had dropped open.

"Okay," she finally managed. "We'll make sure no one goes through on this end."

Caitlin and I ran to the realm gate but the guardian suddenly charged at us, screaming, "For the revolution!" and brandished a dagger.

I stepped into the attack and smashed my forearm into his throat. He staggered back, but refused to drop the weapon, instead swinging it back toward me. I grabbed his wrist and brought my arm down on the elbow joint, which broke his arm. I twisted the limb once again, noticing bone protruding from his joint and kicked out his knee, snapping his leg with a crack that sounded like a gunshot inside the confines of the room. The guardian dropped to the ground in agony.

"He's yours," I told Rebecca and kicked the dagger over to her before stepping through the realm gate with Caitlin, directly into a battleground.

I disarmed three people, one without serious lasting injuries, as I made my way to Harrison, who had a litter of bodies at his feet. He swung a huge hammer of marble at one attacker with enough force to cave in his chest.

"Fucking hell, not you too," Harrison seethed. "Don't we have enough shit to deal—"

"Shut the fuck up and listen," I snapped. "Karl Steiner and about a hundred and fifty people are on their way here. And according to him, at least ten thousand citizens of Shadow Falls are already waiting on this side, ready to attack. Although it appears that last bit has started."

"You're not fucking kidding, there's a war on the streets. About a hundred men stormed the temple not long ago. Most of them are dead now, but they just keep fucking coming."

"I need to get to Galahad. I need to warn him."

"I'm not letting you near my king—"

"Think for a second. I'm not here to hurt him, but if several thousand people start trying to attacking the palace, how long to do you think it'll be before someone among his own people shows their true colors and goes for him?"

"Fucking hell," he snapped. "What about Simon?"

"One thing at a time, Galahad first, then Simon. Karl wants this temple taken, so he's going to send everything at it. You need to hold this place like it was the king himself."

"Ah, will you look at that," Patricia said as she stepped into the temple and saw me. "I guess you killed some more of my lions."

"Yeah," I smirked. "Bianca's probably not in any state to join your little sojourn to this fair city."

Joshua glared at me. "You murdered my girl."

"Oh, that's right you two were a couple," I said. "Yeah, sorry about that. If you like you could keep her head in a bag. It's already detached so, it's easy enough to do."

Joshua roared at me and changed into his werebeast form mid-stride.

"Get behind me," I whispered, which Caitlin did immediately, followed by Harrison a second later.

"You're in the wrong fucking realm," I snapped and threw a blast of air at Joshua.

In our realm it would have knocked him back, maybe causing some bruises and cuts. It was a sizeable amount of magic in the scheme of things, but nothing compared to what I'd done to the cave troll a few hours earlier. But here in Shadow Falls, with the particles of magic in the air, it was devastating.

The wall at the front of the temple vanished as the air slammed into it like a jet. Patricia sprinted for cover, avoiding the majority of the blast, but Joshua had been right in the middle of it, and I noticed him slam into the ground outside the temple.

"Holy shit," Harrison whispered before quickly remembering who I was. "Yeah, that was pretty good."

I'd slammed my hands into the floor of the temple as I tried to switch off my magic. The rock was breaking up, disintegrating before me, but after a few seconds I managed to will my magic off.

"I'll deal with Joshua," I said. "Just keep that gate free."

The other defenders of the temple, all of whom had finished fighting, were staring at me with a mixture of fear and awe. I wasn't about to tell them that I couldn't keep using magic, it was too unpredictable, too powerful. Innocent people would die if I started using it in populated areas.

The feeling of power was overwhelming. I'd always been warned of using magic in Shadow Falls, and the small amounts I'd used before had only confirmed the dangers. The huge amount of force I'd just used was similar in scope to what the most powerful sorcerers in the world could easily access outside of Shadow Falls. If Merlin ever came to Shadow Falls and used his magic, the results would be like detonating a nuclear bomb. It was no wonder they guarded their realm gates so completely.

I strode across the temple floor in silence, walking down the steps past dozens of huge chunks of granite and marble. Dozens of men, all armed and armored, darted into the mouth of the temple as I made my way around to the side of the building to deal with Joshua. He was too dangerous to leave alone, and Caitlin, Harrison, and his men had more than enough to deal with.

Joshua was crouched by a huge piece of stone, his body bleeding from a multitude of cuts and tears in his flesh.

"I have to put you down," I told him. "I'm sorry your mum is psychotic, but you're never going to change. People like you don't get better. They just keep killing."

"You'll never kill me," he said with a defiant roar.

"Back in our realm, this would have been a close fight. You're far too strong and fast for me to think it would have been an easy victory for me. But here in Shadow Falls, it's not even a contest."

Joshua ran at me, swiping wildly with animal ferocity. I used a small amount of air magic, enough to extinguish a candle, and blasted his arm aside, then slammed a palm of air into his chest. He spun and landed roughly on the ground several feet back.

"You and your sick kin killed people I cared about," I said as I walked toward him. "You wanted me here to kill me, to show me all the pain and sorrow you were going to inflict."

"Caitlin will never forgive you for killing me," he said with a snarl.

"That's just something I'll have to live with." What was meant to be a whip of fire turned into a plume, which not only tore

Joshua apart but also incinerated his remains before they fell back to earth, leaving the ground scorched beneath him.

Once again, I placed my hands on the ground as my magic refused to stop. By the time it did, the earth beneath my hands would probably never support growth again. I stepped over the body and made my way down toward the trams, which were still working. Apparently Karl's men hadn't managed to find their revolution as easy as they would have liked.

There was a battle behind me in the temple, one I hoped Caitlin and Harrison were winning. I wanted to help, but I knew that getting to Galahad was more important. An explosion sounded out from the king's district, rocking the very ground beneath my feet.

CHAPTER 36

The trams moved too slowly. That was my overriding thought as I watched the fire and smoke rise from the king's district of Shadow Falls. Far below me, the people of the town had begun to figure out what was happening and started fighting the attackers in the streets, defending their loved ones and homes.

I was almost clawing at the tram doors by the time I reached my destination. As the doors opened, I heard a loud horn. I had no idea what it was signaling, but I soon found myself sprinting off the platform and into the crowd of people, who were trying to get away from the insanity that had engulfed the city.

A man wielding a curved sword, screamed obscenities and charged the crowd, ready to attack a group of women and children. I moved to intercept him, grabbing his sword arm as he swung toward me and snapping the elbow. He released the sword and I caught it before it fell to the ground. I swung around intending to cut through his neck but remembered there were children watching. I moved the sword at the last moment and caught the attacker in the temple with the hilt of the weapon. It opened a sizeable gash above his eye and knocked him unconscious, but at least he remained in one piece.

I passed the sword to a nearby woman, who had a child no more than five or six clinging to her leg. "You need to find somewhere safe to stay until this is all over."

"We're going to the temple."

"There's fighting happening up there, it's not safe."

"You don't understand, we're not going there to hide. We're going there to send our children through the portal and then we'll join the fight. This is our home, we will not let it fall."

There were maybe forty women and half as many children. I wanted to tell them that their plan was foolish, that they were putting their own lives in jeopardy. That they should find somewhere to hole up until it was finished. But I couldn't. Based on their fierce expressions, they wouldn't have listened to me. Hell, I wouldn't have listened to me in the same circumstances.

"Look, I know you're keen to help, but if you go up there with kids, some could get hurt."

"What do you advise?" she asked

"We know what we're doing," another woman said. "We wouldn't risk our children."

"Then be careful and give me five minutes," I said and ran off as several more explosions came from Leonardo's side of the district. As I got closer, I found several people already dead or unconscious in the street.

Another explosion tore off part of a nearby building, showering me in stone and dust as I dove for cover behind a wall.

"Fucking hell, Leonardo, will you stop that shit?" I screamed as loud as I could, hoping he'd hear me from within his now fortress-like house.

"Nate, is that you?"

"Most of me," I said and stood. "I think you may have blasted some bits off."

Leonardo opened his front door and motioned for me to hurry toward him. "I can't, there's a lot of women and children by the trams. They need safe haven. They want to go fight at the temple, but it's too dangerous. Do you have room?"

"Of course," he exclaimed. "My home is safe as can be. I already have most of the neighborhood in the back."

He disappeared back inside, giving me the chance to study the building, which had grown considerably since I'd last seen it. The windows had changed to small slots, and the corners had been smoothed and rounded.

Unless the enemy had siege machines, I was confident that Leonardo could not only defend himself, but could probably repair any damage to the building quicker than it could be inflicted.

Antonio appeared a moment later and I told him where to find the women and children. He ran off, a huge battle-axe strapped to his back and a sword in his hand.

"You feel like telling me how you're blowing things up?" I asked.

Leonardo produced several thumb-sized crystals. "A quick application of alchemy and then let them go," he said. "They make fantastic explosives when applied correctly."

"You heard from Galahad?"

Leonardo shook his head sadly. "No, I'm afraid to say. I'm sure he's okay, although if these bastards have already infiltrated the palace, he's probably got a hell of a fight on his hands."

I heard the sound of Antonio and his rabble of refugees soon after. He carried at least four children either in his arms or draped around his neck, a big beaming smile plastered across his face.

"No, you can't keep them," Leonardo mocked as Antonio stopped beside us.

"I think by the time we're done, I'll be more than ready to hand them back to their parents," he said, and his face soon took on a serious expression. "Some of these women were attacked by their friends. Why would they do that?"

"Money, power, and stupidity," Leonardo said. "You're all safe here, I promise you," he shouted to the women.

"We want to fight," the woman who had spoken to me earlier said.

"Well, the door is right there, I'm sure you'll find some people who can accommodate you," Leonardo told her. "Alternatively, you can stay here and help defend this little patch of city. I'd rather ensure that no one made their way into this house." He paused and stepped away from the door, but no one moved.

"You may think that I'm under the impression that women can't fight," he continued. "I care little for that way of thinking. We all know that women are more than capable of fighting battles. But these children need their parents, be that male or female, and make no mistake, there are men here already, waiting to defend their families and homes from all comers.

"So, your options are easy; if you'd prefer to wander the streets in search of battle, I wish you good luck. Or you can sit here and wait for the inevitable battle that will surely take place, not leaving your children alone and afraid while you go and find a war, which will come to you." The last sentence was said with an ice-cold stare, and no one else spoke out about going to find someone to fight again.

"I need to go," I told Leonardo and Antonio. "Keep yourselves safe."

Antonio offered his hand, which I took. "Keep safe, give them hell."

Leonardo and I watched his assistant walk off, trying to keep busy. "I worry for him," my friend said as we walked toward the front door, which was devoid of any of the house's newcomers. "He used to fight a lot, in the army, as a mercenary, whatever was available. I'm not sure he is dealing very well with the sudden increase in violence in the area."

"He'll be fine, just remind him of the things he has here if he starts to slip back into old habits."

Leonardo stared at me and it took a lot of effort not to grin.

"Yes, well, keep my king safe. He's the best one we've had, and quite frankly I don't think many others would indulge my whims quite so readily."

"Galahad is a better fighter than I am," I said honestly.

"Yes, he's probably better than even his father, but we both know that being a great fighter doesn't win wars. Arthur learned the hard way that being whiter than white doesn't do anything, except make you a big bright target. Galahad may not see the world in quite the same polarized way, but he's not exactly cut out to do things that may need to be done. And you ...."

"I am cut out for it."

"Sorry, Nate, but Galahad chose you for a reason back in '77. His line was drawn long ago. Until he was convinced to move it and lie to you, it had been rigid for a long time. Yours is always in flux depending on the situation. It makes you a much more dangerous person than Galahad could even comprehend. It's not about power; it's about the willingness to do something that will stop your enemy cold. The willingness to win at any cost."

"What are you getting at?"

"Galahad needs your support. He needs people to know the power of his friends. Specifically one friend."

"Me?"

Leonardo shook his head. "You need to go make sure people know whose side you're on once and for all. You need to make a statement. Or rather, Hellequin does."

I left Leonardo's house soon after and raced toward the palace as the horn rang out once more. The closer I got, the more bodies were littered across the ground, most in the armor of Galahad's personal guard. I continued up the stairs as quickly as possible until I heard the almighty crack from one of the lightning rods above, and the screams that followed. Apparently, Leonardo's invention worked quite well.

The top of the stairs was mostly empty, although the remains of the palace doors could be found with every step. There was also an increase in the number of bodies, although very few of them wore any kind of armor.

I jogged up to the doors and stepped inside as the sounds of battle overwhelmed my senses. Dozen upon dozens of people were fighting one another in the large hall just inside the entrance, and blood was flowing freely, having already stained the floor and walls. I strode through the insanity, pushing people aside if they got too close. I made it about half way when two men stood in front of me.

The first, a stocky older man with a bald head and bloody face, raised his sword toward me. "You are not one of us."

"I'm wondering," I said, mostly ignoring him. "Why the sword? Of the fighting I've seen, a lot are using their alchemy as a weapon, but the closer to the palace the more sword and dagger cuts. Why is that?"

"We do not wish to waste our power on those who can die by the sword. These scum do not deserve to die with the honor of having alchemy used on them."

I whistled slightly. "Wow, you two are going to die quickly."

Another five arrived around me as the fighting died down.

"Care to change that opinion?" the first man asked.

"No," Galahad said from on top of the balcony above us before launching himself down at his enemy.

He used a sword of brightest silver, something I was sure he had created himself as the battle reached him, and every single blow he landed was deadly. I consider myself good with a sword; in some circles, I would be considered an expert. Next to Galahad I looked like I was moving in slow motion. He was, and always had been, the finest man with a blade I'd ever met. The seven men died as I stepped back to let the king work. He was in no danger. He was barely even breaking a sweat. He was however, covered in blood. I would have bet every penny I had that not a single drop of it was his.

When he was done, the silver blade morphed into a forearm guard. "You killed many?" he asked one of the soldiers nearby as his surviving men bowed to him, the enemy vanquished. For now.

"Yes, my king," the soldier said and bowed his head further.

"None of you men bow to me today," Galahad said. "Every single man here is defending his home and his life. We are not king and subject. We are one." He pulled the nearest man upright and placed a bloody hand against the soldier's heart. "We beat as one. We bleed as one, and we sure as hell fight as one."

A tear fell down the man's face.

"No one here bows to me. And any man or woman in this room who survives this will never have to bow to me again," he shouted the last sentence and every single man and woman in that room stood a little taller, their chests welling with pride.

He turned to me, the only one in the room who hadn't bowed in the first place and rested his hand on my shoulder. "Where is Caitlin?"

"The temple, dealing with her mum and a few other assholes. Harrison is helping, so he should be able to spot the assholes pretty easily. They can tell their own kind, yes?"

The soldier nearest me smiled and looked away.

Galahad and several of his soldiers helped wounded men hobble up the stairs before they were taken further into the palace. We stood looking down at the thirty of so guards who remained, most of whom were exhausted.

"And Leonardo?" Galahad asked. "What's he up to?"

"He's blowing up large chunks of your city in its defense. And he's doing an admirable job of it too."

The loud horn rang out across the city once again, the noise almost deafening. It had been about two hours since the first blast and after so long since the last one, I was beginning to think it had finished.

"What the hell is that?" I asked.

"The prison has been broken," Galahad said, remaining remarkably calm. "Simon is free."

The doors to the palace were no barrier to the dozens of men who entered, brandishing weapons and using alchemy to knock back soldiers, killing more than one.

"If I don't live through this," Galahad told me, his guard turning back into a sword. "Tell Caitlin I'm sorry, I didn't ...."

"Oh shut up, you big girl," I said with a smile. "We've faced worse odds."

Galahad returned the smile as even more men piled into the palace, making the odds against the remaining soldiers loyal to Galahad at least five to one.

"You think you can break into my home?" Galahad said as he methodically walked down the stairs, his sword's point dragging along and making a noise that no one ignored. "You think that I am some weak baby that you can just push over. I am your king."

"Not my king, you're not," one of the men, I called him The Stupid One, said.

Galahad's smile was not one of joy. It held a lot of anger in it. "Nathan, would you kindly show these men the door?"

I jumped up onto the balcony edge and crouched down as everyone below me watched with a mixture of interest and worry. "My name is Hellequin," I said, and for some that worry became fear. I noticed a few exchange glances as they backed away slightly. "Apparently none of you had the presence of mind to knock before you came in. That's pretty bad manners. Why don't you leave and try again?"

I gathered as much air magic as I dared and leapt off the balcony. I hit the floor and released every single bit of magic I had in the direction of those who would dare threaten my friend. The magic kept coming flowing out of me as twenty of the men were picked up and thrown back dozens of feet, taking the door and part of the palace wall with them. They landed by the steps, many of them falling further and bouncing down them at high speed. For those who remained in front of the palace, I gathered the air around them and pulled it toward me, cutting off any oxygen.

"For those of you who live, remember what happened today. And pray I never find you again." And then I gave them their air back in the form of a hurricane. Bodies sailed over the edge, slamming into the buildings below with sickening force.

I managed to turn off the magic quicker than earlier, before anything else was destroyed. But the temptation to keep using it, to show Shadow Falls what I could do, was growing.

When the opposing force was decimated, there was nothing but silence left outside, but the battle inside the palace raged on once more.

"Nate," Galahad said from behind me after a few minutes. "I've not seen anything like that since Merlin."

"This place, it's . . . it's not good for me," I whispered. "Too much temptation to use magic to fix everything."

"Well you certainly left an impression."

"I need to get to the prison, I need to stop Simon."

"You're too late," Karl Steiner said. He was in werebeast form, his fur matted with blood, as he exited the castle and dropped the body of one of the guards to his side. "I know all the secret little entrances and exits," Karl said.

I flung fire at him, but one of his men rushed up and raised a huge piece of granite, blocking it. The next thing I knew I was sailing through the air as the ground beneath me shot up and caught me under the chin. My head spun and I checked my jaw to see if it was broken, but luckily I was okay.

"You're not needed here, Hellequin," Karl said. "It appears that the man can't live up to the legend."

I picked myself up and took a step forward, but Galahad blocked me. He had eyes only for Karl. "Go, Nate," he said. "I'll deal with this little problem."

"You sure?" I asked glancing over at Karl and the half a dozen warriors he had with him. They weren't to be taken lightly, despite Galahad's fighting skills.

"Nate, go stop Simon. Karl and I are going to have a nice long chat about the virtues of not pissing me off."

"Enjoy."

Galahad cracked his knuckles and smiled, this time it was a smile of joy. "I plan on it."

CHAPTER 37

The prison was in flames by the time I reached it well over an hour after the initial horn alarm. A massive hole sat in one side of the building, although there was no rubble. The brick itself had just been moved aside. Several bodies, some in guard uniform, but many more in prison clothing, lay on the ground. A dozen or so soldiers sat around, clearly wounded and exhausted. They'd had a hell of a day.

"What happened?" I asked the nearest guard, a huge man who was cradling his broken arm against his chest.

"You were here before, one of them who arrived with the king?"

I nodded.

"The prison broke out," he said. "All of them at once. Someone had put runes all around the building; once they were activated every single prisoner suddenly had their alchemy back. Most weren't concerned about using it against us. And then some of the guards started fighting us too."

"You know who set the runes?"

He shrugged and immediately winced. "I'm going to guess it was someone who knows runes, but what the fuck do I know?"

"Does having a broken arm make you more sarcastic?"

"Look, we all barely escaped with our lives, so you'll have to excuse me if I'm not keen on answering questions where the answers will just piss me off."

"And Simon?"

"Bastard did a runner. I saw him head off toward the mountains, but we were a bit too busy to try and stop him. Most of the prison staff were ordered to the city to fight these damn invaders. There was only a small handful who remained."

"What happened to the guards who turned against you?"

"They died or they ran," he took a deep breath. "Some did both. The prisoners didn't really care if their keepers had suddenly switched sides. To them, we're all the bad guy."

"Thanks for the info," I said and walked away.

"Hey, how's it going in the city?"

"Crazy, but Galahad's forces appear to be winning."

The big man smiled. "Good, bastards coming here to take our homes from us. Take our king from us. That man has done great things for this city, ungrateful little pricks decide they don't like how he works. Fuck every last one of the self-entitled little assholes."

I couldn't help but like the guy. "You guys going to be okay out here?"

"Yeah, I imagine so. Why, what else can we do?"

"You know Leonardo?"

"Everyone knows him, he's either a genius or a crazy bastard, depending on your point of view."

"Get yourselves to his place, there are a lot of families with children there. They could use more hands to help keep everyone safe."

The big man stood. "Right, lads, you heard ...." He paused. "Sorry, what's your name?"

"Hellequin," I said.

He paused and a few of the other men stared at me. "Seriously? Fucking hell, I thought you'd be taller. Right, lads, let's go help that crazy bastard."

They all walked past me as the enchanter, Martin, the one I'd met on my last visit staggered out of the tower and fell to the ground. "Help," he called out.

"You guys get going," I said. "I need to figure out a way to catch Simon."

He's about three hours ahead of you," the big man said. "And he was running."

I thanked him and looked back at Martin. "You helped him escape." It wasn't a question. Despite his blood-soaked clothes, there was little doubt he'd been in on it.

I moved aside his robe and noticed the deep stab wound on his side. "Put your hands here," I said moving them. "Press firmly and don't move." I went into the tower and grabbed a shirt, ripped it apart and used it to help stop the blood flow.

"They threatened my family," he said softly as I used another shirt as a makeshift bandage. "I had no choice."

"You put the lives of many in jeopardy today, other people's families died because of your decision."

He hung his head. "How can I help fix it?"

"Did you get him messages?"

He nodded. "They were given to me by a prison guard and I relayed them to Simon." He pointed behind me. "That guard there, I don't even know his name."

"What did they say?"

"They were just telling him about the people with tattoos, about guardians. I told you back then about the guardians and their tattoos. I helped how I could. "

"Yeah, thanks for that. It's probably the reason I haven't left you here to die."

"Thank you."

"Don't say that, don't try to be polite and nice. You could have gone to Galahad. He would have helped. How long has this been going on?"

"About two years, ever since I started working here. Before then, the messages had been sporadic. He'd had no one for nine years."

"Well that explains why Patricia didn't commit any crimes for such a long time. She didn't have her orders. Although why wasn't Karl or Charles giving her the orders?"

"Simon had them meet about a year ago, I had to send a message telling Patricia who Karl was. Simon was concerned that introducing Karl would mean he'd be left out of the plan."

"Simon thought Karl was trying to take over his position while he was in jail."

Martin nodded. "And then Karl offered him the chance to kill Charles Whitehorn in exchange for his fealty, instead."

"How did Simon take that?"

"He was pleased. We used to talk once a week, while I checked the runes in his prison. The rune that lets you hear him would need to be replaced every few days, so we had an hour to talk without anyone else around. The guards were all scared of him."

"Even with your family captured, you still chatted like buddies?"

Martin shook his head. "He would make sure I got pictures. They live in your realm. I tell them I'm away on business and then come work here. I trade what I make here for dollars and send it back to them. No one knows they even exist, but Karl had someone follow them. I got updates every few weeks, pictures of them at home, school. One time, when I'd displeased Simon for some reason, I received a picture of them all asleep in bed."

I believed his story. There was too much real emotion in his voice to think he lied. I assumed Patricia and her friends were the ones to take the pictures, just another reason why I was glad they were destroyed. "Do you think you can make it to the city?"

Martin tried to move, but yelled out in pain and returned to lying on the ground. "Probably not," he said.

"I can't use magic to heal you, not without Blood magic. And even if I could use it, in this realm I'd more than likely tear you in half."

"I can just wait here."

"Yeah, not going to happen. You were working with Simon, by choice or not, Galahad is going to want to talk to you."

"I'll accept my punishment, I will not try to run."

"Yeah, it's more what happens if any of his friends come back. You're not exactly in the position to defend yourself."

There was a roar that traveled up the nearby pathway toward Martin and me. At first I thought it was another attack of unknown origin, but soon after the cause of the noise came into view and I realized it was a motorbike. Or at least an approximation of one. Ridden by a very nervous-looking Leonardo. He pulled the brake too late and skidded to a stop beside me.

"Nate, I wanted to come help with the effort to stop the prisoners' escape, but apparently I'm too late to stop them or Simon. The guards I bumped into told me he'd escaped. So, I bring you your transport," Leonardo said as he put on the bike's kickstand and got off.

"I thought this thing had a tendency to blow up," I said, unimpressed.

"Don't use your magic on it, and it should be fine. It's a little skittish on the brakes—I just fitted them. Even so, it should get you after Simon quicker than running."

I took the handlebars and swung my leg over the bike, only to find it surprisingly comfortable. "Martin was working for Simon against his will, he's injured and needs someone to keep an eye on him until help arrives."

"Antonio is on his way, he refused to use the bike after all."

"He's wiser than either of us then," I said and pulled at the throttle slightly, lifting the kickstand and spinning the bike in place. "Martin, one last thing. If you're lying to me and you try to escape or you hurt anyone, I'm going to find you and I'm going to make that stab wound look like a splinter. We clear?"

All the color went out of Martin's face, which told me he wasn't lying, but he nodded anyway and I roared off on the bike to track a fugitive.

As it turned out the bike rode like a dream. Leonardo, as per usual, had built a supremely smart device. It was responsive, fast, and at no point did I feel out of control or concerned for my well-being, even on roads that hadn't ever seen a bike before, let alone been paved for smooth riding. There were only two problems.

As I pushed it faster and faster, the crystals powering it clearly warmed up from use, and after about ten minutes I could have fried an egg on what counted for an engine. The second problem was more concerning. There was no speedometer. I had no idea how fast I was actually moving, other than *very quick*. The scenery flew by at pace, and unfortunately it's very hard to figure out exactly how fast you're going without a gauge to tell you. To combat this slight oversight, I pulled the brakes harder and more often than I would have probably done normally, and the smell of what I hoped was Leonardo's attempt at brake pads soon filled my nose.

Fortunately I didn't have far to go. When I'd seen Charles and Karl through the realm gate, I knew that they were in the mountains. However, I also knew that the gate was near an old rundown hut, one that had previously belonged to Leonardo when an old king had given him the ultimatum of either creating weapons for him, or leaving the city. He'd chosen the latter and had built a nice hut for himself up just outside the mouth of the mountains. In fact he built it in the one place that the mountain range didn't cast a long shadow every day. Even though I'd been there on several occasions and had never caught a glimpse of a second gate, I was certain I knew where I was heading.

As I got closer and closer to the mountain range, I saw a large number of men in the distance. All of them wore bright yellow prison uniforms, which told me I was, indeed, heading the right way. Leonardo's old hut was maybe three or four hundred yards south from where the congregation was taking place, on a small hill. Several of the men were dropping items onto the ground, and from the way the sun bounced off them, I guessed they were crystals.

I stopped the bike by the hut and sat back, immediately moving as the engine burned my leg slightly. I used the kickstand and climbed off. Leonardo would never forgive me if I damaged his bike, and quite frankly, I didn't want to ride a bomb into a confrontation. The walk was done without anyone coming out to meet me. I had no concern of guns and the like, Karl would never want to be the king who had to use guns to win. That would show him as weak in many eyes.

I stopped about fifty yards outside of where the prisoners had dropped the crystals and tried to figure out what they'd done. The ground was littered with rocks of all shapes and sizes, which hid them from view. I took a few more steps and paused.

"One chance to leave," I shouted. "Go back to jail, or your homes or wherever you came from, but if you stay here, you will feel my wrath. I promise you, it won't be good."

Simon walked out of a tent and stood at the opposite side of the ditch. "This realm gate was hidden in a cave inside the mountain for over a thousand years. There's not a damn thing you can do that will make us give it to you or anyone you know. It's ours, and soon this whole damn realm will be ours."

"Does this man speak for all of you?" I asked. Eighteen men, all of them large and most of them in their prison fatigues, stood behind Simon. None of them moved or tried to give up. I was pretty certain the others would have killed any one of them who'd tried.

"Hellequin, I think you have your answer," Simon told me with smug satisfaction.

I nodded and began walking forward once again. I'd made another twenty feet and noticed the crystals on the ground, when one of the men used a match to light a rag in a bottle and then threw it on the ground.

Several of the prisoners held crystals and then threw them toward me. They exploded as they touched the rocks, causing the crystals that had been dropped there to do the same. The world in front of me changed to shades of purple and red and orange. The heat was so intense that I had to put my hand up to shield myself as I stepped back a few feet. I may be able to wield fire, but fire can hurt me just as much as an earth magic user can be hurt by a falling boulder.

A semi-circle of flames, twenty-five foot long and twenty-foot wide separated me from the prisoners, Simon, and the realm gate. Leonardo's words came back to me, that when the crystals burned, they used up all the magic in the atmosphere, meaning my magic was normal, or as normal as it could be in Shadow Falls. I really hoped he was right about that as I created a shield of air around me. I waited for it to explode outward, but it never did. It stayed exactly where I wanted it, like a second skin directly over me.

I walked toward the fire without feeling any of the heat, I wasn't sure how long I would have before the magic particles started to reappear, and I didn't want to be in the middle of an inferno when it happened. But I also couldn't rush it. Running through the fire meant using more magic to ensure the shield stayed in place, and I didn't want to use any more magic than I had to. Instead, I took one step inside the fire and breathed in deeply, before taking another.

Simon turned and ran back toward the realm gate as I slowly and surely continued walking through the twenty feet of hell.

When I was about halfway, I tried something very stupid. I coated my throat and lungs in fire magic and then used the shield to draw some of the heat into my mouth and down into my lungs. It meant having to hold my breath as I continued my journey, but I hoped it would help me in the long run.

As I reached the other side, the fire was dying down and I felt the surge of power that would start forcing my magic to go out of control. I continued walking toward the eighteen men, with the shield extended about ten feet. Every one of the men had eyes upon me, waiting, eager for a fight. Then I breathed out, mixing the heat I'd gathered inside me with my own magic.

I'd planned on it being a little stream of fire, just something that would jolt them into thinking twice about picking a fight with me. Give me an edge. Instead, I breathed a ten-foot-long jet of flame along the ground. The shock caused me to shout, which came out like a roar, making the fire buck and twist as if I were trying to ignite everything before me.

When it was finished, I unintentionally exhaled steam and smoke through my nose. I tried very hard not to let anyone know that I hadn't meant to do any of it, and when I looked up at the men, they bolted. They dropped whatever weapons had been in their hands and sprinted around the flames and back toward the city as if the fires of hell were directly behind them.

I continued unobstructed and walked up to the realm gate, where one solitary man stood brandishing a knife. He was shaking like a leaf. "You're from the town of Stratford," I said.

He nodded. "I saw what you did. That ain't normal."

"No, it's not. Wanna guess what I'm going to do to you if you don't activate that gate for me?"

"Not a damn thing," he said and walked over to his side, dragging Fern out from behind an overturned table. He held a serrated knife to her throat, and his eyes told me he'd be happy to use it.

"You think you can hide behind her?"

"You have two options, you turn and leave, or I kill her."

"Actually it's you with the options. See, you can either open that gate and I'll take Fern back with me. Or you hurt her and then I make you open that gate for me, after which I tear your throat out and let you bleed to death in this place. Either way, you're gonna be opening that portal."

"You can't force me to do shit," he said.

Using magic now that the particles were back in the air would kill both him and Fern, and that wouldn't help me get the realm gate open.

Fern made the decision for me by cracking the back of her skull against the nose of the man. She threw herself forward and I darted forward as fast as possible, grabbing the man's wrist, breaking it as I forced him to drop the knife.

"You don't need both of your hands to do this," I explained and picked up the knife. "But if you test me again, we'll see just how many bits of you I can cut off before you can't open the gate." To make a point, I placed his bad hand on the nearest table and drilled the point of the knife through his little finger, removing it entirely.

"Wanna go for something bigger?" I asked as he bucked and twisted in my grip. I pulled the knife free and raised it again.

"I'll do it," he said and I released him.

He staggered over to the realm gate and opened it.

"See, that wasn't so hard," I said. I punched him in the stomach, doubling him over, and then snapped his neck before dropping him to the ground.

Fern spat on his body, "No one threatens me," she told the dead man and grabbed his knife for herself before we both ran through the portal.

CHAPTER 38

Father Patterson was the only person waiting for us on the other side of the realm gate. He was up against the far wall of the room.

"I assume Simon came through here," I said.

"I tried to stop him," Father Patterson said. "It's nice that I'm immortal when near the gate, but it does little to stop me feeling pain."

"Where did he go?"

Father Patterson pointed toward the door. "He said you should go find him at the house. The evil little bastard will be waiting for you. I'm sorry I couldn't slow him down."

"That's okay, you did more than you could have possibly been expected to do. He's an experienced killer, you're a priest. They're sort of polar opposites."

"I'm staying here," Fern said. "You don't need me, but he does."

"That's fine," I told her. "Thanks for your help back there."

She glanced down at the dagger, as if hypnotized by the blade. "I'm glad he's dead."

"Did someone hurt you?" Father Patterson asked.

Fern shook her head.

"Take care," I told them and ran off, making my way back upstairs and through the ruined wall to the graveyard outside. If what Simon had told Father Patterson was true, he would be waiting for me. Which, in and of itself was insane; the last time we fought I nearly beat him to death and when we were in his cell, he showed me nothing to think that any return match wouldn't have a similar ending.

I found Caitlin's truck where she'd left it, outside the church, which certainly added to the feeling that Simon was goading me into going after him on his level. It was either a trap or he had a plan that I just couldn't see. Either way, I didn't care, I was going to break him in half and nothing he could place in my path was going to stop me.

I got the car moving and drove at legal speeds toward the House of Silent Screams. If Simon wanted me to come get him, he could damn well wait. I wasn't going to do anything on his timetable.

I stopped the car on the road, away from the house, and made my way through the woods until I was crouched opposite the house's open front door. Lights were on inside the building, but I couldn't see anything or anyone.

After several minutes of walking through the woods to get as much of a look around the house as possible, I risked exposure and stepped out into the open. And nothing happened.

Nothing continued to happen as I made my way to the front door and risked stepping inside. There were no trip wires or devises that were designed to hurt me and give Simon an edge, so I took another step into the house. I stayed quiet, I didn't want to give away my position if Simon was waiting, but I moved through the ground floor without interruption.

When it was apparent that the floor contained no one, I stepped out of the back door and used my thermal vision to prove to myself that there was no one waiting outside in the darkness either. A weird feeling came over me; nearly twenty-four hours had passed since I'd entered Shadow Falls, even if it felt like no time at all. Twenty-four hours since Rean had died and I'd been forced to leave his body in the basement. A warming anger filled me. Simon was here somewhere, and I would find him.

I removed my thermal vision and stepped back into the house. I didn't want to search the basement until last. I was hoping that I'd be able to find Simon and then leave Rean alone until he was ready to be removed from the hellhole his body lay in.

Each of the stairs up to the first floor creaked loud enough to let anyone in the house know exactly where I was, but I still made it to the top without interruption. I walked the length of the hallway, opening each of the doors in turn, but every one of them revealed nothing. Except for the body of Bianca, which remained where she'd died, there wasn't even a hint of anyone being there.

I was beginning to suspect that what Simon had told Father Patterson, was just a feint to get me to look away from where he was running.

I stood at the top of the stairs, looking down on the floor below, when a crystal landed at my feet. It exploded almost immediately, launching me down the stairs.

I slammed into several wooden steps on the way down, but managed to use my air magic to keep from being too badly injured. Simon had changed the staircase into a slide and was racing toward me. When he got close, I hit Simon in the chest with a blast of air, throwing him across the room and into the nearest wall. I managed to roll away and quickly checked myself for injuries, but found nothing too serious.

Simon touched the wall with his hands, and it exploded out toward me. Not even a shield of air stopped the thousands of pieces of wood, metal, and brick shrapnel. It left me with several lacerations and fragments of wall imbedded in my arms and legs.

I threw a plume of fire at him, turning it into a whip at the last moment to try and cleave Simon in two. Simon dove aside, allowing the fire to destroy the wall behind him, rending the remains to ash.

I drove a wall of air at Simon's chest, throwing him back toward a dividing wall, which he crashed through, into the room beyond.

Simon appeared a moment later, blood oozing from a cut on his forehead. "Do you know how long I've waited for this?" Simon asked as he moved along the side of the landing, toward the front 'door. "Back in '77, I never got a chance to fight back. I wasn't expecting you to assault me, and by the time I knew what was happening, you'd already scored several hits. Then back in the prison, it took so much for me to let you think I was an easy opponent. I wanted to break your neck for what you did, for trying to humiliate me again. But I had to just let it go."

"You're an arrogant little prick," I said as I removed a three-inch-long piece of wood from my bicep and threw it onto the floor. "You know, you may have managed to get away with all this, if you hadn't involved me in the first place. If you hadn't killed Bill."

"Ah, Bill." Simon grinned. "I heard he screamed in fury as they tore him apart, and then, after a while, he just screamed. Patricia so wanted you both dead, and I had to give in to that demand. Unfortunately, she fucked up and led you here before we were ready. Shame, really, but she was always going to die."

"Why run? Why not stay and fight?"

"Because I wanted you here. I needed you here." Simon placed his hands on the doorframe and it started to disintegrate as something inside it began to cover Simon's skin.

I realized what he was doing too late. I threw a massive ball of fire at him, but as Simon stepped through the flame unharmed, I knew that I was going to have the fight of my life. Simon's entire body, except for his face, was covered in a silver layer. It gleamed in the light of the fire at his feet, which he soon extinguished with a single stamp.

I'd let my anger and need for revenge cloud my judgment. As an alchemist, Simon could easily use any part of the house against me, but I'd assumed I'd be able to combat him with my own magic, able to beat him as I had before. But I was wrong. And I was certain I would pay for that mistake.

Simon sprinted toward me, and I tried to dodge aside, but the banister itself sprung toward me, catching me in the face and knocking me to the floor, where Simon punched me in the kidney as I tried to roll away. I rubbed my side as the pain made its way through my body and noticed that I was bleeding.

As if to make his point, Simon showed me his knuckles, which were raised sharply, almost spike-like.

"You can't win this," he said and darted forward, feinting a punch with his right, but instead going with a left jab to my side. It was a blow I saw coming a mile off, but with the silver, even blocking it hurt, the force of the blow burning the skin on my hands and arms.

He followed up with a huge right, which rocked my head, sending dark spots into my vision. I tried to get away, but my legs wouldn't move and I realized that the floor had literally swallowed me up, pinning my arms behind me and forcing my head and neck forward. Then he removed most of the silver from himself, covering the wood that surrounded me in the substance.

"I saw what you did to Bianca," Simon said, and I noticed his hands still had the silver on them. "Saw the burn marks on her mouth. Stupid cow didn't realize that you could use magic without your hands, I assume." He punched me in the jaw with another right and then a left, leaving me disorientated. I saw his knee come up, but could do little about it as it connected with my nose, breaking it.

"Am I right? You should answer me!"

I nodded weakly, although I had no idea why I was letting him know he was right. But then, I barely knew where I was or even my own name.

Simon took a few steps to the side of me and then ran back at me, kicking me in the head as he passed. If I'd been a football, I would have sailed across the field with ease, instead I think I blacked out momentarily.

"I've got something for you," he said with enthusiasm and ran into the nearest room, returning a second later with half a dozen small crystals. He touched the silver by my chest, which moved apart. "I just want to see what happens. I was going to bring loads with me and sell them to the highest bidder, but using them here, that's just more fun." He used alchemy on the crystals and quickly stuffed them against my chest before resealing the silver.

The explosion tore into my body as if it were made of paper. They crystals were too small to kill me, but the pain overwhelmed every part of me.

"That must hurt," Simon said, cupping my face in his cold hands and forcing me to look at him. "Does it hurt?"

I muttered something, but my mouth was full of blood and the words just came out in a cough of gore.

"I think you've lost a tooth when I kicked you," Simon said, picking up one of the white molars that I'd spat onto the floor. "I've always wondered, do you grow new ones? I know your kind can heal well, but can you grow teeth? Maybe we should check?"

He punched me over and over again, and I felt another tooth give way. I spat it onto the floor to join the first one.

Simon sat beside me. "I think your face is fucked. It's all puffy and broken. I think I smashed your jaw pretty good with that last blow." He opened the silver again. "And your chest looks like raw hamburger. Do you feel like the big man now? For beating me nearly to death? Did you feel good for doing it? How does it feel now? You feel like saying sorry?"

I mumbled something unintelligible.

"Is that an apology? What the fuck kind of apology was that?" Simon got back to his feet, raging at me. "You think you can mumble some shit and I just buy it, what kind of fucking idiot do you take me for?"

I mumbled something else. My brain was beginning to clear, but with that came the pain from the shattered bones and broken skin that used to be my body. I sucked it down and tried to figure out a way to escape. I had to get away from Simon, that was my only option. Well, that or being beaten to death. I closed my eyes, or eye considering one of them was already shut, and it hurt to keep them open.

"Fuck me, you can't die yet," Simon said and slapped me. But the silver had gone, there was no damage done to my face.

I stayed silent and kept my eyes closed, hoping that Simon was just that revenge obsessed. That he wouldn't let me die until he said so.

I was right.

The prison holding me tight vanished and I slumped to the floor. I didn't need to pretend that I was unable to stop myself from hitting the floorboards, I was pretty certain that even with full vision I wouldn't have been able to do a damn thing.

"Are you dead, you fucking dick?" Simon said and pushed me onto my back.

I felt him kneeling down by my head. He started tapping my cheeks.

"Well, if you're just going to lie there," he said and moved. A few seconds later, I heard the unmistakable sound of trousers being unzipped. "I could use a piss break."

With the tiniest movement of my hand, I shot fire up toward where I thought Simon was, and he launched himself back at the last second, the smell of burning hair hanging all around me.

"Fuck," he said and started patting down his head.

I rolled onto my side with the greatest of effort and managed to get onto my feet. I was surprised to find that both my eyes opened, although the pain in the rest of my body was still substantial.

"Not gonna be that easy," I told him.

Simon crouched down and once again the floor around me changed, rising up to trap me. But like before, I'd noticed something about Simon. When he used his alchemy, he had to remove the silver armor from his body; he couldn't concentrate on both at once. I threw a blast of air at him, knocking him sideways, and jumped over the splintered floorboards, which had stopped moving in mid-air. I ran at Simon as he tried in vain to get the silver back in place.

It covered up to his waist when I reached him and punched him in the nose. The blow broke bone and blood began to flow freely down his chin, at the same time he lost control of his concentration and the silver ebbed away, pooling on the floor beneath us.

"My turn," I said and grabbed him by the back of the neck and brought him toward me, head-butting him as hard as I could. I followed up with an air-assisted punch to his side and then another to his stomach, both of which hurt me as much as him. He staggered back, slightly dazed from the attack, and tried to punch back. I deflected his arm and stepped around him, sweeping his legs as I moved and cracking him in the side of his head with my knee when he fell back.

Simon rolled away, desperate to get some distance between us, but I grabbed his ankle, wrapping my legs around it. I held on tight as I twisted it sharply, applying pressure to his Achilles tendon, until I felt the muscle snap, his foot going limp and useless. Simon screamed in agony and I released his leg, rolling back to my feet.

"Now you're done," I said, staggering to my feet and producing a blade of fire from one hand. I felt spent and wasn't sure that I'd be able to continue the fight at any high level. But with one useless foot, neither would he. I had to end it quickly.

"I say when I'm done," he shouted and the silver threw itself at me, turning into a solid block as it struck me, knocking me back to the floor.

The air rushed out of me all at once as I fell back toward the ruined floor, gouging myself across the ribs on the jagged edges. All of a sudden the floor beneath me vanished and I fell, connecting with the concrete floor of the basement some fifteen feet below me. Any air that had remained from the attack above vanished as I fought for breath.

"You stay there," Simon mocked. "I'll be down in a second."

The fall had taken whatever energy I had left; I was exhausted and in agony. The previous few days had been one injury after the next, with very little time to heal.

I rolled over onto my back as Simon cursed above me, every step bringing with it fresh horror. I made an approximation of a smile, but my face hurt too much for anyone else to think it was anything other than a grimace. As I glanced to my right, I saw Rean's body. It was undisturbed and for the briefest of moments, I was sorry that he wouldn't receive the burial he'd deserved. Then I mentally slapped myself and forced my body to get to a standing position, using a nearby gurney to keep some sort of stability.

I wondered how many people Simon and his friends had murdered in the basement of this house. How many people had died for nothing? Had died in pain and agony? Had died protecting the ones they'd loved? I paused. How many people had died fighting? I closed my eyes and searched outward, trying, hoping, to find something that I could use.

Rean's spirit was right there, in the room with me. I'd never tried to use the spirit of anyone who wasn't human, I wasn't even sure it was possible. But as I absorbed Rean's spirit into me, I felt the overwhelming strength of a wood troll surge through my body. I crashed back to the ground, hugging myself and screaming as my body began to repair itself, using Rean's strength to accomplish in minutes what would have taken days with only my magic.

After it had finished, I didn't just feel healed, I felt ... whole. My body was repaired, but the toll the previous few days had taken on my own spirit had been hefty. Rean's energy had corrected that.

As before, with Caitlin's dad, Norman, I knew exactly what was happening and why. I understood how the spirit worked, how my body allowed itself to be healed and nourished by the necromancy. I knew how to control that energy to make myself strong, better. And as Simon was going to find out, a lot more dangerous.

I stood up and felt woozy as more spirits came to my attention. Dozens of them, every single one who had died fighting, died never giving in. There were so many people, so many lives taken. Something inside me reached out to all of them at once and invited them in.

The result was insanity personified as I absorbed them. More and more of them, increasing my power until my body could barely take it. Every movement caused magic to leak out of me, the concrete floor cracking beneath my feet from the power.

"Hey, Nate, miss me?" Simon said as he opened the door.

His foot was covered in a silver boot, which allowed him to walk, albeit slowly, down the stairs toward me. His hands were once again covered in silver. "I'm glad you're down here, I'm going to take my time with you. I'm going to show you what I used to do to the people we kept here."

I nodded. "Those people would like a word," I said and sprinted toward him.

He grinned and threw a punch, but at the last second noticed that my face was no longer a ruined mess and his smile vanished. I avoided the punch and grabbed him around the waist, picking him up off the floor, before my body decided that I had too much energy and released it without me having any say in the matter.

The resulting explosion pushed us both up onto the floor above. I'd tried to control the gargantuan blast of air and fire but it had been as if I were still in Shadow Falls, and I was lucky not to turn the house into a smoking crater. I hit the wooden floor hard, rolling toward the door. My body ached more than I'd remember it did when I'd hit the basement in the first place.

Simon dragged himself back to a standing position. "So, you've got some extra juice." He stood up straight and allowed the silver to flow over his body once more, covering everything but his eyes and nose. "But you can't possibly think it's going to be that easy."

I breathed out slowly and got back to my feet. Necromancy doesn't have an ability where you can turn the spirit into pure energy to wield like magic, and unlike Hades, I couldn't just fuck around with Simon's soul. But I knew what I had to do. And I knew I could do it.

I walked toward Simon with purpose, all the while Simon moved his neck and rotated his shoulders, mocking me, as a grin remained on his face.

When there were only a few feet between us, I stopped and stared at the psychopath before me. "You can come in quietly," I suggested. "It's the best way for you now."

Simon laughed. "I'm going to fuck you up."

"No," I said softly, "you're not."

I moved my hands behind me and felt the shimmering of power that filled them. The power increased in intensity until it felt as if I were holding something solid in each hand. I swung one hand forward, and was slightly surprised to see a battle-axe down by my feet. The other hand held a *jian*, a Chinese sword. My soul weapons: a weaponized manifestation of a necromancer's power.

Simon charged me, expecting the silver that covered his body to be all he would need to beat me.

I didn't move. I took a deep breath and as Simon got close enough to reach out for me, his hands aiming for my neck, I snapped the axe up in one lightning-quick motion. It caught Simon under the chin and passed up through his skull. The blade didn't leave a mark, but Simon stopped dead in his tracks, his hands dropping to his sides and his eyes glazing over.

The silver melted off of him, and I kicked him in the chest, knocking him to the floor, where he blinked.

"Soul weapons hurt you without leaving a mark. I'm assuming you can still hear me, although I'm guessing the fact that I went through your brain means everything is really fuzzy."

Simon blinked again and opened his mouth, but nothing came out.

The *jian* vanished from my hand, and I rested the battle-axe's handle against my shoulder. "You should have taken the offer," I told him and snapped the axe down, burying the blade in the top of Simon's skull.

CHAPTER 39

Simon had, unfortunately, survived, although his brain had pretty much turned to a form of mushy pudding. He couldn't speak or do anything that didn't involve blinking or drooling.

Even though I was exhausted after our battle, I'd driven a comatose Simon to Portland and dropped him off with Rebecca before promptly passing out on one of the sofas that sat in the bar area of the Mill.

When I'd woken a few hours later, Rebecca had informed me that the fighting was over. Galahad and his forces had won. It was pretty much the best-case scenario on all fronts. Unfortunately, no one was allowed through the realm gate, but Father Patterson and Fern had traveled through the gate to try and help anyone they could in Shadow Falls. It made my decision to hang around at the bar an easy one; I wasn't going to get through a realm gate any other way. Although, after twenty-four hours of sitting around, I decided to be more productive and sat at the bar, nursing a large scotch. Rebecca wasn't exactly thrilled.

"You could go home," she said for the hundredth time as she walked past.

"Could do a lot of things," I told her and knocked back the scotch. "But I'm not going anywhere until I get through that realm gate."

"And I told you, I'm not letting anyone—"

I held my hand up to interrupt the same speech she'd made every few hours since I'd arrived. It was rude of me, but I didn't care. I understood her reasons. She'd given the order presumably to ensure that no one escaped or that reinforcements didn't arrive. Four of Rebecca's people had betrayed her, killing three people before they'd been stopped. She'd been on edge since then.

I poured another scotch for myself and grabbed a second glass, pouring her one too. "Drink," I said. "Galahad is fine."

"So why haven't you left?"

"Because I want to see Simon handed over. I lost a good friend during all of this; I'm not leaving until I know the people I care about are safe. I know you're anxious to hear about how people are doing, but pacing around and trying to get me to leave won't help."

Rebecca sat beside me and knocked the scotch back, pouring a second. "I'm sorry for your friend," she said and placed a hand on my shoulder. "Simon and his followers are no longer a problem, and I have you to thank for that."

"Rean too," I told her. "So, why are you constantly trying to get me to piss off?"

She knocked back the second drink and made a third. "You make me nervous."

"You think I'm going to hurt Galahad again?"

"Did you know we don't allow sorcerers in without the king's personal approval?"

I shook my head, but noticed she hadn't answered my question. "I assumed we weren't allowed to use our magic, but I didn't know we were banned. How did I get in the first time?"

"King Galahad told us the last time you were here in '77, that if you ever asked to go through again, you were to be allowed. I didn't like the idea, not after what happened between you, so I fought it when you came. I needed to make sure you were going for the right reasons."

"Thanks for that. I assume Harrison wasn't a fan either."

"He was serious about not letting you in. If I hadn't been there, you would have stayed put and he'd have suffered our king's wrath alone. Fighting alongside the king's guard probably endeared you to a lot of them, showed them you weren't the bad guy."

"So, why can't I go back through now?"

"Because you can't be the city's savior. You came in throwing huge amounts of magic around as if it were nothing. You saved people. Galahad has already told them of the aid we received from the great Hellequin. But you won't always be there. The people have to realize they can't be saved except by their king."

"That's a pretty flimsy excuse," I told her. "You don't trust me, do you? Do you think that I've set all of this up with Simon? Is that why he's still dribbling under guard downstairs?"

"No, I don't think you set this up," she said and took another drink.

"But?"

"But, I don't trust you. The power you wield, it's immense out here; in there you're basically a god."

"That's ridiculous. I'm not even one of the most powerful sorcerers in the world, nowhere near. But what the hell does it matter anyway?"

"What's stopping you from deciding you like that power? What's stopping you from taking that power on a permanent basis?"

"You want a list?" I should have been offended, and truthfully I was a little, but getting angry and showing it wouldn't do anything to help me in the long run. I held up a finger. "I'm Galahad's friend, I'm Leonardo's friend—I don't want to jeopardize either of those."

A second finger. "I'm not interested in obtaining power. In fact, I don't actually like ruling anything, ever."

A third. "I have a life away from this, one I enjoy, with people who trust and like me. I wouldn't swap that for all the money and power in the world."

A fourth. "I'm not a gigantic asshole. Do I need to go on?"

Rebecca smiled slightly and shook her head. "You're really not interested in power, are you?"

It was my turn to shake my head. "Power is fleeting, and I like not having the responsibility of people who look up to me and need my guidance. Life is simpler that way."

"You saved a lot of lives by helping." Rebecca stood and offered me her hand. "Including people I care about. Thank you for that."

I shook her hand; it felt nice to finally prove to her that I wasn't the bad guy. "Who told you I was Hellequin?"

"Galahad mentioned it in '77. I think at the time he was trying to stop me from going after you."

"Probably worked out for the best," I pointed out. "So, can I go see my friend now?"

Rebecca nodded. "Give me a few hours, I need to ensure that everything is okay on their end."

I pushed myself off my stool and stretched. "I'm going to go eat something; can I assume that if I make a sandwich, I won't be upsetting anyone or get threatened by your staff?"

"Most of my staff think you're a damn hero already. If you go ask for food, you're likely to find them happy to assist you."

I smiled. "In that case, you may want to get that realm gate open sooner, before I eat you out of house and home."

Six hours later I was standing in the temple in Shadow Falls. Several alchemists were rebuilding the part that I'd ruined, moving huge blocks of stone as if they were weightless.

"Where's Galahad and Caitlin?" I asked Harrison, who was shouting at some of his men.

He turned around to glare at me. He was missing one of his hands.

"What happened?" I asked.

"Some fucker got too close. I'll manage. Leonardo said he'd make me a new one, a better one."

"What about here, what happened in here?"

"There was a hell of a battle. That girl of yours is a tenacious fighter. She took out a bunch of guys without breaking a sweat."

"And her mum?"

Harrison shrugged. "Don't know, didn't see."

"You're a terrible liar."

"Yeah, well maybe it isn't my place to tell you. You ever think of that, smart guy?"

I wasn't in the mood to play games. "Fine. So, where is everyone else?"

"Palace. I was meant to be going, but there's too much to do."

"What's happening at the palace?"

He shrugged again. "Go find out."

"Thanks for your help," I said with as much sarcasm as possible and walked off toward the still working trams.

"Hey, asshole sorcerer," Harrison called after me, the acoustics of the temple making his already loud voice boom.

I turned around and readied myself for an argument for whatever reason Harrison had decided.

"This is the one and only time you will ever hear me say something nice about you. You did good. You saved lives. Thank you."

"You're welcome, you did well yourself. Thanks for keeping Caitlin safe."

"Yeah, now fuck off, I've got people to shout at and not enough time to do it."

I walked away shaking my head, but the exchange had made me smile. Hopefully I'd proven my worth to Harrison as well as Rebecca. Maybe in the future I wouldn't have guards watching me when I arrived in the city.

I caught the tram to the king's district and made my way through the area. I passed dozens of people who were repairing their homes and streets until I reached Leonardo's house, but found it empty.

About halfway up the steps to the palace, I heard the noise of construction, and upon reaching the top saw the reason. A huge hole sat in the side of the palace and several smaller ones pockmarked the side of the building. Several men and woman were all using alchemy to move brick and mortar around, but everything still had to be set in the correct place and organized with efficiency. It was a job that Leonardo appeared to take to like a duck to very wet liquid.

He stood beside a wooden table, with drawings littered across it, shouting orders at people and gesticulating wildly on a regular basis.

"Have you turned into a tyrant?" I asked as I walked up to him.

"I'm surrounded by people who all think they know what they're doing."

"Do they know what they're doing?" I asked.

Leonardo thought about it. "Some do, but I have a vision that King Galahad was keen to recreate and I plan on sticking to it."

"What's the vision?"

"Ah well, the palace was partially destroyed in the fighting, so I've been tasked with not only rebuilding it and its defenses, but also to make it more efficient. I plan on placing more crystals inside, I have a design that will make them much less unstable and hopefully a lot more capable to provide more than just light."

"Sounds like a lot to work on."

"It is," he said, full of enthusiasm. "I've also got to redesign the Tesla coils; they didn't maintain a charge for long enough." He waved his hand dismissively. "But weaponry is hardly at the forefront of my mind."

I searched the area around us. "Where's Antonio?"

"He's helping some families below rebuild. He made some friends during our time with them all and suggested that people should always help their neighbors. He's also involved in training some of those who live there in more advanced uses of their alchemy."

"You don't sound convinced of the wisdom in this."

"I'll be convinced once they manage not to destroy their surroundings every few hours as they practice. They've rebuilt some of those roads three or four times since the fighting ended."

"Can't make an omelet," I said.

Leonardo glared at me. "You appear to be smiling at my discomfort."

"I'm just glad to see you're still alive."

"Of course I'm alive. I survived this long, some up-jumped little prick is hardly going to be enough to end me."

"Jumped-up," I corrected.

Leonardo stared at me, which made me smile even more. "Galahad is looking for you," he said between clenched teeth. "He's in the great hall at the other side of the palace."

"How'd Karl get into the palace anyway? I thought this was the only entrance."

"Apparently the designer forgot to add the secret tunnels that he'd built to the blueprints. I say apparently, because I think he's a lying little shit who sold out his king, but considering he's one of the people I've been yelling at all morning, I guess that this is Galahad's idea of punishment."

I placed a hand on Leonardo's shoulder and followed his gaze to a young looking man with long, dark, curly hair. He didn't appear happy to be there, and everyone else avoided him like the plague. "I think he needs to be repeatedly reminded how bad he is at everything he does," I said with a grin.

"That's my thought too."

I walked off toward the palace, only stopping when Leonardo called my name. I turned back to see my old friend.

"I'm glad you're okay, life would have been considerably more boring without you in it. No one else would have tried my bike. Which, by the way, I thank you for not blowing up."

I grinned and nodded in his direction before making my way into the remains of the palace.

I walked up the stairs, carefully avoiding the busy workers, and almost tripped over Caitlin as I stepped around the corner into one of the long hallways. She was seated against a wall eating a pear. She saw me and smiled, finishing the fruit before offering me her hands to help her stand.

"I'm a bit achy," she said as she stretched. "The last few days have taken their toll; apparently I'm not as fit as I thought I was."

"Battles really take it out of you," I told her. "How are you doing?"

"Getting there." She smiled, but there was a tiredness behind it. "I've decided to stay in Shadow Falls for a while. I want to learn more about my alchemy, and I want to spend time with Galahad ... sorry, my dad. That feels weird. I had to bury one father only to find another."

"It's not weird, you've had a lot to come to terms with in a very short period of time."

"How are you?"

I told her about what had happened since we'd separated, something that felt like a lifetime ago.

"I'm sorry for your friend."

"Thanks. I'll have to arrange a burial for him with his colony. That's if they accept the body. He told me he'd left them. But he's at peace now, so that's something."

"I saw my brother's body," Caitlin said, breaking the uncomfortable silence that had descended after we discussed Rean. "Or what was left of it."

"I'm sorry about that. He didn't—"

"I know. He didn't give you a choice. He was a murderer and an evil man, but he was still my brother. I'll miss the boy he was, not the man he became."

I wasn't sure how to broach the subject of her mum, but I figured head-on was the best bet. "What happened to your mother?"

"We managed to subdue her. Harrison wanted to take her for questioning; it took a lot of effort. We're going to find a pit just for her. Will you be staying in the city long?"

I shook my head.

She leaned over and kissed me on the cheek. "You sort of turned my life upside down, you know that, right?"

"I'm aware of it, yeah. Sorry about that. I never meant to."

"Not your fault. But I think I need some time to let things sink in. Next time you're in the city, come say hi. Until then, take care of yourself, okay?"

I promised I would and let her walk off down the stairs. I wasn't sure if she really was okay with everything that had happened, but I hoped she would be. The previous few days had been a lot for any one person to absorb, but if anyone could do it, it was Caitlin.

It took me a while to find Galahad—I got wildly different directions from the people I asked. In the end I found him outside on the same balcony where he'd found me only a few days previously.

"Hello, Nate," he said, turning from the balcony railing as I opened the door and closed it behind me.

He wore a suit with a pair of trainers and held a glass of scotch in one hand. The rest of the twenty-five-year-old bottle was on the table beside him, one of the benefits of being king, I guessed.

"You were hard to find," I said as he poured me a drink and passed it to me.

"I've been in the dungeons all day, hence the drink. Patricia has proved to be as stubborn as Simon in answering questions. I should be helping people repair my palace, my city, but instead I'm talking to psychopaths and ordering the jail terms for any of Karl's men who surrendered."

"You don't have to explain yourself to me," I told him and took a drink of the scotch. "Wow," I said, holding the glass up.

"It's good, isn't it? I never used to drink the stuff, but recently I found myself enjoying the odd glass. I've got a dozen bottles of this, help yourself."

It was a very tempting offer. "No thanks, this gives me a reason to come back and say hi."

Galahad laughed for a moment, but it was quickly replaced with a somber expression. "This could all have very easily gone wrong. If not for you, they could have beaten us."

"I wasn't about to stand by and do nothing, Galahad. What happened to Karl?"

"I removed his head. Keeping him alive would have been a foolish idea and I had to show that I could carry out what needed to be done. There's a time for mercy, but that wasn't it."

"What are you going to do with Simon?"

"Rebecca tells me he's damaged in the head now. It would be inhumane to execute him when he's incapable of even taking care of himself. There are people here who would like to see him lose his head no matter his mental or physical condition. I will have to think on it and make a decision when the city is repaired. Maybe cooler heads will agree with me."

"And until then?"

"You remember that little hut of Leonardo's, up near the second realm gate? Well, he's decided to outfit it as a prison in the interim. He assures me it will be able to hold Simon, but I'll be placing a considerable number of guards around it. He won't escape again. I'm going to contact Hades, something I shouldn't probably allow, but he knows more about necromancy injuries than anyone I know. Maybe he can tell me if Simon will ever regain his old memories."

"Hades would probably relish communication between his people and Shadow Falls. It could be the start of this place becoming less insular."

"I'm not sure how my citizens will feel, but I think it's something we need to do. We need allies outside of Shadow Falls. We don't have many and I'm setting to change that."

"What about Father Patterson and Fern. How are they doing?"

"Well … actually, I'm not sure. They're not exactly the most open of people. I think Fern only talks to the Father, and he's not the trusting type. We'll be able to arrange something so we can keep them safe. I'm going to be stationing a garrison in the city of Stratford. Not officially, you understand, but that city is going to be safer than anywhere else in the country by the time I'm done." I thought he was going to say something else, but he quickly closed his mouth and glanced out over the balcony.

"So, you have Patricia in the dungeons. How's that going for you?"

"She's a stubborn, nasty little woman. I have half a mind to throw away the key and let her rot, but she may know of more people who are working against us. She thinks she's Vanguard, did you know?"

"It came up, yeah."

"The Vanguard are a concern at the best of times, but having some psycho spout nonsense about them is only going to cause problems for us. If it gets out, it would worry people about another attack. And if she did actually work with any of the Vanguard . . . well, that could mean some very bad people might come looking for her."

"I doubt very much she was working with anyone from there," I admitted. "Karl, Simon, and company were just stringing her along."

"I think the same, but I can't rule it out. One of the bad parts about being in charge is having to think of every conceivable terrible idea and trying to work out which ones I can actually prevent."

I knocked back the rest of the drink. "If you need me, you know where I'll be. Caitlin has my number."

"Don't wait so long to visit next time," Galahad said and offered me his hand, which I took. "Thank you for everything you've done. I thought you'd like to know, Martin's family are safe. They had no idea what he did, but we're going to bring them here. Turns out his fourteen-year-old daughter is an enchanter too. We're hoping she might be interested in training here."

"Good luck with that and with getting your realm back together."

I'd just turned to walk away when Galahad spoke again, "I'm sorry about Rean."

I froze and glanced over at my friend, who had his eyes closed and was shaking his head slowly. He opened his eyes and we locked gazes. "I'm so sorry, Nate. He was one of the good guys."

My mind flashed back to his dying moments on the floor of the blood-covered basement. "Yes, he was. He went down swinging. Wasn't about to let them kill him without a fight."

"I'll ensure he has full military honors; if you have any trouble with the colony, just tell them that. Songs will be sung about him."

I knew he felt guilty over what had happened all those years ago; being responsible for the deaths of Rean's family would have left a stain on all but the blackest of souls.

"He said that you two sort of came to an agreement," I said. "That you made up in a way."

Galahad nodded. "I wanted to give him reparations, arrange for a day of mourning for his family. He wouldn't allow it, he said that his grief was his alone to shoulder, but the gesture appeared to create a bridge between us. I gave him free rein of the state of Maine to do as he wished. I'm led to believe that he helped people."

"He did. He's at peace now. I don't know what the troll version of the afterlife is, but he'll be with his family. That's all he ever wanted."

"That was the worst decision I ever made. I pledge to his soul that I will do everything in my power to ensure I never make another like it."

I walked over and grasped Galahad's shoulder. "My old friend, don't let the burden of your position overwhelm you. You are only one man. Just remember that."

A smile broke through the solemn expression on Galahad's face. "Thank you. I will try. You sure you don't want this job?" He waved to the scotch. "King Nathan?"

I laughed, a deep belly laugh. It felt good. "Not for all the scotch, women, and money in this or any other realm."

EPILOGUE

I received the first phone call from Galahad six weeks after leaving Shadow Falls. He asked me to come talk to Simon. Apparently, the psychotic bastard had decided to stop being a dribbling mess and had asked to see me. To say I wasn't interested was an understatement, but Galahad had insisted until I agreed.

It wasn't until I saw Simon that I realized why Galahad had been so eager for me to talk to him. Simon said that he remembered nothing of his life before waking up in the hut that Leonardo had decked out as a one-man prison. He said he knew names and faces, but nothing of his past.

When confronted with the information about what he'd done, he actually had the audacity to look shocked, even saddened by the news that he was a mass-murdering fuckwit.

The interview had been short, me asking him questions and him never having an answer. I wanted to know who he worked with, was there any truth to the notion that he was only a cog in a bigger machine, but there were no answers coming.

Once a week for three months, I traveled to Shadow Falls, in an attempt to trip Simon up and get him to reveal that it was all an act, but he never did. Which only made me the more determined to find the truth.

"This is the last time," I told Father Patterson as Fern activated the realm gate.

"You say that every single time," he said with a smile. "I'm beginning to think you're enjoying the challenge."

"Sorry to disappoint you, but this really is the last time." I shook his hand and nodded toward Fern, who smiled, before I stepped through the realm gate.

Caitlin met me on the other side, along with several dozen soldiers. The huge fort that was built in the mountain protected the realm gate, but also served as an impressive introduction to anyone using the realm gate in the church. A show of power, Galahad had called it. And it worked.

"Last time," she said with a smile.

"One way or another, yes," I told her. She'd dealt with her brother's death and mother's imprisonment as well as could be expected. She appeared to be settling into living in Shadow Falls.

She wore a simple, but elegant, dark suit. Her once long hair was cut short. She was in charge of the fort and did an excellent job. She'd taken to carrying a dagger in a sheath worn at the small of her back.

We walked through the impressive fort, past even more soldiers, all of who snapped to attention as we passed them. Rumor had it, Caitlin ran a tight ship, but that she was a fair and good commander.

"How's the police force coming along?" I asked as we exited under the enormous fort entrance into the plains beyond. Caitlin had arranged for a standing force to take the place of the militia that had mostly turned against Galahad.

"Going well, training is slow, but it's not like we have a huge amount of crime to deal with. All of the prisoners who escaped were captured or killed, the prison has been rebuilt and the enchanter, Martin, is making up for his mistake by working his ass off on a regular basis. In fact that's him there."

She pointed toward a lone figure beside the hut, which was my destination. Twenty soldiers stood guard in one of four huge watchtowers, keeping the hut in constant examination night and day.

We stopped a few hundred feet away from the hut and I turned to Caitlin. "This is going to be it for a while. Good luck with everything."

She hugged me, kissing me on the cheek and drawing a few glances from her subordinates, who quickly looked away when she turned towards them. "Take care, Nate. Don't be a stranger."

I nodded and walked off toward the hut, where Martin saw me and jogged over. "It's all set for what Galahad and you have planned. You sure it's a good idea?"

"We'll see, I guess."

I pushed the door open, and the runes placed on it burned brightly. I wasn't really sure what would happen if Simon tried to escape, but the words "smoldering crater" were used, so I wasn't sure I wanted to find out.

Simon sat at a desk, reading one of the dozens of books that littered the two-room hut. The bedroom and kitchen made up one room, with the bathroom being separate.

He put the book down and glanced up at me, smiling as I stepped inside and closed the door behind me.

"Nate," he said with genuine enthusiasm. "Is it that time of the week already? I'm burning through these books faster than they can be given to me." He showed me his latest acquisition, a horror story about a clown.

"Yeah, I've read that one. It did very little to change my opinion of clowns as being creepy assholes."

"It's amazing that someone can come up with a story like that, with a monster who is so dangerous."

"Like you?"

Simon sighed. "I know I used to be a monster, and I know that whatever you did to me was utterly deserved, but I'm really not that man anymore. I lie in bed and try to remember the horrible things I used to do, but I can't. The idea of hurting someone . . . it makes me feel sick."

"Well, this is our last time together."

For the tiniest of moments, I thought I saw the tug of a smile at his lips.

"Oh, why's that?" he asked.

"A decision has been made about you. You're going to be taken away from here, allowed to go back to our realm."

"You're freeing me?" he asked, hopeful.

I shook my head. "Not exactly." I sat on the bed beside Simon. "Just one last time, do you remember anything? You sure you want to continue telling me you can't recall anything?"

"Damn it," he snapped. "I can't remember a thing. I told you, Nate. Don't you think I want to remember?"

"Do you?"

Simon paused. "I'm not sure. If I was the evil man you claim, I'm not sure I want to know what I did. But if I don't remember, how can I make amends for it?"

"Fair enough." I stood. "You can leave whenever you're ready."

I motioned toward the door and Simon stood tentatively, knocking over a stack of books onto the floor. Then he ran toward the door, bursting through it as I remained in the hut.

I poked the books with my toe and dislodged a sheet of paper. On it was my name, written over and over again until it filled the paper. I glanced up at the screams outside. I smiled. I couldn't help myself.

The screams turned to pleas as I left the hut and found Simon kneeling in the dirt, begging Galahad to spare him. Hades stood beside the king of Shadow Falls and stared at Simon with a look of anger and contempt.

"I assume you've already met your new jailer," I said to Simon.

The murderer turned his gaze toward me and sprang up, almost foaming at the mouth as he screamed obscenities. I didn't even flinch as Martin stepped forward and touched Simon with one hand, freezing him in place.

"I put runes on you," Martin said. "You can't scare me anymore, or threaten my family."

"I'm going to find them, Marty," Simon snarled. "I'm going to flay them in front of you."

"You are coming with me," Hades said and took hold of Simon's arm in an iron-like grip. "You're responsible for your friends trying to kill the people I care about, including my daughter. You will answer for that."

"I'll get free," Simon snapped. "And once I'm done with this pissant, I'm coming for you, Nate. I'm going to make you watch me butcher your friends."

"How long have you had your memories?" I asked.

"Fuck you," he shouted and spat at me.

"You've always had them, yes? After today, you'll be someone I'll never again give thought to." I turned toward Martin. "Release him, give him one last chance."

Martin touched Simon on his arm and hurried back out of range.

Simon snarled at me and took a swing. I dodged it and slapped him around the side of the head. "You can't use your alchemy can you?" I asked as Simon tried running at me but only met my knee, breaking his nose and sending him sprawling to the ground.

"Fuck you," he shouted again and spat blood onto the dirt. "Fuck all of you, you have no idea what's coming for you. What's going to burn you to the fucking ground."

"Feel like telling us?" Galahad asked.

"You'll see. A cleansing fire is coming for all of you, it'll change everything you know and take everyone you care about. And when it comes, I'm going to stand atop the mountain of corpses that used to be your loved ones, and I'm going to laugh."

"Overly dramatic, isn't it?" Hades said. "That's okay, we're going to have a very long time to work on your people skills."

Simon got back to his feet. "Stick me in any prison you like, I'll escape."

I glanced at Hades. "Can I tell him, or do you want to?"

Hades grinned and walked toward Simon, who dropped to his knees. When they were inches apart, Hades spoke, "You are going to become a cautionary tale for what happens to people who hurt my family. People will tell stories about what I'm going to do to you. Whatever horrific acts you think you've done on others, I'm going to revisit on you a thousand times over. Over an indeterminate period of time, I'm going to tear your soul into tiny pieces and then put it back together over and over and over and over until you can no longer remember what species you are, let alone your name. The suffering you're about to go through will be total."

Hades stood and motioned for several guards to drag Simon away. Any fight and bluster he'd possessed was all lost as the realization of what was going to happen settled in.

"You're not really going to do all that, are you?" Martin asked.

"Young man, if I tell you what I told him, would you ever hurt my family?"

Martin shook his head so hard I thought he'd get whiplash.

"Simon's going to have a long journey to think about the terrible fate that's about to befall him. He will be partially broken before I ever start. Be assured, Simon will pay for his crimes and pay dearly. He will never be able to destroy or harm anyone or anything, ever again." Hades turned to Galahad and bowed slightly. "Your majesty, it's good to see you again. Nate, I'll see you later."

I watched Hades walk away toward the realm gate as the soldiers around us began to dissipate.

"So, you off too?" Galahad said a few minutes later as we reached the fort.

"Yeah, I just have one more thing to do," I said and bowed toward Galahad. "Your majesty, if you are ever in need of Hellequin's services, you need only ask."

Every single soldier in the fort heard my words and saw me bow.

"Nate, what are you doing?" Galahad whispered.

"I never showed you the proper respect, I'm correcting that. And now everyone here has heard that I'm willing to help at a moment's notice. Should help to have the bogyman's phone number on speed dial."

Galahad motioned for me to rise. "Thank you," he said and hugged me. "This is a manly hug, right?" he asked after a few seconds.

"It was until you started whispering in my ear," I pointed out and he released the hug, which made us both laugh.

"Take care, King Galahad." I walked off toward the realm gate, where Simon was being placed on a stretcher; rune inscribed straps tied his body to the silver gurney.

"That was either foolish or selfless," Hades said as the realm gate activated. "But it was a nice gesture."

"Well, if what Simon said is true, there are people out there helping these little bastards. We still don't know who killed Jerry back in New York, or who the man who visited the House of Silent Screams back in the 1970s was. We have less answers than I'm normally comfortable with."

Hades glanced down at the prisoner, causing him to flinch. "Well, I'm sure this man here will be more than forthcoming with answers. Whether he wants to be or not."

ACKNOWLEDGMENTS

I'm on my third one of these now, a situation I wasn't sure would ever happen. I was considering just making it up and see if anyone noticed, but smarter heads prevailed.

As always, I have to thank my wife for basically just being her. She puts up with my need to be left alone to work while keeping our three young daughters occupied, even when all she wants to do is lock herself in a bedroom with a bottle of wine (if you don't have kids you won't understand the joy they bring, along with the desire for alcohol).

To my three beautiful daughters, who I love more and more every day. Behave yourselves.

To my parents, thanks for always being so positive about my writing and for asking how things are going. But mostly, thanks for sounding interested when I start talking about whatever research I've done that no one but me would ever find interesting.

The rest of my family and friends have been nothing but supportive. I thank each of you for that.

My crit partners, D.B. Reynolds and Michelle Muto, are two of the best writers I've ever met. But more importantly, they're also two of the nicest people I've ever had the pleasure to call my friends.

Speaking of writer friends, all of Kelley Armstrong's OWG, the Rebel-Misfit Alliance, are awesome. Each and every person there is a talented writer and good friend. You all made me a better writer, and I can never thank you enough.

To the massively talented Eamon O'Donoghue. I couldn't ask for a better artist to continue do the covers.

David Pomerico, 47North acquisitions editor, who first asked if I'd like to work with them, thank you for giving me this opportunity. Jenni Gaynor, my editor, I've very much enjoyed working with you. To everyone at Public Relations, the 47North Author-Team, and anyone else I've had dealings with: Thank you all for making it so easy to work there. You all do an awesome job and should be thanked individually, but you all know who you are.

And lastly to everyone who has supported me and my work, to those people who send me e-mails or leave reviews, or even reply on Facebook or Twitter. Thank you. The fact that people are enjoying what I write means the world to me.

ABOUT THE AUTHOR

 Steve McHugh is the author of the popular Hellequin Chronicles. He lives in Southampton on the south coast of England with his wife and three young daughters. When not writing or spending time with his kids, he enjoys watching movies, reading books and comics, and playing video games.